ANTHOLOGIES BY WRITTEN BACKWARDS

PELLUCID LUNACY

International Book Awards – Winner
USA Best Book Awards – Winner

CHIRAL MAD

Eric Hoffer Awards – Grand Prize Finalist
ForeWord Reviews Book of the Year – Finalist
International Book Awards – Winner
London Book Festival – Winner
Indie Book Awards ® – Finalist / Silver Medal
Anthology of the Year by This is Horror – Runner-up
USA Best Book Awards – Finalist

CHIRAL MAD 2

Bram Stoker Awards ® (HWA):
Superior Achievement in Short Fiction – Nomination: "The Geminis" by John Palisano
Superior Achievement in Long Fiction – Winner: "The Great Pity" by Gary A. Braunbeck
ForeWord Reviews Book of the Year – Finalist
Independent Publisher Book Awards – Finalist / Silver Medal
International Book Awards – Winner
Indie Book Awards ® – Winner / Gold Medal
Paris Book Festival – Runner-up
USA Best Book Awards – Winner

QUALIA NOUS

Benjamin Franklin Awards – Winner
Bram Stoker Awards ® (HWA):
Superior Achievement in an Anthology – Nomination: Editor, Michael Bailey
Superior Achievement in Short Fiction – Nomination: "Ruminations" by Rena Mason
Superior Achievement in Short Fiction – Nomination: "The Vaporization Enthalpy of a
Peculiar Pakistani Family" by Usman T. Malik
ForeWord Reviews Book of the Year – Finalist
Nebula Awards ® (SFWA): Nomination: "Vaporization Enthalpy…" by Usman T. Malik
Rhysling Awards (SFPA): Nomination: "Shutdown" by Marge Simon

THE
LIBRARY
OF THE
DEAD

CHAPEL
OF THE
CRIMES
COLUMBARIUM
CREMATORIUM
NICHES
URNS

THE
LIBRARY
OF THE
DEAD

EDITED BY MICHAEL BAILEY

ILLUSTRATED BY GAK

INTRODUCTION BY NORMAN PARTRIDGE

WWW.NETTIRW.COM

PUBLISHED BY WRITTEN BACKWARDS

Original concept by Gene O'Neill and Gord Rollo

Cover artwork, photography, layout, and "The Librarian" by Michael Bailey

Illustrations by gak

Introduction by Norman Partridge

Afterword by Mary SanGiovanni

FIRST EDITION

ISBN: 978.0.578.15675.0

CATALOG
OF THE
DEAD

COLLECTIONS

NORMAN PARTRIDGE

I had this shrink one time. I didn't see her very long...well, only as long as I had to because of the probation deal. Anyway, she was the one who suggested that I get into library work. She said I led a highly compartmentalized life.

I thought everybody did, but the shrink disabused me of that notion. Her name was Rebecca. Of course, I could never call her that out loud. In our sessions she always insisted that I address her as Dr. Nakamura. But in my head it was always *Rebecca Rebecca Rebecca*. I guess you could say that I thought about her a lot.

Rebecca was tall. She liked to wear boots and long skirts and cowl-necked sweaters. Her hair was curly and a shade of blonde that made you wonder what color it really was. And she wasn't Japanese, so I have no idea where the *Nakamura* came from. Your guess is as good as mine. Maybe that name was all that remained of an ex-husband or a misplaced father. I never did figure it out, even with all the internet stalking I did.

(And, yes, I know none of this really matters when it comes to the story I'm telling you—unless it's to say that there are just some questions you never can answer—but bear with me. I have an eye for detail, and I admit that I can be more than a little garrulous at times. It's just me.)

Anyway, Rebecca had firm viewpoints on compartmentalization. I didn't argue with her. Only an idiot argues with a court-appointed shrink. Besides, it's true that I like things neat and orderly. And, sure, as Rebecca pointed out you can get carried away with that approach to life ... but then again, you can get carried away with almost anything, can't you?

Of course you can. That's only human.

But let's get back to keeping things neat and orderly. General topic: compartmentalized devices. Specific frame of reference: boxes. If you approach life the way I do, you probably use a wide variety of same without even thinking about it. There's a toolbox for your work behavior, and a toy box for behavior at home. There's an easy-to-open box that holds the public you, and a Japanese puzzle box that holds the unvarnished real deal. Maybe there's even a little glass dollhouse for your spouse, and a gone-to-seed Barbie playhouse where you can fool around with your lover while Trailer Park Ken's out back cooking meth. And last but not least: a big metal safe full of secrets you'll never ever face, and a nailed-down coffin where you keep dreams so dark you wouldn't want to see them even if you dared to yank nails and open the creaking lid.

That last kind of box ... well, I guess the contents would look something like Dorian Gray's portrait, wouldn't they? Meaning: You don't go traipsing up to the attic and pull the curtain on that one unless you absolutely have to. If you dare bring along a light, it's just a flickering candle so you won't have to eyeball the entire Goyaesque mess in a hundred-plus-watt glow. And to be honest, it's probably a better idea to expose the naked guts of that thing in complete darkness. That way, the only sensory input you'll receive is auditory—like grave worms wriggling on slick, oily canvas.

Just imagine that sound inches away in the darkness. Those little worms churning in a face that's as much rot as paint, burrowing into bloodstained canvas ... digging and devouring, writhing and twisting...

Pretty creepy, right? I mean, you wouldn't go tactile, reach out blindly, and bury your fingers like five little corpses in those wriggling worms, would you? Uh-uh. No way. But that's exactly the way it is with the dark things we file away, in life and in libraries. If you want knowledge, you have to reach out and touch it. You have to take a chance, perhaps even suffer the consequences. Information—and secrets—aren't always pretty or pleasant. Sometimes they can be dangerous, like hungry worms crawling through the winding tunnels of your mind. That's why information management is so important... believe me, I know.

Think three c's: codify, consign, and care. This is especially important with managing dangerous information. Libraries deal with lots of things like that. Often they're consigned to Special Collections. Such materials demand careful oversight and limited access—sometimes so limited that the items are almost forgotten... except by a select few, or (sometimes) only one.

And really, to close the circle, you might say that's the way things ended up with Dr. Nakamura, my court-appointed shrink.

She was consigned to Special Collections.

In other words: I put her in a box.

Actually, I put Rebecca in several of them.

All it took was a little foresight, and a few very sharp knives.

⸺◆⸺

I don't want you to get the wrong impression. I really made an effort to listen to Rebecca... at first, anyway. And I took her advice about libraries to heart. I'd actually worked in one when I was in college. So I started submitting applications, hoping they wouldn't be checked too carefully. This was the late nineties, and you could still manage that. In those days there was barely an internet, and the term "computer literacy" was cutting edge.

I had a few interviews. Nothing surprising about any of them. Sit through enough interviews and you'll realize that search committees end up settling way more than anyone would ever admit. Basically, they see who walks through the door and pick the best of the lot. In the end it's mostly about personalities.

I knew I wasn't much of a personality, so I developed a basic game plan to become one ... long enough to get what I wanted. I built a box from good old-fashioned aromatic cedar and filled it with photocopied stories. I found them in library trade journals, and most of them were pretty funny. Then I looked up some articles about the basic interview questions, and I matched the stories to the questions. The whole exercise was *easy-peasy, lemon squeezy*.

In most library interviews—at least for public desk jobs—there's always a question about handling problem patrons. Which, of course, demands quick thinking and good people skills. I found a great answer for that one. It was about a homeless guy who sat in a library children's room, clucking just like a chicken. Different staffers talked to him, but no one could shut him up. He'd quiet down for a few minutes then start up again: "Bawk bawk bawk!" Finally one staffer tried a different approach. You know, very understanding: "Sir, I'm really sorry to bother you, but could I ask you to keep your pet chicken quiet in the library? It's disturbing the other patrons."

The way the story went, the homeless guy didn't make a peep after that. He just sat there pretending to pet his (equally quiet) chicken, every now and then telling it to *shush*. End result of this patron interaction: *You could have heard crickets*.

Anyway, you should have heard the search committee howl when I dropped in that last line. It set up the clincher, and that was this: "Working in libraries isn't just about reading books. It's about reading people, too ... and I'm very good at that."

Boy, you should have seen their collective eyeballs light up when I said that.

If only it had been true.

———————▲———————

I got the job. It was a night supervisor gig at a little college library. The campus had a reputation for social justice advocacy, and maybe that's why they overlooked the minimal stuff I included on my application concerning my criminal record. Or maybe it was because the dot.com boom was still going strong. With a good portion of the emerging workforce making big bucks moving jillions of pixels around millions of screens, pickings were slim in the non-virtual playground of real-world joe jobs.

Anyway, the library was open late—you know how college students like to procrastinate. I didn't have much to do . . . not at first, anyway. Just make sure students didn't bring a six-pack into one of the group study rooms, keep the student workers busy at the desk, and lock things up at the end of the night.

My boss worked with me the first few weeks, then turned over the keys and the alarm system passcodes. After that, I could pretty much do things my own way. I liked hanging out in the old bindery in the basement. Part of my job was managing book repair, so spending time downstairs was expected. Besides, the student workers at the front desk could buzz the bindery if they needed me . . . but that never happened much.

Anyway, I built a big plywood box—long but not too deep, and not very high. One of the bindery work tables had a piece of base trim at the bottom, and it wasn't much of a problem to install a hinge in the trim plate so I could hide the box beneath the table. I kept my woodworking tools inside, and I decided I'd make a present for Rebecca during my downtime. My probation was almost over, and after landing the library job I was her star pupil. I figured a gift was the least she deserved for giving me such good advice.

That's what I told myself, anyway.

Rebecca was usually tight-lipped, but she let slip that she was attending a conference in a few months. She planned to present a paper that referenced my case as a positive example of her rehabilitation methods. I wasn't sure I liked that, because it was information I couldn't control. But I had a kind of unspoken attraction to it, too—because, in the end, Rebecca was the one in control.

For some reason that excited me. So did the present I built for Rebecca. It was a *himtsu-bako*, or Japanese puzzle box. I made it from Hinoki wood, decorating it with a classic Koyosegi pattern. Fifty moves were required to open it. Up to that point the box was probably the finest piece of woodworking I'd ever produced, and I was especially proud of the combination of dowel pegs and sliders which I installed. A few of those sliders were actually lead, should anyone ever decide to x-ray the box. Back then I thought that was pretty clever.

Put me to the test, and I'd have to admit that opening Rebecca's *himtsu-bako* was a challenge for me—and remember, I'd designed the thing. But make those fifty moves, and you'd find a real treasure inside—a duplicate key for one of my storage units. Talk about dangerous stuff, giving something like that to a person who could put me away with a single phone call. Looking back on it, I can't believe I took such a risk. Not that I thought Rebecca was the kind of person who'd figure out how to open such a complicated puzzle box, let alone turn detective and search out my storage unit. In truth, I figured she'd probably just put the box up on a shelf in her office and let it collect dust. Certainly, that would have ensured a smug and tasty victory for me. And if I'm honest with myself, that's probably why I took a chance by giving Rebecca the box in the first place ... after all, it was a pretty sizable thrill to put one over on the oh-so-brilliant Dr. Nakamura.

But you can't ever predict what people will do. Not really. The way things turned out I spent a lot of time worrying about the puzzle box, even after I decided to murder Rebecca. I suppose that added some spice to the whole exercise. All those worries were locked up in different places in my skull, in boxes large and small, and sometimes they'd get opened before I even realized it. That was scary. It was like some stranger breaking into your house and rummaging through your most personal possessions when you're not even there.

Or to put it another way: It was information that was way out of control.

I hate to admit it, but that kind of excited me, too.

It's crazy the way your mind works, isn't it?

You bet it is.

A few months into the library job, I found out the place was haunted. Everyone thought so, anyway. The Public Safety officers said they got weird vibes in the building after closing, and the motion detectors for the alarm system would indicate movement when the building was empty. There was even a story about a custodian quitting the job cold after she saw one of the second-floor statues move ... just its head, as if its stone eyes were tracking the young woman as she worked above the dimly lit atrium. She claimed she heard laughter bubbling up from the old fountain on the first floor below, and the sound was like something that belonged in a cave.

Weird, right? Of course, I didn't worry about those stories ... not at first, anyway. When it comes to the supernatural, I rely on my own sensory input. And that usually means that in the end everything adds up to a big fat zero ... except this time.

The incidents that bothered me most happened when I was alone in the building. I could write off several of them pretty easily—like, the elevator running by itself. The cab would come down to the first floor, and the doors would open. I'd be sitting at the Circulation Desk after closing, and I'd stare across the darkened lobby into that empty box bathed in its internal halogen glow. It was like a king-sized *himtsu-bako* waiting just for me, and you can probably guess that the very idea gave me a pretty sizable shiver.

The elevator doors always seemed to remain open just a little too long before closing automatically, but I figured that was just my imagination. Even so, I could write off the elevator antics as some kind of electrical glitch. But I couldn't explain away other phenomena so easily. Like the elevator, these incidents only occurred when I was alone in the building. For instance, I'd hear doors slam upstairs when I knew no doors were open. Or I'd be shifting books on the second floor, and I'd hear footsteps coming from the Periodical stacks on the third.

One night I even heard drawers sliding open and slamming closed in some old microfilm cabinets stored on one of the third floor breezeways. When I went upstairs to check things out, I found a spool loaded on the oldest microfilm reader and the machine humming away. I knew that no one had been using that equipment before closing... but there it was. Of course, I looked at the screen. Someone had been reading an old *Life* magazine article about Jack the Ripper. That was a little too creepy for me. I put away the microfilm and turned off the equipment, then set the building alarm and called it a night.

When I came to work the next afternoon, I ran into one of my closers in the quad. Stephen worked a lot of late-night shifts, and he'd go for a run around the campus after we closed the library at midnight.

"Hey," he said, "were you in the building last night around one a.m.?"

"No. I cut out about ten minutes after you did. I was already home by then."

"You sure?"

"Sure I'm sure."

Stephen paused, as if he was hesitant to say more. "That's weird."

"Weird how?"

"Well, I was running past the library around one o'clock. You know. Along the access road. And I had this weird feeling someone was watching me. I glanced up at those big windows overlooking the parking lot, and I could see that breezeway on the third floor where the old microfilm readers are. The lights were off, but someone was up there. I only saw his silhouette, but I got the feeling he was staring right at me."

"Spooky," I said. "Unless you're just yanking my chain to get out of working more night shifts."

"Not at all. You know I like nights the best. I just thought I should tell you."

"Thanks."

Stephen hesitated.

"Something else?" I asked.

"Yeah...but you'll think I'm crazy."

I laughed. "I'll let you know."

"Well... don't judge, but the guy I saw up there on the third floor?"

"Yeah?"

"He was wearing a top hat."

———————◆———————

Ghost or man, I kind of forgot about the wearer of the top hat... at least for a while. There was a lot going on in my head, and some of it wouldn't shake loose no matter how hard I tried. Mostly I was hung up on Rebecca, the puzzle box, and the hidden key to that storage unit. I just couldn't stop thinking about it. And the worst thing was that no matter how much I thought, I couldn't decide what I should do about the whole mess...so I didn't do anything.

I hate inertia. Don't you?

Anyway, I knew I'd go crazy if I kept spinning on a (metaphorical) hamster wheel, so I went looking for distraction. The college Archivist suggested that I ought to move up the food chain and get a Masters in Library Science. It sounded like a good idea, and maybe an answer to the Rebecca problem, too—school would keep my mind occupied during the day, and work would keep me busy at night. At the time I figured it was best to think less and do more.

So that was the way I played it. I was accepted to a program at a state college just before the semester started. Remember, this was the nineties. There weren't a lot of online classes yet. So I spent a good chunk of time driving to the campus, which was about sixty miles south of my apartment. Three hours of class, and then I'd make the drive back to work and put in my eight hours. For the first semester, I barely spent any time in my apartment at all...and when I was there I was (almost invariably) sleeping.

Some classes were dull, some interesting. It was the same with the people in them. There was one girl in a couple of my classes. Her name was Daphne, which is one of those names that conjures two very disparate sources—either the seductive niad from Greek mythology, or the hot chick from *Scooby-Doo*.

And maybe in the end Daphne was a little bit of both. In those days most people would have (mistakenly) called her a Goth, but she was really more of a fifties throwback with a rockabilly twist. She wore a lot of black, and had these tortoise-shell glasses and a Betty Page hairstyle. Residing on her left arm was a tattoo of Elvis with a raven perched on his shoulder. Just those three sentences were enough to tell me that she really didn't see life the way I did at all. Meaning: Forget secreting things away in compartmentalized boxes; Daphne seemed to wear her boxes on the outside.

That was a strange enough concept for a fellow like me, but it wasn't what—dare I say it?—sparked my attraction. Not really. What I liked most about Daphne was that she'd say whatever she felt like saying without worrying about stepping on someone else's blue suede shoes.

Ha ha. Just a little Elvis humor there.

What I mean to say is that Daphne didn't care what other people thought of her. Plus, she was really funny . . . if you got her jokes and references, anyway. Most people in the class didn't have a clue, but I did. Sometimes I'd laugh out loud at something she said. More often I'd just arch an eyebrow, or grin. Daphne didn't let on that she noticed, but she did . . . and pretty soon I'd catch her checking me out after she said something just to gauge my reaction.

Anyway, I'm getting ahead of myself. Before I knew it I was thinking about Daphne a lot, especially during those drives between school and work. I even bought some CDs with artists I knew she liked—Elvis (of course), but also Wanda Jackson, Robert Gordon, and The Collins Kids. Sometimes I'd get lost in those songs while driving, just thinking of Daphne. I even ran over a dog on the way home one Friday night, so wrapped up in Gordon's version of "Only Make Believe" that I barely even noticed.

Bow-wow.

Clunk clunk.

Daphne Daphne Daphne.

Pathetic, right? I know. But that's the way my world turned… for a while, anyway. Of course, I still thought about Rebecca, too. It wasn't the same. Not at all. And then one night while driving home from work, I realized that I'd finally decided what to do about the oh-so-troubling Dr. Nakamura, and the puzzle box, and the whole horrible mess.

The solution was simple, once I realized what had changed between me and Rebecca. My brain had already moved on, along with the small little knot of muscle that passed for my heart. It was time for the rest of me to follow, and (metaphorically speaking, anyway) put Dr. Nakamura in the rearview mirror.

There was only one way to do that.

I'd have to kill Rebecca.

And close her box for good.

<hr>

I'm like most people. There are some things I'm proud of, and (if I'm honest with myself) more than a few that I'm not. Take my criminal record, for instance. It's embarrassing. I can't even bring myself to tell you some of the things I've been convicted for. Stupid stuff, and more than a little compulsive … which is even more embarrassing, because it's hard to admit that a compulsion can overcome your natural intelligence.

But that's the way it was with me. The only good thing about my rap sheet was that it didn't match the profile for the type of perp who committed the crimes that were actually my *forte*. In other words, I was very successful at not getting caught for anything that mattered. In a way, I imagine that was why things went as smoothly as they did for such a long time. My record created a kind of blind alley sure to send inquisitive cops on equally blind detours … until that last thing with Daphne, anyway.

But there I go again, getting ahead of myself. I warned you I'd do that occasionally. Back to the upside—the things I'm proud of. One of them is my woodworking, and the true shame of that is that very few people ever saw the things I made. Like the boxes I built for Rebecca. Not the Japanese puzzle box. The other ones— the custom-made caskets I built to put her in after she was dead. They were beautiful, especially the box I made for her head. It was made of Zelkova wood seasoned for twenty years, and it was as lustrously blonde as the highlights in Rebecca's hair. I worked with the Zelkova to bring out its glow and inlaid a dark forest of stained hemlock fir against it—the latter wood harvested from Aokiaghara, the Japanese forest at the base of Mt. Fuji which was infamous for its suicides.

Of course, Aokiaghara was famous for its ghosts, too, but I didn't think about that then.

I think about it now, though...and often.

To this day I wish I'd never touched that wood.

It was a night in May, just before the Memorial Day Weekend. I'd closed the library, and (now that Rebecca's boxes were finished) I'd been sitting in my office for hours planning her murder. From out of nowhere, a door slammed upstairs. A moment later, that sound was followed by a short burst of *down in the bottom of a cave* laughter.

That laughter didn't scare me. It made me mad. After all, I already had more than enough on my plate to keep me busy. The last thing I needed was a supernatural side-order of ghostly laughter crowding out the main entree. I was just about to grab a mallet from my woodworking tools and head upstairs to see if I could pound ectoplasm into cobwebs when the office phone rang. I grabbed the handset, said my name and the name of the library, so off my game that I didn't even bother with "How can I help you?"

"Riddle me this, Batman."

"Huh?"

"Where do you find narrow houses that last until doomsday?"

"The graveyard, of course. Now who is this, and—"

"Well, my name isn't Ophelia."

"What?"

"C'mon, slowpoke. You must've guessed by now. It's Daphne, from cataloging class."

"How'd you figure out where I work? I never mentioned the name of the library in class."

Daphne only laughed. "I'm a librarian, Sherlock ... or I'm going to be, anyway. Have you tried this new search engine called Google? It's pretty amazing what you can find."

"I'm more of an AlltheWeb guy," I said.

"That's a good one, too. I like the way you can search by specific dates."

"So what's up?"

"Well, you answered my riddle, so you're still in the game. And Memorial Day Weekend is just around the corner, which means a certain destination is *de rigueur*."

"So we're back to graveyards?"

"Dig it. We should excavate and investigate. You can be Mr. Burke, and I'll be Ms. Hare."

"You're kidding, right?"

"Certainly, silly. After all, we're a couple of purely straight-up individuals, embarking on careers as library professionals. So no shovels, no holes in the ground ... just a nice little picnic lunch among the tombstones."

"That sounds kind of morbid."

"Indeed it does, but I'm kind of a morbid girl. And you're not too far off the mark ... if I read you right, anyway. Besides, the cemetery I'm thinking of has something special."

"What's that?"

"A library. You need to see it."

A library in a cemetery—now I was curious. Really curious. We exchanged a few more words, and somehow they seemed heavier now, as if everything we said had some kind of double meaning. I couldn't even tell you what it was, only that it carried a particular edge ... and a certain weight not unlike secrets or truth.

Whatever it was, it was unsettling. I was relieved to hang up the phone. But I'll be honest—any trepidation I'd had turned to (more than rabid) curiosity . . . and something much stronger. Something I'll have to let you name. I'll simply say that I didn't have to be in Daphne's presence to realize the power she had over me. It was there, even over the phone. Those lips of hers, painted black, smiling just a little bit. A simple arch of an eyebrow, and a gleaming pupil (nearly) dilated past the color of its iris. All of that a vision in my head, so strong that I had to close my eyes and hold my breath.

"*Daphne Daphne Daphne*," I whispered.

Speaking her name to myself.

And no one else at all.

I don't like dreams. I've never trusted them. They don't fit well into compartments, and you can't control them. That means they're dangerous . . . and the one I had that night after talking to Daphne was the most dangerous dream I ever had in my life.

It began in the library, and things were just the way they had been a few hours before. Only Daphne didn't call me, and I wasn't sitting in my office. No. I was sitting at the Circulation Desk. The library was closed and the building was dark except for that particular square of workplace illumination, which was surrounded by three counters and several metal shelves.

A door slammed somewhere upstairs, and that sound was followed by a short chorus of (by now familiar) *bottom of a cave* laughter. The dual sounds spurred my anger, just as they had in real life. And just the same way, I was ready to grab one of my hammers and make a trip upstairs to see if it was possible to pound a hole in a ghost.

So I stood up, and quickly. The rolling chair shot out behind me as if launched from a cannon, banging into the Reserves shelves. But that didn't matter, because I didn't move an inch. Instead, I just stood there, my feet suddenly buried in cement, frozen in place by a man standing on the staircase landing on the other side of the lobby. He wore a top hat, and (from a distance) his face seemed as narrow as it was pale. The rest of him was black—frock coat with a strange twice-buckled collar, riding boots, trousers, leather gloves.

That the man had not been there on the landing a moment before was a certainty . . . I was sure of that. But he was here now, and that was just as certain. Only five stairs separated the landing from the main floor. The man glided down them the way a marionette does, as if he were an apparition pretending to descend a staircase to create an expected impression.

Soon he was halfway across the lobby. As he came closer to the desk, into the light, the pale face beneath his black top hat came clearly into view. Only it wasn't a face. It was a translucent mask, imprinted with a slight smile that didn't seem like a smile at all. And the voice that came from behind it betrayed nothing more than did the expression—it was neutral, and little more than a whisper, with just the slightest hint of a British accent.

The man said, "I'd like to place an item on Reserve."

"You're a faculty member?"

"No, but I am a teacher, and I do have pupils. And I would like to—"

"If you're not a faculty member at this institution, I can't help you."

"Oh, but I'm certain that you can. You might say I have specific knowledge of an item housed in Special Collections here, and that knowledge is accompanied by certain privileges. I wish to share those privileges . . . with you, to begin."

"Well, I'm not a student, so I don't quite understand your request. What's the item, anyway?"

"As I said, it's housed in Special Collections. It's an autopsy kit from the Victorian era, an item of some particular import. I'd like to make it available for your inspection . . . and use."

Now I laughed. The idea of an autopsy kit in the library was completely ridiculous. "We don't have anything like that here."

"You most certainly do have. If you doubt me, look on the

prep shelf behind you."

I did, and there it was, on the shelf with the other items waiting to be added to the Reserves Collection—a long case with leather straps, similar to ones I'd seen in medical histories of the Victorian era.

"Who are you?" It was the only question I could ask, but the man in the top hat didn't reply. He simply stood there, not moving at all ... as if waiting. And then, he did move. Or at least his lips did. Not the pair on that mask, but the lips barely visible beneath that translucent plastic seemed to writhe, and curve, and—

Quite suddenly, the man reached up with one black-gloved hand and removed the mask from his face. Beneath, there wasn't a face at all. Just a mass of wriggling grave worms—pink, and gray, and blood red—balanced in a large horrible knot atop the twice-buckled collar of his heavy coat. The mass bulged and wobbled, and for a moment I was afraid it would topple and spill those horrid creatures across the desk. But it didn't topple at all. Instead it seemed to grow tighter, like a clenched fist. And then several bloated specimens twisted across the space where a mouth should have been, approximating lips ... approximating a smile.

"You really want to know who I am?" the thing asked, its voice holding a horrible tenor of amusement.

I managed a nod.

"You're certain?"

"Yes ... I am."

My words seemed to hang in the air. Those worms writhed and twisted, as if trying to snare them. The thing's smile became larger, the lips becoming a thick woven hole that widened over a patch of blackness. Soon enough, other words came from within that hole.

"Then you must do as I say—slip your fingers into my mouth like a good lad, and I'll tell you my name."

If I'd had any control, it was gone now. I closed my eyes and reached out as if hypnotized. My fingers slid inside that hole rimmed with worms, and the thing's mouth closed around them.

Suddenly everything around me, and everything I heard, was a whisper. I was inside it, in a very small space no larger than the *himtsu-bako* box I'd built for Dr. Nakamura.

And, then, for a moment, I was nowhere at all.

The next thing I knew, I woke up in my apartment.

Screaming.

For a smart lady, Rebecca did some really stupid things. Like most people, she was a creature of habit. That was lucky for me. It was also lucky that the conference where she was presenting her paper took place on Memorial Day Weekend, just far enough north so it'd be a tough drive to make in a single day. Which (of course) meant I'd have to do just that, kill Dr. Nakamura, then make it back home in time to set up a solid alibi.

So pedal to the metal all the way up Highway 5 and across the Oregon border, cutting over to the coast and hitting the little resort town just as twilight fell. A long spike of beach jutted into the Pacific just south of the place, and I didn't park anywhere near it. No. I parked a mile away at a rocky beach unpopular with tourists, and I grabbed the backpack that contained my murder kit and humped it double-time down a state park trail that connected the two.

You wouldn't have recognized me. I was wearing an army-surplus jacket and had greased my hair so it looked a lot darker than it was. If you didn't look twice—and why would you?—you'd take me for a grad student who'd just finished finals and was hitting the Pacific Northwest trail for a summer adventure. And that was the story (exactly) I would have told had I run into a park ranger.

But I didn't run into a ranger. I didn't encounter anyone at all, except the person I was looking for. The one who liked to go for a run every night after dinner, no matter where she happened to be.

"Hi Rebecca," I said as I stepped out of the trees.

Rebecca's Nikes were new and expensive—electric blue with coral stripes, probably fresh out of the box. Her back was to me, but her little stutter-step told me she recognized my voice. Just that fast her toes dug firmly into the sand, and she stopped cold.

"Don't turn around," I said. "It'll be easier that way."

Even as I spoke, I knew Rebecca wouldn't heed my warning. Her sharp inhalation cut the silence, and then a big wave broke across the beach and slapped the sound away. The sea wind caught Rebecca's blonde hair, masking her face as she turned. She just couldn't help herself—I'm certain she already had a few persuasive paragraphs worked up to lob my way.

"I warned you," I said, and I fired the Taser before she could say a single word.

That was that. Dr. Nakamura hit the sand face-first. I dragged her into the forest. An hour later I was back on the road. Several hours beyond that, I was home. Rebecca's corpse was tucked away in one of my storage units, wrapped up nice and neat in a GE freezer. I'd finish with her later. After all, I had a date with Daphne the next day at noon, and it was already long past midnight.

I needed to get my rest.

⸻

If I shared it, you'd recognize the name of the cemetery where Daphne and I had our first date. It's famous. But I think I'll keep that information to myself. I suppose I'm a little sensitive about the place after the way things turned out. You'll have a better understanding of why later.

Anyway, as prominent as the place was, I'll bet no one had ever picnicked there. That's exactly what Daphne and I did on an afternoon that was as still as it was sunny—May light filtering through the trees, chill patches of shadow not quite ready to warm despite the change of seasons, the scent of pine and cut grass, the cool appraisal in Daphne's guarded glances.

Daphne (of course) had done her research. She said that cemeteries had been akin to city parks in Victorian times, when families would spread tablecloths on the grass and share memories of their dear departed along with roast squab and pickled eggs on sunny

Sunday afternoons.

I can't speak for Daphne, but I certainly had no one to mourn with that level of sincerity. What I did have was Daphne's company and the picnic lunch she prepared. A pleasant Pinot gris, nicely chilled. Fried chicken, a loaf of sourdough with wedges of Irish butter, and an apple and grape salad with sour cream dressing. Cherries and chocolate cake.

Unfortunately, the conversation didn't match the food. The words that passed between us were simple chit-chat, with none of the electricity of our phone call. Just some mundane gossip about classmates and instructors, with a few conversational detours concerning the cemetery's more infamous residents. All that was entertaining enough as far as it went, but it wasn't the kind of conversation I'd hoped for . . . and I'm sure Daphne felt the same way.

All that changed as soon as we emptied the bottle of wine and packed the picnic basket.

"Ready to check out the library, Mr. Burke?"

"Definitely, Ms. Hare."

"I should warn you—it's a library with spirits."

"As in: distilled?"

The exchange passed so quickly it seemed we had rehearsed it, as chipper and quippy as dialogue in an old William Powell/Myrna Loy movie that was about to get much more twisted than Warner Brothers would have ever allowed. But neither of us laughed when it was over. For the truth was that we had simply progressed to the next point on the agenda, as in: I followed Daphne down a path that led to the edge of the cemetery grounds.

A cathedral stood at the end of the path . . . or at least a building I took for a cathedral. Inside was something else entirely. Instead of a large room with a vaulted ceiling, the building was a tangle of twisting corridors and oddly shaped rooms. The walls of each were lined with golden books that weren't books at all, but instead boxes bearing the cremains of the deceased with their names etched on the spines. The correct term for the place (I knew) was *columbarium*, but indeed it was a library, and it felt like one. For just as books do, each of these boxes held a particular story.

Of course, I never would have believed those stories could be shared. Daphne, I soon discovered, thought otherwise. Even her walk through the place was a lesson in that, for she brought with her the percussion of coffin nails. Her heels clicked along the empty corridor, each step a seeming precursor for a small ending, and as she walked she ran one black-nailed finger along those golden spines, as if searching for the beginning of a tale that struck her particular fancy.

I followed her down the corridor, listening to the scrape of that nail. Without turning to face me, Daphne asked: "So ... do you believe in spooky stuff?"

"What do you mean?"

"You know—001.64."

"We're talking paranormal phenomenon?"

"You can close down the parameters a little: spectral manifestations ... shades and revenants ... your basic things that go bump in the night."

"Well, I suppose I'm the kind of person who believes what he can see."

"You mean, you're a *proof is in the pudding* kind of guy?"

"I suppose so."

"Then let's see what we can see, Stagger Lee ... or maybe what we can feel."

Daphne turned and smiled at me, and that same finger she'd run across a hundred etched spines brushed my lips and crossed my chin. Only for a moment. Then she turned away, advancing down a narrow hallway. Her hips swayed beneath her skirt, and her fingers arched into claws, a fistful of nails scratching over spines.

The briefest moment later her fingers stopped, very quickly, index finger poised on one particular spine. "Ohhhh," she said, and it was the kind of sound I'd never heard from Daphne before. It echoed through the columbarium hallway like a sound from a cave.

"They say some people are mediums," Daphne said. "They stir shadows, raise the past and the dead, hold them in their grasp. For a while, for a time ... and then that time is gone. In that regard they're like imperfect vessels, I suppose. But they're something more, too."

"People say all kinds of things."

"So—no verdict on that particular form of perception?"

"Uh-uh."

"Let's conduct a little experiment then. For example, it's my perception that this particular box is filled with firecrackers, psychically speaking. I'd like you to touch it and see what happens."

"I don't know."

"C'mon. Take a chance." Daphne smiled. "Do it and I'll guarantee a reward ... later."

"Not my thing, really."

"Well there's a surprise."

"Uh." I stammered. "Well ... maybe it is. Sometimes."

"Okay. You're the boss, applesauce ... but just one other thing —our date's over."

Daphne turned away. From me. From the columbarium book. She started walking and didn't look back, heels clicking down the hallway, those little nail-driving steps marking percussion to my thoughts. Quite literally, she was disappearing into the shadows, and before my very eyes.

My hand reached out before I even knew it, fingers touching that yellow spine. But it wasn't a spine at all ... at least not one you'd find on a book, or a box. No, it was too cold and slick, its ridges mimicking movement like those grave-worms knotted across that horrible face in my dreams. And then there were words, and they weren't Daphne's. *You see, my friend. We meet again.*

And now that face hung before me, above a buckled collar cinched from dead whore's nightmares. The thing wore a top hat, and it leered with that knotted-worm smile. One whiff of its breath and a wave of dizziness hit me so hard that for a moment I imagined I was back on that beach with Rebecca, cold Pacific tides pounding me to the ground as she escaped down the beach in her blue-and-coral Nikes. And even in the moment I realized that was only a fantasy, one shorn of every notion of personal power possible. I tried to focus, managed just for a moment to read the name on the spine of the book, and then the letters were lost in a wet, smeared sheen.

So was everything else.

My knees buckled. I was about to pass out.

I started to fall. Daphne didn't allow that. Suddenly she was very close, holding me up. "I've been coming here for a few years," she said. "Touching a spine here, a spine there—collecting impressions. I remember the first time I touched that book, and he told me who he was. I couldn't believe it, not at first. Later, I couldn't deny it. And now he's my special friend, one of a kind, no one like him anywhere. At least, I always thought so...until I met you."

Daphne's wine-dark lips drew closer, close to my ear. But her voice was far away, as if deep inside a seashell ... or a memory boxed away. "Remember that day in class? When you loaned me a pencil? It started then. I got my first little tingle of you. And now there's nothing I don't know about you. I've been inside your storage units. Those are nice boxes you built for Dr. Nakamura ... they should be a good fit. I've even held your knives. In fact, I borrowed one a few weeks ago, the night we took our final for AARC2. Remember that little dweeb who always sat in the front row? The one who asked the same question three different ways in every class? Well, his questioning days are over."

"I need to sit down," I said. "I think I'm going to pass out."

"Don't get fried, Mr. Hyde," Daphne said. "Not during our very first dance. He wouldn't like that."

I said something, but I can't imagine what it was. Moments had passed ... perhaps minutes. The next thing I knew, Daphne was already moving away. I toppled sideways, leaning against the wall, trying to steady myself. Daphne's heels clicked over the tile floor. I tried to measure time by her footfalls. I still couldn't move. I was buried in a dream—her dream or mine, I couldn't be sure—and those coffin-nail footfalls were driving deeply ... over and over and over again.

Daphne was further away now ... very far.

And then she was gone.

A door swung open, and a breath of wind washed over my back.

Outside the door Daphne voice rose over the marble forest ahead, and lingered behind.

"Come along now," she said. "After all, I keep my promises."

I don't know how I managed it, but I began to follow.

The darkness followed behind me.

No doubt Daphne had made promises to it, as well.

———▲———

No one had ever been in my apartment before. Except the land-lord, and a plumber when I had to have the toilet replaced. But now that we were there the rooms seemed too small and the things they contained even smaller. And the bed, well ... it was only a sin-gle bed, but Daphne said it wouldn't matter because our real bed was darkness itself, and without borders. That was fine with me. I welcomed darkness wherever I found it.

That night, I hoped the shadows would deliver my mind to other places ... alone. But you can't be alone with lovers, even in the dark. And so it was with us and the thing from the columbari-um. Daphne and I, alive on a hideous canvas, our hearts pounding, the two of us writhing in the night as worms that twist and couple in a ripe grave. That thing an oozing mess around and under and over and in, free of its buckles and clothes, ripe and corrupt.

Whether it was climax or prelude was a matter of perspective. As act or ceremony, the grave was the grit of it, and blood was its heart. Still Daphne burrowed in and so did I, like hungry little grave worms seeking the choicest morsel. There was no other choice, but any pleasure found was quickly lost between lips and belly in the manner of a ghoul's meal.

Or, to put it more succinctly:

"A nightmare?" you ask.

"Of course," I reply.

What else could I call it? For in truth or imaginings, nightmares must be endured. And as I drifted off to sleep, I thought it would have been better if we were all past enduring. If (on this night) we'd all worn knives for fingers instead of flesh and shadow. Make that simple adjustment, and the three of us would have slashed the darkness to ribbons and left nothing for the coming dawn but a puddle of gore fit only for the coroner's pail.

It would have been better that way, I think.

For in the end, the worms indeed had their way.

When I awoke in the morning, Daphne was already gone. She had a waitress job not far from the college where we attended library school, so she'd probably put my apartment in her rearview mirror long before the sun came up. The only thing she left behind was a lipstick message on the bathroom mirror:

Stay loose, Dr. Mabuse.
We'll see you soon.
Xoxoxo,
364.1523³

Of course, I knew that Dewey Decimal number by heart long before I ever picked up a knife.

Amping it up to the third power was a nice touch, though.

Then again, I've never been much of a joiner.

I left my apartment not long after that, grabbing coffee, then waiting for the cemetery gates to open. Once inside, I made my way to the library...or the building that passed for one.

No one was there, of course. At least, no one living … not at this early hour. That was fine with me. There was only one thing I was after—I wanted another look at the name on the columbarium box I'd touched the day before, and I wanted to write down the dates of birth and death. That seemed as good a place as any to begin my research.

I hurried down the hallway, retracing my steps. Of course, I remembered the spot, and for a moment it was as if I walked in my own shadow, and the echo of my footsteps was an echo of Daphne's from the day before.

I shook those impressions away. All I wanted was that book, and the information on the spine.

My hand traveled upward, fingers spreading.

The nail of my index finger traveled spines, as Daphne's had the day before. And then it came to a gap.

To the place a book had been.

In its place was another box—the Japanese puzzle box I'd built for Rebecca. It sat on the shelf, as open as open could be and just as empty. There was no storage-unit key inside.

I grabbed the box and hurried away from the chapel and the cemetery. Feeling, with good reason, like an exorcised spirit.

<hr />

It would have been a relief to go to work the next day, except for the eight a.m. phone call from the library director requesting that I come in early for a meeting. A few hours of uncomfortable tension passed before the appointed time arrived and I dropped my backpack on a chair in his outer office. His administrative assistant led me inside.

"I know you're a creature of the night, working the shift you do," the director said. "Thanks for coming out in the light of day."

"I wore my 666 sunblock," I said, "just to be safe."

"Good one." He laughed. "Now let's get to it. Looks like you really knocked out all the repair work we've been throwing at you. I think it's time you put the scrapper and glue away for a while. Now that you're getting your Masters, we'll give you something really interesting to work on."

"Such as?"

"Let's take a walk, and I'll show you."

I followed the director, waiting for the other shoe to drop. We took the three flights to the Archives office, my suspicions mounting with every step, just waiting for him to say something about my hidden toolbox or some other troubling evidence. But the only things the director talked about were his doctor and his cholesterol numbers. Needless to say, he wasn't happy with either.

By the time we reached the third floor, I'd begun to relax. Obviously, this wasn't about me. The Archives itself was empty at this time of day. The main office adjoined several workrooms, and the director used his master key to make the trip down a narrow hallway leading to the very last one.

"You really won't believe this stuff," he said. "It's been in a warehouse over in Oakland for close to a hundred years. The place is changing hands, so the college had to relocate a ton of material that's been stored there since Moses was a baby. Mostly papers that belonged to a doctor who left his entire estate to the college years ago. He was a Brit expat who did pretty well for himself after immigrating in the 1890s, and he didn't have any relations ... at least on this side of the pond. After his death, the college got his money and the library was stuck with rest of it—you know, the usual story. Who knows what the collection amounts to, but I think you're the man to give it a look and decide what's what. There's a ton of books on esoteric religions and cults—but I have a feeling a lot of that's just landfill waiting to happen. Seems the silverfish got to it long ago... or something that was hungry, anyway."

"And the rest of the collection?" I asked.

"Well, who knows? Turn-of-the-century scuttlebutt was that our doctor friend might have been the abortionist of choice for the privileged class of his day, so there might be something interesting. Buddy up with someone in the Women's Studies department, you might even get a juicy paper out of it."

The director unlocked the door. Even before it swung open, I had an idea what I'd see . . . and my gut told me it was something I knew I'd recognize.

"First off, here's your full box of *morbid*," the director said, pointing at an object on a table in the center of the room. "That's a Victorian autopsy kit. Saws and knives and the whole nine yards. Can you believe it?"

"Yes," I said. "I certainly can." It was a true statement, because (of course) I'd seen the box before, in a dream, and I recognized it down to every strap and buckle, ones that matched the buckles on a certain walking nightmare's collar.

Next to the autopsy kit was another box. This one was wooden. I'd never seen it before, but it was definitely a style with which I was familiar.

The director picked it up. "Judging from what I've found on the internet, this is a Japanese puzzle box—well-crafted, practically a museum piece. I believe it's in the Koyosegi style. No idea what's inside it, however. Who knows . . . maybe it's a diary or something. They say our friend the doctor spent a few years in Japan before immigrating to the States. Could be a find. Maybe he hung out with Lafcadio Hearn and took notes." He sighed. "Anyway, want to give it a look and see if you have any luck opening it? From what the students tell me, puzzles are your thing. Stephen told me you can knock out a Rubik's cube in less than thirty seconds."

"Actually, I'm not very good at puzzles," I said, realizing quite suddenly that I spoke the absolute truth. "Not at all."

———————⬥———————

There were a million things I should have done that night, but I suppose the only one that matters is the one I did. I paid a visit to my main storage unit, where I butchered Rebecca's frozen corpse and placed the parts in individual caskets. This itself was an exhausting process, and afterwards I embarked upon my usual ceremonies for secreting the caskets that held my victims. But in truth that was little better than indulging an avoidance mechanism. There were far more pressing matters at hand, most of them involving Mr. 364.1523 and/or Daphne.

I should have called Daphne ... or perhaps kidnapped her. I should have found out if the game we were playing was of her design, or Mr. 364.1523's, or perhaps both. I should have found out if she opened Dr. Nakamura's puzzle box, or if it was opened by ghostly hands. And then we should have had a frank discussion about statistical improbabilities of certain coincidences involving serial killers both dead and alive, and the dangerous course (and absolute, incontrovertible outcomes) of certain obsessions. Namely those that fell within the parameters of 364.1523.

Or I could have done research about the infamous killer who dominated that particular number, and plugged the dead doctor's name into any number of search engines along with "Jack the Ripper." A little history lesson, if you please. And perhaps a lesson in connect-the-dates, because I was more than familiar with the timetable of Jack the Ripper's crimes. If the doctor were indeed a suspect, dates and places would not be hard to match.

Perhaps I could have even gone to the college and opened the doctor's puzzle box, still waiting for me in the Archives on the third floor. Perhaps there really was a diary inside. If that were true, it no doubt held answers.

In short, there were many things I could have done.

Many questions I might have answered with just a little effort.

But none of that was to be. As a result, many of those questions still haunt me today. Perhaps I could never have answered them, but I would have liked to say that I tried. I didn't. For one night, at least, I had hit my limit. So I washed Rebecca's blood off my hands, and I locked the caskets in my storage unit and drove home.

Then (in the manner of Mr. Poe) I quaffed Nepenthe and slept the sleep of the dead.

But not the dreamless.

This time the dream didn't take place in the library. Instead it was in the graveyard, outside the columbarium. Mr. 364.1523 stood there among the tombstones, his double-buckled collar cinched tight, his top hat perched above the little mountain of worms that masqueraded as his head.

"So, you're beginning to understand now?" he asked.

"I'm beginning to see a larger picture," I said. "I'll admit that. But I'm not sure I understand much at all."

"Come, come. You're a bright lad, and it's all very simple. I won't have to draw you a diagram, will I?"

"No. I'm perfectly capable of adding to three."

"Bravo. So nice to hear."

"Then you'll like this even better: I make my own choices, and I always have."

He laughed, as if highly amused by my audacity. The sound shook him from within. The worms ringing that familiar black hole in his face circled it the way gore-flecked water circles an autopsy table drain.

"It's funny, is it?" I said.

"Oh, yes. Dreadfully so."

"I'm not so sure I see the humor in the situation."

"Perhaps not. But you must realize there's much I can teach you. And we obviously share common ground—a very nice patch of it. On that subject: Did you like it? The three of us? I suppose that is the primary question, simply put."

"I can't say as I did."

"Oh, now you're lying, sir. Shame, shame. Or perhaps you're simply not the kind to admit the particulars of your pleasures. Perhaps, in the end, that evening's work put you exactly where you belong. You're simply not accustomed to tucking your tail between your legs as of yet, but this too will come. You'll learn your place in the new order quickly enough ... just as a well-used knife finds a new home in the barnyard when a sharp new blade arrives for the china cabinet."

"The fact is I've always seen myself as a lone wolf."

"You're not a wolf, my friend. That is my particular prevue. But perhaps you're a dog. Yes, I think that's the role that would suit you best. An obedient and loyal servant. After all, you learned all the tricks, just as a good dog does. You learned from books, from histories of true wolves like myself. Not a lot of originality in your methods, but you're quite the talented imitator. In that role, I can use you."

"You're asking me to fetch and carry?"

"No. I'm saying you already are." Again, those worms were twisting where his lips should have been. "Would you like me to show you?"

"I wish you would."

The dream-wind was higher now, scoring my skin, brushing the worms across Mr. 364.1523's brow. He removed his top hat and held it aloft … just for a moment. And then his fingers set it free and it tumbled on the wind.

"There's a good dog," he said. "Fetch and carry."

I stood there for a moment, not believing the words he'd spoken. The top hat tumbled through the air, traveling between wind-twisted boughs, and then it touched down between the tombstones. Before I knew it I was chasing after it, running through the graveyard. For a moment I even dropped to all fours, charging ahead without a care for whatever came afterward … without a care, forevermore.

And then I stopped, quite suddenly. I knew what had happened … what was happening. Mr. 364.1523's laughter whipped me like the wind and rang in my head. That sound chilled me as nothing ever had. And suddenly I understood just how it would be if things stayed that way … just how it would be, forevermore.

I couldn't allow that to happen. So I fought the dream. I started to awaken. I know I did. I tried to swim up from deep black water, the way you do when you rouse yourself from a nightmare.

But something held me back. Or someone. At first I thought it was Daphne. She stood at the edge of the graveyard, in shadows that hung from the trees. Her pale face was flushed with excitement. "Can you imagine what it will be like?" she asked. "Using that kit? Carving up a victim with his knives? It's time to get started. Hurry and join me . . . I'm ready. Let's go to the library. Let's get that case—"

I wanted to warn her. I wanted to tell Daphne what Mr. 364.1523 had asked. I wanted to tell her what life would be like as a hunting hound, and say that I'd never spend my life in a dead man's kennel. I opened my mouth, ready to tell her everything. I ran my tongue over my lips, for that graveyard wind had dried them. But all I tasted on my lips were the slick excretions of carrion worms, and the words that came from my mouth were not my own.

"It's time to make a new start," he said, his voice coming from a hollow place inside me. "A red parade—that's what it will be. Meet me at the library. We don't need him at all. Tonight it will be just the two of us. That's all we really need . . ."

———◆———

When I awoke, I found myself standing in the kitchen of my apartment. The handset of the wall phone was wrapped in my fingers, and my mouth was open. But the words he'd spoken were gone and it was too late to replace them with others.

A dial tone buzzed from the receiver.

Daphne was gone.

I dropped the phone, grabbed my keys, and left my apartment in a rush. I was barely awake when I started the car and headed for the library. But soon my mind was ticking away, running different scenarios the way it always did, searching for a way to come out on top in the confrontation that lay ahead.

Of course, in truth I was still running like a dog in a dream.

I just didn't know it yet.

———◆———

I have wondered if I was the one responsible for everything that happened that night. I mean, if I was the real murderer. Certainly, I might have been. Certainly, my brain didn't function the way other brains function, and I was clearly capable of the acts which occurred. So I won't blame you if you read this and think: "That's it, exactly. He was crazy. He imagined half the coincidences that led up to that night. He probably imagined half of everything. Hell, he was probably alone when he ate that picnic lunch in the graveyard. And I'll bet he barely spoke to that Daphne chick at all, just stalked her like a creepy little mouse. Just listen to what he says, do the math, and it all adds up to *beyond batshit*. Even if you go best-case scenario, that Ripper stuff was already hard-wired in his head... and if Daphne really was tuned in to all that supernatural jazz the way he said she was then she was probably a couple cans short of a six pack, too. And when they bumped up against each other it was dead-on destiny that it'd end up badly... in no uncertain terms."

And who knows? If that's the way you read the cards, maybe you're right. I can't convince you otherwise. After all, they say that perception is everything. But so is honesty. And while I understand there's no real reason that you would accept the latter quality as part of my makeup, I can assure you that it is.

Or was.

I can also assure you of a few other facts of which I'm absolutely certain.

First: When I arrived at the library that night, the front doors were already open.

Second: Daphne was already on the second floor, screaming bloody murder.

I wish this were another kind of story. If it were, I could provide you with a more satisfying ending. One that involved pulp heroics, or noirish anti-heroics, or perhaps a Hitchcockian twist or two. One with full measures of shadow and darkness and a triple-play of bad business and murderous intent. Or, to put it simply for those who appreciate the classics, I'd love to be able to provide you with a twisted version of "The Most Dangerous Game" times three.

But doing that with the facts at hand would be just as impossible as making a butcher shop display case seem exciting. No matter how hard you try, you can't do it. In the end, it's just dead meat. And that's the kind of ending I found at the library. I didn't have to see what the man in the top hat left upstairs to know that was true, for I'd studied his methods for years. I could imagine well enough what remained of Daphne after he finished with his knives and assorted autopsy instruments. To paraphrase a comment from my dream: I didn't need him to draw me a diagram.

Not that he would have. Not that he needed to. Not anymore. If I'd been useful to him at all, the time had passed. At that moment we'd circled back to the beginning. Meaning I was frozen in place when he descended the library staircase—I had been for several minutes as Daphne screamed her last—frozen just the way I had been that first night he appeared on the landing after the library was closed. He wore no leather apron, just the black clothes he'd worn that very first night. And for a ghost he seemed to handle material objects just fine. In one hand he held the old puzzle box that might have contained a diary, and with the other he carried the autopsy kit. It was buckled and secure the same way his collar was buckled, and swung in his gloved hand the way a pendulum swings in a funeral home, marking time that no longer matters.

He spoke as he approached me, his head writhing and alive now, no longer approximating anything human at all. "You don't realize what I offered you. The secrets I know, the things I was willing to teach. The nightmares we might have shared, the three of us. The boxes we might have opened, together. But now they are shut, forevermore. For you, for her ... for eternity. I will always walk alone."

The words washed over me. I stood there like a statue as the Ripper's smile writhed across those lips one last time. It was almost wistful. I couldn't say a single word. Not as he patted my cheek with a bloody hand. Not as he crossed the lobby to the Circulation Desk. Not as he picked up the phone and dialed the extension for Public Safety. Not as he reported a murder using my voice.

In a moment, he was gone.

The darkness closed in—for seconds, for minutes—and then sirens rose in the distance. And soon I was running. Just as I had in my dream, like a starving dog in a cemetery, charging over bones that lay buried much too deep to be enjoyed.

I ran farther than you'd expect, and finally the sirens and lights closed in on me.

The light was followed by bullets.

In some measure, that was another ending.

And a beginning, as well.

Of course, you can probably guess how the remainder of my journey progressed. Autopsy table, crime lab, a long blast of crematorium fire. All of it leading to a final destination that is a given: the cemetery where I picnicked with Daphne, and a box in that very same columbarium chapel where hallways led one to another, and the rooms did the same ... all of them (given the circumstances) ultimately leading nowhere at all.

Who knows about Daphne. Perhaps she's here, too. If she is, I haven't found her yet. I've checked the shelves at least a hundred times, scoured every room searching for a golden box which bears her name. But perhaps that isn't the kind of box I should be looking for. Perhaps I should look for a puzzle box made of laurel. In a perfect world (or a perfect myth), I'm sure that's exactly where Daphne would be.

As for my own box, it's really no different than all the others here. That may surprise you, but it really doesn't matter to me. There have always been boxes hidden away, in my life and in my mind. But I have never really inhabited a single one of them. I have never shut myself in. I won't change by doing that now.

Instead, I think of the boxes here as books. Each one holds a story, and I've come to know many of them. I am their curator. Of course, if you asked anyone on staff, they'll tell you there is no librarian here. But there is. It's me. I walk the halls, and I know the stories. You'll learn a few of them soon.

For my own part I listen carefully, searching for another story that will inform my own. One that will tell me more about Daphne, or answer the questions which remain in the Ripper's wake. Was he ghost or demon or something stranger, I don't know. Maybe I never will. But you can never tell where an answer might be hidden, or the unexpected places a tale might lead. In life and in stories there's always another panel to slide, another puzzle box to open.

Perhaps it's that way in death, too.

For here, in this place, there are always more boxes, always more stories.

They arrive every day.

Maybe someday I'll find the one I need to finish my own.

Until then, there are other stories.

Listen, and I'll share some of them now...

THE LIBRARIAN

1

Stars hide behind late-rolling fog as you make your way around the winding labyrinthine paths of Mountain View Cemetery. Crocker Mausoleum casts lighthouse-like shadows over the semi-paved walkway called Millionaires Row, which you follow to a more straightforward path you recognize, leading back to a fountain near Piedmont Avenue, leading further to a small circular path near the main gate, which may or may not be locked at this hour, you realize.

And hold your breath.

Chapel of the Chimes glows in the distance as the night rolls into early morning, but as you approach, the color of the building is not so much white, but golden in hue. Interior light escapes the multitude of windows behind arches and cloverleaves and other such carved patterns in the exterior, giving life at night to this sizeable yet plain-looking adobe building in the day. Before the sun died, you remember an ordinary gray—perhaps stucco—exterior beneath a roof of burnt-orange clay tile. Now, with the moon taking the sun's place, the building nearly breathes with color, and pulls you toward its warmth to escape the chill Oakland night, and you breathe out, realizing the gate is still open.

All is silent but for the trickling and splashing of water from the fountain, the soft buzz of old streetlights, and the yelping of a faraway dog or perhaps a coyote. Your car is parked somewhere on the street, and on the way to it you pass the first of what appears to be three entrances to the eerie building at your side. Above a high arch, the first entrance reads:

CHAPEL OF THE CHIMES

Each capital letter, carved intricately into the stone façade, follows above and along the arch. A dozen or more paces leads to the second entrance, which, like the first, has a small fountain and is nearly identical, with the same arching capital letters. The only differences are those same words as above, newer, displayed in black on the left-hand side of the entry, followed by 'Oakland,' and below that above six Asian symbols:

Funeral Home
Crematory
Columbarium

The third, and what appears to serve as the main entrance to the building, stands nearly twice as high and twice as wide as the others, and the archway leading to the main double doors is even more intricately carved in stone. In large capital letters above this impressive gaping maw is a single word:

MAUSOLEUM

It must be past midnight, yet these main doors to the building are wide open. Cold chills bubble like champagne poured down your spine, yet the doors are open arms, inviting, calling you to come inside. The golden glow emanating from within pulls you closer, and then closer, until you are no longer on the sidewalk at all but standing on the first steps, and then you are suddenly under the framework of the doors, your head peering through, then the rest of you, and finally you are inside and wide-eyed.

The foyer is nothing spectacular, resembling a hotel lobby more than a mausoleum, and the golden glow does not emanate from this particular room, but permeates from the maze of rooms further inside.

What startles you is the hooded figure.

"Welcome to The Library of the Dead," the figure says, sweeping a gangly arm in an arc matching that of the entryways. *The voice is chant-like and neither masculine nor feminine.* He or she turns in a fluid motion and gestures for you to follow, then disappears into the first of many rooms.

The cloaked arm sweeps the next room, pointing out the endless shelves of golden books encased in glass. The oversized books create the glow, you realize, for there are countless volumes, thousands, hundreds of thousands on display in the building, you imagine, most gold or etched in gold. Vaulted ceilings leading to beautiful stained glass, rooms leading to more rooms, and then more rooms, and then even more rooms, each unique, each glowing differently because of their design, a Moorish- and Gothic-inspired maze of rooms, with ornate stonework at every curve, mosaics at every turn, statues, fountains—yes, that is water you hear—and gardens—green and colorful and growing within the building, and yes, that is life you smell—and private chapels. All of it seems endless, or perhaps eternal. 1909, you remember reading about this place, and not a library, per se, but—

"Called so because each of these golden tomes contains the entombed ashes of a fascinating person."

The hooded figure bows politely.

Cinerary urns.

"And I am your guide, your librarian."

The librarian, whose features remain shadowed by a cowl, continues: *"Here, within these golden covers, are ancient legends, ethnic myths, and much realistic magic."*

The figure floats to the topmost shelf as if lifted on a gust of air, withdraws three golden books, and descends.

"Like these," your librarian says, opening the first of the three.

THOSE WHO
SHALL NEVER
BE NAMED

YVONNE NAVARRO

January 9, 1947

The girl was a waitress and her name was Elizabeth. He'd had coffee in the restaurant several hours earlier and flirted with her just enough to where she'd remember his face when he "happened" to run into her on the street later. He followed her for a couple of blocks to make sure no one from her job saw him, then made his move, calling out to her and flattering her because he remembered her name from where she'd written it on the check. She was a looker, pale and young with curly black hair and light blue eyes. There was a faint, unfocused desperation about her, like she didn't know where she was going or what to do next, and was looking for someone to take over for her. He was just the guy to show her the way.

There had always been a darkness in his soul. Hungry, waiting beneath the surface of his barely contained humanity, knowing that someday its will would win over his. Tonight, surrounded by the damp, chilly breeze, he surrendered and let it take him where it would, down a path that could never be reversed. He thought that when this happened—and he'd known it eventually would—he would regret it. He'd thought he would be heavy with guilt, remorseful. Instead, he reveled in the freedom of letting go, even wallowed in it. It was joyous and sweet and indescribably evil.

January 15, 1947

Tommy Milner was walking along the side of the road in Leimart Park when he realized he was coming up on a car parked off to the side with its headlamps angled just enough to spill light into the abandoned lot next to it. He froze, watching as a dark-haired man hauled first one, then another oversized package out of the trunk; they were clearly heavy and he carried them a few feet off the road one at a time and set each carefully down. Always the enterprising teenager, Tommy crept closer, instinctively making his footsteps soundless as he extinguished his cigarette and pocketed the butt to finish later. Maybe the man was a robber, or a mob guy burying a load of money to be dug up after the heat was off him. Tommy wasn't particularly bright but he knew the score—or thought he did—and he figured he'd hide out and pick up the loot after the guy was gone. He dropped into the ditch about twenty feet behind the car, huddling into his leather jacket for warmth and ignoring the clammy, unpleasant dirt, convinced that this was going to be the luckiest night of his life.

That all changed when the man unwrapped the parcels.

─────▲─────

He was a fastidious man, precise, thorough to a fault. It took time to decide how to place her—her hands, her hair, the top and bottom. He wore gloves, of course, even though he had done the bulk of the work and the cleaning up in the privacy of his home; although this was his first time, he knew it would not be his last and had therefore amassed a profusion of implements for just this occasion. He wanted her to be relaxed in her slumber, exquisite with the modifications he had given her. Her beauty would be preserved forever; there would be photographs taken, books written. Not by him, of course, but about him, and her, and what he had done to her.

He backed up, inspecting his work with the critical eye he knew would be forthcoming by law enforcement and journalists alike. No, the arms weren't right—they had to be above her head, as if she had thrown herself back on a bed, her dark curls arranged just so. She was smiling, ear to ear as he had insisted, although the ropes had left marks around her wrists that he couldn't erase—too bad. There were some other marks that also couldn't be disguised, like the part of her breast that he had cut into—

He jerked and raised his head from where he had been bending over her, then looked back toward the road. He'd heard something … maybe. He strained to see but the headlights of his own car blinded him, turning everything behind them to an abyss. Straightening slowly, he walked back to the car, then stepped behind the lights. It took a few moments for his eyes to adjust, but although he scanned the area carefully he still didn't see anything. He waited, always patient, for several minutes, but the noise didn't come again. Probably a stray cat, or perhaps a rat. The thought disturbed him as he went back to where Elizabeth lay, wrapped in the sleep of eternity, and he hoped she would be found before animals maimed his perfect handiwork.

A few more adjustments, a gathering of materials, and he was finally finished. As he drove away, he relished the thought of the days to come, and the way everyone would marvel at the wonderful piece of art he had created.

It took the man a few minutes to strip off his gloves and push the blankets, or whatever they were, into a paper bag. By the time the car was rolling slowly away, Tommy had wiggled up close enough to the road to read the car's license plate. He had nothing to write on so he repeated it to himself over and over, knowing that otherwise he'd never remember it. Half an hour later he made it home and scribbled it on a piece of paper, then he could finally sit down and think about what he'd seen, the whole picture. He should tell the cops, but his old man was on the force and he and Tommy had been going at it for the last year, ever since Tommy had graduated high school but not found a job. Truth was, Tommy was more interested in hanging on the street corners with his pals; the senior Thomas Milner—Tommy was a junior—routinely called them all street thugs. He'd probably accuse Tommy of killing that woman and then things would get a hundred—no, a thousand—times worse. Nah, better to dig around on his own. He'd learned a few things by listening to what his father said about finding public information at the library. Once he traced the license plate number and found out who the murderer was, it was a short hop from there to heroism. He couldn't wait to see the look on Detective Milner's face.

———————▲———————

A week later he was on his way to eat at a nice little diner a world away from the one in which he had first put Elizabeth Short—he had learned her full name from the newspapers—in his sights, when he realized he was being watched. He stopped and bent over so that it looked like he was tying his shoe-lace, and a quick scan of the area across the street confirmed it. There, leaning just on the other side of a lamp post, was a young man in a beat-up leather coat and baseball cap. His face was lowered and indistinguishable, but the outfit was solidly blue-collar: checked shirt collar crushed beneath the top of the leather coat, denim jeans, white socks and dusty black shoes.

He straightened and moved forward, walking at a crisp pace but keeping his watcher in sight without actually looking straight at him. The man paced him along the sidewalk across the street with almost no skill at concealing him-self. Obviously not the police, but being followed was irritating and made him discard his plans for dinner and head for his car instead. He would leave this foolishness behind and find somewhere else to enjoy a meal. A coworker had told him about a place called Philippe's over on Aliso Street and recommended a sandwich they had called a "French Dip." It sounded interesting and he'd lost his taste for anything more . . . involved this evening anyway.

———————▲———————

When the killer did an about face and headed back to his car, Tommy figured he'd been made. Even so, as long as he kept his distance he ought to be okay. What was the guy gonna do, call the coppers? He had it all thought out, and the guy's choice of a one way street had made it even easier; Tommy was driving his buddy's car and he'd found a parking space three cars up; unless his target tried a U-turn to go the wrong way in the middle of the evening traffic, there was nowhere for him to go but right past Tommy. Tommy pulled out behind him and stayed just close enough to where he could jump on it if the man tried to lose him.

Six blocks later, that's exactly what the murdering bastard tried to do, and an hour later Tommy couldn't have recounted their route if he'd tried. The guy had started by turning left and right seemingly at random, then he'd finally made a flat-out run for the highway. That's where they were now, on 101 and headed north. That was fine with Tommy; he'd filched some cash from the rent money jar his old man didn't know he'd found, then filled up the tank and bought himself some cigarettes and snacks. That wasn't all he'd taken from the house this morning, so he was feeling pretty good about what the evening would hold. Damned good, in fact.

Tommy dropped back a little, letting a car pass him and get between him and the killer. That would give the guy a false sense of security and it might make him think he wasn't being followed anymore; there weren't many turnoffs and Tommy was staying close enough to see him around the car in front of him— he'd catch it if the car turned onto some side road. Grinning, the young man settled back and turned up the radio, ready to see where this ride would take him.

<hr/>

He was still being followed. Although the vehicle had dropped back a car or two, there was so little traffic on this road that it wasn't hard to keep the headlights in his rearview mirror. At first he wasn't sure where he was going—he was just driving, vaguely turning over routes that might let him throw the guy off. Logic told him that the longer he was followed, the safer he was, if for no other reason than it led away from his home in the Los Angeles area and Leimert Park, where he'd killed the girl. It couldn't be the police following him or he would have already been arrested, or at least questioned. As he was driving, he had a flash memory of the night he'd sent Elizabeth Short to her maker and that moment when he'd thought he'd heard something. Perhaps it hadn't been a rat after all, or at least not the rodent kind. If that was the case, he was going as far as this guy was willing to follow him.

Almost nine hours later, though, he'd had enough. He was running out of patience, low on fuel again after stopping nearly a dozen times, and he wanted nothing more than a hot plate of food and a warm bed. He swung off the high-

way toward Oakland, heading east with the thought of finding somewhere—anywhere—that he could put this farce of a car chase to an end. He made random turns but the smaller streets and the traffic, even at this late hour, worked against him. Eventually though, destiny threw him a bone, and a few miles into Oakland proper, the answer was right in front of him:

MOUNTAIN VIEW CEMETERY

What better place than a graveyard to take care of this problem and hide the results?

Tommy followed the killer at the turnoff to Oakland, staying close to make sure no one pulled between them. He was done with any pretense—the guy knew he was there and it no longer looked like he was making any effort to get away. They were headed to a showdown, but Tommy was okay with that. His cash was about gone and he was bone tired; he'd filled up every time the other man did and almost lost him every damned time. It was almost 5:00 AM, and unless the guy he was chasing was some kind of Superman, this cat and mouse had to come to an end. The guy was a killer but his weapon was a knife, or a saw, or maybe both—who really knew? Tommy had read about his dirty work in the paper, how he had cut that poor girl's face up and then chopped her body in half. Tommy half-grinned, half-grimaced, then reached over and touched the .38 Colt he'd taken out of the backup holster hanging in his dad's closet. The metal was cold and filled the air around him with a heavy scent of gun oil that couldn't be overcome by his cigarette smoke. Somehow its presence didn't give him nearly the feeling of security he thought it would, but he wasn't going to turn back now. He might not be the expert at shooting that his old man was, but how hard could it be? You just had to be close enough to the target, that's all.

Still, Tommy couldn't help a feeling of the creeps as he followed the killer into Mountain View Cemetery.

He'd hoped to finally lose his follower within the twisting, circling lanes of the cemetery. No such luck; his own car was a fine automobile, but the vehicle tailing him must have been "souped up," as the young people were saying nowadays. Nothing he did would shake the guy, and he was starting to feel like a mouse trapped in a maze with a hungry weasel—no matter which way he ran, the predator was always just behind him.

Enough. He'd managed to navigate the routes sufficiently to see that he was nearly back where he'd started, but a glance at his fuel gauge showed that the car was already close to empty. He was angry now, so much so that he was ready to have an in-person meeting. The whole thing might be a prank, some initiation cooked up by one of the street gangs that were so prevalent in Los Angeles, and the thought really fed his temper. On the other side of the ornate gates was a huge stone building, but he couldn't tell in the dark if it was a chapel or an expansive mausoleum. He swung his vehicle to the curb then leaned over and slid a black briefcase from beneath the front of the passenger seat. Rather than open his bag of tools, he took it with him as he stepped out of the car and hurried toward an arched, deep-set doorway that seemed to be the building's main entrance. As he ducked into the shadows he heard the slam of a car door as the other driver exited his car.

Excellent.

Tommy ran after the killer, his old man's Colt clutched so tightly in his right hand that his fingers ached. He'd never fired a gun but it didn't take a college degree to point the thing and squeeze the trigger. He'd seen pictures in the paper that showed what this guy had done to that woman, so if it came down to it, he was sure he could step up. In fact, maybe that would be the best thing all around—kill the killer, right? Rid the world of the sicko and pull in the credit. He could see the headlines now: TOMMY MILNER A HERO FOR CATCHING MURDERER! There would be radio and television interviews, maybe even book deals. He grinned, but that expression disappeared as he edged up to the arch that covered the doorway the other man had gone into. This wasn't going to be a cakewalk so he'd better pay attention.

"Come out," he ordered. "I've got you covered." He cringed,

partly because his voice sounded so loud against the quiet of the empty street, and partly because the words were so corny. "I'm not kidding," he added.

The only reply was a chuckle, so low that at first Tommy wasn't sure he'd heard it at all. Then it dawned on him that the man was laughing at him. *Laughing!* His face flushed. His father laughed at him just like that every time Tommy tried to talk about things he wanted to do, as though he believed Tommy wasn't smart enough to do anything at all. The similarity between the two adults made his temples pound and he pulled in a breath to steady himself.

"I've got a gun," he said. This time his voice was hard and flat. "I'm not so stupid I'm stepping in there with you. I'll shoot first and let the cops ask questions later."

At first there was nothing, then Tommy stepped back as he saw a darker man-shaped shadow shift inside the archway. But instead of coming toward him, the figure swung sideways. In the next second a door opened and light, bright and golden, cut through the darkness, making Tommy squint and instinctively raise a hand to shield his eyes. Darkness returned as the door swung shut, and this time Tommy swore and leaped forward. He yanked the door open again and saw he was facing the center aisle of a chapel; a dark-haired man was turning past the front pews at the far front, heading toward another closed door.

There was no more time to hesitate. Tommy went after him.

He hadn't bargained on firepower, had assumed—stupidly, it turned out—that the thug following him would be armed with nothing more than brute force and scarred knuckles. It wasn't, however, an idle threat; there had been enough of a glow from the streetlights to see the revolver aimed in his direction. He was more sure than ever that his stalker wasn't a cop, but that just made him more dangerous. The police were brutal but they were far less likely to shoot someone who didn't have a gun than a nervous, would-be vigilante. Based on that, any attempt at getting close enough to use one of the knives in his case would be unwise; he'd be shot and if he didn't die outright, his identity would be splashed all over the tabloids. Unthinkable—he would have to put enough distance between them so that he could hide and then attack.

So he ran. He was in good shape for his age, but the voice of his pursuer had pegged him as much younger. The mouse in the maze feeling rose again as he lurched around turns and sprinted down dozens of hallways. He'd never seen a mausoleum such as this—it looked like a library, with rows upon rows of oversized books and urns that resembled more decorative vases than containers for the ashes of the dead. Words and dates flashed past as he fled, but he didn't have time to stop and ponder those who had been immortalized in this exquisite, multi-roomed building. Fine statues and fountains, benches and small trees, luminous stained glass windows and opulent plants—everywhere he turned was beauty that he could not take the time to appreciate. At last, nearly at the end of his stamina, he rounded a doorway and faced, of all things, a fireplace.

And froze at the sight of the figure standing next to it.

Tommy cursed under his breath. He'd stopped running a while ago, thinking that would make him able to hear the footsteps of the man as he was fleeing. That hadn't worked—either the place was super soundproofed or it was so huge the killer had gotten away. Still he searched, going from room to room, trying to put himself in the other guy's shoes and figure out which way he'd gone. What a crazy way to be buried, he thought as he hunted. Get your body burned up and then poured into a box that looked like a library book, like your relatives could check you out and take you home for a couple of weeks. Would there be an overdue penalty if they were late bringing back the dead? He would've laughed at the idea if his circumstances had been different, but right now he needed to find that murderer. If he didn't, his plans to have everyone know who he was were going to fall apart.

Tall and stick-thin, the man was bald and had skin so white it seemed to glow. He wore a loose-fitting black suit and tie, exactly the garb one would expect an undertaker to wear. His eyes were so deep-set that their color was ambiguous, and the lips on his hairless face were a strange shade of unhealthy gray. His hands, folded placidly in front of him, displayed fingernails that were the same disturbing color.

"Who are you?" His voice came out as a whisper, but somehow he wasn't surprised.

"I am the Guardian."

He winced. The words had slipped into his mind but the mouth of the man standing by the fireplace hadn't moved. "Excellent." He somehow made his voice almost normal. "I seem to have become turned around. Perhaps you can direct me to an exit."

"There is no exit for you."

He opened his mouth to protest, then realized that he had moved to stand directly in front of the fireplace against his will. The Guardian or whatever he claimed to be was only a few inches away. "I-I'm s-s-sorry?" It took everything he had to say the words, and even then they came out as a thick stammer, barely understandable even to his own ears.

"No," the Guardian said. "You're not sorry at all. You're evil, which is why you will never leave this place."

He tried again to speak but found he couldn't. His tongue had become as unresponsive as his limbs, and although inside his mind he was screaming, the only thing he did was tilt his head a little to the right, like a dog that didn't understand its master's command. Without knowing why, he had a death grip on his black bag.

"The young woman you murdered will be buried nearby," the Guardian continued in a placid voice. "It is unspeakable that you should be free to repeat your atrocities upon others. She would never rest if I did not ensure that was not the case, nor do you deserve ... shall we say, recognition *for what you have done." The pale man shook his head. "No one will ever know you were responsible for the depravities visited upon her."*

His breath hitched in his throat as the Guardian leaned over and extended two fingers towards the fireplace. The tip of the flames swirled, then reached out, curling around his hand and settling on the tips of his fingers as though they were living matchsticks. The Guardian stepped back from the fire and turned to face him. His voice was soft but as cold and flat as an arctic night.

"And you shall never be named."

He could do nothing but stand, paralyzed, as the Guardian bent and brushed the bottom of his slacks.

The flames consumed him.

———▲———

Shaking, Tommy hid on the other side of a doorway, trying to process what he had just seen. He was lightheaded, barely breathing because he was so afraid he'd be heard. All thoughts of fame and heroism were gone, burned as fast as the killer he'd been following. Now the only thing he wanted was to get out of here as a whole person rather than the pile of white ash that the so-called Guardian had scooped up and was carrying away.

Instinct made him want to run in the opposite direction, but he knew better—he was as hopelessly lost as the now dead murderer had been. He would follow the Guardian he decided, because when the strange man was done disposing of the ashes, he would have to leave. Surely the Guardian wouldn't want to be here at dawn or whenever the daytime property caretakers arrived, and at that point Tommy would find his way out. His father's backlash be damned, he was going straight to the nearest police station.

More turns and hallways, left, then right, maybe even doubling back on himself. He kept the Guardian just in view, hanging back as far as was safe without losing the other man. After a good quarter hour—was the building really that large?—Tommy finally came around a corner into a room that led nowhere . . .

Except face to face with the Guardian himself.

He cried out and scrambled backward, then spun and leaped—right into a solid wall. The doorway through which he had just stepped was gone; in its place was heavy floral wallpaper and walnut wainscoting. The space where he'd slammed against the surface was flanked by a pair of matching gold brocade wing chairs, standard funeral home style. He turned back, twisting in each direction, but there were no exits—no doors, no windows. The .38 had come out of his waistband and gone sliding across the carpet until it was out of sight. He was unarmed and trapped.

"There you are," the Guardian said. He was standing at a table in front of a wall of shelves, carefully pouring the ashes of Elizabeth Short's killer into a book-shaped container. His voice was absurdly cheerful as his head swiveled and his nondescript gaze settled on Tommy. "I was wondering when you would catch up."

"Let me go," Tommy croaked. His voice was a little choppy but at least he could still speak; in his mind was the clear picture of the killer trying unsuccessfully to voice what would ultimately be his last words. He flexed his hands and shuffled around the chair, moving along the wall in the opposite direction. So far, so good.

"You have to stay," the Guardian said. Finished with his task, he brushed his hands off. "Otherwise everyone will end up knowing about him."

Tommy shook his head as the white-skinned man turned and carefully removed several more book urns from a shelf; the ornate containers had names and dates etched into their spines. The shelf was deeper than it appeared and he could just glimpse the dark spines of more urns hidden behind those in front. "No, I won't tell anyone. I swear. I don't even know who he is—"

The Guardian made a *tsking* sound. "Lying is never good," he said. "You do know who he is, and you will make the knowledge public. I'm afraid that cannot be allowed."

Tommy turned to run instead of answering, only to find himself right back where he started—the chairs behind him, the Guardian at his table a few feet away. "Please," he said desperately. "I got nothing to do with him. My name is—"

Before Tommy could finish, his throat closed up as the Guardian suddenly raised his forefinger and pressed it over Tommy's lips. "No," the man said softly. "You do not have a name anymore."

He wanted to protest—*Of course I do!*—but he couldn't pull in air to form the words, he couldn't exhale, he couldn't *breathe* anymore, and his blood was pounding in his head. Tommy clawed at the collar of his jacket, then at his shirt, and finally at his skin; his nails dug in, leaving long, bloody grooves, but he didn't feel the pain. He crashed onto one of the chairs when his legs gave out and his vision shifted from color to black and white, then faded quickly, as though someone was piling filmy black fabric over his face.

Tommy Milner's final view of the world as himself lasted nine seconds.

The Guardian brushed his hands off again, his task almost complete. The old one's ashes were now in a second book-shaped urn, a match to the volume containing the remains of Elizabeth Short's murderer. When he put them together, he could see the previous Guardian's name etched in ornate font along the spine of his container, and the name of the young woman's killer on the spine of the other one. That wouldn't do, not at all.

He snapped the thumb and forefinger of his right hand and a small, white-hot flame appeared. The old one hadn't really needed the fireplace earlier, but it had been good for a show, a bit of momentary distraction from a task that had become tedious to him after so many decades. It took only a few moments to draw the flame down the spine of each urn and burn away any chance that her killer, or that of the old man whose place he had taken, would ever be identified. That done, the Guardian pushed the two urns to the far back of the shelf with the others, then meticulously arranged a row of labeled urns in front of them.

Because like him, there were those who shall never be named.

THE
LAST THINGS
TO GO

MARY SANGIOVANNI & BRIAN KEENE

The last things to go, Sharon Coulter supposed, were the hardest. There in her driveway, the slanting late-afternoon California sun softening the edges of a darkening world, she blew an errant piece of hair from her eye and continued scraping at the yellow ribbon on her trunk. The ribbon was the sticker kind, and not the magnet kind. Her Kia Sportage was made with fiberglass, so the magnets wouldn't hold. That had been okay; there had been something lasting and almost superstitious about the sticker on her trunk. So long as it remained, her fervent belief in it would keep Cameron safe, keep him alive until he came home from Iraq and scraped it off himself—and thereby scrape off the war and all its baggage.

But Cameron had never come back to this home in West Oakland that they had briefly shared, a home they'd purchased just four months before his second deployment. Sharon had originally been hesitant about buying it, even though owning a home—a place of their own—had been her dream, but Cameron had convinced her, citing the more affordable housing prices and its proximity to San Francisco via the bridge and BART. Without Cameron, this home felt empty, even though it was full of reminders of him.

She still had the letters he'd written to her, and print-outs of all the emails, Facebook postings, and other things he'd sent when he wasn't out on patrol and had access to his laptop. She had a box of dried petals from every flower or bouquet he'd ever given her, and the empty Sweet Tarts box he'd bought her at the movies on their first date, and the ceramic kitty cat tree ornament he'd given her on their first Christmas together. She had two dresser drawers full of his t-shirts, socks, and underwear, and half a closet still occupied by the rest of his clothes. His aftershave and cologne still occupied a shelf in the medicine cabinet, and a six pack of his favorite beer still lurked in the back of the refrigerator, untouched since his departure. She had a removable hard drive full of pictures of the two of them together, and a bed that felt bigger and emptier with each passing night.

She was surrounded by Cameron and yet he was gone.

The first thing to go had been his impression on the pillow. That had faded a few days after his deployment. The second thing to go had been his scent, washed from the sheets and pillowcases when she did laundry. Some nights, on the rare occasions when Cameron had been able to Skype with her, she'd found herself missing him so badly after their call that she'd spray his pillowcase with a hint of his cologne. But it had never been the same, and her longing for him then was nothing compared to the deep and mournful sense of loss she'd experienced when she learned that he'd never be coming home again.

There would be no more letters and no more phone calls, no more conversations about how much they missed each other or how weird the time difference was between California and Iraq. Never again would he buy her a box of Sweet Tarts or help her decorate the Christmas tree. There would be no more flowers, and the beer still sat in the fridge, unopened.

Cameron was gone.

How then, Sharon wondered, was it possible life still went on?

After finishing with removing the yellow ribbon sticker, Sharon decided to re-read some of the letters Cameron had sent her. She wasn't sure that was the healthiest activity, given her current state of mind, but she wanted to anyway. Maybe it was like picking a scab. She knew she shouldn't, but she couldn't help it.

It was Friday. She didn't have to work again until Monday. She could have gone to the movies or taken a drive to Napa for the weekend, or spent some time antiquing. But all of those activities seemed empty somehow, without Cameron there to enjoy them with her. Looking through their old correspondence was a connection—an intimacy that helped to keep her loneliness at bay.

She'd read all the letters before, of course. She'd read them so much that she almost knew them by heart. Mostly, Cameron wrote about how much he missed her, and how he couldn't wait to get back home, and all the things they would do together when he returned. He talked about his buddies, serving over there in the desert with him—guys like Don Bloom and Kowalczyk (who everyone called Planters "because he's fucking nuts"). These were men who Sharon had never met, but she felt like she knew them well, just from the things Cameron had told her. She wondered where they were now. After all, their stories hadn't ended just because Cameron's had. Were they still out there in the desert somewhere, or had they made it home? Were their loved ones waiting for them to return, and if so, were they as alone as she felt?

Sharon turned on the air conditioning as she walked inside, pausing for a moment as the unit sighed, filling the house with cool comfort. She sighed along with it, and closed her eyes. When she opened them again, the room seemed to spin. She reached out with one hand and touched the back of the sofa to steady herself. When she felt better, she walked down the hall into the bedroom.

Sharon kept Cameron's letters in a box beneath their bed, alongside another box containing the dried flower petals. As she knelt, peering under the bed, she spied both boxes, along with dust and debris. She reminded herself that she needed to vacuum under there the next time she cleaned. Then she pulled out the box containing the letters and opened it.

Sharon gasped. Cameron's letters were gone.

A sick ball of anxiety weighed in her gut. There was some superstitious part of her that had always believed words—written
words even more so than spoken ones—had a kind of lasting power, that if something was written down, it was somehow more real,
more concrete. It was that belief that had prompted her to keep
every text, every email, every Facebook post and card and chat
transcript. Hell, she even had, folded neatly in her box of letters,
the last shopping list he'd written out before his deployment. She
saved every "I love you and miss you," every "You're so beautiful,"
every "You mean the world to me" because it reminded her in the
cool gray-blue hours of pre-dawn that she wasn't imagining a soul
mate way on the other side of the world. He was real, and his feelings for her were real. She knew it in her heart, of course, but liked,
all the same, to have it in her hand, too.

But those little mementos of proof were gone, somehow. The
dizzy feeling returned for a moment, less intense but threatening all
the same. Could she have moved them? She didn't think so. But
there wasn't any other explanation for it. No one else had come to
visit since last she'd pulled out the correspondences to look at, and
there were no pets, no cleaning people, no children...

Sharon thought of that pregnancy test she'd taken the night after he left and tears blurred the sight of the empty box in front of
her. She hadn't wanted to say anything until she was sure, but God,
how she'd hoped that test would come back positive. She hadn't
realized how much she wanted it—had, in fact, firmly believed the
opposite until the digital window had returned the result NOT
PREGNANT and a wave of intense, almost biting disappointment
surged through her. Now, there was no one to tell anyway, and she
found herself relieved it had turned out as it did. She couldn't very
well mourn that they, as a couple—a family—would never hear
tiny voices learn to laugh and talk, or small feet scampering to welcome him home, if those things didn't exist. She couldn't cry about
their never holding curious small hands or seeing reminders of his

smile in tiny upturned faces that would never be. The written words had spoken. She couldn't dwell on something that never really was, right?

She wiped her eyes, stood up, and leaving the box where it was on the floor, pulled out a second box. In it, she found the dried flower petals of every bouquet he had ever given her and all their movie and concert ticket stubs, but no letters. She huffed, a slow leak of frustration and sadness, and peeked under the bed. Nothing but the dust bunnies.

Next, Sharon searched the night table drawer on her side of the bed, then the one on his side, just to be sure. She dug into the pile of shoes on the closet floor and sifted one by one through the contents of cluttered boxes labeled "Old Bank Statements" and "Important Papers." She looked under the bed again, in every drawer of the dressers, and behind every major piece of furniture in the room. She repeated the same methodical search in the bathroom (although she knew nothing would be there, but just in case), the guest room, the small towel closet in the hallway, and that third spare room she had intended to use as maybe a craft room (or a nursery, if ever). As she went, she did her best to ignore the lump in her gut. Her cheeks felt cold. She thought to turn the air conditioner down, and then realized she was crying.

There were times since the Official Visit and the letter, since the flag they had given her when he was buried in Chapel of the Chimes in Oakland, that the grief came over her so strong she felt like she was being swallowed alive by a thick, heavy fog—dark, all encompassing, dulling to her senses. It was likely she'd taken out the letters then and set them somewhere to read, and just forgotten where that was. During those times, it was like moving outside of real time and space, and thus, hard to remember later every little detail of where she'd put things and what she'd done around the house. It was usually less disconcerting to her then it should be, she supposed, but then, she'd never lost something as important to her as the letters.

It took her the better part of an hour and a half to comb through the downstairs as she had the upstairs. She searched the basement and her car. She even searched all of the trash. The letters were just plain gone.

Her head had begun to ache. She was exhausted. Sharon pulled one of Cameron's t-shirts from the dresser and pulled it over one of his pillows. Then she climbed into the big empty bed, pulling the shirted pillow to her. She didn't bother with the covers.

She closed her eyes, gave in to the aches within and without, and burst into tears, crying until sleep crept up on and overtook her.

On Saturday, over her morning tea (her stomach, unsettled, put her off to the idea of breakfast), Sharon glared at the stack of bills to be paid and thought about the night before. She'd awoken that morning feeling incredibly drained, more than usual, and knew that it had been a tough night, but found that try as she might, she couldn't remember why. Something... something had been... taken? Lost? She wasn't quite sure.

Maybe the feeling came from some part of a nightmare. She certainly had them often enough, when she managed to sleep. Likely, she'd dreamed of Cameron; often, those dreams evolved one of two ways, both equally painful. In the first kind, he would be somehow suddenly mad at her or worse, utterly indifferent to her, and would spend the dream either avoiding her and her attempts at communicating reconciliation or he'd be outright nasty to her, spitefully flaunting his attempts to drive her away. Those dreams were bad, but the other kind were worse. In those, they were blissfully happy and deeply in love, having fun, having adventures, making love, and planning their present and future lives together. She'd wake from the former knowing, at least, that those weren't true, had only been bad dreams. But the latter... it was harder to be torn into wakefulness after those, to an empty house that was supposed to have been a home and an empty space beside her where all those dreamed moments should have been.

She never dreamed of his death. There had never been the good-bye dream, where Cameron appeared to her to tell her he was okay, that he was safe and would be waiting for her and where he was going was so, so beautiful. Other military wives posted about having dreams like that after, but for her, Cameron was just gone.

Usually when she had those kinds of dreams, it offered her some comfort to go through the box she kept under her bed, the one with all the flower petals from every bouquet he had ever given her, and all the ticket stubs from the movies and concerts they had gone to together. She decided to do that now. Maybe the rest of the day would be easier, and maybe this strange disquiet would dissipate, if she looked through those old memories.

As she walked to the bedroom, Sharon found herself wishing that she had kept Cameron's letters and emails, as well. He'd never been much of a writer, preferring instead to call or Skype with her when he could. But surely, he'd sent a few cards and letters, hadn't he? For her birthday, at the very least? She couldn't remember.

When she pulled the box out from beneath the bed, and lifted the top off, Sharon gasped in dismay. All of her treasures, all of the mementos of their time together, were gone. The ticket stubs and flower petals had vanished. Even the empty Sweet Tarts box was missing.

She moaned, low and mournful, turning the box upside down and shaking it, as if the keepsakes would magically fall out. When they didn't, she peered under the bed again. Maybe she hadn't put them back in the box the last time she'd looked through them, or maybe she had the wrong box. She rifled through the nightstand drawers and searched the closet, and eventually all the other rooms in the house, but the treasure box was gone.

Just like Cameron.

Her melancholy lingered for a few hours. She searched for the missing items one more time, but to no avail. She sat in the kitchen and cried over a second cup of tea. But eventually, Sharon decided to get out of the house. She had no particular place to go, but just the act of leaving, of getting away from this temple to Cameron's memory, seemed preferable to sitting here grieving all day.

She showered and dressed, and managed to hold back tears during the process. Then she grabbed her purse, locked the door behind her, and walked out to the car. As she thumbed the remote to unlock the doors, Sharon noticed a weird stain on her Kia's rear bumper. Frowning, she touched it. Her fingers came away sticky. The residue felt like bumper sticker glue, but that was bizarre. She'd never had a bumper sticker on the car. She hated those things. She remembered the Yellow Ribbon sticker a friend had given her shortly after Cameron's deployment. She'd stuck it … somewhere. She couldn't remember the exact location. Probably in a drawer or on top of the fridge. Maybe even in the box beneath the bed.

Sharon sighed.

Was she sad that the mementos were gone? Of course she was. Each item had been a part of her life with Cameron. But, she reminded herself, she still had pictures of their time together. And she still had this home they'd shared. And most importantly, she still had her memories.

On Sunday, Sharon paused on her way down the hall. She'd been stumbling from the bedroom to the kitchen. Her head hurt and she'd planned on making a cup of tea, but something else had caught her attention.

On the wall was a picture frame—the type that held multiple photographs. There she was with her parents. Another showed her with some girlfriends. But there were several empty spaces where photographs were missing. Sharon frowned, trying to remember what they had been. After a moment, it occurred to her they'd been various snapshots of her and her old boyfriend, Cameron. She'd been crazy about him at one time, but then he'd joined the army and … well, she supposed they'd drifted apart. She still thought of him from time to time, but she hadn't heard from him in ... well, a very long time. She couldn't remember removing the pictures from their frames, but she must have at one point. The frame looked uneven with those empty holes, somewhat ... unsettled, and she didn't like that. She made a mental note to find some replacements for them.

Then she continued with her day.

On Monday morning, Sharon left her apartment in North Oakland and drove to work. It was a ritual she repeated five days a week, and had done so since moving into her place. She'd always wanted a house, somewhere to really think of as a home, but it was a big responsibility financially, and she just couldn't swing a California mortgage alone.

Sharon smiled in bemusement. Wasn't it funny? She'd dreamed of a house the night before, and a man who shared a home with her. She only remembered snippets of it—pictures of them in frames though the dream-faces were blurred, drawers with his t-shirts, socks, and underwear, a closet with her clothes hanging on one side and his on the other. She remembered a shoebox under the bed where she had been plucking and placing petals from flowers she knew, in the dream, he had given her. And she had been sitting on a big, soft bed in the bedroom with pillows that smelled like his cologne. It had been a pleasant enough dream, although she knew it was little more than her mind fantasizing about a life she wanted, but would probably never really have. She thought for a moment about the man in the dream. She couldn't see his face, but remembered his arms—there had been tattoos, one of them military. And she thought his name had begun with a C—Casey? Cameron? Chris? Eh, it didn't matter anyway, she told herself, because it had only been a dream. But the smile had slipped off her face.

Her daily commute took her through West Oakland. While stuck in a backup due to road construction, Sharon happened to glance out the passenger-side window, and saw a house there. It was a cute house, just the kind of place she had always dreamed of living in some day, but for some inexplicable reason, the sight of the place filled her with unease.

Maybe it's haunted, she thought, and then traffic began to move again and within another block, she'd forgotten all about it.

On Tuesday, the house was gone, but Sharon Coulter never noticed.

A
RAVEN
IN THE
DOVE'S NEST

ROBERTA LANNES

Dead center in one of her amitriptyline dreams, Ruth waded through ever more vivid memories, drawn out and melded together into the nonsensical and fantastic. Four-thirty in the morning, a stunning progression of vignettes put her first in a plush chair in the Chapel's lush, well-appointed mourning room. She grabbed onto the chair's plump arms, staring into the glass case. There, the engraved marble book urn holding her husband's ashes stood alone, awaiting the company of his family's volumes to follow. Ruth felt the weight of expectation.

Sunlight streaming through the atrium cast her bent shadow onto the tile floor. That shadow took on the shape of a large beaked bird, lengthening and expanding over the pale expanse. As the bird's head bobbed in a pecking rhythm, its shadow grew black as India ink. The void of light spread until it eclipsed the room. Ruth's heart raced as she was consumed. Startled at the touch of someone grasping her shoulders, she flung them away with a shriek!

She wrapped herself tightly with her arms, blinking away the

utter darkness. Freckling pinpricks of light grew slowly into a dazzling constellation. In a filmic fade, she stood in an amber lit hotel ballroom. The air, perfumed with pomade, cheap cologne, and sweat, vibrated around her as a swirl of soldiers, sailors and pretty young women moved feverishly to a band playing *"Organ Grinders Swing."* Then, there was Louis; all six foot two and boyish twenty-three years of him, slim-hipped in his sailor whites. He flashed his future salesman's radiant smile and she bought it. Falling into his strong arms, their feet took to jitterbugging as if they'd danced together for years.

When the music slowed to a romantic tune, Louis held her close as they slow-danced in her childhood bedroom. They kissed. Deeply. Easing her gently onto the bed, Louis told her she was lovely. Ruth, naked and filled with a double whiskey of courage, trembled in Louis's arms. When he kissed and stroked her breasts, her nipples went so rigid they ached. Her body responded to his touch with gooseflesh and electric warmth all at once. He whispered her name, kissing her belly, moving her legs apart, his mouth focused between. Tenderly yet unrelentingly, his tongue nudged and prodded until she disappeared into an explosion of rapture!

Euphoric, her body still pulsating, she lie alone, naked on the cold tile floor of the mourning room. Her eyes fluttered at the sound of the Chapel's chimes, clear and beautiful. They pealed again and again, their sound increasingly dull, like a doorbell. She shut her eyes, tumbling onto an ultramarine cloud, the sun on her back.

A more insistent ring jolted her. Annoyed at being ripped from her pleasure, Ruth swam up from slumber. *The doorbell!*

Her every joint squawked with pain as she rolled her ninety-three-year-old body out of bed. Drug-dragged, with slatted eyes, she wobbled along in her routine of sliding on her slippers and her purple robe, then went to her dresser mirror. Her fingers moved like wooden pegs, weaving her long white hair into a haphazard braid as she shuffled toward the toilet. The doorbell went *again.*

Padding through the house, the amitriptyline stupor took her balance. She thumped against the walls, then down the stairs she nearly missed steps. Had she ever felt this intoxicated? Ruth flicked on the hall light, blinking toward her front door. She supported herself, hands against the walls, as she swayed onward. Too numbed to wonder who'd wake her at this hour, she brought her eye to the peephole. Even under the wan, yellowed light and a very long time having passed, Ruth recognized the woman's face. The woman. The one whose name she could never remember from somewhere she couldn't recollect.

Damn this medication, she thought as she pulled open the door.

"Oh. Hello." Ruth's hand flew over her mouth to cover a gasp. Her eyes fell to bloody nightgown and slippers, then back up to the woman's wild green eyes and blue-black hair.

"Please. Can I come in? It's cold out here." The woman shivered, her hands tucked under her arms. "I'm lost."

Baffled, Ruth squinted at her. "Are you hurt?"

The woman put her bloody hands out, flipping them palm to back. She stared at them as if they weren't her own, her head cocked. "I don't know."

"Well, come in." Ruth frowned, her speech slurred. "But, take those slippers off. Leave'em outside."

The woman kicked off the slippers as Ruth peered out toward the street for signs of the woman's car. She felt silly, then. How would she know the woman's car from any other after all these years?

"I don't know why I'm here. I just thought of you. Your kindness. You *are* kind, aren't you?"

"I hope so. People've been kind to me." And they had. She took a chance. "You were."

"Was I?" The woman stepped gingerly down the hallway in her bare feet, clearly remembering her way to Ruth's kitchen. The woman glanced back over her shoulder, smiling blandly. As she followed, Ruth noticed the blood staining the hem of the woman's robe ombred up from near black to a ruby red, as if she'd been dunked in it and hung up.

Ruth turned the oven on low and left the door open a crack to warm the neat Tuscan-styled kitchen. Ruth went into a sort of drunken hostess mode. She started the coffee machine, searched for pastries, hoping the woman wouldn't sit in Louis's chair. Louis's place was set as if he might wander in and sit down any moment. Everyone, friends and family, knew not to sit there. Ever!

Coffeemaker started, cookies in a decorative tin put onto the table, Ruth set dish towels on a chair. "Here. Don't want that stuff on the chair." Ruth patted the seat cushion, nearly tipping over. Her face went red, her scalp tingled as the woman sat down. She recovered, straightened.

Ruth leaned against her counter. "What happened?"

The woman flipped her hands palm to back again, grabbed at her bloody robe, mystified by it all. "I don't remember." She gazed up at Ruth. "Can I call George?" Then she fixed her eyes on Ruth's cordless phone, sitting on the counter beside the paper towel stand and a knife block.

Ruth's mind wouldn't clear as drug and a dull dread saturated her. "Of course, if you want to." George. Who's George?

The woman nodded like a stunned child. "He'll wonder where I am."

Ruth picked up the phone, pressed for the directory, as if she'd somehow recognize the woman's name if she saw it. "Tell me your phone number. I'll dial."

The woman chuckled mirthlessly. Eyes to the ceiling, she muttered, "Ahh...510. Wait, no. That's the area code. Try 619-2030."

Ruth dialed, her eyes crossing, fingers half off the buttons. The phone rang and rang. A machine caught it. *You've reached Sal and Mercia. Leave a message. You know what'll happen if you don't!* There was laughter and a beep. Ruth pressed END.

"Sorry, that's not it." Ruth's hand shook as she put the phone in her robe pocket.

The woman pressed her fingers over her eyes. "I can't think straight."

Ruth turned away at hearing the coffeemaker squeeze the last of the water through its filter. Hands trembling, fingers aching, Ruth sloshed coffee onto the saucer and counter as she filled two cups. Ignoring her mess, she set a cup in front of the woman, another at her place. Ruth plopped onto her chair, jostling the table. The woman paid no attention.

As the coffee cooled, they both stared unfocused at their hands. Ruth surreptitiously cast an appraising eye at the woman. In her unreliable mind, two thoughts danced. The woman was in dire need of her help; why else show up on her particular doorstep, covered in gore and clearly desperate unless someone had harmed her? Or, had she'd been involved in the harm of another? The stultifying amitriptyline loosened its grip a moment as her belly turned icy cold.

The woman glanced up at Ruth, whose eyes shot back to her hands. Ruth strained to summon the businesswoman mask she'd worn all the years she'd run the elder care facilities she and Louis owned. Something to hide her burgeoning panic, like the 'Everything's-Just-Fine' look with a touch of 'Trust us, we've-got-it-all-under-control.'

Coffee cooled, they drank the bitter brew. Ruth grimaced, then ladled sugar into the cup. The woman seemed unfazed by the strong stuff and drank it down.

The woman picked up a cookie, smelled it, then took a bite. "Mm, that's better. Can I get another cup?"

Ruth nodded and hauled herself up. She barely remembered when getting up from a chair had not been punishing. Thinking of Louis, how he'd soldiered on through eleven years of cancer treatment, she always felt petty for thinking her arthritis was the most horrible of afflictions. She poured the woman another cup, making less of a mess.

Twenty minutes, they sat in dazed silence. Ruth took the

phone from her pocket and stared at it, struggling to recall the woman's name. Perhaps, she thought, she'd never known it.

"Should I try George again?"

"Oh!" The woman sucked in her breath, her reverie snatched away.

Ruth stared at the phone. "The number?"

"Okay. Home. 523-1180." The woman turned her head toward the wide kitchen window facing out to the garden as dawn turned the pale golden kitchen walls a mottled peach.

Ruth pressed in the number. It rang once, then went to voicemail. "You've reached the Miramontes. Leave a message." Miramontes? She had no recollection of knowing anyone by that name. Someone who worked for them in one of the care facilities? She'd have to leave a message.

"This is Ruth Scavone. Your wife's here at my home and needs your help. Can you call here?" Ruth glanced at the woman who looked baffled. Ruth rattled off the phone number. "Please. It's important."

Ruth put the phone back in her pocket. "He didn't answer. Could he be at work already?"

The woman shook her head. "My husband should be there. Why isn't he worried about me? I've been gone for days."

Days? Ruth's heart raced a moment as she dipped in and out of her inebriated fugue.

The woman clasped her hands under her chin. "I'm sorry. I'm so confused. He *is* going to call, isn't he?"

Ruth gave her the *Everything's-Just-Fine* look. "Why wouldn't he?" She straightened up, groaning with the pain in her back. "Do you need to use the toilet? I have to. Will you be all right?"

The woman nodded, staring into her coffee. Dried blood had begun to flake onto the saucer and table. Ruth rankled at the mess.

In the bathroom, Ruth ran cold water and splashed her face. As she dried herself, she whispered to Louis, gone sixteen years now.

"I'm scared, Lou. Something's wrong with this woman. I don't want to think about her mental state. Or what happened to explain all that blood. And where is her husband? She's been missing days! If only you were here, you'd help me figure it out."

Ruth brushed her half-braided hair out, twisted it into a loose bun and secured it at the nape of her neck, chatting away quietly. "I'm so out of it. This medication. I'm trying to remember how I know her, and I think I met her after you passed away. She left an indelible impression somehow, but, I can't seem to remember her name." Ruth closed her eyes. Handsome sailor Louis from her dream floated into mind. She felt his hands, remembered his youthful skin, his mouth on her, and blushed. "Oh, Lou. My Lou."

Louis prepared his naïve bride to live a life less sheltered than the privileged one she'd grown up with. He loved his soft, supple Ruth, but encouraged her to get tougher out in the world; brittle if she had to. It had to be his way; how they would raise the kids, and ran the businesses he inherited from his father, Fausto. Just as his father had taught him, so it would be with his family. Only Louis didn't want the weak-willed nervous wife his mother had been; in and out of a sanitarium his entire life.

A beauty, but awkward and shy at eighteen when they met, Louis made sure that over the years Ruth developed into his equal, a force to be reckoned with in business and at home. Ruth worked side-by-side with Louis when the kids were in college, and the moment they were out on their own, Ruth became a businesswoman full-time. Louis insisted she take over the elder care business, telling her she didn't need his approval or advice anymore. She'd become a true Scavone; smart, sensitive when she needed to be, and most importantly, powerful.

Ruth thought of Louis, how he'd have advised her to take care of the woman for now. She needed help, but keep a keen eye on her. If Ruth needed to get tough, she had it in her.

On her way back to the kitchen, Ruth stopped at the hall closet and took out a bag of neatly folded clothes planned for Goodwill.

She chose a wool sweater, a pair of baggy pants, and boots with heels that constituted a health hazard for Ruth, who'd been eighty-eight when her granddaughter gave them to her. She stood staring into the closet, a memory of Lucy at four trying on Ruth's high heels, falling over, and bursting into tears. Her innocence. Jolted then by the realization of what sat in her kitchen, Ruth ambled back.

The woman stood at the window, her arms hanging at her sides. She didn't move as Ruth set the clothes on the table, shifted a chair, clanked her coffee cup in the sink and cleaned up the mess she'd made.

"Don't you want to sit?"

The woman shook her head. "Why can't I remember what happened?" She gave Ruth a quick glance, then stared out at the garden. "This ..." she put her hands up, "isn't my blood."

My God, then whose? Ruth sat down with a grunt. Her voice felt strangled in her throat, still slurring off her tongue. "Well, maybe George'll know."

The woman shuddered, but didn't budge. "I just remembered when I met you. Where. At St. Stephen's. Do you remember?"

Ruth winced as memories flooded her. "Grief counseling. You and the other women were so helpful. Were we friends?"

The woman shrugged. "I remembered this house. I was here a lot then wasn't I? That has to mean we were friends."

Yes. Something like that. "We were." At that very same table; talking for hours about Louis, her great loss, her kids, grandkids; slowly recovering.

Back then, most of her closest friends had died or moved away. She'd relied on her son and daughter through Louis's illness. But, when Louis died, they too were felled by grief. Once they'd gravitated around her, but with Louis gone, they flew out of her orbit to the comfort of their friends and families.

Then, Ruth saw only lonely, pain-filled days, unbearable without Louis. She let herself go. She stayed in bed, sleeping or weeping. Without an appetite, she lost the stubborn fifteen pounds she'd struggled with in her seventies, plus another fifteen, then another ten. She stopped cutting and coloring her hair, doing her nails, putting on makeup. Though she feigned her breezy businesswoman's voice when anyone called, she refused requests to visit. People came anyway, bringing meals, groceries, her medications. But Ruth made little effort to be the usual hostess or pretend she was glad for the support. Sometimes she railed at her visitors, cursing them and her lot for outliving Louis. No one stayed long.

Then, one day Lucy showed up. She cleared the house of rotting food, opened the windows, and forcibly shuttled Grandma Ruth to the hospital where they hydrated and fed her. But, they couldn't heal her heartache. So Lucy found a church that had a volunteer community doing outreach for Bay Area folk. Ruth balked at going to a church; she'd had her fill of the Scavone Catholic zeal, and was sorely disappointed at the paltry solace it provided when Louis died. As it turned out, the grief support group ladies were more like a secular band of sisters with a sense of humor and a lot of warmth.

There had been six women. Ruth remembered a Sheila and a Bernice, older like her. They oozed the rapturous kindness of the deeply religious, yet they made everyone laugh, feel less alone. And the woman who now sat across the table from her? Though thirty years Ruth's junior, she bore a weight of loss Ruth found familiar and oddly comforting. Ruth sought the woman out over the others, and in time the woman became vital to her. Out of all the sweet doves nesting in the St. Stephen's community, Ruth chose that woman to be her friend.

The woman saw the clothes on the table and clapped her hands like a kid at Christmas, startling Ruth. "Are these for me?" She came over, lifted up the sweater, held it to her bloody robe, then grabbed one of the boots. "These are so cute!"

Just as she'd gained a surer footing in this waking nightmare, Ruth came unmoored at the woman's sudden shift in mood. She thought of Louis. Get businesslike. Now.

"Yes. These should fit. You don't want to sit in those things. Just put it all … there." Ruth motioned toward a trash bag hanging in her laundry room off the kitchen.

Ruth was about to remind her where the bathroom was, but the woman had already begun peeling off the robe. She let it drop, making the muffled sound of cardboard as its dried bloody edges hit the terracotta floor. Ruth knew she should turn away, but just then a remnant of the amitriptyline brought on a wave of stupor. She felt like a double exposure; one misaligned self, and an unfamiliar marionette-like Ruth, controlled by medicinal strings.

The woman pulled her nightgown over her head, revealing olive skin, still smooth except for a caesarean scar. No bloody wounds. Her breasts were still relatively high. Ruth felt the malignant envy only vain old women knew. As the woman reached out for the sweater, Ruth saw the scars along her wrists; waxy pale exclamation marks marching toward her palms. Those lines roused the memory of that one day, the pivotal day when things irrevocably changed.

Over that last month, Ruth had noticed how the woman appeared distracted, melancholy. Then the woman, very much out of character, suggested lunch out at a casually classy restaurant Ruth had mentioned. Ruth thought about the woman's cheap clothing, bottle-dyed hair and twelve-year-old Nissan, and prepared to get the check. The woman deserved this treat, though she'd done the inviting.

The woman had worn her Sunday best. She waited outside the restaurant, fingering her written directions as if they'd continue to be of importance for posterity. Ruth was late.

"Ruth, you made it!" The woman awkwardly embraced her. "I've never been to a restaurant like this before. It's a five-star kind of place, isn't it? It's so thoughtful of you to think of it." The woman beamed at her.

"Forgive me. My son drove and insisted we stop by his house

and then... Never mind. I'm hungry!"

They were seated quickly in a small booth. Though it was one in the afternoon, the woman hoped they might get wine. Ruth laughed, delighted. Her kids would be upset at her having wine before dinner, which made the idea even more delicious. They tasted a Chardonnay that Ruth approved. Once poured, the woman quickly drank down one glass, then another.

The woman kept up with Ruth's small talk, but as their food arrived, the woman grew solemn, pulling into herself.

"What's this? You're supposed to cheer *me* up." Ruth relied on the woman's joviality, even when she sensed it was all façade. They had little in common, and came from worlds apart, but women found threads to bind them, and in Ruth's bottomless sorrow they had. It seemed the woman needed her now. Ruth slipped naturally into her take-charge businesswoman mode.

"You tell me what *you* need." Ruth smiled warmly.

The woman took a tissue from her purse as tears fell. "Sorry. I didn't want to bother you with my troubles. I'm here to help *you*." She wiped her cheeks, pinking with sadness. "George's always taken my troubles on his shoulders. But he tells me this is *my* problem." She slapped a hand against her chest.

Ruth cocked her head. "Go ahead and tell me. We're friends."

The woman blinked tears away, hopeful. "Are we? I hope we are. Really."

Ruth took a long swig of Chardonnay, poured the last of it into her empty glass. She worried that in her current state, her fragility would make her pathetic as a shoulder to lean on, so Ruth turned up her wattage.

"Let me take some of the weight. You've helped me. It's my turn!"

The woman examined Ruth. Her animated face shifted from wary to cloudy with anger, then woeful to wary and then hopeful.

"I'll start at the beginning." She looked down at her pasta, avoiding Ruth's ardent gaze. "The first five years we were married,

I lost three babies. Every miscarriage wrecked me. They wrecked George. But with that third one, I snapped. The doctor told me I had a hormone disorder, prescribed stuff for me, and said I'd get right in my head in time. I wanted it to be true, but inside I felt crazy, you know?"

Ruth looked away. She didn't know. She and Louis had no trouble when it came to having children. They'd wanted a happy, healthy boy and girl, and that's what they got.

"That sounds frightening." Ruth heard the patronizing tone in her voice and grimaced.

"Oh, yah." The woman barely restrained a scowl, but went on. "Then I got pregnant with my daughter. A great pregnancy. No problems at all. George couldn't be happy for us until I got to seven months. Ruth, she was wonderful!" The woman became radiant with joy. "You know. The kind of baby people stop and stare at and say 'What a beautiful baby!' She never cried unless she was wet or hungry, and she slept through the night. We couldn't have asked for more!" She smiled to herself, remembering.

Ruth nodded. "My daughter was like that. I don't know where she got that thick blond hair as a baby, but everyone commented. Everyone!"

The woman pursed her lips, shut her eyes, and made a wounded animal sound. Ruth, taken aback, crammed a roll in her mouth. A minute ticked by. Ruth swallowed. The woman straightened, opened her eyes and gave a tight smile.

"When I met you last year, Mercy had just turned fifteen. We had a little trouble with her the year before; bad grades, fights with other girls over silly things like clothes and boys. Then she started wearing extreme makeup, like blackening her eyes and powdering her face a pasty white. She got jewelry that looked like the stuff people put on their pit bulls. Then she started sneaking out and I'd find her bed unmade in the morning. George said it was a phase, and she'd grow out of it. I suspected sex and drugs and the wrong crowd.

"I probably tried to shelter her too much, but isn't that what a good mother does? George *never* punished her. It was always me! To her, George was the moon and she'd jump over it to please him."

Ruth chuckled, the wine relaxing her. "Isn't it 'the cow jumps over the moon'?"

At that, the woman put her palms on the table, then made fists, squinting at Ruth. She growled, "Whose side are you on?"

"Yours, of course." Confused, Ruth put on her executive's grin. "Go on. Please."

The woman softened. "George won a cruise from a raffle ticket at church. I didn't want to leave Mercy alone. Sheila said she was happy to stay with her for the week. George argued that Mercy would never show us she deserved our trust if Sheila babysat. But, I *insisted.*"

"I'd have done the same thing, and my children were angels!" Ruth caught herself, steeling for the woman's spite. The woman merely sighed dismissively.

"I got so seasick on the cruise; we had to fly home early. I ruined this once-in-a-lifetime thing!" The woman dabbed at a welling tear. "When I finally got ahold of Sheila, she said George had told her *not* to stay at our house, and that Mercy had been on her own for four days! I got *so* angry!" The woman's voice rose and nearby diners turned towards them, glowering. Ruth feared hushing her. "But, I didn't tell George I knew." She balled her fists. "I wanted to kill him!

"I couldn't even look at him when we got home, so I let myself in while he got the suitcases out of the car. The minute I got inside, I heard grunts and cries, like someone being tortured! I would've waited for George, but I was *so* mad at him. My first thought was something horrible was happening to Mercy, so I tiptoed down the hall toward the sounds. They were coming from our bedroom!" The woman went red-faced, her voice punching at the space between them. "*Guess*-what-I-found?" The woman waited, but Ruth didn't want to say. "They-were-fucking…on our bed!"

The woman covered her face. Ruth reached out to touch her, show her sympathy, but the woman pulled away. Someone called a manager over, and Ruth imagined it was to complain about them. She was about to warn her, but the woman lowered her voice and went on.

"She was with this *man*. Long ratty hair, lots of tattoos, and metal things attached to his face, his chest. Wrinkled. He had to be in his forties! I stood there, paralyzed. I couldn't look away…" The woman put her hand over her mouth, muffling a primal whine. "Mercy had nothing on. I saw she had rings on her nipples and a tattoo on her belly. How could she do this to herself and I didn't know? I screamed!

"George rushed into the bedroom and all hell broke loose. I've never seen him go crazy mad. He beat the guy up while Mercy was on the floor shaking, yelling at him to stop!"

"Oh, my." Ruth whispered, glancing around, catching stares. She'd stopped eating midway through the story, her stomach clenching as the woman's voice, peppered with muffled growls and whines, grew ever louder.

An officious-looking gentleman approached.

"Anything I can help you with?" He held their bill in his hands. Ruth sheepishly shook her head, then reached out to take it. This had been her fear, that her usual steely reserve and take charge attitude would desert her in her delicate emotional state. She felt the flush rise up from her armpits to her neck and face.

They skulked onto the street, walking along in taut silence. The woman twisted the straps of her handbag, alternately cursing under her breath and sobbing quietly. Two blocks on, they stopped in the shade of a jacaranda tree.

"What can I do?" Ruth wanted to know the end of the story. Say the right thing. She shook her head, dazed by it all.

The woman fixed Ruth with glaring indignity. "How *dare* you judge me? You with your *perfect* house, and *perfect* children, and *per-*

fect dead husband! I lost Mercy that day. She ran away and we haven't seen or heard from her since!

"You selfish old bitch, complaining about Louis dying with that *oh-woes-me* bullshit, while the rest of us have real problems!" The woman leaned forward, shaking, her shoulders set, arms straight, fists ready for a fight. "Go fuck yourself!"

Ruth put her hand to her face as if she'd been struck. She watched the woman stalk off, fuming. Confused, feeling as if she'd been run over by a truck, she made it back to the restaurant to call her son. In his car, she thought about telling him what had happened. But, as he drove along, her mind emptied. Everything the woman had been to Ruth, as well as her name, was gone. Just like the woman's daughter. Vanished.

"I think I need the bathroom, now. When George gets here, tell him I'll be right out." The woman's grin was no more than a slash across her face.

When George gets here? The woman listened as Ruth left a message for her husband. How could she think he was coming to get her? Ruth had no idea what might happen next, but recalling their lunch fifteen years ago, she felt sure she needed to call George again. Or her son. Maybe even the police.

The moment Ruth heard the bathroom door shut, she pulled the phone from her pocket and hit redial. Again, no answer. How does a wife go missing two days and her husband ignore a phone call?

"George, this is Ruth Scovone again. Your wife is here in her night clothes, covered in blood that isn't hers. She just showed up at my door and is acting crazy. I'm getting frightened. Please call me back!" She hurried the phone back in her pocket, her eyes stopping on the knife block.

Ruth glanced at Louis's seat at the table, imagined him there, watching her take care of the problems, one at a time. She saw his amazing smile as she decided she needed to protect herself. She swiveled as she rose, groaning at the pain in her hips and shoulder, and reached out for the chef's knife from the block. She pushed it under the chair cushion and situated herself as benignly as possible. She reddened as her heart felt as though it would break through her ribs.

When the woman returned, her hair had been brushed and she'd washed her hands and face. Ruth tried to gauge her temperament, but the woman went to the window, her back to Ruth.

"Better?" Ruth felt the knife's handle beneath her.

The woman nodded, standing taller, more composed. "Some of it's coming back." She turned toward Ruth, her fists under her chin, eyes wide. "George knew where my Mercy was, you know. They'd been talking the whole fifteen years. He saw her, knew what her life was like. But, he never told me. Not one word." She dropped her fists to her sides, stiffening.

"How did you find *that* out?"

The woman threw her head back and barked a laugh. "How? I found her myself. *She* told me the truth!"

"What? How could George betray you that way?" In a morning of shocks, this stunned Ruth.

The woman stepped toward Ruth and slammed her palms onto the table. "Well, he will never betray me again!"

"You mean, you," Ruth set her elbows on the table, put her chin in her palms, "ah...took care of him."

The woman nodded, grinning conspiratorially. "That's right. After I saw her." The woman's voice came steely. Cold. "I found her in Emeryville. That's not far from here in Piedmont! She was with the same old tattooed guy. He's my age, for God's sake!" The woman paced, wide-eyed, fierce. "She looked awful, Ruth! Fat, wearing teenager's clothes, her belly flabby and hanging out. And she smoked! Blew it in my face! When I started to cry and beg her to let me back in her life, she spit at me, told me I was embarrassing myself. Wasting my time!" She stepped to the window again, pressing her hands on the glass. "He sniveled like a beat puppy when Mercy punched him in the arm to get him to ask me to leave." The woman chortled at the memory. "When I turned to go, I saw photographs on her mantle. Her and that pedophile and *kids!* I had two grandchildren! And George knew!" She whirled around, spitting as she shouted, "She said I was never going to see them! What right did she have keeping them from me?"

Ruth felt for the knife again. George was *not* calling her back.

"I knew they were there, the kids. Upstairs. It was after ten at night! I started to go to the stairs then, and he grabbed me. I turned and saw Mercy reach into a drawer and pull out a gun. A gun! What kind of people keep a gun in a house with children?"

Ruth shook her head, her resolve growing. "Low-lives. Trash. You couldn't let her do that to you."

The woman's shoulders relaxed. Her tone became plaintive, almost childlike. "George ... he didn't understand how painful it was not to know where she'd been all these years. Not to know if she was dead or alive. He knew I was looking for her, but he put her before me. His own wife!"

Ruth waited calmly as the woman appeared to flip between self-righteousness and wounded victim. "So what did you do?"

The woman sat down across from her, gripping the table edge. "When I got home, I told George I found her. He got angry, said he didn't want me hassling her. He said I should let her live her life." She hiccupped away a sob. "He didn't know. I already took *that* away from her."

"You didn't tell him then." She could hear Louis in her head. *Everyone's a potential client. Put them at their ease. Make them think you're with them all the way.*

She looked wild-eyed at Ruth. "I thought how he'd feel when he found out what I'd done, and that felt good. So yah, I told him. Every detail." She shook her head, resigned to tell Ruth now.

"When I was at her house, she threw the whole last fifteen years at me. She said George thought I was crazy, that I might hurt her. My precious miracle daughter? George was the one who beat the crap out of that scum she screwed in our bed ... the guy she was still with! And they thought I'd hurt her? That was insane!" The woman got up and began pacing again, wringing her hands. "I tried to make George hear how I felt. I asked him if he understood. But, he just laughed and called me *delusional.* Then, I just didn't care if he understood." She stopped, turned to Ruth. "He couldn't tell me anyway, after I cut his throat."

Ruth's bullet-proof poise took over as she cocked her head and mirrored the woman's conspiratorial tone. "You took care of *them.*"

The woman went blank for a moment, studying Ruth. She folded her arms and rocked back and forth in the new boots. She shook her head. "So *you* understand." Unconvinced, the woman chuckled darkly.

Ruth nodded slowly, surely, furrowing her brow. She struggled not to let her gaze slip from the woman to the knives. "It was *criminal* what they did to you."

The woman balked. "Mrs. Perfect thinks I'm right? Yeah, sure." She recovered, the now familiar storm clouding her face.

Ruth remembered the woman's wrath the day of that lunch debacle. Thought how if they'd been in her kitchen instead of out on the street, the woman might have done more than just hit her with foul words. She slowly took the knife from under the cushion and held it carefully under the table.

Ruth looked up at the woman. "I'm sorry. I failed you. You were so good to me and I ..." Ruth blinked as if trying not to cry. "Can I make it up to you now?" Louis would be proud. *When you screw up, you offer to fix it. Act penitent. Nothing shuts the client up faster.*

The woman stepped toward Ruth, put a hand on the table. "What could you possibly do now?" She bit the inside of her cheek, eyes going wider. "*What?*"

Ruth tensed, her twisted misshapen fingers howling with pain as she gripped the knife even tighter and swung it up and into the woman's stomach. The woman pulled away and the knife fell. She grabbed her belly, screaming. Ruth bent to retrieve the knife and fell with a crack as her knee hit the terracotta floor. She felt a jagged pain go up to her hip and knew she wasn't getting back up soon.

The woman wrestled the sweater up as if it was on fire, backing away from Ruth. Blood pulsed out onto the floor. The woman stared down at the wound, disbelieving, as the heel of one of the new boots hit the wet tile. As if in slow-motion, the woman slid sideways and hit the floor, her head bouncing hard with a hollow thud. She didn't move. Her eyes still wide, stared blankly upwards.

Ruth pulled herself up to lean against the chair. Dazed, she thought of the phone and patted her robe. She felt the hard lump of it and pulled the phone from her pocket. Staring at it, she wasn't sure who to call first. What would she say?

She let out a deep quaking sigh, fearing everything might empty from her head just as it had all those years ago. Then, Ruth glanced at the woman, now harmless, and remembered her name.

FOR JEAN SEALEY
WHO ACTUALLY OPENED THE DOOR

THE LIBRARIAN

2

The hooded figure closes the third book, and it is then you notice the titles etched on their spines: THOSE WHO SHALL NEVER BE NAMED, reads the first, followed by THE LAST THINGS TO GO, and finally A RAVEN IN THE DOVE'S NEST, now neatly stacked side-by-side-by-side by your guide.

Each golden book contains the ashes of the dead; amid those ashes lies the tale, and upon opening, the tale recounted.

Tales the ashes tell, you muse.

"One story in this building goes by that name, which we'll get to later," the librarian says, as if reading your thoughts, then gracefully floats to the top of the shelves once again to return the three books to their rightful places, and it is in that same stacked order the librarian places them.

"There's a story in all of us."

Each volume fits neatly alongside the next, as if placed is in a predetermined or perhaps preternatural and not-to-be-altered order.

"When we pass, stories remain to be told, over and over again. If a story is good, that is. The good ones are here, in The Library of the Dead. If a story is not good, well, those stories are kept elsewhere."

The librarian glides over the floor to the next room.

"Come with me. More good stories must be opened."

Fewer golden books fill the next room than in the previous, and some of the shelves contain urns instead of books, or other various relics. Nearly a third of the shelves are filled, as opposed to every available spot, such as in the last. Some of the books seem old, oiled and bound in leather, although they all appear metallic, as if dipped in bronze. Some books are dark brown with gold text and some are black with gold stripes across their spines, and some are completely golden and smooth-spined. Not all have labels, however.

A white cherub statue observes the room, alone, in front of a blue- and yellow-tiled wall that is still under construction.

"This is an unfinished room," the librarian says, "but in time this room will be filled like the others; yet there are three on these shelves to show you now, one of which is a very recent addition by someone who left us recently, yet who left us with many marvelous stories."

A covered hand reaches to what looks like a recently added shelf reaching from floor to ceiling to retrieve a book labeled I'M GETTING CLOSER; *the second,* A CHIMERA'S TALE, *is taken from the highest shelf on the opposite wall, and the third from the nearest shelf where many books await, although he or she chooses only the middle:* I'M NOT THERE.

"Let us start with this one."

I'M NOT
THERE

KEALAN PATRICK BURKE

"What am I doing here, Joe?"

Lacy was uncomfortable, as he knew she would be, but he couldn't afford to get hung up on that now. There were far greater concerns than her passive aggressive efforts to ensure he knew she was doing him a monumental favor, that her being here was highly inappropriate.

"I think I'm losing my mind, Lace."

Still standing just inside the door, still wearing her coat, her Prada bag slung over her shoulder, she frowned. "What are you talking about?"

He stood a few feet away from her, the distance meant to reassure her that even though he'd meant what he said, he didn't represent a threat to her. Given how he must look—and he had no idea how that was, exactly—he knew he had to be careful to avoid frightening her. She had never seen him this way before. Couldn't have. He'd never had cause to be this way when they were together. The closest he could think of was maybe in the days and weeks after his mother passed away. He'd been a wreck. But that was different. It was grief, and therefore natural.

About this, there was nothing natural.

"Something's wrong," he said. "I'm not sure what's happening, but I needed someone to see if they see it too. To verify whether or not I'm going crazy. I'm sorry that it's you. I just didn't know who else to call."

A slightly smug look crept over her face as her shoulders relaxed. *She's enjoying this*, he thought, *getting off on it*. Momentary regret pulsed through him that he hadn't waited for his best friend Thad to finish work. Thad would not have judged him, nor reveled in his panic. Lacy, on the other hand, was already looking at the situation—without yet knowing what it was—as validation for her abandonment of him six months ago. Clearly, her parents had been right in coaching her away from him and his limited prospects and toward that plastic surgeon in Burbank. He wondered how long it would take before her natural beauty was stretched and lifted and tightened by her new beau, until she looked like a wax dummy.

"Fine," she said, shrugging out of a dark gray ankle-length coat he was sure cost more than his condo. She held it in the crook of her arm and raised her eyebrows. "So? What's the problem?"

He wrung his hands together like an old maid, found it difficult to meet her gaze, in which he saw the worst combination of things flickering in the green: pity, contempt, satisfaction. He had lost weight and his clothes reeked of cigarette smoke and bourbon, looked, in other words like the failed and desperate screenwriter she had always thought him to be. And in that moment, despite her presence, he had never felt more alone.

"It's this way." He turned his back on her, relieved to be free from her harshness of her attention, and started toward the bathroom.

"Wait," she said, and he did, but turned only his head to indicate he was listening. "First I want to know why I'm here, because—and no offense, Joe—but if you think I'm going to waltz back into the bowels of your condo with you while you stink of drink, seconds after you told me you think you're losing it, then you have another thing coming. My parents didn't raise an idiot."

No, Joe thought, *they didn't. They raised a sweet, smart, wonderful woman whose only flaw I could find was ambition because it didn't include me.*

A woman I loved and love still, even though I don't recognize her anymore.

And now he did turn to look at her, his head bowed a little, weighed down by the preposterousness of the words he was about to deliver. Did her face soften a little at the pathetic sight of him, at the brief flash of some distant memory of better days? Perhaps it was just his imagination. Perhaps all of this was. In a moment, he would know for sure.

And what then?

He didn't know, and didn't want to think of the implications for his future either way.

"Three days ago," he said, pausing to lick the dryness from his lips, "my reflection disappeared."

They stood together in his bedroom, facing the tall free-standing mirror in the corner next to the window. The blinds were closed but glowed like bars of hot iron as the midday sun beat mercilessly against the other side. In the mirror, Lacy was a vision, her honey-colored hair piled high on top and free falling in lustrous ringlets at the back and sides. Her makeup was light, eyes darkened by kohl to emphasize the emerald green. Lips he could still taste if he closed his eyes were parted slightly to reveal perfect teeth.

"Do you see?" His guts were aquiver.

He watched her reflection frown. "Assuming this mirror, like all others, is fulfilling its intended purpose, then yes, I see perfectly well. What is it that's supposed to be wrong?"

Joe felt his insides collapse, a thunderous roar of water in his head as the dam threatened to break. He realized now he had put all his hope on the horror of the situation being immediately evident to anyone who looked into the mirror with him. But apparently he was there in the glass with her, as he was supposed to be, except *he* saw everything reflected but himself. In the mirror, Lacy stood by herself before a bed with sweat-stained sheets and alcohol stains and a nightstand piled high with screenwriting books, memoirs, and an overfull ashtray.

KEALAN PATRICK BURKE

"You can see me? In the mirror, I mean?"

She turned to look at him and for the first time he saw a note of concern on her face. "Of course I do. You don't?"

He shook his head, sweat gathering at his hairline.

"You said this started two days ago?"

"Yes."

"You just woke up and couldn't see yourself in the mirror?"

"Yes."

"Is it just this mirror?"

"No. The bathroom mirror. The mirror in the hall. But it's not just mirrors. Anything reflective: the faucets, the glass on the coffee table, the windows, even my laptop and TV screens when they're turned off."

Her frown deepened, but cleaved the concern, and now the distance was back, the kind of cold, clinical detachment expected of a stranger when faced with someone who has clearly lost their marbles. "Have you been outside?"

"I was afraid to. I didn't know if anyone could see me. Didn't know what I'd do if that had been the case. But...*you* see me, so at least I know that now."

"I would think being invisible to people might make things kind of interesting."

He tried to mirror her smile but came up short, and instead returned his attention to the glass and the absence of his reflection.

"Maybe you're a vampire," Lacy said, her voice still tinged with humor he didn't appreciate.

"I'm scared," he said.

"Look, it's whacked, there's no doubt about that, and if it happened to me, I'd be terrified too. But whatever's wrong is clearly something in *you* and not a glitch in the universe. *I* can see you." She poked a finger at the place in the mirror his reflection should have been. "You're still there. Which means that you've probably suffered some kind of blood pressure incident, a mini-stroke or something, and you probably made it worse by drinking so much."

"I wasn't drinking before this. That started when I thought I was going nuts."

"There's not a shrink on the planet who would prescribe that as a wise course of action in the wake of a mental…episode…or whatever this is." She put a hand on his shoulder and guided him away to the bed, where she forced him to sit down and stood before him, blocking his view of the mirror. "Look, I know this has you completely messed up, but panicking and certainly drinking isn't doing you any good. You need to get yourself to a hospital, get an MRI, let them poke around and be sure something serious hasn't gone rogue up there. I can drive you if you like."

"I'm afraid," he said again, hating how true his voice made that sound.

She lowered herself down beside him and put an arm around his shoulder, gave it a squeeze. It was a maternal gesture meant to comfort. It had the opposite effect, and something cold writhed within him. He had to resist the urge to pull away.

"It'll all be fine, I promise. Weird things like this happen to people all the time. The brain is a fickle bitch. Sometimes it revolts."

He nodded, looked down at his hands, at the dirt beneath his fingernails. "You're right," he said. "Thanks."

She removed her arm and stood, startling him when she clapped her hands like a coach rallying the team for a game. "Okay, so how about you take a few minutes to freshen yourself up? You look like a turd on a swing set. I'll wait in the car and bring you to Alameda when you're ready."

He spoke without looking at her. "Will you stay with me? Just until they tell me what's wrong, assuming they can. I don't know what to do, Lace. I feel like I'm falling apart."

Her pause was brief, but enough for him to sense the deliberation, the unwillingness to accompany him this far down his own personal rabbit hole, her fear of what it might mean to him after it was all over, whatever dreadful and life complicating form that ending might take.

"Yes," she said then, a heartbeat too late, and put a hand over his. "Of course I will."

He nodded, but could not bear to look at her again, not because of what he would see in her face, but what he might not.

———◆———

As he'd feared, the tests revealed nothing out of the ordinary other than high blood pressure, which he had suffered since his early twenties, a condition which culminated in ischemic strokes in his early thirties. Since cutting down on smoking and drinking and taking three aspirin a day, he hadn't suffered one since. It was the doctor's contention that his "hallucinations" were related and that it was something best monitored via consultation with a "medical health professional." Lacy seemed buoyed that the doctor condoned her advice, and when she deposited Joe back at his condo, she was positively cheerful.

"Get some rest, stay off the booze, and go talk to someone tomorrow," she told him as he eased himself out of her husband's silver Audi A7. "You'll be your old self in no time."

How I wish you *were your old self,* he thought.

He stood for a moment on the sidewalk, one hand on the open car door, his gaze fixed on the condo, which looked to him now like a mausoleum for dead reflections. The dying sun glared like a baleful eye over the flat roof, the sky bruised purple around it. It seemed to him the worst possible idea to enter that place and yet he had nowhere else to go.

"Joe?"

Slowly, feeling as if he were underwater, he turned to look at her.

She gave him an apologetic look. "I have to go."

After a moment spared to study her face, to take a mental snapshot of the true beauty behind the brittle mask of forced concern, he nodded and summoned a smile for her benefit. "Of course. I'm sorry, Lace. And thank you for, y'know, being there."

"It's no problem." She gunned the engine. "Keep me posted, all right?"

The lack of sincerity galled him, but he kept it from his face. Why shouldn't she want nothing more to do with him? He was the one being unfair, his dilemma creating unreasonable expectations of a woman who had a life of her own to live. A life that no longer included him and never would. The fact that he wanted it to was redundant. He had signed away all rights to her when he'd resisted her suggestion that he get a "real" job, that he have more faith in himself. He had done neither of those things, had indeed resented the notion that his creative pursuits didn't constitute *real* work. *Real artists get paid*, she'd once said, a statement that led to the first of the worst arguments, the ones that undermined the foundation of all that they had once been. The beginning of the end. And all the while she'd gone to work at the insurance company and made enough to keep them both afloat while he waited for his ship to come in, only to watch it wreck itself upon the reef.

And now he was alone, so much so that it seemed not even his reflection wanted anything to do with him. The absurdity of that thought brought a smile more genuine than he'd managed in days, and Lace mirrored it. "Keep your chin up," she said and, because he didn't seem inclined to do it himself, she leaned across the passenger seat and pulled the door shut. Joe backed up a step as she gave him a cute little finger-wave and drove away. He watched until her tail-lights were mere embers in the deepening twilight.

Inside, the shading of the fading light against the shuttered blinds made the condo seem even colder and emptier than before. For a long moment he stood by the door, considering the benefits of fleeing. But where could he go? Everywhere out there were mirrors because people need to see themselves. Without them, part of our identity is lost. We need to know what we look like, we need to know that yes, we are here. And whatever the cosmic calamity that caused it, Joe was *not* here, not according to the mirror. He wondered what it would be like to be alive in a world in which he couldn't see himself, could never know what he looked like, the long term mental impact of having something so trivial and yet critical taken away, and being the only one denied it? And yet, others could see him in the glass, which meant that maybe he would show up via other methods too. In photographs, perhaps.

Emboldened, he tossed his keys in the wicker tray on the table by the door and made his way to the bathroom. Hit the fluorescent light and gave the oval mirror over the sink a distasteful glance as he fished in his pocket for his phone. It was still jarring to be standing before a mirror he had looked into every morning and night for two years and see nothing. The specks of toothpaste and water on the bottom of the glass seemed almost like mockery now, the harsh light unobstructed by a presence that had every right to be there in accordance with natural law. Worse, however, than the bizarre lack of a reflection, was the probability of what it meant to be the only one who couldn't see himself. He did not believe in the supernatural, had been intimidated into willful ignorance by science, and had only the most rudimentary understanding of psychotherapy, gleaned via research for a script that had, like most of them, ended up in the bottom of his filing cabinet. He knew only enough to concede, as anyone would, that whatever had happened to him, its origins likely existed inside his own head. Any relief this might have afforded him—the idea that he actually *was* there in the mirror and had somehow simply been blinded to it—was dashed by the greater implication of what that meant for his sanity. Somewhere up there, a cog had slipped so badly it had managed to alter the reality available to his eyes.

He brought the phone up before him, the camera's eye focused on the mirror, which showed only the phone floating magically in the air before the glass.

The phone's display screen showed a smaller version of the same impossible image.

Joe clicked the button and the phone made a ratcheting sound as it captured the moment.

He lowered the phone, clicked the small preview thumbnail to enlarge it, and looked down at the photo. He stared at what was there to be seen, and what wasn't, and then attached the photo to a text message and wrote:

THIS IS WHAT I WAS TRYING TO TELL YOU.

JUST TOOK THIS.

I'M NOT THERE.

Fingers trembling, he hit send. Looked straight ahead, wishing he could see his eyes, wondered what he might see in them if he could.

Could it be that whatever strange selective blindness he was suffering extended to phones too? When Lacy received the message, would she see him in the photograph? Mouth dry, he pocketed the phone and brought his hands to the glass, pressed them hard against it. Yes, he could feel the coolness of the mirror against his skin, the tactile confirmation that he was real and he was here. It did not yield to him and he was relieved that the sudden fear that he might sink through it and find himself in some awful netherwhere of negative space was not realized. He pushed harder against the mirror, heard the glass creak as it bowed against the pressure.

I am here.

He could smell the soap, the disinfectant, the stink of his own sweat.

"Show me," Joe told the mirror. "Please. I've done nothing to deserve this. Let me see me."

Teeth clenched, he leaned harder into the mirror, his arms quivering from the strain.

"For God's sake, *show* me," he pleaded, his voice cracking under the weight of imminent tears.

The light above his head flickered and buzzed.

"Please…"

When it became clear that whomever or whatever power controlled such things wasn't listening, he screamed at the top of his lungs, drew back a fist, and slammed it as hard as he could into the mirror. On impact, a jagged silver crack shot upward like lightning in reverse, a smaller crack radiating outward from the side of his hand. The mirror shuddered in its frame but did not break. He imagined the glass falling away only to reveal his reflection behind it where it had been hiding all along. Weeping, Joe put his forehead against the glass.

His phone chimed to signify a text message received. With a shaky almost child-like sigh, he fumbled it out of his pocket and brought it up to his face.

The message was from Lacy.

I C U JUST FINE, BABE.
U NEED 2 TALK 2 SOMEONE, STAT.

A grim smile through the tears. So to everyone else, he did appear in photographs, just like he did in the mirror. He would just never be able to see it, a revelation that greatly decreased the likelihood that anyone would ever believe him anything other than mad. There was, after all, absolutely no proof of what he was going through other than his own testimony.

He released the phone, let it clatter into the sink.

Where there was blood.

Blinking away the tears, he looked from the smattering of crimson on the porcelain to his knuckles. The skin was broken and torn across all but one of his knuckles, blood smeared across his fingers and dripping from his hand. He raised his eyes to the mirror, saw the smudge of his blood on the glass.

And something else. Something which made him jolt and back away from the mirror as if it had burned him.

"Jesus." A spear of elation shot through his chest and he brought his hand up, turned it this way and that. A smile spread across his face, though he could not yet see it in the mirror. He would though, that much was clear. He was coming back.

He thought about calling Lacy, decided to wait. First, he needed to be sure, or risk compounding the impression that he was mad.

Almost afraid to hope, he looked down at the faucets, saw the slightest distorted blur of movement there. Next, heart thundering, he ran into the bedroom, not caring that he was leaving specks of blood on the beige carpet, and stood before the free-standing mirror in which he had last seen only Lacy's beauty, and beyond it, her struggle with apathy. A prayer to a god he had never believed in on his lips, he looked into the glass.

And saw what he had hoped would be there.

A laugh disguised as a sob burst from his mouth and he dropped to his knees, the relief almost unbearable. He chuckled and wept and whispered thanks. A week ago, back when things were normal, what he was seeing in the mirror now would have horrified him as much if not more than the absence of his reflection. But things were no longer normal, and the sight of his disembodied bloody hand floating in the glass gave him the hope he needed to keep going, to do what clearly now needed to be done.

Excited and terrified in equal measures, he rose, took one last look at his hand in the mirror, and hurried to the kitchen to get the sharpest knife he owned.

A

CHIMERA'S

TALE

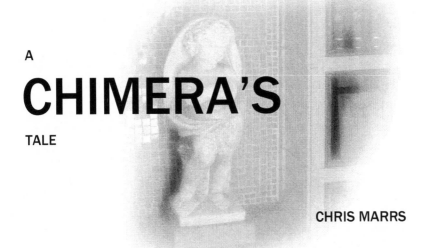

CHRIS MARRS

The Mortal

Josh trudged down the sidewalk as he debated whether to go home to Lisa-Anne and her feeble attempts to murder him or not. She wouldn't know his meeting with the building inspector down in the Tenderloin District ended early. Then again, she had a way of sussing things out of him. He'd quarreled with himself since he was a child and believed an angel sat on his right shoulder and a devil on his left. It drove his wife nuts. Their two teenaged boys, though, had always found it humorous and teased him every chance they got.

The heat rose off the pavement in shimmers and thickened the air. His sport coat, hooked over one shoulder with his thumb, bounced against his lower back with each step. Sweat dripped down his sides but he was so engaged in arguing with himself, it didn't register. Neither did the sandwich board sitting on the concrete. Josh walked into it, caught it before it tipped over and, when setting it back in place, noticed the board listed beer specials for a pub named Gary's. A gentle tug from deep within his gut propelled him inside.

———————▲———————

The Immortal

I was messing with the barflies at Gary's when I sensed the presence of an approaching chimera. My hand paused in mid-air as the familiar pins and needles sensation rippled across my skin.

A tattoo on the hairy arm of the biker hunched over a bourbon on the rocks begged to be stroked, but my fun would have to wait. Not that he'd see me touch him. Feel it? Yes. And with luck, might have thought the geeky dude sitting beside him trying not to make eye contact with anyone was getting touchy-feely.

The prickling sensation deepened into sharp stabs, indicating the reshaping of my present form. Colors bled until everything I saw was cast in black and white. The scents of beer, disinfectant, piss, and mold heightened, yet the change never affected sound. While I rode out the transformation, Sammi, a cute little bartender, laughed with four guys seated near the pool table. The hooker, Jane, provided the soundtrack by coaxing a lively Hungarian piece from her violin in hopes of receiving tips or booze or a trick. A junkie in the corner twitched and scratched as he waited for his dealer.

When my pieces settled into their new place and the ache receded, I knew my appearance had become that of a female. A bartender, too, based on the black skirt, apron, and tight shirt with the name *Annalise* stitched over one breast. Which meant the approaching chimera was a male, and unfortunately a mortal, just a man born with two sets of DNA. He may be earthly; I, on the other hand, am not. I'm a celestial chimera, a creature genetically angelic and demonic, light and dark, and I'm the only one in existence. The *Powers that Be* deemed me too good to be accepted by the dark and too evil for the light, so until they made up their minds, I was stuck here. Sucked to be me.

I shook out the last of the tingles. Then, because I could, and because the last couple of chimeras had been female, I flashed the bar. No reaction. Ha! So I did it again, but the satisfaction wasn't there that time. I felt a little pathetic and gave up the game to lean against the back counter and wait.

Impatience crawled through me. I wanted him to show up now. After all, he'd be able to see and talk to me and we'd be spending copious amounts of time together, at least until he grew old and died. My last chimera passed away over fifty years ago. The excitement caused my angelic side—the right half of me—to glow with a soft blue light and suffused me with happiness. Finally, he walked in.

The Mortal

Goosebumps pimpled Josh's arms and the sweat quick-dried when he stepped into the air-conditioned bar. He spotted an empty table in the corner and, ignoring the stares from the bikers playing pool, plopped down onto a wooden chair, varnish worn thin in spots.

A cute bartender with short blonde hair nodded at him in acknowledgement as she tipped a mug beneath the spigot. While she poured, an old man chatted her up while he leaned forward to gaze down her shirt, but she ignored it. After giving the letch his draught, she sauntered out from behind the bar. Her short skirt revealed a great pair of legs to go with the ample cleavage.

"What'll it be, hon?" she said.

"Mug of draught, please, Sammi," he said as he read the name on her shirt. "You pick the flavor."

"I recommend the lager or the lager." A slight grin brought a dimple to the surface of one cheek.

He laughed then said, "A lager then."

Off she went, seductively twitching a perfect ass with each step. While he admired her butt, the little hairs on the nape of his neck stirred. He checked to see if the bikers were watching him but they were engrossed in their game so he scanned the room for the culprit. Then he saw another bartender leaning against the back bar counter.

She looks just like Lisa-Anne. The long black hair and trim body was an exact replica of his wife's, but the violet eyes staring back at him clinched the illusion. He noticed a pale blue glow surrounded one side of Lisa-Anne's doppelganger. Josh blinked, hoping the heat was affecting his mind, but the aura still clung to her. Sammi blocked his view to set down his draught, moved to another table, and the other bartender slipped onto the chair across from him.

Up close the similarities were more apparent, right down to their Roman nose, full lips, and diagonal scar running through one eyebrow. According to the name on her shirt, even their names were alike. Josh deconstructed Annalise's face, examined her for any little flaw or difference to shatter the resemblance, but found none.

In his mind, the angel and the devil started to yammer.

The Immortal

"I'm Annalise. Mind if I join you?" I said.

By his narrowed eye expression, I thought he might tell me to leave, but he said, "You look like my wife. She's trying to kill me."

"Wait. What?"

"No, she isn't. Don't be paranoid."

I wished I could, just once, meet a normal chimera who didn't have a private war going on inside them, but then they wouldn't be a chimera, would they? It's a curse of the dual natured genetics and one even their closest loved ones never suspected.

"Why do you think she's trying to kill you?" I said.

He frowned at me over the lip of the mug, drained it, then said, "I didn't say that." Hands trembling, he brought out his wallet, fumbled out a few bills, and tossed them on the table. "Sorry, can't stay."

Panic swept through me; this wasn't going like it should. He was not supposed to leave. I reached out and gripped his wrist. The spark of contact trilled across my nerves and out of surprise, I jerked away, but my fingers refused to open. Then I *saw*. I knew his name was Josh, his wife's name was Lisa-Anne, and they had two teenage boys. She didn't look like me, nor I like her. Yet, there was an imbalance surrounding her and, on impulse, I reached deeper into the connection to find out what it was. Josh ripped his arm out of my grasp, breaking the spell.

"I don't know what the hell that was about," he said. "But don't touch me again." Then he stomped out.

Instead of chasing him down, the combined shock of rejection and revelations kept me seated. When I touched my previous chimeras, nothing like this had occurred. Normally, we both felt a sense of calm, a balanced serenity, and the kinship of meeting a kindred spirit. A bond to tie us together as the mortal grew old and died. As for the newfound knowledge, the *Powers that Be* had to be behind it. What were they trying to tell me? Why now?

The answers lay with Josh, so I resigned myself to wishing for his hasty return.

Hands on hips, I stood at the window and watched eddies of fog twist and swirl as people walked through it. Every so often, someone would drift in for a beer or to check the score on the football game playing on three of the ancient TV's; the fourth broadcasted the news. Three weeks had gone by with no sign of Josh. This wasn't right, yet there was nothing I could do but wait, as usual, or maybe I didn't.

Two centuries ago, I'd chosen to hang exclusively around bars, especially after I'd discovered they attracted chimeras for some unknown reason. I'd always allowed them to find me, never attempting to seek them out myself. Now I questioned why. The answer I found was pride; it made me feel wanted in the face of my exile by the *Powers that Be*, made me feel as if I mattered. I didn't know if I could even locate Josh but it wouldn't hurt to try.

I closed my eyes, breathed in and then out, long and slow, and pushed all distractions from my mind until I was neither angelic nor demonic, a perfect balance. Recalling his face, I concentrated on going to him. Damp air pressed against me. I opened my eyes. Standing in a garden at the front of a newer suburban home, I wondered if I'd always been able to travel like this or if the *Powers that Be* had granted me a new ability.

A woman's voice floated through the open window and distracted me from my musings. Because I heard only one side of a conversation, I assumed she spoke on the phone.

"Yes, it's all going according to plan," I heard her say. "No, I don't think he suspects a thing … A week next Saturday … I can't, sweetie …"

Her voice began to fade as she moved deeper into the home so I leaned toward the window in an attempt to hear her better. A shadow coalesced behind the screen.

The Mortal

Josh wandered around the house, mumbling as he considered the pros and cons of eating dinner tonight, Mexican judging by the spicy aroma floating through the rooms. The boys were upstairs playing computer games and Lisa-Anne was on the phone with a friend. He heard the murmur of her voice as she went from the kitchen to the laundry room, but wasn't quite able to catch the words. His meandering took him into the dim living room. Movement within the fog outside caught his attention so, curious, he crept to the window.

The bartender from the dive bar stood in the garden. He froze. *What is she doing here? How did she find out where I live?* The angel and the devil offered conflicting answers, but for once he wasn't listening. Instead, he recalled when Annalise had touched him in the bar and the sense of calm it'd brought. How it'd silenced the opposing voices and left him feeling balanced yet terrified. As if by remembering the fear, it had overwhelmed him.

"What are you? Some creepy-ass stalker?" he said. "I don't

know how you found out where I live, but go the fuck away."

Annalise hopped back a step, as if in surprise, then said, "You don't want to send me away, Josh. I know you can feel something you can't describe that attracts me to you. A wholeness, maybe?"

He didn't want to admit she was right, especially since he knew he hadn't told her his name. The alarm inside him intensified.

"How did you know... never mind," he said. Lisa-Anne's heels clicked on the kitchen tile. Soon she'd walk into the living room so he said, "Go away or I'm calling the cops."

"You don't want to do that," Annalise said.

Josh got the impression that she smirked when she replied.

"Don't try me," he said, then Lisa-Anne walked into the room.

"Who are you talking to, babe?" she said.

Tell her, the angel whispered. *Don't*, the devil said. He shifted from foot to foot, watched Annalise, and waited for his wife to notice her. She didn't. The angel won.

"Some deranged bartender I met a couple of weeks ago who thinks stalking customers is okay." Instantly, he regretted saying it.

Lisa-Anne came over to the window and peered into the fog.

"I don't see anyone," she said.

He looked at Lisa-Anne, then outside. Annalise was still there.

"She's right in front of the window," he said. "You can't miss her unless you're blind."

"There's no one there." Lisa-Anne put her arm around Josh's waist. "Would you like me to book an appointment with your psychologist, love?"

You'd like to do that, wouldn't you? Then you could admit me to the crazy house in place of murder.

"No, I'm fine."

"If you're sure." She turned on her heels. "Dinner's going to be ready soon and I'd appreciate it if you'd eat with us for once."

A retort came quickly to his tongue, but he clamped his lips shut before it flew out.

When he heard her opening and closing cupboards in the

kitchen, he chanced a glance outside. The woman was gone.

Good riddance. Yet, why did he feel a twinge of disappointment?

The Immortal

I spent the next two days sitting at Josh's table and contemplating whether I should go to him again. The previous experience had left me a little discombobulated. First, the conversation I'd overheard led me to believe Lisa-Anne may be trying to kill him after all. My good-natured angelic side, however, harbored a smidge of doubt. And second, he still didn't want to be around me and I wasn't able to understand his rejection, nor did I want to accept it. The best way to handle Josh might be the subtle approach, something at which I wasn't proficient. The familiar tug in my gut told me that I wouldn't need to make a decision; it had been made *for* me.

Josh slunk over to the table, his sideways glance and twitch when the pool balls clacked gave him the appearance of a junkie looking for a fix. Sammie poured a pint and brought it over as he removed his overcoat. Her memory for recalling what someone drank, even if they'd been in once, always amazed me.

He slid into the seat across from mine.

"Now who's being the creepy stalker," I said in an attempt to open with humor.

He stared into his glass as if he'd never seen bubbles and found them fascinating.

"I didn't know where else to go," he said. Josh heaved a sigh then looked up.

I blinked in rapid succession, thinking the haunted eyes peering at me from sunken pits, as well as the sharp cheekbones and pale skin, was an illusion. They weren't. He thrust his hands at me, almost knocking over his drink in the process.

"Do you see them?" he said. "The lines on my nails. They're called leukonychia striata. Arsenic poisoning does that."

I didn't see any lines on his fingernails so I grabbed his hand for closer inspection. Again, images of Lisa-Anne, the boys, and the sense of imbalance swept over me, yet I still wasn't able to capture the reason for the vision. Josh pulled his hand back, breaking the tie, and laid both palms down on the table out of my reach. When my mind stopped reeling from the mental visuals, I decided to indulge him and see where it went.

"A slow poisoning, that's pretty harsh," I said.

"Oh, she was trying, but I outwitted her by refusing to eat anything she makes." He smiled in a way that was somewhat smug and partly lost. "She'll have to find some other way to kill me before my fortieth birthday." Josh stared back down at his nails.

The chimera looked so pitiful examining his hands, as if they held the solution to his problem. I wanted to wrap my arms around his thin body and tell him everything would be okay, but wasn't able to convince myself to touch him again; I wouldn't be able to without physical contact, at least not until I figured out what the visions meant

Exasperated, I slammed my hand onto the table as my skin warmed and heat rose from my demonic side in shimmery waves. The beer mug joggled and Josh snapped his head up, his face paling, and it struck me how much he resembled a skull.

"Lisa-Anne looks at me like that when she's angry," he said. "Did I do something to make you mad at me?"

The mention of Lisa-Anne and his inability to do anything about her supposed plot rankled more than my conundrum.

"Wouldn't it piss you off to listen to someone complaining about how his wife is trying to murder him, yet he's doing nothing about it?" I found the solution to my problem hidden in the question. "Run away with me. Somewhere Lisa-Anne can't find you."

Josh sat back with enough force to rock his chair onto two legs. For a second, I thought he'd passed the point of no return and topple backward, but the chair settled onto four legs again. He remained quiet. I knew if he agreed, I'd have what I desired—an answer to the visions and an end to my loneliness—so I pushed.

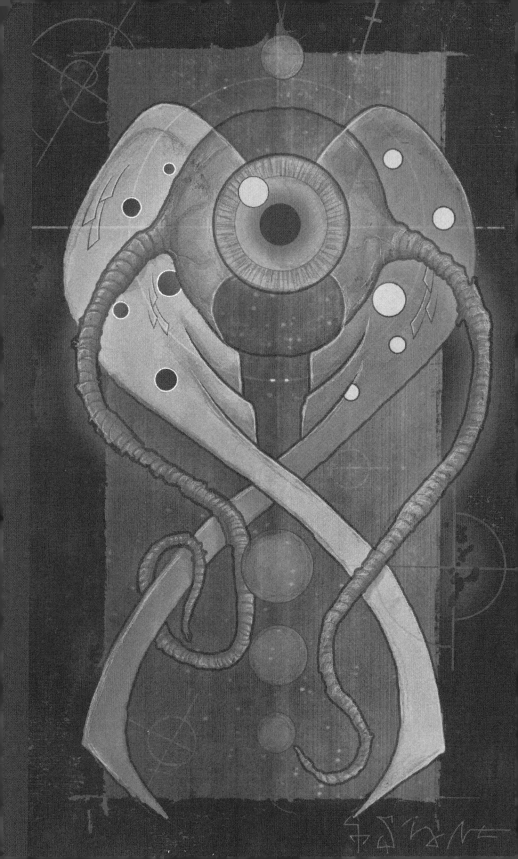

"I know I look just like your wife. So why don't you come with me and start new?"

He furrowed his brow and massaged the sides of his temples while mumbling under his breath. I strained to catch what he said.

"Is everything okay, hon?" Sammi said.

I hadn't noticed her approach and wished I'd had the ability to strangle her. She must have caught the negative vibe because she moved a step away from me.

"Yeah, I'm fine," Josh said.

"If you say so, but you don't look fine."

"Really, I'm good. We're just having an intense conversation."

She cocked her head, "Uh, okay? Flag me down if you need another draught." Sammie scurried back behind the bar.

"So?" I said. "What will it be?"

Josh shrugged and returned to contemplating the bubbles in his ever-warming beer. My ire reached a peak. The fingernails on my demonic side blackened and the skin cracked to reveal a glowing red liquid not unlike molten lava.

"I'm tired of this game. You can leave now," I said while ignoring the angelic side's urge to take back my words. "A piece of advice, though: if I were you, I'd kill her before she does it to you."

He flinched like I had hit him, then tossed down a few bills, grabbed his overcoat, and dashed out.

I traced the cracked skin on my forearm and decided this chimera wasn't worth the trouble. I didn't care if it would be another fifty years or so before another came along. Josh's extreme dual nature had really, really pissed me off.

The Mortal

Josh snuck into the house and closed the door as gently as possible. All week he'd been preoccupied with the thought of Annalise and her offer. *Damn her to Hell for heaping another conundrum on me.* He hung his coat, stashed his briefcase on the shelf, then left the mudroom and walked into the warm, meaty scent of roast beef. It made his mouth water and drew him to the kitchen.

While he tiptoed down the short hallway, hoping Lisa-Anne had already gone upstairs, the inner argument continued. Should he leave with Annalise? *No, said the angel. Yes, said the devil.* She was Lisa-Anne's exact replica, though, but would it be enough for him? Would he able to leave the boys or should he take them? Again, his mind offered the same yes and no answers. It was enough to drive him insane.

Lisa-Anne was in the kitchen when he entered. He wanted to breeze right on through to the living room, but the guilty expression on her face halted his feet. She tossed something into a cupboard, slammed it shut, then smiled.

"Hey, sweetie, I saved you some dinner," she said. "Roast beef with all the trimmings."

"I ate already," he said.

Frowning as she started moving pots off the stove to the sink to be washed, she said, "You're getting too thin. Come on, I'll get your plate out of the oven and we'll sit down and talk about what to do for your birthday Sunday while you eat. Forty. A big one."

He'd forgotten Sunday was his birthday. Now that she'd reminded him, he wondered if her preparing his favorite meal was to be his last. And what had she stashed in the cupboard? *Kill her now. No, don't.* Then his wife gazed at him with those violet eyes of hers and all he saw was Annalise. He heard her urging him to leave with her, to begin again. It was like she offered to rewind time for him and he found the notion appealing.

A carving knife lay on the counter. The overhead light reflected in its shiny surface, the black handle pointed toward him. *Should I?* For once, the two voices provided the same answer: *yes.* Josh grabbed it and lunged. Lisa-Anne screamed, raised her arms. The blade sliced into the flesh of her forearm. Blood splattered onto the tile floor. She pushed past him and ran.

"Jordan! Matt! Stay in your rooms!"

Josh heard the hysteria in her voice, but instead of bringing him to his senses, it ignited the desire to be happy again, to fall in love with Annalise the way he used to love Lisa-Anne.

He followed the sound of her footsteps up the stairs. Red droplets sunk into the carpet and led to their bedroom. Josh tried the knob—locked—so he leaned his forehead against the door.

"I'm sorry, sweetie," he said, keeping his voice soft. "Open the door and we'll talk this out." No reply. "Maybe I should go see my psychologist in the morning."

Low murmurs came from the other side of the door and he knew what she'd done. Panic wound its tentacles through his innards. He rattled the doorknob as if it would magically fall unlocked. A hollow metallic sound caused him to turn around.

"Leave Mom alone!" Matt stepped out of the den.

The world went dark, and when the light came back, he stumbled into Gary's. Annalise sat at the table as if waiting for him. He ambled over, sat, and slammed the knife down.

"I did it. I killed her," he said. He spun the knife in circles. "Why did you tell me to do it?"

The Immortal

"I only gave you a piece of advice," I said. "The choice was yours."

Despite the copious amounts of blood stiffening Josh's white shirt and dried splatters on his face, no one screamed or made any indication that they noticed.

"And the boys," he said. "My brave boys tried to protect her and now they're gone too." Tears poured down his cheeks, met the blood and turned pink. "You did this!"

He picked up the knife and dove across the table to plunge the blade into my chest. Instead of stopping at the hilt, it carried right through. He scowled and tried again with the same result. Using both hands, I wrapped my fingers around his wrist, then *saw* everything.

"Lisa-Anne wasn't trying to poison you," I said. "She was planning a surprise party for you."

I didn't hear if Josh replied since the information continued to flood into me. I saw my path and why the *Powers that Be* had suddenly gifted me with visions and the ability to travel to a chimera. Even the reason for the imbalance I sensed in Lisa-Anne became clear.

The disparity hadn't come from her, but from Josh. Lisa-Anne was good, pure, what one—if this were the Middle Ages—would call a saint. I was shown how years from now her and the boys would overcome the tragedy and band together to change a portion of the world for the better. Under her direction they'd touch many lives with their natural goodness and grace. In this, the *Powers that Be* let my purpose be known and it wasn't about being accepted by one side or the other, but about balancing the light and the dark in humanity. I'd been approaching my experiences with the chimeras from a selfish angle. Stupid me.

Lastly, I saw Josh laid out in a cardboard coffin while awaiting cremation at Chapel of the Chimes. In spite of what he'd tried to do, Lisa-Anne held his cold hand while tears dripped off her jaw.

"And now you're the one who's dead," I said.

"No, I'm not." He tried to pull out of my grip.

"Unfortunately you are. When you wouldn't stop trying to get at his mother, your eldest son shot you with the gun kept in the desk in your den."

Josh sagged under the weight of my words.

"No," he said. "I killed them."

"If you don't believe me, check out the TV in the corner. The one playing the news channel."

We both turned to watch. A reporter stood outside Josh's home. The volume was off, but we could read the banner on the bottom. It declared one-person shot in what appeared to be an attempted murder-suicide. A stretcher rolled past in the background and a body lay hidden under a white sheet dappled with red splotches. Lisa-Anne, her forearm bandaged, talked to an officer. The boys were nowhere in sight.

"See?" I said.

He nodded. Once he'd acknowledged his death, I released his wrist. Dark tendrils reached through the ether and caressed him. His body shook and crumpled in on itself at their touch, smaller and smaller until he popped out of existence. My angelic side sighed and a blue aura emanated from my pores, but to my surprise my demonic side surfaced too. With one half of me glowing blue and the other red, I found my own balance.

A month slipped by before I gathered the nerve to test my new-found purpose. I still haunted Gary's so I went to Josh's old table and sat down. I closed my eyes, took a few deep breaths to calm my mind and center myself before I began the search for a new chimera. A tingle raced along my skin and then I felt the rush of air against my body.

By the time my ass hit the concrete somewhere in the heart of the Tenderloin, my transformation was complete. I'd become a male this time, and a stinky one, too, judging by the smell coming off the trench coat I wore. Cars crawled by with bass-heavy music blaring and pushing the fetid air around. Pedestrians crossed in front of me but one pair of feet clad in orthopedic shoes stopped. I looked into the face of an older woman, her hair in a scarf and thick make-up cracked. She knelt.

"Can you help me?" she said.

"I don't know," I said. "What do you need help with?"

She smoothed her hair through the scarf before she said, "I'm looking for my daughter. I lost her a long time ago and recently discovered she lived down here. It's important I make amends with her soon."

"What's her name and I'll see what I can do."

"Jane."

"Does she play the violin by any chance?"

"She used to. Why? Do you know her?"

"I do." I stuck out my hand. "I'm Allan, by the way."

"That was my son's name." After hesitating, she took my hand. I *saw* my purpose. "I'm Susan, and am I glad I ran into you. It's all about balance, isn't it?"

More than you know, Susan.

I'M GETTING
CLOSER

J.F. GONZALEZ

It was Friday night, and Sarah and Jessica were walking aimlessly down 1st Street because they had nothing else to do. They'd spent the earlier part of the evening at Gott's Roadside where they'd hung out with their friends and chowed down on burgers, fries, and milkshakes.

The evening was pleasant with a nice breeze. It was dark out but still early, and streetlights kept the areas they hung out at very well lit. Jessica was nattering about a sophomore they knew at Napa High named Steve Beck. "He's been, like, checking me out every day after school when we gather outside for the buses."

"Sure, Jessica," Sarah said.

She held her iPhone in one hand. Jessica thought every guy at Napa High had the hots for her.

"You don't believe me?" Jessica said.

"Oh, I believe you," Sarah said. Her iPhone chimed and there was a text message from her mother.

Honey, it's getting late and I'd like you to start heading home now.

"Ughhh!" Sarah groaned.

"Is that your mom?" Jessica asked.

"She wants me to start heading home! It's not even nine o'clock yet!"

There was another cell phone chime and Jessica pulled her

iPhone out. She groaned. "My mom wants me to come home *too*."

Sarah and Jessica resumed heading towards Silverado Trail.

"Is your mom worried about the stalker?" Jessica asked.

"Stalker? What are you talking about?"

Jessica shrugged. "Some weirdo's been following girls around town, trying to break into their homes. Apparently he's, like, making this lame attempt to copy Bart Shafley."

"Who?" Sarah had no idea who Bart Shafley was.

"You've never heard of Bart Shafley?"

Sarah shrugged. "No. Why should I?"

"So you didn't hear that he died?" Jessica was a sucker for those stories and memes on Creepypasta and other websites. Sarah had the vague feeling that Jessica believed most of that stuff.

"I don't even know who he is!" Sarah exclaimed. "What blog did you read about him on?"

"I didn't read about him on a blog. He was on the *news*," Jessica said, emphasizing the news part, as if this lent it more legitimacy. "Bart Shafley went to our high school ten years ago. Apparently he was a computer nerd and hacked into the school's network and changed grades around, even hacked into their phone system. He was a stalker. He'd, like, follow girls around like a pervert. Anyway, he got fixated on this one girl named Amanda Brady. He hacked into her home computer, read a bunch of her diary entries and learned all about her. She had no idea he was obsessed with her until he snuck into her house one night and killed her."

"How'd he kill her?" They'd resumed walking up 1st Street and had reached the crosswalk on the green light and started across Silverado Trail. Jessica lived on Willow Avenue, the first street on the right after they crossed Silverado.

"He smothered her," Jessica answered. "Her parents found her. Shafley's lawyer tried to have him committed to a psychiatric hospital but that's really tough to do. He was tried as an adult and got a life sentence." She paused. "Apparently he was really into the occult, too."

"The occult? You mean like, black magic and stuff?"

Jessica nodded. "There was a story on the Internet that said his cellmate was scared of him because he was doing weird rituals and shit. That's what got him killed."

Sarah didn't respond for a few seconds. She'd honestly never heard of the Bart Shafley story and she and Jessica shared an affinity with websites like Creepypasta and sites of a similar ilk. The difference is, she saw these sites as entertainment, unlike Jessica who believed pretty much everything she read on the Internet.

When she finally responded, Sarah asked, "So somebody's like, trying to copy what this guy did?"

Jessica nodded. "Apparently he's been following girls around Napa Valley and if they're using a smart phone he somehow hacks into them and, like, messes with them."

Sarah scoffed. "That's dumb! What's so scary about that?"

They reached the other side of Silverado Trail and beneath the glow of the streetlamp Sarah caught a glimpse of her friend's face. For the first time since she'd known her, Sarah thought Jessica looked scared. "Two girls have disappeared."

"Disappeared? What do you mean, disappeared?"

"They disappeared! The hacker/stalker guy, like, kidnapped and killed them."

"Are you even *sure* he's killing them? Before you said two girls have disappeared."

"Isn't that what usually happens when girls turn up missing?"

Sarah nodded. "Guess you're right."

They said little as they resumed their walk up 1st Street toward Willow Street. The stalker/hacker story must have spooked Jessica, because she turned to Sarah and said, "Will you text me as you walk home?"

"Sure." Sarah offered her friend a smile. *Everything will be okay.*

"Okay," Jessica said, stepping off the curb to head down Willow Street toward her house. "Let me know when you get home."

"I will."

Sarah had a few blocks to go until she reached her own house.

They said goodbye, and as Sarah made her way down 1st Street nearing Alta Avenue, she heard the chime of an incoming text message. It was from Jessica.

I'm home, but I'm not going inside. My mom just pissed me off. Can I come to your house?

Sarah stopped and looked at her iPhone. She couldn't see Jessica, but could picture her standing on the sidewalk in front of her home. Still walking she carefully typed her response.

Sure. I'll wait for you to catch up. I'm still on 1st just past Alta.

She pressed Send and waited.

A moment later Jessica's response came back.

Keep going. I'll just walk to your house and we can talk outside. I don't want my mom to see me.

Sarah frowned and looked back down 1st Street.

Okay, whatever. I'll wait for you outside my house.

She hit *Send* and started heading home.

A moment later there was a chirp from her iPhone. It sounded like Siri. She pulled out her phone and slowed down. Siri had been activated and Sarah was about to press the Home button to deactivate it when the app's computerized voice came through the iPhone's speakers.

"I'M GETTING CLOSER."

"What the fuck?" Sarah said aloud. She looked down the street where Jessica would be coming from but there was nobody there yet. Sarah had already reached East Avenue. She was about to head back the way she came when Siri spoke again.

"I'M GETTING CLOSER TO YOU, SARAH."

This time, Sarah almost dropped her iPhone. Her heart hammered in her chest and she felt ice freeze in her veins. Her stomach fluttered as she brought up the phone. She pressed the Home button and went back into iMessage to type out a message to Jessica.

Are you still heading toward my house?

No response. Then the Siri app launched again almost immedi-

I'M GETTING CLOSER

ately and Sarah gave a frightened yelp as it answered.

"YES. I AM HEADING TOWARD YOUR HOUSE."

Sarah bolted. She made a left on East and continued on up to East Spring Street. By the time she reached it, she was panting. She slowed down, a stitch forming in her side, but she didn't turn back to see if Jessica was behind her—surely Jessica would have rounded the corner of 1st Street by now.

"I'M GOING TO YOUR HOUSE, SARAH," Siri said.

"Fuck this," Sarah said. She started running again, but then stopped as the stitch in her side stabbed into her. With her heart pounding from adrenaline, she pressed the Call button on the iPhone and called home.

Her mother answered. "Hi honey."

"Mom, can you come pick me up?"

"Sure. I can have your dad come get you. Where are you?"

"I'm on East Spring on the corner of East Street."

Mom's voice grew concerned. "Are you okay, Sarah?"

What should I say without sounding like an idiot or making her worried?

"I'm just really tired and I have a stitch in my side. Can you have Dad come and get me?"

"Sure, he's leaving now." She heard Mom tell Dad where Sarah was, and then her mom came back on the line. "He'll be there in about a minute."

"Thanks." She closed her eyes for a moment and took a deep breath. She opened them and looked back down the street. No sign of Jessica. "Will you stay on the line with me until Dad gets here?"

"Are you sure you're okay, Sarah?" Mom asked. That tinge of concern in her voice was amped up a bit more now.

"I'm ... I'm just kind of freaked out ... that's all."

"About what?"

Sarah checked out her surroundings. The houses she was standing in front of were occupied; she could hear a TV in the background and she also heard a dog bark a few doors down. People were home. Nothing could happen to her out here. "Jessica and

131

I were talking on the way home," she began. "And Jessica told me about this guy copying Bart Shafley."

She repeated what Jessica told her about Bart Shafley's past crime, the copycat who was going around town harassing teenage girls and how two girls in the area had already disappeared.

"There's been nothing in the news about girls disappearing," Mom said. "Besides, that stuff doesn't happen here. In Oakland, yes, in Napa, no."

Sarah thought, *Yeah, of course shit like this happens in Oakland where all our relatives are buried in that creepy Chapel of the Chimes place.* "But Jessica said—"

"I know what Jessica told you, but it just isn't true," Mom said. "It's true that a guy named Bart Shafley was recently killed in prison. I remember when he was arrested for murdering that girl."

"So that really happened?" Sarah asked.

"Yes, that really happened," Mom said. "But he went to prison and he was killed. That happens to guys who hurt or kill kids. The thing about girls disappearing, though? It isn't happening or I would have heard about it. I check the news sites every morning."

"Then why would she say that?"

"I don't know, honey. You know Jessica is prone to telling stories."

Sarah felt a little better. She also felt a little embarrassed that she'd felt scared in the first place. She looked down the street toward Meek Street where she lived, but her Dad's car hadn't approached yet. She glanced back down the street; no Jessica, either.

"You okay, honey?" Her mom sounded concerned. "You weren't harassed by anybody for real, were you?"

"I think I was," Sarah said. "Mom, can Jessica—"

Headlights from down the street. Sarah looked up and saw her Dad's car heading toward her. "Here's Dad!"

"Can Jessica what, honey?"

"Jessica wanted to come by tonight," Sarah said, making up the story quickly. "She had a fight with her Mom." She did a quick check to see if Jessica had caught up to her yet—she hadn't. "Is it okay?"

"I guess it's okay with me if it's okay with your dad."

"Great! Thanks!"

Her Dad pulled up. Sarah told her mother they would be home soon, disconnected the call, and got into the car.

As the car pulled away from the curb, Jessica said, "Can you make a left on Spring and see if Jessica's there? She said she was following me home." Sarah quickly brought her dad up to speed on what happened and how Jessica asked to hang out at their house for a little bit. Dad listened and they retraced Sarah's route from where she and Jessica had split up.

Sarah sat in the passenger seat of the car, leaning forward expectantly, looking out the window for her friend. She wasn't anywhere in sight.

They made a right on 1st Street and headed toward Willow Street where Jessica lived.

"Maybe she decided to head back home," Dad said.

"If she did, why didn't she call me?" Sarah said.

"Why don't you call her and find out where she is?"

Sarah pulled out her phone and checked her Recent Call log. There was no record of Jessica, and Recent Texts showed Jessica's last text was sent shortly before her Siri app got all weird.

"Let's just go home. I'm sure she just changed her mind, went home and decided not to tell me. That would be just like her."

Dad drove them home. After parking the car in the driveway, Sarah got out of the car and went in the house. Mom was on the sofa in the living room. The TV on, tuned in to some Home Improvement channel her mother wasn't even watching. She was fiddling with her laptop. Their pit bull mix, Lady, came off the sofa and greeted Sarah, her tail wagging so hard her entire hindquarters were swishing from side to side, as if she was doing some weird interpretative dance. Dad was in the house almost immediately.

"Mom, some weird stuff was happening with my Siri app."

Sarah pulled out her phone and, after greeting Lady, who insisted on being petted, she sat on the other end of the sofa and told her parents what happened.

Mom and Dad glanced at each other.

"I haven't heard about girls disappearing," Dad said.

Sarah then told them about how she and Jessica had been texting and how Jessica's texts to her seemed to activate Siri. "It was, like, I texted Jessica 'Where are you?' And Siri responded, 'I'm following you, I'm heading to your house.' I would text back to Jessica and it was Siri who answered!"

Dad held out his hand. "Can I see your phone?"

"Dad, it's no big deal!"

"Give him your phone, honey," Mom said. Mom's tone was absolute and firm. Sarah handed the phone to her dad.

"Do you know Jessica's home phone number?" Mom asked.

"Yeah." She rattled it off to Mom, who handed her the house phone. Sarah dialed the number and watched as Dad fiddled with her iPhone.

After a dozen rings, Sarah looked at her mom. "Nobody's answering."

"I can't tell if Siri has been used or not," Dad said. He looked confused. "It's not like the application keeps a log or anything."

"Try her cell phone," Mom said. She turned to Dad. "Give Sarah back her phone so she can call Jessica."

Dad handed the iPhone back. Sarah quickly brought up Jessica's profile and called her. After three rings, Jessica picked up. "Are you okay?" Sarah asked. "Where are you?"

"I'm at home," Jessica said. She sounded sheepish. "Sorry. I was heading toward your house, but ... I realized my mother would be even *more* mad at me if I decided to go to your house so I just came home."

Sarah turned to her mom and mouthed the words, *She's okay.*

Mom nodded. Dad just stood there. Why did dads just stand around like dorks when there was nothing going on?

"Omigod, you are not gonna believe what happened!" Sarah moved toward the stairs to the second floor, already dismissing her parents. "You know that thing you told me about—"

Her Dad's voice stopped her as she headed upstairs. "When you're finished talking to Jessica, come down with your phone."

Sarah nodded and headed upstairs. The fear she'd felt when Siri had spoken to her had dissipated, being replaced by a sense of relief that this was all behind her now. She went to her room, closed the door, and told Jessica what happened and how it felt like Jessica's texts were coming through Siri.

When she was finished talking to Jessica, she pulled out her laptop and got online. She was just logging on to Skype to talk to her friend in Canada when Dad called up to her from downstairs.

"Jessica!"

"Ugh!" Jessica grabbed her iPhone and scampered down the stairs. "Sorry," she said, handing Dad the phone as she entered the living room. "I forgot to come down when I was done."

"It's okay," her dad said. "Let's see what we have here." He took the iPhone and accessed it. Jessica hovered close to him, biting her lower lip nervously. Her Dad worked in the IT field and was sometimes overbearing when it came to how she used her laptop and phone, but he'd fixed things pretty quickly in the past too. She watched as he went through the Settings screen. Mom was watching TV, their dog curled up beside her. After a moment Dad shook his head. "It doesn't appear to be tampered with. You're sure the voice that came from Siri said that she—meaning Jessica—was following you?"

Sarah nodded. "I was texting with Jessica and asked where she was. That's when Siri started and said, 'I'm following you home.'"

"So that response is something Jessica would have texted back to you?"

Sarah nodded again.

"And Siri said it a second time, right?"

"Yeah." Remembering sent a shudder through her body. "She

said something like, 'I'm almost at your house, Sarah...' It called me by my name! It was creepy!"

"And the Siri app activated when the voice came through?"

Sarah nodded again.

"Do you know how Siri works?"

"You ask her a question and she answers."

"Right. I suppose while it's possible for Siri to interact with the iMessage app, I don't think Apple has even considered using the two features together." Dad was facing her, the iPhone still in his hands. "When you ask a question, a recording of your voice is sent to an Apple server. The recording is broken down in a process called feature extraction, which numerically transforms the sound wave and pulls out relevant features from your question. This is run through a speech recognition engine to interpret what you're saying and turns it into text. The Siri app then uses resources from your iPhone that includes the Internet, your contact list, and your GPS location to respond to your question. All this works within seconds."

Sarah didn't know how to respond.

What the hell did Dad just say?

As if he'd read her thought, Dad smiled at her. "There has to be a glitch in your iPhone somewhere, honey, probably in a bunch of them for this to happen. Your phone doesn't appear to be tampered with, and what we've heard on the news regarding this so-called stalker has only happened in this area. My guess is a batch of iPhones that got sent to our area are defective and everybody is attributing it to a stalker who probably doesn't exist."

"Bart Shafley's death a few weeks ago have sparked a lot of urban legends around here," her mom said from the sofa. "I did some research online. I'm surprised you haven't heard about it. It's been all over your school."

Sarah shrugged. "I'm sure Jessica heard about it and that's why I didn't pay attention. All that stuff is just..." She didn't really pay attention to rumors, especially those not grounded in reality.

"From what I'm reading," Mom said, "there've been a few cases where girls are reporting strange activity on their smartphones, as if somebody is trying to communicate with them. There's only one other mention of Siri acting weird. In all these cases, there has been no police involvement."

"So there's no stalker?"

"There's no stalker," Dad said. "And if there was, it's very difficult to remotely access somebody else's iPhone. It still wouldn't hurt to enact some security policies just to be safe."

"Like what?"

"Password protection for one." He held up her iPhone. "Give me a few minutes and I'll set up a password for you and make sure some other things are in place, then you'll be good to go. Okay?"

"Okay. Thanks, Dad."

A few minutes later, Dad handed back the phone. Sarah got to pick her own password. After getting a short lesson on the security features he'd enabled, she thanked him, gave him a goodnight hug, and dashed upstairs.

She watched a movie on her laptop for a while in her room, then she Skyped with Jessica. Around 11:30 she heard her Mom come upstairs, followed by the dog, who slept at the foot of their bed in her own dog bed. Dad came up a moment later. The house was now locked up, the security alarm enabled. They were safe.

Sarah dimmed the lights in her bedroom with the remote and crawled under the covers of her bed. She chatted with Jessica on iMessage. Jessica was still freaked out by what happened earlier that evening.

Don't be so paranoid, Sarah texted to her. *My Dad says it was probably just a glitch.*

It's still freaky!

I know! We're going to contact Apple tomorrow. Maybe those other girls reported the same thing.

Those other girls are dead, Sarah.

Sarah sighed.

She thought carefully about how she'd respond. She tapped out the message and read it over before hitting Send.

My Mom said there are no dead girls. There hasn't been anything on the news about them, and she's a news junkie. If two girls had been abducted in this area, she would have known about it.

There was no response from Jessica.

Sarah waited a while, then texted back.

R U There?

No answer.

Bitch probably turned off her phone and went to bed, Sarah thought. She set her phone on the nightstand and settled against her pillows, closed her eyes, and turned over.

She was on the edge of drifting off to sleep when Siri's voice filled the room.

"I BEAT YOU HOME."

Sarah shot up in bed, grabbing for her iPhone. Heart pounding madly, she saw that the Siri app was open. She swiped the screen and typed in her new password to unlock the phone.

"What?" Sarah said.

"I SAID, I BEAT YOU HOME."

Her bedroom door was closed.

All she had to do was leap across the room, open the door, and dash down the hallway to her parent's room and she'd be safe. She debated what to do—she had to tell Dad! He had to see this!

"DID YOU HEAR ME, SARAH? I SAID, I BEAT YOU HOME."

Sarah looked down at her phone with growing terror.

"Who are you?" she whispered. "What the fuck is going on?"

Siri answered.

"I'M YOUR NIGHTMARE. AND I'M RIGHT BEHIND YOU."

A cold, clammy hand pressed on the back of Sarah's neck and another one cut off her scream.

IMMORTAL LOVE,
FOREVER FULL,
FOREVER FLOW-
ING FREE,....
FOREVER SHARED,
FOREVER WHOLE,
A NEVER EBB-
ING SEA......

THE LIBRARIAN

3

The next room glows even brighter, everything—even the air around you—gold and radiant. The room is quiet, respectful, and reverential. Much of the light comes from a ceiling composed of yellow and white and orange stained glass, with a few shades of purple in seldom locations, which offer impossible—yet can only be—sunlight, for there are no artificial lights and the two eye-level candelabras in the room are unlit. You attempt to estimate the number of books in this smallish room, and guess five hundred.

It is another room of golden books, but so is the next, and the next, and the next, for the hooded figure leads you through half a dozen rooms and down windy paths that expose the building's three stories. And then you stop in a large vestibule overlooking both bookcases—yes, even more books—and granite walls, and from here your path offers multiple directions from which to explore.

Life joins you amongst the dead in this gateway between rooms. Plants of various height fill decorated pottery and planters from tile and granite; round pits and statuettes sprout from gravel- and rock-filled enclosures as if to force you away from the center of the room toward the walls, which you cannot help but touch. Where there are not glass-enclosed shelves filled with book-shaped cinerary urns, the walls are bare and polished-granite white and as smooth as glass. Names and dates of the dead are etched onto the surfaces of each square section that tile the walls—at least fifty feet from floor to ceiling, it seems, and stretching all three floors in places. These are tombs as well, you realize, perhaps entire families, perhaps generations of families.

The librarian allows you to explore the many outlets here as he or she seeks out the next three books. As you peruse, the librarian pulls a book from a waist-high bookshelf covered with a planter; some sort of ferns hang over the sides and the hooded figure leans down to reach a brownish-copper volume.

"RELIVING THROUGH BETTER CHEMISTRY," the figure reads, and in a softer voice says, "This one you may find most interesting, as it contains a story pertaining to the very ashes this book contains."

Quotes etched onto walls at the ends of a few hallways are haunting, with letters bigger than hands. On one wall, towering over you in Dalek font:

IMMORTAL LOVE.
FOREVER FULL.
FOREVER FLOW-
ING FREE . . . . .
FOREVER SHARED.
FOREVER WHOLE.
A NEVER EBB-
ING SEA . . . . . .

Two angels embrace in a kiss: a statue standing six feet high, either carved from white marble or plaster-cast from a mold. Soft droplets from twin fountains surrounding a palm tree break the silence. And around the corner, broken by your line of sight from the corner of another floor to ceiling book-/urnshelf, are more words:

SHALL THINK
OF DEATH AS
DOOM .

"CTHYLLA," says your guide, and you instantly picture the word etched onto the wall with the others, although you realize it's another title of a book

soon to be opened. The librarian spots it from a distance, floating diagonally from one side of the room to the other, to a vast amount of books with similar metal bindings at least twenty feet up from the floor. From this distance, the books look solid black with silver text.

"Actresses and actors, athletes and Olympians, politicians, scientists, historians, authors, critics, mathematicians, physicians, war heroes, homemakers, good souls and bad; they are all gathered here, their stories waiting."

The vestibule seems to go on forever, in all directions, and you stand in the middle of it. Ashes from thousands and thousands of dead must be entombed in these halls, you consider. Contained in these books, these urns, trapped in the walls with past loved ones, lives spanning centuries, all gathered together—

"Some of the tales stored within The Library of the Dead are older than the building that houses them," says the hooded figure at your side. "Some offer histories of this land, and some offer reason to this land's unstableness."

The figure glides to a wall of glass-covered shelves half-filled with brass volumes, and you follow. One book stands out from the rest because of its size, nearly twice as wide at the spine—a longer story, you can only imagine, perhaps containing the ashes of more than one storyteller: FAULT LINES.

Together, the three books look heavier than one should be able to carry, yet the hooded figure, your guide, carries them under an arm to a the end of a hallway where a lone, black, wire-mesh patio chair awaits; the free hand gestures for you you to sit, and as you do, you can't help but look past the towering shelves of books at either side to the ceiling where most of the light emanates.

The first of the next three books opens before you. As ash billows from the absence of pages, you cannot avoid inhaling the dead.

RELIVING

THROUGH BETTER

CHEMISTRY

WESTON OCHSE

Why is it when you're fifteen that eighteen seems so far off? I swear to you it seemed a lot closer when I was twelve. My mom says it's because I'm impatient. I'm not impatient. I just want to grow the fuck up. This waiting around to become an adult bullshit is just that...bullshit. If this was a hundred years ago, I'd already be an adult, on my own, and have a job so I wouldn't have to borrow money all the time.

Mom was working the night shift again at the Oakland Regional Hospital so she left me ten for pizza. I grabbed three value burgers from Mickey D's instead, pocketed the rest and stood waiting for Randy and the guys to pick me up. Of our little group of four, Randy was the only one with access to a car. Ricky was like me and couldn't even come close to affording one. Lamont had one but he'd thrashed it against a tree five days after he used his life savings to buy it. As much a piece of shit as Randy's Saturn was, it was a car and any car was golden to us.

I watched a red-headed MILF in a minivan, an old man in a Buick, and some girl I recognized from school in a Camaro with her boyfriend make their way through the drive-thru before Randy showed up in his Saturn. I hopped inside and we were soon heading towards the cemetery.

"Do you have it?" Lamont stared at me eagerly, tapping his fingers on the glass and jiggling his leg up and down. He was rail thin, black as night, and twitchy to the point of locomotion.

"Yeah. Two tabs."

He began to hyperventilate. "Only two? That's not going to be enough."

Randy glanced in the rearview mirror. "Dude. Easy. Maybe you should take some. Calm your hyperactive ass down." Randy was the sort who would have been the high school quarterback and dating the head cheerleader had it not been that he was home-schooled.

Lamont grinned sheepishly and wiped away a little spittle. "Can't do it. You know the mix. We need four then two then ash. Four then two then ash. It's fucking chemistry."

I cringed a little inside, wondering if all this extracurricular activity might be having a permanent effect on Lamont. Not taking the Ritalin was one thing, but this seemed like something else entirely. I glanced at Ricky, but noticed he was staring miserably down at his hands.

"Yo, Ricky? Whassup?"

"Dad's moving us." That got everyone's attention.

Randy asked "Where?"

"Fucking Rhode Island."

"What's in fucking Rhode Island?" I asked.

He balled his hands into fists and laid them against his thighs. "His new job. Can we not talk about it?"

I noticed the bruising on the back of his neck—purple dark lines. Ricky was always moving. He'd only been with us for six months and was already on his way out. Whatever the job was, we all knew the real reason.

We reached the cemetery by nine. I'm not sure where the idea of snorting the ashes came from, but it had become an addiction that I knew was going to kill us. Randy had invented the game, using a concoction of X, Ritalin and ash, we'd find a soft piece of grass, snort the combination up our noses, then lay back and relive.

Here's the deal. You can snort someone's ashes and live part of their life. Usually it's the last moments before they die. Sometimes it's an important moment in their life like their honeymoon or the birth of a child. Other times it's even better because it's sex. Sex is a powerful memory. When you find one of those it's hard not to try and snort it one more time.

What happens if you snort it twice?

Nothing usually. But we'd all agreed that three times was the ultimate limit. I mean, I'm not the expert, but it's like pieces of the persons soul were in the ashes and every time you snort it, they get in you, infect you, become you. That's how we'd lost Trey. He'd been Randy's best friend. He'd found this one old man whose ash memories were always him having sex with some women. His name was John Henry Chaney and we looked him up online. He spent thirty years in the Navy, always going to different ports— especially Asia. Trey couldn't get enough of it. I mean, we all tried Chaney's ash. Don't get me wrong, it was good. Real good. We might have tried more of it, but Trey bogarted it, keeping it all for himself.

That is until he went bat shit crazy.

Lamont checked for the security guard. It was football season, so he was entranced by the glow of the game. We had at least forty five minutes before the game ended so we were cool. Then Randy took the two tabs of X I'd scored from my cousin Donny, got two tabs of Ritalin each from Ricky and Lamont, then proceeded to select an urn from the several thousand on display. He finally settled on one none of us had tried before. His name was James Robert Franklin and he died at the age of twenty four.

Four, then two, then ash, then up our nose and we lay back on the grass and...

Blam! Ten seconds of drifting followed by a slick shot through a memory coaster, down time rails, swooping into the fuzziness at the edge of vision, then I'm locked in. I'm on a boat on a lake. I'm fishing with my dad—his dad. The sky is only a shade lighter than the water. I'm staring at my dad—his dad—as he's lost in thought fishing. I love my dad—his dad—so much I feel my chest expanding with the volume of it, cracking with the purity of it. I sit and stare at him for a while, happy, fulfilled, knowing that my love for him is at least equal to his love for me. A fish strikes my dad's line. He stands and I grab the net. The fish is a fighter. It leaps twice from the water, its long glistening frame flinging wet drops and fear as it pirouettes through the air. Then...

The ride was over.

I'm back in my own brain with my own problems living my own suck ass life—one with no father, no chance of a father, and completely without the possibility of feeling what James Robert Franklin felt for his. A niggling voice scolded me, telling me that if this is how I feel afterward, then I shouldn't continue. I ignored that voice. It didn't know me. It didn't understand that I wanted to live someone else's life because mine was so mind-numbingly dreary. It didn't understand. This way I get to experience emotions I'd never otherwise feel, probably for my entire life.

Lamont sat up, eyes wide, his hand on his forehead. "Holy shit did you guys relive what I just relived?"

Randy grinned. "I was having sex."

We all groaned. He always gets the sex moments.

"I was fishing with his dad. It was cool," I said.

Ricky smiled grimly. "I got that one too. It was uber cool."

By the way he said it and the way his eyes stared through his hands, I knew he wished his father was more like that.

"You all are boring me to death. I went skydiving. Jumped out of a freaking plane with some military unit. I don't know what was happening, but it was about the coolest shit I've ever done."

"You mean relived," I corrected. "It's not like you actually did it."

"Yeah. Whatever."

"Wonder if that's how he died?" Randy asked.

My eyes got wide. I'd never relived a death and didn't want to. "Dude, what if the parachute didn't open? It might have—

Lamont waved me away. "That shit ain't true. I've relived many deaths. They don't kill you. Hell, some of them were the best reliving I've done."

Which was a defining statement about how exhilarating our lives were.

Randy pulled me aside two days later at school.

"We've got to do something about Ricky's dad."

I stared at him. What did he think we should do? We were just a bunch of kids.

"I'm serious." He glanced around to make sure no one could hear. "We've got to do something or his dad's going to kill him one day. I've relived men like his dad before. I know how they think. I know how it ends."

"I thought all of your reliving was about sex?"

He frowned. "I just say that. I've never actually relived sex before." When he saw my surprise he added, "I mean I've had it, but not someone else's."

"Then what'd you relive?"

"Death. Murder. I've been killed several times and twice," he held up two fingers, "I killed someone else."

"You relived that? Who was it?"

"Remember that old man we did last month. Him. He shot a guy in an alley and stole his wallet when he was young."

"That old guy? I relived his seventy-seventh birthday party. He didn't seem the type." Even as I said it, I questioned by ability at fifteen to know what the murdering type was. "Who else?"

"That girl with the rhyming name."

"Mary Carey."

"Yeah, that was her. She shook her child to death then pretended it died of SIDS."

"No wonder she committed suicide. You know, I think I was

at a party with her too. How is it that I do parties and you do death?"

He shook his head. "Maybe it has something to do with who we are."

I thought about that for a moment. It sounded like maybe we should be more careful with the ash. I finally asked, "So what's it like to kill a guy?"

He grinned mournfully. "Scary. Exhilarating. Powerful."

Four days later we had a plan in place and were waiting down the street from Ricky's dad's favorite bar. Pouring rain slammed against the Saturn's windshield creating a constant background static to our nervous conversation. I sat in the backseat beside Ricky. He wore a bruise across the left side of his face and walked funny. He'd been speechless when we'd told him our plan. Then he'd cried. At first, I thought it was out of sadness, but it turned out to be grateful tears. We were about to do what he couldn't get the courage to do himself. Lamont sat in the passenger seat checking his email on his phone. Randy sat behind the wheel, his fretful fingers drumming against the dashboard.

I checked my phone. It was 11:00 PM. My mom wouldn't miss me, but being out this late made me nervous.

"When's he going to be done?"

Ricky spoke in a low voice. "He stays there and drinks until he can barely stand, then he staggers home."

"Why doesn't he drink at home?" Lamont asked.

"He says only alcoholics drink at home alone."

Randy laughed. "Yeah, right."

Ricky rubbed the side of his face. "It was after we did ash the other night that he gave me this. He came home early already drunk. But he was in a different mood, you know? Wasn't angry... he acted like a real dad, wanting to know how my day was, what I did at school, you know, like dads do on TV."

Randy had stopped rattling his fingers.

Lamont wasn't looking at his phone.

"We talked for like five minutes. An actual conversation where he didn't yell or ... Then I asked him about fishing. I thought maybe I could possibly have a moment like that boy had with his dad. Remember that, Brandon?"

I nodded. "Sure. I remember that."

"That's when he changed. All I said was maybe we could go fishing sometime and it was as if I'd flipped a switch. I could see his face turn red, then his hands start to tremble."

"Did you run?" Lamont asked softly.

"I don't run anymore. It just makes him madder."

I saw Randy's eyes in the rearview mirror as he said, "So you sit there and take it." They were angry eyes.

"I sit there and get it over with."

In firm and even words Randy said, "You'll never have to do that again, Ricky."

We were all silent for the next twenty minutes until Lamont pointed out the window. "There he is."

The rain was still hammering down. A lone hunched figure exited the bar. A red and green neon sign with the image of a crashing wave with the words *The Cove* beneath it bathed him in a pool of pale light. Through the rain shrouded window the scene reminded me of one of those French painters we'd learned about in art. He started down the street.

Randy put the Saturn in gear and we drove towards him. As we pulled past, I spared a look at his face—swollen, red, angry, drunk. We continued to the corner, then turned left. The road was deserted. We stopped on the other side of an abandoned house.

"Get ready," Randy said.

We had Teenage Mutant Ninja Turtle masks Lamont bought at the Dollar Store two towns over. I didn't know which one was which. I never did get into that retro bullshit, but I put mine on nonetheless. The others did the same. It wasn't long before Ricky's dad passed by our car.

Randy opened his door. "Showtime."

Lamont and I did the same. Ricky didn't open his and no one said a thing about it. The three of us held metal baseball bats.

"Hey, Asshole." Randy stalked towards the man. "Yeah, you drunk ass bitch, I'm talking to you."

Lamont and I exchanged looks, but with his mask on, his face was unreadable.

Ricky's dad turned. "Whas theesh. Hallo—Hallo—shit?"

"It's Halloween, you bastard." Randy removed his mask. "And I don't need this for what I'm about to do."

Shit was getting too serious too fast. I didn't know what I thought was going to happen. I mean I knew we were there to kill Ricky's dad, but I think I really thought we were going to scare him, maybe make him join AA or something. Now that Randy had his mask off—

He swung the bat and took out the drunk's right knee. He fell hard.

Randy swung three more times, hitting the man in the stomach with full swings of the bat. He turned onto his side and puked out an oily mixture of bile and booze.

"He just wanted to go fishing." He swung again. "Fishing!"

Randy glanced back at where we were rooted into the pavement. His face held a crazy smile. His eyes gleamed. Then he dropped the bat, and pulled out his folding knife. He opened it, kneeled beside Ricky's dad, and without hesitation pushed the tip straight into the center of his throat.

He stared at his handiwork for a moment, then stood. The water beside Ricky's dad was already beginning to turn red. He grabbed the bat and said, "Let's go."

The next morning the police woke Ricky and told him that his father was dead. They called his grandfather, who got on a plane that afternoon to fly down and settle his son's things.

Three days later they cremated him.

On the fourth day was the funeral.

On the fifth day we snorted him.

We weren't going to do it at first, but Randy insisted. He said that it was important that Ricky do it so he could see and remember what his father was thinking and feeling so he'd never become that person. Break the chain, he'd said. But I think he was hoping to relive the man's final moments and be able to see himself in the starring role of murderer.

Ricky's grandfather was going to take him away from us the next morning. He was moving to Bemidji, Minnesota, which I knew was just north of Bum Fuck Egypt and about as far away as any human could get from this miserable town. So it was also a celebration of sorts. Because of that, Randy had a six pack of Coors.

We all drank from the same can, passing it around. We talked about our favorite relives. Randy boasted about all the sex he'd had, only glancing my direction once. His secret was safe with me. We didn't talk about the murder. We didn't talk about Ricky's dad at all. But the more we didn't talk about it, a bigger deal it became, until finally, we all kind of wanted to get it over with.

Four, then two, then ash, then up our nose and we lay back on the grass and...

Blam! I drift for a moment, then I'm in a boat on a lake in the water. Two fishing poles rest on the bottom of the boat, but they aren't being used. I'm on my knees and the metal is painful to my skin. But not as painful as what's going on behind me. Someone, something, was inside me. My hands gripped the side of the boat. Larger hands gripped my shoulders and pulled me backwards. I'm trapped in the reliving of something terrible and I can't stop it can't stop it can't stop it...

When I return to myself, my face is covered in tears. My stomach heaves and I vomit on the grass beside me. I can almost still feel it inside of me. But even that paled to the pain I'd felt in my heart as I realized it was my own daddy—his daddy—doing it to me—him.

Ricky was blubbering.

Lamont stared into the distance.

Randy was angry. When he saw me, he said, "You too, huh?"

I nodded.

"Where?"

Not what did you relive, but where did you relive it. "In a fishing boat."

He nodded, slammed back the beer, then said, "Me too."

"I was in a fishing shack on a lake," Lamont said. "It was winter." He rubbed his knees. "It was so cold. He had me naked while he sat back and..."

I'm glad he didn't finish the sentence.

We all waited for Ricky to come around. When he was about ready to talk, he held his hand out for a beer. We only had one left. It was all his. He drank it in less than two minutes, taking a lot of small sips as his eyes sought something beyond the grass.

"I know now. My dad, he was abused."

Randy shook his head. "Doesn't make it right."

"My grandfather ... now I know the reason we never visited him. My father was trying to keep me away from him."

I couldn't help but ask. "Did your dad ever...?"

"Never." Then he paused. "I used to see him standing at my door at night staring at me. I used to think it was because he was sorry and couldn't bring himself to tell me. Now I wonder if..." He shook his head. Then he shook it again. He shook his head, his arms, his hands, his whole body, as if he was trying to shake free of his skin. When he next spoke, it was with a raw voice. "You know what I think? I think my dad tried to keep me away from him all this time and now I'm going to live with the bastard who made him like he was." He laughed. "My dad was probably a kid just like me."

"Doesn't make it right," Randy repeated.

"No, but it makes it real," Ricky said with as much force and power as I'd ever seen him give.

"We can protect you," Lamont said. He had a sheen in his eye like the one I'd seen in Randy's when he talked about killing Ricky's father.

"Like you protected me before? Look where that left me. The man who abused my father abused me and he wasn't even here." He turned to Randy. "Give me your knife."

Randy's eyes narrowed. "What are you going to do?"

"Break the chain."

"I can take care of this for you. Like I did before."

"I want to do this myself."

Randy stared for a moment longer, then grinned. "If you say so." He pulled the knife from his pocket and handed it over.

Ricky stared at the weapon in his hand. Then took two steps back and opened it.

"Careful, Ricky. That's sharp."

"There's some synchronicity here." He held the blade up to the light. "This is the blade that killed my father."

"And we just relived him, too."

"Think we should relive Ricky's grandfather after we do him too?" Lamont asked.

I shook my head. "I don't want to be anywhere near that sick guy's life. Neither giving or receiving. He's a terrible fucking pervert."

Just then Ricky gave me a curious look. "But don't you see, he was once a boy just like me. He wasn't grown that way. He was made to be that way."

"But your dad didn't do that," I countered.

"Did you ever think that maybe the reason he drank so much was so he couldn't do it. Like maybe the urge got so bad he felt like he had to drink. Why else wouldn't he drink at home?" He shook his head. "How sad of a life do you have to live to always be so afraid you might do something terrible that you have to maintain a level of drunkenness so it won't happen?"

"We don't know if that's why he was like that," Randy said.

"Oh no?" Ricky's voice raised two full octaves. "Where'd my grandfather fuck you? In the mouth or the butt?"

"Okay, now." I took a step forward and held out my hands.

"It's easy to say that your dad was being an honorable drunk now that he's dead, but he wasn't honorable when he was beating you."

Randy nodded. "Yeah, beating and fucking, it's still abuse, Ricky." He looked around. "Dude," he said to me, "We need more beer."

"What the hell you telling me for? I'm fifteen?"

Lamont screamed, "Ricky! No!"

We turned to a scene of gushing blood. Ricky had slit both of his arms from wrist to elbow, slicing through a dozen veins in each arm.

I rushed to him, but he held the knife out with a shaking, bloody fist.

"Leave me. Let me break the chain."

Randy was crying. "I didn't mean like this. I meant—"

"I know what you meant." His face was already white. "You were hoping to get permission to kill someone again. Well, you can't have it." He staggered a little. "Randy, you need to deal with your own shit and figure out what's you and what's not."

"What do you mean?"

"This whole reliving thing is so we don't have to be in our own heads. Remember Trey? Remember how he got to feeling sad, the same sadness he'd relived became part of him. It might have been all sex, but what came with it was no wife, no family, no kids, and a lifetime full of regret. I felt it when I was reliving Chaney. Sure there was sex, but dude, the regret was terrifying."

I don't know why we were watching him bleed to death. We needed to get help. We needed to save him before it was too late. I glanced over and Lamont held his phone in his hand, I could see the 911 on the screen and barely hear the voice of the operator. But he was so transfixed by the scene, he couldn't respond.

"Like you. You've been reliving murders and death."

Randy glanced at me.

"He didn't tell me. I already knew. Something you said once, a slip. The feelings of the killers, being in their minds, it's not right. It confuses your own memory, your own mind. It makes you like doing things you shouldn't like doing." His eyes widened. I need to sit down. He sat down hard. The knife fell to the grass.

"Let me give you a tourniquet," I begged softly.

"Promise me you'll stop, Brandon."

"Why me?"

"Because you're the only one of us who isn't ruined."

That last word hung in the air like an emotional supernova.

Then he turned to Lamont. "Lamont, get help."

Lamont nodded.

Ricky's face was white and sagging. He looked a hundred years old and like a wizened old man, he had a special wisdom he'd never had before.

"And Randy?"

Randy hesitated. "Yeah, what is it Ricky?"

But Ricky said no more, his eyes staring to a place far removed from this one.

Randy sobbed hard. He rushed to Ricky and knelt in front of him, grabbing his shoulders. "What was it you were going to say? What was it, Ricky?" He sobbed harder. "Tell me."

The sound of sirens soon came upon us.

I've thought of that night for the last nine years. Randy and I used to talk about it before he joined the Army. We both thought the same thing. Ricky could have told both Lamont and Randy to get help, but he hadn't. He'd specifically singled out Lamont for help, like Randy was beyond it. He probably was. Although I never said this to Randy, I think Ricky was going to tell him to break the chain. I think he expected Randy to kill himself before he could kill anyone else. Randy did in his own way. He kept redeploying to Iraq and then Afghanistan enough times that the odds caught up with him. He was guarding a market in Kabul when a kid the age Ricky was back then came up to him and self-detonated. His funeral at Chapel of the Chimes was the first time I'd seen Lamont since we were kids. He'd changed. He was no longer the handsome slim teenager. He was balding and overweight. He had an acne problem. He was going to counseling, he said. He was working on it. There was happiness in his eyes.

That moment changed me too.

I straightened up. I graduated high school, then college. I just got a job teaching high school kids about English and literature. Good thing, too, because my wife and I just had our first baby. It's a son and we've named him Richard—Ricky for short. The others relived terrible things. I'd seen it and felt it that once, but all of my other reliving was about happy times. Family times. Times I'd never had growing up. The others might have wanted to break the chains of their reliving, but not me. With the exception of the very last one, I wanted to be those dads I'd relived. I wanted my son to feel about me the way I'd relived the feelings of those strong, responsible men. Without reliving, I never would have known how to be that man. Without reliving I might have been someone terrible.

Not anymore.

Never going to happen.

Four then two then ash.

CTHYLLA

LUCY A. SNYDER

We move among the volumes until we come to one whose spine reads "Natalya Moroz, Artist and Muse and Misguided Soul." An incomplete summation of a life that burned short and very bright. But the label does not tell anything close to the whole story of the ashes in this lovely work of ceramic and paint. For that, we need to take a closer look at a young woman named Kamerynne Craigie, whose story we know from diary entries, recovered texts and email…

———▲———

Grayce Aberdine (her mother had kept her maiden name) used to call Kamerynne "my little changeling" and it wasn't until the girl read a book of fairy tales that it dawned on her the term had nothing to do with diapers. After her Oscar nomination for her role as the priestess in *Cthylla*, Kamerynne's mother got a lot of acting offers. Grayce wasn't ever the leading lady, but she was often her best friend or a quirky neighbor. She always had a shoot someplace, or an appointment with her shrink or her acting coach, or she was off at a spiritual retreat.

Kamerynne sometimes wondered if she'd just been prettier, like an actress, if things would have been different. She wondered if her mother would have found reasons to be home instead of worshipping some goddess at the beach or centering her chakras. On the other hand, the other kids at her school complained bitterly about their parents getting up in their business all the time, so maybe her mother's being gone was for the best.

Her father was gone a lot, too, but he had his company to run. He'd dropped out in his freshman year at Cal Tech to start up a software company in a friend's garage, back when that was a legitimate career move for whiz kids. Years later, Kamerynne would realize his absence was just as much a choice as her mother's.

Her parents met at the Sundance party for *Cthylla*, nine months before Kamerynne was born. As far as Kamerynne knew, they hadn't shared a bed since then, but they both grew up in old-fashioned households and they believed in the institution of marriage, particularly when a child was involved. Past that, neither of them carried any particular expectations into the marriage.

Her mother's sister Cherity stepped in to fill the unspoken maternal void when Kamerynne was three. Where her mom was willowy and elegant, Cherity was stocky and strong. Her aunt played softball for a team called the Oakland Outlanders, and Kamerynne loved going to games. She and her aunt had the same way of smiling and laughing and they both really loved *The Muppet Show*. Once, when they were hiking in Redwood Park, someone mistook them for mother and daughter, and Kamerynne was secretly pleased.

But then her aunt started feeling too ill to play ball or go hiking, and she went to the doctor and found out she had blood cancer. She still took Kamerynne out places, not as often because the chemo really took it out of her, but everyone spoke of it as a temporary thing. Almost two years after her diagnosis, Cherity died.

I'm going to die, too.

Her body would turn into something like that steak her mom had forgotten in the trunk of the Jaguar for a week, stinking and slimy and crawling with maggots. She'd cease to exist. Would her soul go to heaven? What if there *wasn't* a heaven? What if *this*—this frustrating, confusing, unasked-for existence on Earth—was all she'd have?

Her parents had their fame. People wrote her mom fan mail and, because *Cthylla* had become a cult favorite, some people had tattooed her character's face on their bodies. Nobody got her father's face tattooed, but his picture had been on the cover of *Time*. His software ran computers that ran hospitals that kept people alive. They were both heroes. They'd be *remembered*.

Her teachers and her parents spoke of everyone having an individual calling, a place in the world. But what if that wasn't true? What if she was only ever going to be pretty good at things that didn't really matter, and there wasn't a place for her soul to go afterward?

"Let a kid be a kid," her father always said—but as the years went on her mother bore a palpable air of disappointment. Kamerynne tried singing and school plays but she had a hard time remembering lyrics and lines and standing up in front of a bunch of strangers inevitably tied her tongue. Nobody seemed eager for her to get up on stage anyhow, not with her unfashionable pudge and poofy hair.

Was there a reason she was here on Earth, other than that one night her mother and her father both went to a party, got a little tipsy and didn't bother with condoms?

What if her life was just a meaningless accident?

It was suddenly hard to breathe. An enormous, cold, unfathomable blackness had opened up inside her, and she was teetering, about to fall into it. She wanted to run screaming down the street, as though she could outrun death and the pain of mediocrity. But some kid at school had run naked down the street once and a paparazzi took a picture and his whole family was embarrassed. The kid had to see a shrink and surrender his thoughts and feelings every week like one of the kids in *Oliver Twist* giving his money to Fagin.

Kamerynne didn't want to see a shrink. She was afraid that talking about her fears out loud might make them real, like saying "Bloody Mary" three times in front of a mirror.

Three years passed in which Kamerynne went to school, didn't cultivate any friends, and played video games and read thick fantasy novels (when she wasn't reading one of her father's endless book assignments) to keep herself from thinking about death and the probable meaninglessness of her existence. She wasn't getting into drugs or drinking like some of her classmates, so her parents mostly just vaguely fretted about her lack of fresh air and exercise and made the housekeeper take her to the gym three times a week. Her mother sometimes spoke of getting her some liposuction and plastic surgery when she was ready for college. Her father started sitting with her to show her how to code, and he took her to work with him more often, showing her bits and pieces of his business. She was being tested, she could tell, and although she tried to please him, she couldn't work up much enthusiasm.

"You like games, right? You could become a game designer," he said as they got ice cream at the company cafe. "It would be harder, because you're a girl, but you could do it."

"I could." She swirled the hot fudge into her sundae with her spoon, not sure if he meant it would be harder because girls just weren't very good at designing games or it would be harder because people would be dismissive if she tried. "But would it matter?"

He frowned, puzzled. "Matter? What do you mean?"

She realized she'd said the first "Bloody Mary" and quickly shrugged, blushing. "I don't know."

Kamerynne might have spent the rest of her teen years and young adulthood in a video game cocoon if her mother hadn't caught Darla, their housekeeper, smoking a joint by the pool. Her mother fired Darla and three days later brought in a new woman named Olga Moroz who was very pretty; her mother said she'd been an actress back in the Ukraine and they'd met at a spiritual retreat. Olga went about her chores with quick, silent efficiency. After Kamerynne tried to make small talk, she realized the woman couldn't speak much English, which was probably why she hadn't been able to get many acting jobs in the U.S.

On the third weekend of Olga's tenure as their new housekeeper, she brought a teenaged girl with her.

"Is my daughter, Natalya," Olga explained. "I hope you do not mind."

"It's fine," Kamerynne replied, her throat suddenly dry. Natalya was like nobody she'd ever seen before. Certainly she'd seen the individual parts of Natalya's wardrobe on a hundred other girls: the magenta-and-black bob, the silver nose ring, the black jeans and Doc Martens and Bauhaus tee shirt. But it wasn't her wardrobe, or her porcelain skin, or her dark green eyes. There was something *luminous* about the girl, something beyond mere physical beauty that Kamerynne would never have the words to describe.

Natalya never noticed Kamerynne gawking at her because her own eyes were fixed on the huge painting of the *Cthylla* movie poster on the living room wall.

"Oh. My. God! That is my *favorite* movie!" Natalya gushed. She stepped forward and touched the polished mahogany frame reverently. "Grayce Aberdine was *amazing* as the priestess. She should have won an Oscar. She was *robbed*."

"She's my mom," Kamerynne said, trying to sound cool. "This is her house."

"What!" Natalya looked shocked and did a little dance as if she was trying to levitate, afraid to have her mere-mortal feet touching the creamy white carpet of her movie idol. Then she danced around to face her mother. "Mom...?"

"Is true!" Her mother beamed, clearly aware that she'd just earned herself premium Cool Mom points.

Natalya let out a delighted shriek and practically bowled Olga over giving her a bear hug. "You are the best! Ohmigod this is the best!"

"Loves you, too. But work. I have to." Her mother gently pushed her away.

"Hey, um, Natalya." Kamerynne had fallen out of the habit of trying to impress anyone, but now every neuron in her brain was firing, fixed on solving the problem of making this amazing luminous girl like her.

"Nat. My friends call me Nat." She pushed her magenta bangs out of her eyes.

"We could go watch the director's extended cut of *Cthylla* downstairs in the theatre if you want."

Nat frowned and squinted as though she suspected Kamerynne of playing a prank. "What? There's no director's cut."

"Oh yeah there is. It just isn't out yet; they haven't even told the trade mags because the director is still messing with it. He had to cut some scenes to get it down to an R—"

Nat clapped her hands and pogoed excitedly. "Omigod yes!"

Kamerynne led her down the big spiral staircase to the theatre that her mother always called a screening room. It seated twenty-four people in three rows lined with little blue LEDs along the aisles. The screen was a genuine antique her parents had rescued from an old theatre before it was torn down. Her mother said it was the first place she'd ever seen a movie.

"If you want, there's soda and candy and stuff." Kamerynne waved toward the wet bar at the back of the room.

"You got any Sprite and vodka?"

"Um … yeah." Kamerynne felt a pang of guilt; her mother was into clean living and would not approve. But she felt far too anxious to tell Nat "no."

So she just turned on the media server and queued up the movie while Nat made herself a tall drink. They settled down on the front row, the screen huge above them, and Kamerynne hit PLAY on the remote.

Kamerynne hadn't actually seen more than bits and pieces of her mother's movie; her parents said it wasn't suitable for children. She wasn't a child anymore, but she hadn't gotten around to watching it, either. It seemed like old news somehow. She'd heard everyone chat about it so much that she'd *felt* as though she'd seen it about twenty times over.

But the talk and the trailers hadn't truly prepared her for the film, and as the opening credits rolled, she found herself mesmerized by the dark, strange story about a cult of women raising an ancient goddess from the ocean. The goddess was like a mermaid, if the bottom half of a mermaid was an octopus instead of a fish. She wondered if the animators at Disney had seen the movie and ripped off the goddess to create Ursula the Sea Witch in *The Little Mermaid*. But Ursula was all cartoon wickedness and the goddess in *Cthylla* was terrifying and breathtaking.

"It's all real, you know," Nat whispered as the eight-legged goddess rose from the water flickering above them.

"What?" Kamerynne blinked at her, feeling disoriented; she'd gotten so engrossed in the movie she'd nearly forgotten Nat was there.

"Well, it's not real now, but it *will* be, someday."

"Oh." Kamerynne blinked again, suspecting she'd missed something important, and then she realized that Nat's hand was on her knee. Suddenly she felt as though her stomach was filled with a hundred buzzing, stingless bees.

"This is so hot," Nat breathed, staring raptly at the screen.

Kamerynne looked up again, and her mother had dropped her red priestess robe and was standing there completely bare-ass naked, embracing the glistening goddess, whose purple tentacles were creeping up her bare legs . . .

"Jesus. That's my *mom*. I can't watch this." Kamerynne could feel herself blushing right down to the soles of her feet.

She began to stand, but Nat grabbed her wrist.

"Don't go," she said. "Sit on my lap and look at me instead."

Nat was pulling her wrist insistently, not letting go, so Kamerynne knelt across the girl's slender legs and blinked at her as she gazed at the screen over her shoulder. Kamerynne tried to ignore the moans and wet noises coming in crisp remastered Dolby audio through the speakers. Nat held both of Kamerynne's hands very tightly, her breath perfumed with alcohol.

"When I first saw you, I didn't think you looked anything at all like your mom," Nat whispered, not taking her eyes off whatever

was happening on the screen behind Kamerynne. "But now I can see it. You have her neck and her ears."

And suddenly, Nat was kissing her just below her left ear, and Kamerynne's body filled with decalescent electricity, and she no longer gave a damn about what was the cephalopod goddess was doing to her mother in the movie.

———▲———

A month later, the two girls sat making out on Kamerynne's bed.

"Could I, like, show you something?" Nat asked, oddly shy.

Kamerynne had seen Nat top to bottom, so what could possibly make her this bashful? "Sure, anything."

"Okay, but I mean, don't laugh if you think it's stupid or whatever."

"I'm not gonna think it's stupid. Just show me."

"'Kay." Nat retrieved her black nylon Jansport backpack from the floor, unzipped it and pulled out a sketchbook. "I sorta want to be an artist someday, just sort of wanted you to see my stuff..."

Kamerynne opened the sketchbook, and at first she thought she was looking at a black-and-white photograph of a man with rats' toothed maws where his eyes should have been, but then she saw the smudge of pencil graphite and realized it was a hyperrealistic sketch. She carefully turned the page, and saw another: this was a woman in a tawdry hotel room cradling a baby made entirely of insects' eyes. The book contained page after page of beautiful monstrosity.

"You did all these?" Kamerynne asked.

"Yeah, I mean, they're not how I want them to be, but maybe someday..."

"What do you mean 'someday'? These are amazing, right now! These are, like, better than the art that my dad drops a grand on down at the galleries!"

"Aw, you're a sweetheart. But nah, I'm not that good."

"I mean, okay, I'm not an expert, but my dad made me read like fifty billion art books. This is really *really* good. I mean, you *are* an artist, right now. Why do you think it's not good?"

"I just… I just want to get what's in my head down on paper, you know? I want it to look the same as I see it in my mind, but it never does. It never comes *close*. I'm okay with pencils, I guess, but I need to get better with oil and acrylic. Maybe I need to learn how to work a computer or whatever."

"So learn to work a computer." Kamerynne blinked at her.

"I don't have the money to buy a computer, and I feel weird working on my stuff at the computers at the library. People see naked bits and freak out. And the library doesn't even have Photoshop or anything I could really use anyway."

In that moment, Kamerynne experience another major revelation: she herself might have no talents to speak of, but Nat had a talent that absolutely took her breath away. And it would be so easy to help her become the artist she was clearly born to be. Maybe helping was Kamerynne's reason for being alive on the Earth.

"Put your shirt back on; I'm taking you to the mall. You want a laptop or a desktop?"

Nat stared at her as if she'd sprouted a tentacle in the middle of her forehead. "Are you serious?"

"Totally. Let's go."

A year later, Kamerynne was sticking her finger down Nat's throat in a filthy McDonald's restroom in Oakland, desperately trying to get her to throw up the bottle of tranquilizers she'd swallowed. It seemed obvious to Kamerynne, finally, that someone like Nat who had such wild nightmares spilling out of her imagination might have had some of that darkness seep into and poison her soul. And truly helping her might be a bit more harrowing than spending a few dollars here and there.

"Why'd you do that?" Kamerynne asked, wondering whether she wanted to cry or slap Nat as the other girl retched melting blue pills and orange juice and vodka into the stained toilet. "You're my best friend; you could have talked to me."

Nat collapsed back on the piss-stained floor, shaking her head. "Nah. You'd be berr off wi'out me."

"I love you."

"I hate me," she sobbed.

———◆———

Kamerynne picked up Nat after she was released from the hospital.

"I have to go to the pharmacy to get some meds." She smoothed the crumpled prescription on her lap.

"Okay. Matter which one?" Kamerynne turned the key in her BMW's ignition.

"Nope."

They drove in silence for a few minutes.

"I'm sorry I scared you," Nat said.

"It's okay," Kamerynne replied. "It could have been a lot worse." She cleared her throat. "You know, I wouldn't be better off without you. I love you."

"I love you too," Nat said.

"I *forbid* you from dying, okay?"

Nat laughed. "It doesn't work that way, I don't think."

"You're smart, you're beautiful, and you're so much more talented than anybody I've ever met ... look, if you decide *you* don't deserve to live, how are the rest of us supposed to feel like we deserve to keep breathing, huh?" Kamerynne meant for it to all sound like a joke, but when the words left her mouth, she realized it wasn't the least bit funny.

Nat smiled at her anyhow. "It's different for you. I see the Goddess in my dreams, and I know I'm a disappointment to her."

Kamerynne swallowed. Nat mentioned the Goddess sometimes, just in passing, but when Kamerynne asked her about her religion, Nat always said she wasn't really supposed to talk about it. The whole thing seemed weird, but she didn't want to be disrespectful. "How could you disappoint her?"

"I have a role in her Coming. Not now, but later. And I'm too scared to do it. I'm a coward, and worthless, and She knows it."

"Hey, no, you're not worthless; don't talk about yourself like that, okay?"

"I am." Nat began to weep.

Kamerynne squeezed the steering wheel, feeling lost and help-less, but then she remembered the pills they were driving to get. The meds would surely help clear Nat's mind. Kamerynne vowed to make sure she took her meds on time and stayed away from al-cohol.

Kamerynne's mother swept into the house with an enormous smile on her face.

"Oh, darling, you're here! I have the most wonderful news!"

"What's up, Mom?"

"Charibdys Studios has gotten the funding for *Cthylla: The Rising*! They want me to reprise my role."

"Oh, wow, that's great!" Part of Kamerynne cringed as she remembered the tentacled screen embrace.

"I've talked to your father, and he's interested in being a pro-ducer this time around, so we're meeting with the studio president and some of his execs aboard his yacht this evening. We should be home by 11:00, I think."

Shortly after midnight, Kamerynne got a call from the police. A propane tank exploded onboard the yacht, and the force knocked her parents off the deck. Unconscious and helpless, they drowned. They were dead.

The next morning, she found that *Cthylla* fans had left a mas-sive pile of roses and lilies outside the front gate.

Kamerynne met with her parents' lawyer after the funeral.

"It seems your parents made some changes to their will that I was unaware of and would have advised against," he said gravely. "But nonetheless the alterations are legitimate and legal."

"What changes?" she asked. She'd had a hard time feeling anything but numb since the phone call. Her parents' bodies were too badly damaged for an open casket funeral, and so their deaths still felt unreal.

"Your father and mother have both left 80% and 90%, respectively, of their money to the Messina Strait Foundation."

"What's that?"

"It's a religious organization, one that your mother was apparently involved with most of her adult life. According to the notarized letter she left behind, she apparently joined it either before or during her work on *Cthylla*, and your father became involved recently. It's news to me, too," he added, apparently reading the confusion on her face.

"What does the foundation do?"

"They offer spiritual retreats and workshops. Past that, I'm honestly not sure, except that now they have a great deal of money with which to do it."

Kamerynne couldn't help Nat or anyone else without money. And if she couldn't help...what good was she?

"Am I broke?" She immediately hated how much her question made her sound like a little girl.

"Oh, no, don't worry...you still have your parents' house, and they left you a trust fund that should enable you to maintain the house and pay for your college and personal upkeep indefinitely. You should be able to live comfortably without having to work unless you want to."

"I do want to work," she said. "I want to be...worthwhile."

She and Nat both started their freshman years at UCLA the next year. They left Olga to take care of her parents' house and they split a dorm room on campus. Nat majored in art, of course, and Kamerynne tentatively settled on journalism; she wasn't sure she wanted to try coding games, but writing about them for magazines seemed fun. And if she majored in English she knew she'd have to write a bunch of papers on a bunch of old books that had bored her half to death the first time her father made her read them.

The week before midterms, two events changed Kamerynne's life forever.

The first was that she attended a guest lecture offered by an investigative journalist from *The New York Times*.

"There's *always* a paper trail," the journalist told them. "Every thought that every person writes down or sends through an email is recorded somewhere. Every communication leaves a ghost behind. If you jot down a note on a piece of paper resting on a phone book, and then you tear up that paper, guess what? The imprint of your pen marks are on the cover of the phone book. A good investigator can find that and read that. If you send an email, even if you and your recipient delete it? That message has traveled through a dozen routers, and that email can be packet sniffed or recorded. There's *always* a paper trail, even if it isn't paper."

Kamerynne sat up straighter. Bloody Mary didn't have to be spoken aloud anymore to summon her spectre, it seemed.

She was still mulling over palimpsests and packet sniffers when she arrived back at their dorm room. "Paint it Black" was blasting on the stereo, and Nat was unconscious on the floor, barely breathing in a puddle of pill-spotted vomit.

Kamerynne spent five long hours by Nat's side at the ER. Nat regained consciousness briefly and started wailing and trying to pull out her nasogastric tube and IV. The doctors had to sedate her and told Kamerynne it was best if she went home.

So she went back to the dorm room; the janitorial staff had cleaned up the vomit in her absence, but the air in the room had a sour chemical smell. Kamerynne sat on her narrow bed and wept out her frustration and worry. Nat had seemed to be doing so well; she'd seemed *happy*. And her art had gotten even better! A gallery in LA was interested in showing her work. But clearly she wasn't actually happy... or something bad had happened.

Kamerynne booted up Nat's computer, composed a short, polite letter to let Nat's instructors know that she was in the hospital, and got into her email to start sending out messages.

In Nat's inbox was a message from someone named Dr. Helene Arcanjo:

Natalya,

It's nice that the gallery is interested in your drawings, but remember you must not focus on such trivial things. The Goddess has her plan for you, and you must dedicate yourself to her fully. Do not disappoint us after everything we've done for you.

– Helene

Who the hell was this Arcanjo woman? And what had she been doing for Nat? If Nat had confided in Arcanjo about her earlier suicide attempt, this email was as good as handing Nat a loaded pistol. A quick Web search revealed that Arcanjo had a PhD in divinity from the Innsmouth Theological Seminary in Rhode Island and she was the minister for the Temple of the Deep Mother in Oxnard. As far as Kamerynne knew, Nat had never been to the church…

Not knowing made her sick to her stomach. What was going on in Nat's life? Kamerynne dug through Nat's email, looking for messages to or from Arcanjo. And there was nothing, no messages from other church members, not even any messages referring to the Goddess. If she was deleting the emails, Nat had to believe they contained something incriminating… and that there was a risk of someone looking for them.

Suddenly worried about leaving a search engine history on Nat's computer, Kamerynne went to her own computer. Another query on Temple of the Deep Mother led to an older version of the church page in archive.org containing a list of members. Searches on those names led her to a church member's personal website, which contained a lot of poetry about the Goddess and links to several *Cthylla* fan pages, a couple of which mentioned Charybdis Studios. Whose representatives Kamerynne's mother and father had been meeting with the night they died.

———▲———

The next morning, Kamerynne made some phone calls to former associates of her father's. When she told them what she wanted to know, most of them claimed ignorance or blew her off. Finally, she got in touch with a senior programmer who offered to call her back on another line. He gave her a name, and a campus address.

Kamerynne walked to Boelter Hall and found a small, window-less office on the third floor. The door was open a crack. Inside were two pale computer science students clustered around a Sun Microsystems computer. Their desks were piled high with diskettes, computer cables, and empty Mountain Dew cans.

She rapped on the door frame to get their attention. "Hi, is Chad Barnes in here?"

"Can we help you?" one of them asked, barely looking away from the code on the monitor.

"I hope so. My name's Kamerynne Craigie, and—"

"Are you Cameron Craigie's daughter?" His eyes focused on her like lasers.

Nat had the same star-struck expression when she found out she was standing in Grayce Aberdine's house.

"I am, in fact." She smiled at them, and suddenly they were all on their feet, talking over each other.

"Wow, it's an honor—"

"I was so bummed to hear about your dad, it was terrible—"

"I was hoping one of you guys could help me with a project," she said.

"Sure, what?" the first asked.

"I need everything you can tell me about keyloggers..."

———▲———

Kamerynne disappeared into the computer science underworld at her college. She emerged long enough each day to visit Nat at the hospital, but beyond that she was in the computer lab learning what she could from Chad and his friends or at her own machine. She burrowed into cracking like a larvae in a juicy apple. The search for illicit knowledge and cryptic information excited her almost more than sex.

The day before Nat was released from the hospital, Kamerynne went to her computer to install a program to record keystrokes and copy her incoming email in a separate, hidden file on her hard drive. But as she dug into the computer's core system to install the hypervisor ... she discovered another keylogger already running. It didn't look like any of the standard malware Chad had showed her. Kamerynne was able to decrypt enough of it to see that it was sending the data to a computer in the Ukraine. Nat's native country.

Kamerynne looked up the IP of the receiving computer, not expecting to find anything ... but the address was registered to the European branch of Charybdis Studios.

A week after she picked up Nat from the hospital, Kamerynne downloaded a torrent of *Cthylla: The Rising*, which was still three months away from opening in theatres. She'd figured they'd gotten another actress to play her mother's role ... but her mother's character wasn't in this film. She hadn't been recast; as far as this movie's script was concerned, her character had simply never existed. Had she been written out after her death? Or was she never supposed to be in the film in the first place?

Kamerynne took a screen capture of the list of supporters in the movie's end credits and spent several hours looking up names. Ten attended the Temple of the Deep Mother at some point in their lives. And three seemed to have something to do with the Messina Strait Foundation, the group that had inherited her parents' money.

"What do you know about Charybdis Studios?" Kamerynne asked when Nat stumbled into their dorm room at three in the morning.

Nat paused in the doorway, her face flushed with alcohol. "A little. Not much. They made the *Cthylla* movies."

"Right." Kamerynne paused, not sure if she should continue. "Why would someone from those studios be monitoring your computer?"

Nat laughed dismissively, but also turned pale. "That's silly. That wouldn't happen."

"But it did." Kamerynne nodded toward her computer. "They're watching you. Why?"

Something seemed to crumple behind Nat's eyes, and she got a faraway expression. "To make sure I'm doing as I'm told."

Kamerynne's heart beat faster. Was she going to get the truth, at last? "What are they telling you to do?"

Tears spilled down Nat's cheeks. "Right now? Helene *wants* me help get rich people to donate to the Foundation. But I'm shit at it. Eventually I'm to go in the water, and the goddess will come out. She needs sacrifices to bring her into the world. It's what I was made for."

"Made for? What do you mean?"

Nat gave a shuddering little laugh. "It's funny, you know? You and I were both conceived at parties. Only your parents didn't mean to make you. Mine did. My mom had sex with every man at the temple so nobody would know who my father was. Thirteen guys, and she didn't get pregnant the first time, so they had to do it again during the next new moon. Me and all the other temple babies, we're goddess chum."

Kamerynne tried to get her mind around what Nat was telling her. "You're … you're saying you're supposed to be a human sacrifice?"

"Pretty much, yeah." Nat's face was a sickly grey.

"Why … why do they let you walk around? Go to college?"

"They don't care how I live my life; they just care that I'm there when it needs to end. And who knows when that will be? It could be next week, it could be in twenty years. And if it's in twenty years, I might as well be useful in the meantime, right?"

"Why don't you run away? Look, I'll give you money to run away."

Nat laughed again. She looked like she was going to start weeping at any moment. "There's no place to run. The Foundation is everywhere."

"The Messina Strait Foundation?"

"Yeah."

"How is the Foundation connected to the Temple of the Deep Mother and Charybdis Studios?"

"Isn't it obvious? The Foundation runs the studios and the Temple runs the Foundation."

Kamerynne stared at her for a moment, feeling herself dangling above that terrible, cold, unfathomable blackness she'd feared since she was a kid. "Did the Foundation kill my parents?"

"Probably, yeah. I mean, I don't know anything specific, but yeah. Once a wealthy person changes their will for the Foundation, they don't last long."

"Jesus. Fucking. Christ." Kamerynne wanted to scream. She wanted to cry. She wanted push Nat's face right through the wall. "How can you be so casual about that? They murdered my parents! Does that not mean *anything* to you?"

"It's terrible! I agree! But...they do it every day."

Part of Kamerynne's mind was whispering *This can't be real* over and over. The room seemed to be tilted, the air a suffocating blanket. She looked down at her hands; they felt like they belonged to someone else.

"Why are you telling me all this?" Kamerynne's tongue felt like borrowed flesh, too, and was hard to move.

"Because it doesn't matter if you know or not. They won't kill me for telling, because they need me for the ritual. And they probably won't kill you, not unless you go to the papers or the cops or something stupid … and you're not stupid. They already have your money. And when the Goddess rises, everybody dies and none of this mattered. That's just how it goes."

A month later, Nat and a group of 100 other young women attended a beach-side retreat near Bolinas, California. Helene Arcanjo led them into the water at high tide during a freak storm; all of them drowned. A pair of fishermen found Nat's body washed up on a nearby beach three days later.

Just hours after that, Kamerynne's BMW was found crashed and burned in a ravine; the body inside was so badly damaged it could not be conclusively identified.

Nat's cremains were interred in Chapel of the Chimes, courtesy of an anonymous donor.

Bank accounts and mutual funds belonging to the Messina Strait Foundation and Charybdis Studios developed mysterious electronic leaks, and in the space of a few months their assets plummeted so far that they had to seek bankruptcy protection. And after that, high-ranking members of the Foundation started turning up dead: a few car accidents, an electrocution in a bathtub, a heart attack in a hot tub, a plane crash.

Some people in the hacker community speculated that Kamerynne faked her death, re-emerging as a formidable grey hat named BldyM@ry, bent on destroying the Foundation and groups like it at all costs. Others claimed she was simply a dilettante who died of grief.

Regardless, the Goddess never rose from the depths.

But maybe that's just a matter of time …

FAULT LINES

CHRISTOPHER GOLDEN & TIM LEBBON

Jane traveled halfway across the Pacific to find something precious, only to realize that she'd left the most precious thing behind. Long weeks journeying from San Francisco to Hawaii, a handful of days on the islands, and then just before her departure home she'd received word that her daughter Franca had fallen dreadfully ill. Now she sailed for home, bearing the guilt of her absence at such a time. Franca might be edging closer to death every day, but Jane was not there to hold her, to speak soft words of love and comfort, to pray over her.

She should have remained behind when Neville had summoned her, let him go and find his treasures and artifacts for the museum. Because she was a mother and her place was by her daughter's side.

I didn't know she was so sick, she reminded herself for the thousandth time. But no denial could erase the truth. She *had* known, somewhere deep down, even as Franca stood on the dock and waved farewell. Jane had known that something was terribly wrong and she had ignored it because Neville and his people in Turkey had found something remarkable.

Now, she was half a world away and she would have given anything to be home again. The ship was making all possible speed, but there were still at least six days remaining of their month-long voyage from Hawaii to San Francisco. They churned across rough seas, sharing their passage with people whom Neville increasingly suspected might mean them harm. Jane would have offered her soul up to the devil himself if that would transport her home, now, to sit by her dying daughter's side.

But not the jar. She could never give that up. Not when it might be the only thing that could save Franca's life.

Jane sat on her bunk and willed the minutes and hours away. Unlike some of the other passengers she did not suffer from sea sickness, but still the incessant roll and sway of the vessel troubled her deeply. She could not sleep, could not relax. The ship was never still, and neither were its contents. Doors swung open and closed when not latched correctly. Bulkheads creaked. Contents slipped and bumped against walls. The whole ship was alive, and every sound might have been someone making their move.

There are factions, Neville had said as they boarded the ship for the return passage from Hawaii. He had already accompanied the artifact on its long journey around the globe, from the place of its discovery near Amedi in Turkey, through Asia by rail, and then across the Pacific Ocean to Hawaii. That was where she and the three specialists had sailed to meet Neville, to collect and accompany the object on the final leg of its voyage. *Some of the crew watch us with an interest I don't like. And those two men from the Turkish Museum in Constantinople... Halis and Saygin... I wouldn't trust them for an instant.*

Jane had found the two Turks quite charming, and their knowledge of history gave her and them a comfortable common ground. But from the moment the ship had left Hawaii on its journey east to the USA, the two men had fallen silent, eyes hooded and sad.

Neville she trusted implicitly—she had known him for over two decades, and there had been a time when they might have become more than merely colleagues and friends—and she knew the three specialists well enough. One of them, Bryan, she'd come to know quite well indeed. They had been companionable enough on the crossing to Hawaii, but now that they had collected Neville and the incredible thing he had found, the specialists were too focused on the acquisition to socialize.

A knock at the door startled her from her thoughts. *A telegram telling me Franca has died!* she thought, fear cutting deep. She jumped up and unlocked the door, and Neville pushed his way inside. His gray eyes were wide, scared, and he had evidently been up on deck. He was drenched and smelled of the sea.

"What is it?" Jane asked.

"One of the crew is dead," he said, running his hands through dark, wet hair.

"What?" She blinked, confused and scared. "What happened?"

"It looks like he tried to get into the hold."

Panic took her in its grasp. *They've discovered—*

"Don't worry," Neville said. "The door is secure, and the crate inside is untouched. He had a crowbar, but whoever killed him slit his throat before he could even begin."

"Who was it?" The words seemed to issue from her without her forming the question. She felt numb, distant, somehow both afraid and impatient.

Neville closed the door behind him. He even locked it.

"Neville?"

"The crew is blaming the Turks. And the Turks blame me. They say I'm obsessed with the thing, and now that we're almost at the end of the journey, I'm trying to take it for myself."

"But that's ridiculous! They know the arrangements, this trip is sanctioned at the highest levels."

She did not mean governments. It was the academics, the archaeologists, and those who knew the potential power of what they carried who had made the arrangements. The whole point was to keep governments out of it.

"There's something else," he said. He sat on her bed and groaned, holding his stomach as the ship dropped and lurched. The captain had promised stormy times ahead, and Neville never had found his sea legs. "There's someone else on the ship."

"Another passenger?"

"No, a stowaway. Bryan overheard the crew talking about it. And no one seems to know who it is, or even where they are now."

"You think this stowaway is the killer?"

"I don't know. But whoever murdered the crewman, I'm willing to bet it's the same person who killed those two at the dig."

Two local people, a husband and wife helping with the excavations, had been brutally murdered days before Neville and the others had departed. He had told Jane about it in a telegram, expressing his terror at what had happened and concern that he might be held accountable. But local authorities were not as thorough as they might have been in the United States. He had been saddened by such a tragedy, but pleased to leave it behind.

"And now we've brought the murderer with us."

Neville sighed and tried to smile at Jane, but it did not touch his eyes. He was tired and looked sick, and the pressure of what they had found bore down upon him. Jane worried that it might prove his undoing.

"So it seems," he said. "And we've six or seven days left of this wretched journey." He sighed again, then glanced up guiltily. "No more telegrams about Franca?"

Jane shook her head.

"She'll be fine. We'll get back in time."

In time for what he did not say, but Jane could only pray that he was right. On her journey to Hawaii her mind had been filled with excitement and adventure, the chance to make history, and the staggering idea that she might be about to set eyes upon a mythical object. Popular culture knew it as a box, though it turned out to be more of a small jar, and legend said it had belonged to Pandora, whose very name conjured up grand imaginings.

Now, everything was about Franca. To hell with Pandora.

They had to get back in time.

Captain Gavriil called a meeting in the mess. He and his chief mate carried side arms, and that did not make Jane as comfortable as it should. All but two of the Greek crew—those required to steer the ship—were there, along with the Turks, Neville and Jane, and the three specialists working for the Golden Gate Museum of History. Bryan, and the others, Patrick and Cesare, had been shut away in their large shared cabin, trying to translate ancient writings and hieroglyphics, and they all looked as though they had just woken from a trance and remembered that the rest of the world existed.

The captain spoke in reasonable English. The Turks understood, but some of the crew remained blank-eyed. Jane assumed it was because they did not understand. Or perhaps they simply didn't care.

"Somebody in this room is a killer," he said. He glared around at the assemblage, gaze flitting over the crew and lingering on his passengers. "It has something to do with the cargo. That small box. One single box." He was fishing, she knew. Maybe he himself had sent the now dead crewman to discover just what that solitary box contained.

"What about the stowaway?" Neville asked. A few of the crew stirred, but no one but the captain spoke up.

"There's no proof that we have a stowaway."

"Your crew seems to think we do. This isn't a large ship, Captain. Shouldn't it be easy enough to discover whether there is one or not?"

"As easy as revealing what the cargo is."

"You have been paid very well not to know," one of the Turks, Saygin, said.

The captain stared at him for a loaded moment, then smiled. It was a slick, confident expression, one that Jane suspected had frightened a lot of men and lured a lot of women into his bed.

"My overall concern is the safety of my ship and crew."

"And your passengers, of course," Jane said.

"I am paid to give you passage," he said, the implication clear.

"From now on, no one will be left alone, either around the ship or in their cabins. The hold is out of bounds until we reach port. And Yanni's funeral will be held tomorrow at midday."

The mess was quiet but for the constant creak and groan of subtle movement. When Captain Gavriil left the room his crew followed, whispering amongst themselves and casting suspicious glances at the passengers. One of them looked Jane in the eye and she flinched, but did not turn away. She had seen the man before—small, wiry, strong, and rarely without a smile on his face. Now he looked stern. Worse than that, he looked scared.

When the last of the crew had left, it was Neville who stood and took control. Jane thought he would have made a natural captain. Her friend's character always filled a room, his staggering intellect a large factor. She knew that seasick though he was, he would be feeling so constrained in this ship, as if his life was paused between one shore and the other. Even with what they were transporting.

This jar that might once have belonged to Pandora.

It had been discovered in a subterranean chamber, on the walls of which were ancient writings that had taken weeks to decipher, with some even now still being translated. What had already been determined was that the writings told a variation on the story of Pandora and identified the jar as having been in her possession. The location of the chamber, the historical descriptions of the jar, all made sense. But there was so much more they did not know, and that was why the team was working around the clock. Rumors and whispers down through the centuries spoke of two vessels, one containing all the ills and diseases and bad things of the world, the other filled with goodness and light. The writings in the chamber confirmed this variation. But while one jar might already have been opened, the other—the lost jar, mislaid millennia ago and perhaps now found again—remained sealed against the world.

The true mystery was which of those vessels they had found. Before they reached port in San Francisco, they had to know.

"He didn't seem too concerned that one of his crew has just been brutally murdered," Bryan said, with a worried glance at Jane.

"I suspect he and his crew have been involved in more than a few unsavory situations," Neville replied. He looked to the Turkish men. "I asked you to secure us safe passage."

"You asked me to find *quick* passage," Saygin said. "The two are not necessarily good bedfellows."

"But with a pirate?"

The word shocked Jane. It held so many connotations.

"We've used him before," Saygin said. "He's trustworthy, and once bought, his silence is assured."

"Even if someone starts killing his crew?"

"The dead man was trying to break into the hold to see what we're transporting. You really want them to know?"

"No," Neville said softly, and Jane was surprised to hear such vulnerability in his voice.

"We'll reach dock soon," she said. "Whatever happened, we'll be away from it."

"Really?" Neville looked down, seemed to gather himself, then lifted his gaze again to Patrick and the other specialists. "How close are you to completing the translation?"

"Come and see," Patrick said. "Seems to me that staying together will be safest for us all, anyway."

As they left the mess hall Jane glanced back to see Saygin and Halis sitting at a table, heads close in conversation. Saygin saw her and smiled, then waved her on. *We have things to discuss*, that wave might have said. Or perhaps, *We have plans to make.*

Walking along dank corridors that stank of diesel and sweat and boiled vegetables, listening to the groans and clangs of the vessel flexing and tipping through the ocean's swell, she understood how people could go mad out here. Or if not mad then at least a bit unraveled, their ways of living, moral codes and outlook on life radically changed. Against the vastness of the ocean Man was small, and to be at its mercy every second of your life would be humbling and mind-altering.

She also watched the shadows. Light came from shielded oil lamps set into the walls of the narrow gangways. As flames flickered, so the shadows seemed to stretch and dance, reaching for them as they walked past and then drawing away again. Any one of them might have harbored a killer.

They entered the cabin that Bryan, Patrick, and Cesare were sharing. Neville and the museum director always referred to the men as specialists, but the men preferred the term freelance archaeologists. They were essentially adventurers for hire, traveling the globe and working for the highest bidder, no matter what the commission. Rough and harsh, Jane had also come to know them as sharp and intelligent. In many ways they were more knowledgeable than Neville, because their experience covered vast swathes of the world's buried histories, not just one small aspect of it. Each had his own self-professed specialty. Patrick's was societies and geography, while Cesare's was military history and anthropology. Bryan's expertise was in ancient languages.

Their cabin was a mess. Three cots had been unbolted from the floor and pushed against the wall, and they were covered with tangled blankets, unwashed food plates, and scattered clothing. A fourth cot held a selection of books and papers, while the floor area had been cleared as much as possible. Across the floor lay heaps more papers, all of them indexed with a pencil mark in one corner showing where and when the rubbing had been taken. A white cloth sheet was pinned to the wall, and Jane recognized the general layout of the chamber in which the jar had been found.

"Sorry about the mess," Bryan said, not sounding sorry at all. "We're getting there, though. I know a lot more about the jar than I did when we left port."

"But you know there's a lot more you don't know," Cesare said.

"Every answer poses another two questions," Jane said, and Neville threw her a distracted smile. He'd told her that the first time they'd met, when she had taken up her post at the Golden Gate Museum. It had turned out to be so true, in many aspects of life as well as archaeology.

She thought of Franca and her incessant questioning when she was younger. Why this, where that, when the other. As she had grown into her early teens the questions had come less frequently, but only because the girl asked them inside, keeping more mysteries to herself and not being quite so open with her curiosity. It was an adolescent thing, Jane knew, but it seemed foreign to her because she herself had undergone the opposite change when she entered her teenage years, starting to ask more questions than ever. She hoped that Franca would emerge from this phase soon.

If she doesn't die, she thought, and her daughter's illness struck her yet again. *I'm doing everything I can. If I could fly to you like a bird, I would. And if I can I'll bring something that might make you better, my sweet girl.*

"Jane?" Neville said.

"Hmm, what?"

"You with us?"

"Just thinking about that poor man who died."

"Yes, well," Neville said, and it was evident that he hardly cared at all.

"Death surrounds the jar like sand around a desert oasis," Bryan said. "At least that's what some of the writing seems to say."

"It's quite common to build such myths around sacred objects," Patrick said. "Whoever put this jar down where we found it wanted it left alone."

"And it's worked, at least three times through history," Bryan said. "See here. These sheets are from the walls lining the last passageway down towards the final chamber."

He pointed to the sheet on the wall, climbing onto the grouped cots and kicking aside a pile of dirty plates. The room was cramped with them all inside, but Jane was used to being in enclosed spaces with these people. Holes in the ground, stuffy library rooms, exhibit stores in museum basements. She had known them all for a long time, and trusted them in spite of their roguish approach to their work. That was why Michael had left her several years before. He claimed that she liked her work colleagues more than she liked him, and though that had never been true, she knew there was more to it than that. Michael had always been a traditionalist, and he didn't like Jane's adventurous side. As far as he was concerned, her place was at home with Franca.

Just now she would have agreed with him. But she was not one for regrets. She had chosen this unusual life for herself.

"Alexander the Great?" Neville said, snapping Jane's attention back to the moment.

"From what I can make out he captured the region, discovered these chambers and ordered them guarded," Bryan said. "He didn't even venture deep inside. Just destroyed the entrances he could find and ordered them sealed up forever."

"Forever wasn't quite as long as that, though," Cesare said.

"Nope. The chambers were discovered again four hundred years later. A great battle was fought, thousands died, and their corpses were used to plug the access routes into the underground network."

Jane shivered at the thought. "We didn't find anything like that."

"It must have been a route still hidden away," Neville said.

"So we were working close to thousands of bodies all the time," Cesare said. "Well, that's enough to give me nightmares for the rest of my life."

"If that isn't enough, this last section I've translated will be," Bryan replied.

He knelt close to the sheets he had spread across the floor and looked up at them, and Jane realized that he appeared haunted. The Irishman had never seemed troubled by signs of death and decay, and they had found plenty in their searches of hidden, ancient places. Sometimes the death was ritual, the victims arranged in poses or positions designed to convey certain messages in this world or the next. Sometimes the deaths were violent, evidenced by holed skulls and scattered bones with blade scars across their pale surfaces. Even when they found dead infants, Bryan seemed able to disassociate himself from them. They were archaeological artifacts, not dead people, he would say. Mysteries for people like them to unravel. He was never spooked, and she knew that he held his faith close.

He was spooked now, though.

"So?" Neville prompted.

"These were taken from inside the chamber," Bryan said. "Remember, Alexander wanted this place and its contents hidden away forever. Those who discovered it later fought battles to keep it secret, using the dead to dissuade anyone from digging deeper."

"And now we've gone and plundered it," Jane said.

Plunder was not a word any of them would normally have used, but right then no one questioned her usage. They were too focused on Bryan.

"Maybe we shouldn't have," Bryan said. "There are warnings. They're quite detailed, and fairly intricate in their—"

"Paraphrase," Neville said. One word, and he possessed the room.

Bryan sat back on his heels, no longer needing to read from his sheafs of notes and rough translations. He gave Jane a long, searching look before he continued. "Anyone who enters the chamber of Pandora will be forever damned," he said.

"Pretty standard," Cesare said, shrugging. "In that case I've been damned a thousand times."

"The main part is more important," Bryan said. "It goes something like: If you accept your damnation and dare touch the jar of Pandora or that of her sister Anesidora, the Keeper—which we interpret as some kind of guardian of the jars—will rise, hunt you down, cut your throat and take your eyes."

"Take your eyes," Jane muttered. "That's horrific."

Neville was quiet, staring at the papers in front of Bryan, as if he were taking these warnings seriously. Jane had never seen him troubled by ancient writings such as these, equating them to superstitious words muttered by countless people down through the ages. He was a scientist, he said, with no time for superstition.

"Neville?" she said softly.

"The crew member with his throat cut also had his eyes gouged out," he said.

No one spoke. Jane looked at the rubbings of engravings scattered around the room, the scribbled translations underlined and crossed-out, and feeling threatened by something more than she could understand, she was more terrified for her dying daughter than ever.

There was a knock at the door. Soft, polite. Jane was closest, so she reached out and tugged on the metal handle. The door swung in and Captain Gavriil stood in the opening, glancing briefly at each of them in turn. His gaze settled on Jane.

"The funeral later will be a busy one," he said. "Does anyone know Muslim funeral rites? Your Turkish friends are dead."

The air was thick and close in the gangway that led down into the hold, and yet it was strangely cold, as if the chill of the ocean had made an icebox out of the hull. The seas had grown rougher and the ship listed to and fro, not enough to make Jane lose her footing but enough so that she had to take a wide stance and ride the swaying of the vessel. Seasickness had never been a problem for her, not even belowdecks in rough seas. So it could only have been the sight of the two dead men that had turned her stomach queasy and made bile burn the back of her throat.

She kept her dinner down, but barely.

Halis lay in a fetal tuck on the dirty gangway floor. His abdomen had been cut open, the stinking tangle of his guts in a glistening pile in front of him. He had his hands on them as if they were a newborn infant he had died to protect. His body was turned away from them, and Jane thought that was best. She could see the pool of blood, and if she had seen his torn throat and mutilated eyes, horror would have overcome her revulsion and she would have broken down into a sobbing mess.

Saygin's corpse lay further ahead, in the shadows beneath the sealed hatch that led into the hold. In the darkness, beyond the light of the crew's lanterns, he stared at them with impossible black holes where his eyes ought to have been. Jane couldn't help feeling as if Saygin stared directly at her, baleful and accusatory.

She looked away.

"What were they doing down here?" the captain asked, shooting Neville an accusatory glance. "Not trying to steal your precious cargo, I assume. These were your people, so why were they trying to get into the hold?"

"You had a sentry on duty," Neville snapped. "Where is *he*, I'd like to know."

One of the crewmen shuffled a bit awkwardly, gave a sniff. "A fella has to piss, he has to piss. I was gone all of three minutes and I come back to this."

Seconds ticked by without another word spoken. Jane felt the ship closing in around her, all the breath forced from her lungs. Neville and Captain Gavriil began speaking again, both at the same time, and all she could hear was the fear in their voices—fear that it would happen again. They'd put more sentries in the gangway and two on the deck. Five days remained, more or less, and no one was to wander the ship alone.

"I've…I'm sorry, I need air," she said, and she turned and stumbled along the gangway, up the metal stairs, and onto the starlit deck.

At the railing, she held on tight and threw up over the side. Cool wind swept over her and sea spray dappled her face as she breathed in and out, trying to purge the stink of death from her nose, and her memory.

The captain's question hadn't been answered. He'd asked what the Turks were after, down there in the hold. If they were part of the team, why attempt to break in?

God help her, Jane thought she knew the answer.

———▲———

Sleeping, cradled by the gentle roll of the sea, Jane clung to sleep as if it were a lover who, once released, might never return. Rest had been hard to come by the past few days. Exhausted and on edge, she found herself with no appetite. Each night she lay her head down, body leaden and thoughts muddled, but sleep would elude her for hours. When at last her mind succumbed to weariness, she slept more deeply than she ever had before, and mornings were not welcome.

The knock came softly, but insistently, again and again. At first she thought she must be dreaming, but then she became aware of her surroundings, heard the creak of the ship and the soft knocking at her door, and her eyes opened to find her cabin was still in darkness. Outside the portholes, night still claimed the world. She heard a distant bell clang and sat upright as her mind struggled to make sense of that sound.

Again, the knock.

The ship was not moving. All was silent save the lingering echo of that now silent bell and the wash of the sea against the hull.

And that gentle knocking.

Jane stared at her cabin door a moment, then bolted from the bed. The white blouse and long black skirt she'd had on the night before lay across the top of the trunk containing most of her things, but she reached for the thick robe at the foot of the bed and pulled it on.

The knock came again and she almost went to the door, then thought better of it and dropped to her knees to slide her valise out from beneath the bed.

Rooting in the darkened room—her only illumination what little starlight came through the porthole—she felt first the bundle that did not belong in her valise. Jane had put it there herself but even so her touch was startled by its presence. Then her foraying fingers moved on, brushed the handle of the small Browning pistol she kept in her bag. It fit perfectly into her small hand and she plucked it out and went to the door.

"Who is it?" she whispered.

No answer.

Jane held her breath. They had a murderer on board. Only a fool would open that door. And yet she had secrets of her own, desperate desires that might welcome a soft knock at the door in the small hours of the night.

She turned the lock and drew the door open, stepping back quickly with the gun aimed at the silhouette that now moved across her threshold.

His hands went up and he shifted enough that she saw the thick wave of blond hair that swept across his forehead and the nervous, self-effacing grin that had won her over so immediately when they'd first met.

"Watch where you point that, woman," Bryan whispered.

Jane rasped his name, reaching out to drag him into the cabin. Bryan closed the door, quickly and quietly, then turned to her wearing an entirely different expression. She saw fear in his eyes, and excitement, but more than anything she saw the urgency in him.

"What's happened?" she asked.

Bryan kissed her, cupping his hands on the sides of her head and making it linger, so that before the kiss ended they each were breathing the other's breath, as if they shared one body, one set of lungs. He pressed his forehead against hers and stepped back, seemed to contemplate a moment and then nodded.

"Get dressed, Jane," he said. "We've got little more than an hour before dawn, but we've got to move now if we're going."

Her skin prickled. Nothing made sense to her. Yes, they'd had a plan, or the nascent beginnings of one, but this...

"Where are we?" she asked. "We had a day or two remaining, surely."

"Dress while I explain," he insisted, and she set about it, placing the gun on her bed.

Jane slipped out of her robe and left it in a heap on the floor. She reached for her skirt, unconcerned about Bryan seeing her in her underthings. He'd seen her wearing less.

"Gavriil ordered all speed days ago," he said. "We've been burning extra fuel, straining the engines to make port as swiftly as possible. The crew didn't let on. If I hadn't woken, I'd have been none the wiser until he returned with the police."

She froze, one arm through a sleeve of the blouse from the night before. Her thoughts went to the valise, and to the package inside. "Police?"

"He's gone ashore to bring back detectives," Bryan said. "I guess that rules the captain out as our killer, unless he's run off and never returns. Still—"

"If we're getting off, it has to be now."

Bryan nodded. "Now. Take nothing with you, save perhaps that gun."

Jane sat on the bed and pulled on her boots, lacing them almost unconsciously. Her valise contained the only things of value she had with her—photos of Franca, her identification, a ring that had belonged to her grandmother—and the only thing she had ever stolen in her life. She thrust the gun back into the valise and stood, blouse untucked, hair in disarray.

"Ready," she said.

She held her breath as he opened the door. The valise hung heavy in her grasp. Bryan checked the passageway and then ushered her out. Jane moved past him and led the way, familiar with the layout of the vessel after so many days aboard. Treading lightly, they nevertheless dashed along the gangway, ducked into a stairwell hatch and made their way abovedecks. The April night air chilled her instantly and Jane wished she'd thought to take her coat, but there was no turning back. Nearly everyone would still be sleeping, unaware they'd reached port, but at least one or two of the crew would be on deck. They crouched low, hoping to avoid being spotted. Everything depended on it.

Captain Gavriil had left a whip-thin, cruel-eyed man named Paolo to guard the gangway. The tip of Paolo's lit cigarette glowed orange in the dark. Bored, pistol jutting from a holster at his side, Paolo did not seem like a man fearful that a murderer might attempt to rush him. Nevertheless, there was that gun, and Jane had seen the way the rest of the crew became uneasy when Paolo entered a room. Idle or not, he was dangerous.

She handed Bryan her valise and gestured for him to remain in the darkness beside the chart house. Hugging herself against the cold, she walked toward the gangway, making no effort to muffle her footfalls. Paolo turned and stared at her. He drew a long puff on his cigarette, bright tip flaring, and watched her approach, but did not draw her gun. What threat did she pose?

"Could I have one of those?" she asked.

He glanced down toward the dock as if to be sure Gavriil would not suddenly appear and then reached inside his jacket for the pack.

"Trouble sleeping?" he asked.

"Every night since … well … it gets stuffy down below. Now that I'm up here, of course, I realize I should've brought my coat."

She took the cigarette he offered and leaned in as he lit it for her. Drawing the smoke into her lungs, she felt instantly warmer.

"We're waiting for morning to disembark?" she asked.

"Harbormaster doesn't arrive for at least an hour," Paolo said, gaze turning lustful as he studied her. "We're stuck here till then. You do look cold, miss. Let me give you my coat."

Jane smiled at him, one corner of her mouth curling upward to add a hint of coquettishness. "I wouldn't say no."

As he slid out of his jacket, she shoved him overboard, reaching for his gun as he tipped over the railing. Her fingers missed and she came away with neither gun nor jacket. Paolo shouted as he fell, but not loudly, perhaps too shocked to do more than bark a little. She hated herself in that moment, said a silent prayer while he plummeted, and then thanked heaven when she heard a splash and not the crack of bone against the wooden dock.

She ran down the gangway, trusting Bryan to catch up. When he did, she took the valise from him and cradled it against her chest as if it held her daughter's life within. They ran up the dock and she listened for Paolo, hoping he would surface, weighing Franca's life against the cruelty in his eyes. Would she be damned for what she'd done, if Paolo died?

It mattered not at all. Not in the balance of things.

Neville snorted loudly as he came awake, staring up into the face of Cesare. The man's long mustache made him look a bit like a walrus and with his eyes wide, he seemed about to unleash some kind of Arctic mating call. Sleep cluttering his thoughts, Neville pushed Cesare away.

"What are you—"

Then the puzzle of information around him clicked together. Still dark beyond the porthole. The panic in Cesare's eyes. Neville swept back his covers and swung his feet over the edge of the bed.

"Tell me," he said.

"We've reached port and—"

"What?"

"The captain's gone for the police, wanted to do it before we all woke to surprise the killer, so I'm told."

"All the better," Neville said. "He's a smarter man than I'd have guessed."

Cesare shook his head, wetted his lips with his tongue. This wasn't what had him so fearful.

"He set a guard. Paolo. But now the man's disappeared, and so has Bryan. Patrick and I woke and he wasn't in the cabin. We went searching, even knocked on Jane's door but—"

Neville frowned. "Why would you..."

He caught the look in Cesare's eyes, surprise that he hadn't known and a trace of pity because they all knew that Neville was more than fond of her.

"Bryan's been to her cabin before," he said, and saw the confirmation in Cesare's face. "All right. So you went searching for him there. What did Jane say? Has she seen him?"

"Jane isn't there either. They're both missing."

Cursing loudly, Neville reached for his boots.

They went directly to the hold. The first mate had beaten them there, along with a raggedy looking crewman named Volk, who had a rifle cradled in his arms. The metal hatchway was still locked up tight, and Captain Gavriil and the mate had the only keys.

"Open it," Neville demanded.

"Not until—" the mate began.

Neville rounded on him, fury and a hundred ugly thoughts storming about inside his head. "Open the fucking door. We're in port already. Volk can shoot us if we take anything that isn't ours!"

The first mate opened the hatch.

Inside, the cargo was undisturbed. The crate that Neville had shepherded all the way from Turkey remained sealed. And yet ... was there a certain amount of scoring around the edges of the lid? Panic surged through him as he snapped orders at Cesare and Volk, even as Patrick arrived to aid them. They had the lid off in moments.

A few moments more and Neville's worst fears were realized.

The crate lay empty.

Someone had stolen the jar. His heart sank as he began to understand, and he wondered how long ago the jar had been taken. *But only the captain and the first mate have keys!* he thought, and the whole, terrible truth struck him. The thief had stolen the jar before the hold had been locked, even before they had left port in Hawaii.

Jane had been planning this from the moment she had learned that her daughter was dying.

He wanted to be furious with her, but he understood. He might have done the same thing if it were his own daughter whose life flickered like a candle nearly at its end. But of course, the myths about the jar were just that, and Jane had made a terrible mistake. The police would be after her now. But they weren't the only ones. Whoever had killed the Turks and the others—the barbaric son of a bitch who had slit their throats and taken their eyes—would be pursuing Jane as well.

Neville leaned on the crate, exhaling loudly. He'd once believed that he might be in love with Jane. But there was nothing he could do for her now.

"What do you think—?" Patrick said, but a sound cut him off. A roar of rage, a scream of unrelenting grief, Neville had never heard its like before. It echoed around the hold and multiplied, seemingly growing louder instead of quieter.

Neville and the others staggered, not knowing which way to look or run because the cry came from everywhere. Then he spun around to face to doorway into the hold, and the shadow he saw there loosened his bowels and sent a chill through him like an electric shock.

There, the murderer, the killer, he thought, *but it's no woman or man, not human at all.* As the scream faded at last and the shadow flitted from view, Neville realized that Jane's fate was already sealed.

Heavy, doom-laden footsteps sounded through the ship as the figure raced away, and he experienced only a shred of selfishness feeling glad that it was not coming for him.

———————

"Hurry," Jane said. "Hurry!"

"Not too fast," Bryan replied. "Jane, take it easy. Take it slow. I know you want to get home to Franca, but you won't do that if you're caught. If we run into Gavriil and the police, and they get us, what's going to happen?"

She stared at him, valise clasped to her chest. He looked pointedly at it.

"What's going to happen, Jane?"

"They'll take it away."

Bryan nodded. "They'll take it away from all of us."

A pre-dawn glow smeared the eastern skies above the city, vibrant colors destined to be dulled by factory smoke. They were huddled behind a pile of cargo waiting to be loaded onto ships, heavy wooden crates and thick hessian bags bulging at the seams. A few dockers were already wandering to work, smoking and laughing and cracking crude jokes. But it wasn't these that Jane was worried about. It was Captain Gavriil, who had proven wiser than she had assumed, and the police he had gone to fetch. With several murders on board the ship—and, so the captain hoped, the murderer still safely asleep—he would be rushing as fast as he could.

But Jane's fear was twofold. First, that the murderer was something she could not quite understand, and that he or she was even now following their trail, the lure of the jar as strong as it had ever been. And second, she was filled with a burning terror that everything was happening just a moment too late. She would arrive home and Franca would be lying in her bed, still warm even as the heat of life bled from her, eyes still shining, skin still flushed.

A moment too late. That was her greatest fear.

Clutching the bag against her chest, one hand inside holding the gun, she nodded to Bryan and headed out across the waterfront.

They moved quickly and cautiously, trying to appear as if they belonged. Several men glanced their way, but none took a second look.

"How far to your place?" Bryan asked.

"A couple of miles," Jane said. "Out of the docks area, then south to the Mission District."

"Streets should still be pretty quiet," Bryan said. "Maybe we can—"

"There!" Jane whispered. She had seen Gavriil running from behind a storage building further along the dock, and several police came with him. At first she thought they were actually chasing him, and she hoped that the danger to her and Bryan might have been shifted. Then she realized that they were all running to reach the ship, and it was Gavriil who moved the fastest. Yet another way in which she had underestimated him. He was a big man and heavy around the waist, but that did not mean he wasn't fit.

They ducked behind several wagons loaded with goods, crouching so that she could see the running men through the wheels. She glanced at Bryan and they both remained motionless, fearing that any sudden movement might attract attention. Gavriil would be hoping they were all still aboard ship, but he would also be alert. If he saw them, Jane knew, he would barely break his stride.

The men ran along the dock and disappeared behind piled cargo. Urgency bit at Jane. As soon as they were out of sight she moved off at a crouch, ignoring Bryan's whispered warning to give them more time. Franca was sick and might not *have* time.

A moment too late, Jane thought again. She straightened and started running, hearing Bryan sprinting to catch up. He was a fit man—she knew that well enough—but her own exertions were driven by desperation. He would have to keep up.

She almost ran into the policeman. He emerged around the side of a storage unit as she ran for the corner. A big man, fat, red in the face and struggling with the effort, he gasped as she skidded, slipped, and finally fell. Jane's instinct was to protect her head and body, but good sense prevailed, and her arms hugged tight around the valise.

To have it smashed open now ... She almost laughed at the idea. None of them knew for sure which jar this was, and yet she intended to present it to her sick daughter, open it, exposing the world to whatever lay within in an effort to cure one person's ills.

"Careful, Ma'am," the policeman said. "Here, let me—" He held out a hand but Jane knocked it aside, scampering back on her behind and pushing herself upright against the wall.

"Don't!" she said. The policeman's eyes went wide, then narrowed again, his expression cooler and more considered than before. She might have fooled him, she supposed, if she'd reacted better. But now she had raised his suspicions, and his eyes flickered down to the bag clutched against her chest.

"Jane, no," Bryan said. He pleaded. And as she drew the gun from the bag, she wondered just what he thought her capable of.

"Anything," she whispered, pointing the gun at the man's chest. Her hand shook, but his fear was very real. "I'll do anything for her. You understand?"

The policeman didn't, but he nodded anyway.

"Go that way," she said, nodding across the dock to where the others had disappeared. "Don't look back. I'll know if you do. You believe that?"

He did not, but he nodded again. Then he went, hurrying, and Jane knew he would be feeling a hot spot on his back just waiting for the bullet. She pitied him for a moment, but Bryan gave her no longer. He grabbed her arm and pulled her around the building. She thought he might take the gun from her, try to assume control, but he did not. He knew what she was doing and how determined she was.

"Fast as we can," he said. "We probably don't have very long."

They ran, no longer caring what the arriving dockworkers thought of them.

Two minutes after she sent the policeman on his way, Jane heard a terrible scream, rising from terror to agony before being cut off at its height.

"What the hell was that?" Bryan asked.

An awful thought occurred to her. "We're being followed," she said. "The killer. After this." She tapped the jar.

"After it or protecting it?"

"You really believe that curse?"

"If someone else believes it and acts on it, that makes it true."

They left the docks behind and entered a network of streets, and Jane considered what Bryan had said. Patrick and Cesare had translated and read the curses carved into the catacomb walls, so was there a possibility one of them had taken it to heart? The dangers of what they had found had been discussed again and again, and while none of them openly professed belief in the supernatural aspects of the jar, she knew they all harbored secret hopes. Her, most of all. Why else would she be doing what she was doing now?

But they had all agreed that there might be very sound scientific reasons why the jar should only be opened in a controlled, sealed environment. If it was the so-called 'good' jar, then maybe it would contain tinctures and medicines from long ago, many of which had faded from memory in the intervening centuries. They could prove useful again—imagine a cure for polio, or the plague. But if it was the bad jar, it might have been filled with all manner of infections, illnesses, and germs. One inhalation of the jar's ancient contents could seal the fate of humankind.

She knew the three specialists well, and Bryan more than she had known any man since Michael had left her. But it was still entirely possible that Patrick or Cesare had taken it upon himself to protect the jar. Perhaps even as far as murder.

It was a mile to her home, maybe a little less. Her stomach ached with excitement at seeing Franca again, and the boiling terror that she would be that moment too late. Nothing mattered now but Franca, and the jar, and although Jane knew all the dangers that hung around it, her vision was blinkered, tunneled towards her daughter being well again. That was all that mattered, and the rest of the world could go to hell.

"Something's following us!" Bryan said.

Jane spun around and looked where he was pointing, back along the street. They had passed people on their way to or home from work, and to some extent being in the vicinity of others had given her a sense of safety. But no more.

Bryan's use of the word *something* instead of *someone* rang so true.

A shadow moved along the street. It flitted back and forth across the road, seeking the darkness between buildings, avoiding angular patches of light thrown by oil lamps, moving quickly and smoothly. It passed a small group of men and only two of them paused and looked up, as if none of them had seen it and only a few heard or sensed something amiss.

"What do we do?" Bryan asked, scared. He put his hand to his throat, subconsciously trying to shield it from the blade.

"We run," she said. "Follow me. We can shake it."

But whatever it was, she was nowhere near certain of that.

She knew these streets well, and the alleys and yards behind the streets even better. She had been born and brought up in San Francisco, and while as a child she hadn't lived in this neighborhood, she'd had friends here. They had stolen fish from the dock markets and fruit from street vendors, and a fast and secret getaway route had always been vital. Sure, a few of them had been caught one time or another. But she dug down now in her memories, seeking those retained maps and hoping things hadn't changed much in the intervening years. It had been some time since she'd needed an escape route from anything.

"This way! Follow me, keep fast and low, and don't look back." She slung the valise handles over one shoulder and pulled out the gun, unconcerned whether anyone saw it. She was too damn close to home to care about anything other than getting there.

Jane ducked between two ramshackle wooden houses, nudging against a gate with her shoulder when she saw it ajar, rushing across a yard and out through another gate. She heard Bryan behind her, breathing hard but keeping up, and a rush of gratitude washed through her. She wasn't sure that she loved him, but right then she felt that she owed him everything.

They emerged into a narrow alley, dark and shadowed in the pre-dawn, and she immediately turned right. Memories formed a map she followed subconsciously, sensing the ghost-whispers of old friends urging her on. She kicked through something wet and stinking, heard the rattle of chains, and then a dog leapt at them, barking and foaming at the end of its chain. Jane kicked out and connected with its side, but it was a big beast and felt no pain. They dashed past without suffering a bite and the hound barked them along the alleyway.

Reaching a wall, Jane pocketed the gun and searched for familiar handholds. They were still there, all these years later, and climbing the wall felt like a dream. There was no hesitation. She pulled with her hands, pushed with her feet, and reaching the top she looked over into the small square on the other side. The trees there seemed taller, and there were several automobiles parked outside some of the houses, but otherwise it was as it had been twenty years before.

Just as she swung her legs over and dropped down the other side, Bryan cried out.

"Jane, it's—"

She hit the ground and turned, pulling the gun and aiming at the top of the wall. *I'm so close to home!* she thought, waiting for Bryan to appear, or the shadow, or both of them struggling to reach her first.

Something growled. Bryan shouted, and she heard him dragged down from his hold on the wall, striking the ground hard.

And all that mattered was her dear, dying daughter.

"Bryan, don't give it to him!" she shouted. Then she turned and ran, almost home, nearly there, and behind her on the other side of the wall, following a brief pause, she heard her lover's scream turn into a sickening gurgle as his throat was torn open.

Sorry sorry sorry, she thought, but there was nothing she could do. Bryan would have died anyway, and giving herself just a few more seconds... surely he'd have wanted that?

Swallowing down the stale, poisonous guilt, she crossed the square, and just as she ducked into the street that led to the block where she lived, glanced back.

A shape was hanging from the top of the wall. Dark, small, and as it dropped into the weak glare of an oil lamp she saw the wizened, wrinkled features of an impossibly old woman.

But when she ran it was with an unnatural athleticism.

Jane braced herself against the wall, lifted the gun, and fired three times. The woman staggered and veered to the left, then tripped over a tree root and fell.

Voices called from elsewhere. A door slammed, and a child screamed, and someone else started shouting. Jane ignored them all and kept her eyes on the old, old woman. She was sprawled in the dust, writhing like a wind-up toy reaching the end of its time.

Then she lifted her head and looked directly at Jane. In the half-light she couldn't be sure, but she thought the woman smiled.

She fired one more time and saw the woman's head flip back. Glancing across the square at the wall, knowing that Bryan lay dead beyond, she hurried along the street towards her block, and home.

Franca heard singing, somehow both distant and close, in the same way that her body felt both dreadfully heavy and impossibly light. Her limbs were thin and her body slender, but her bones seemed to drag her down, making every muscle ache. Something within her seemed so wispy and airy that in her fleeting moments of wakefulness she thought she might fly away.

Like tonight.

Her eyes fluttered open in the dark. Damp with sweat, chilly with fever, she blinked several times, trying to focus. Her thoughts blurred along with her vision and she wondered if she might be dreaming—*must* be dreaming, because in a splash of moonlight in the corner of the room stood her mother, staring at her, whispering something that sounded almost like a song.

Oh, my darling, my baby girl, my beautiful sweetheart. Oh, Franca, I'm sorry, so sorry. I never should have left you but I'm back now, Mama's home, and I will make you well. You know I'd do anything for you, even give my own life. Oh, my darling, I'm sorry.

"Mama," Franca whispered, or thought she did. Had her lips moved? Had any sound emerged? She wasn't sure.

The little girl closed her eyes again. *Fever*, she thought. *I'm dreaming.*

I'm dying.

A hand on her arm. The touch alone hurt her. She took a sharp breath, thinking she might have stopped breathing altogether and only that touch—the pain of contact—had brought her back to life. *I could have died in my sleep. That wouldn't have been so bad. Better than the pain.*

Her eyes opened. The blurry silhouette above her couldn't have been her mother. Mama was away. Away, as she so often was. Something heavy lay on the bed beside Franca and she let her head loll, glancing down to see the dark shape of her mother's valise. Her chest clutched, breath rattling with phlegm, and she struggled not to cough because coughing sent spikes of pain through her and made her cry. She didn't want to cry in a dream.

"My love," her mother said.

Franca had no breath to reply.

Her mama reached into the valise and drew out something wrapped in thick cloth, gray in the moonlit room. Her hands trembling, she slipped the cloth away and revealed the strange piece of pottery within. Franca wheezed and began to cough and her mother said *no, no, stay with me darling* as pain lanced through her chest and the phlegm rattled and tears came to her eyes. Her vision went dark and for a moment she saw nothing at all.

The stink of her own sickness made the little girl groan in revulsion.

When she opened her eyes again, she saw the jar in her mother's hands. Ceramic, but ancient. Mama worked with artifacts at the museum. Franca didn't recognize the symbols on the jar—her mother always tried to teach her things and sometimes she paid attention, but these weren't like any of the things she'd seen before. She blinked, vision blurring again, and then through the fog she saw that her mother was trying to open the jar, digging her fingernails into the crusty seal around the lid.

Then she saw the thin, black-hooded figure rise in the moonlight beyond her mother.

The figure reached spindly, bloodstained, shaking fingers toward her mother's shoulder and Franca felt the breath seize in her chest, fear lancing through her where the pain had been and filling her lungs with a scream she could not voice. The hood shifted and she saw the face of the old woman beneath the hood, the *ancient* woman, a crone with gleaming yellow eyes, like a panther's. On her forehead was a terrible wound, splintered bone, but she seemed unconcerned.

The hand fell on her mother's shoulder.

"You must not," the crone said.

Her mother screamed and flinched away from the clutching hand, and the jar fell from her grasp. It bounced against the edge of Franca's mattress and then struck the floor with the sort of dry clink that only came from the sound of something cracking.

Breaking.

Franca heard a faint hiss, like a dying gasp, and wrinkled her nose at the peculiar stink that filled her bedroom.

Her mother cried out, but the crone's hawk-like screech tore through the suffocating air as she batted her mother aside. Franca wheezed, calling for help as Mama struck the wall with a different sort of crack, thicker and wetter, but just as much the sound of something breaking.

The picture frames on the walls rattled. The whole room jolted once, so hard that lines threaded the glass of both windows. Franca's eyes widened, adrenaline surging and focusing her vision as the whole bed quaked beneath her and she felt the world buck. Her hands clutched at the blanket and she mustered a cry.

"Mama!"

Her mother was trying to stand, clutching her chest, one hand on the wall. The floor shook again and she collapsed. She wheezed and coughed. In the moonlight, despite the juddering of the room, Franca saw blood on her mother's chin.

The crone whirled on Mama, whispering a chant that might have echoed the song that had first woken Franca. But these were not her mother's words, nor were they full of love. They carried a promise of fury and terror.

The crone swept towards her mother and slammed her into the wall again, hard. Then she slumped to the floor and stared down at the jar. In those old eyes, Franca saw a glimmer of despair beneath the rage.

"Mama," Franca whispered, but Mama did not reply. She sat slumped at the foot of the wall, crying.

"What have you done?" the crone said, but she remained staring at the jar. When she looked up the despair was still there, but so was something else. Resignation.

"Your mother earned this for you," she said as she drew a rusted, gnarled knife from her cloak and drew it across her own throat.

Blood gushed, dark in the faint light. The ancient woman shuddered, dropped the knife, and pressed a hand to her throat. Then she started smearing her own blood onto the jar, staining the symbols and the thick grey seal, and she pressed it along the crack in the jar's side. Gasping, blood bubbling at her throat, she continued to work until her movements slowed and the flow of blood lessened.

The room stopped shaking.

Franca gasped. For the first time she realized that the low light in the room came not from the moon but from dawn's early light. She stared at the face half hidden by that black hood, then at the jar, and she saw that the cracks had been sealed with quickly drying crimson lines, blood that was no longer blood but a threaded vein of marbling in the ceramic.

The girl inhaled. She heard the thick, choking voice of her mother and turned to see her trying again to rise to her feet.

"Mama," Franca said, leveraging herself up on one elbow and reaching out, sorrow washing over her.

A strange light glittered in her mother's eyes. Franca thought it seemed like relief. Like happiness. Her mama tried to stand but could not. Something inside her was broken, and only her eyes still held signs of life. And then, as Franca watched, even they were extinguished.

"Take it," the crone said. She was offering the jar in both hands, crouched close to the floor in case she dropped it. Blood bubbled at her throat as she spoke, and the second time there were no real words, only the hiss of air.

The jar slowly rolled from the crone's hands onto the floor.

Franca was confused and scared and, most of all, desperate not to believe that she had just witnessed her mother's death along with this old woman's.

But the crone's eyes flickered wide.

And the world began to tear itself apart.

The room had bucked before but now it lurched, shaking so hard that the walls split. The roof dropped, cracked in two. The city seemed to roar outside the broken windows and Franca heard screams. She took a deep breath and slid to the edge of the bed just as it lurched again and threw her to the floor.

The rumble of the earthquake filled her ears as she grabbed the frame of the bed to anchor her and tried to reach for her mother's outthrust leg. Mama sat against the wall, silent gaze full of love for her daughter.

The roof caved in. Thick ceiling timbers crashed down upon them all. The crone closed her eyes in that last moment as if in peace, and then the timber struck her, shattering her dry thicket of limbs and crushing her skull.

A timber fell across the bed, slammed the floorboards at an angle and smashed the wood. The bedframe held. Franca lay in the small space beside it, the timber canted above her, as the jar rolled through a pool of her mother's blood and came to rest in the cradle of her arms as if it belonged there.

If the foreshock had lasted twenty seconds, this bucking, roaring, cracking of the world went on for at least twice that, and felt like eternity. When it eased to a rumble and then ceased altogether, screams and the sounds of chaos continued in the early morning light, and Franca could smell burning.

"Mama?" she whispered, holding the jar to her chest. It felt warm.

There was no reply. She was alone in the room.

But she felt strong.

And with the jar in her arms, a terrible understanding began to dawn.

———◆———

They walked through the devastated city before crossing the bay towards Chapel of the Chimes in Oakland, and Neville told her about her mother.

Franca had known what her mother did, but had never understood the depths of her passion. She had grown used to seeing her disappear for days, sometimes weeks at a time, but she had not truly appreciated the reasons behind the absences, and how much each moment they were apart meant that her mother was chasing her dreams harder than ever before. Neville filled in some of the blanks while fires raged and smoke and dust hung heavy in the air, and Franca had never felt so strange.

In a bag slung across her right shoulder she carried her mother's funeral urn. That urn also bore something else, but she was the only one who knew the truth of that. She was the only one who *could* know. It was danger and wonder, charm and chaos, and even she still did not understand which.

They had talked about it in those days since her mother's and the city's deaths. Neville was glum and sad, mournful, and convinced that the jar had been the bad one. Why else would Jane be dead? How else could the great city still be burning, the ground cracked, aftershocks collapsing weakened buildings and sending a terrified populace rushing into the streets once again?

Franca suggested that the jar was the good one. She presented herself as the answer. The fever was gone, infection vanished as if shaken away by the violence of the earthquake. She said that such fortune would not be allowed by the contents of the bad jar, even amidst such chaos.

But in truth, even she did not know.

She had told Neville that the jar had been smashed into fragments, and then burned in the flames that consumed her house and a dozen others mere hours after she saw her mother die. He was devastated at the loss of the artifact, she could see that, but it was not something he could show. Especially to a little girl who had so recently seen her mother killed.

They passed the ruin of a city block, burned to the ground days before and still smoldering. Dogs scavenged within the fallen buildings. The smell of death hung heavy in the air, and groups of rescue workers made their way slowly across the landscape of devastation. Franca paused for a moment and watched, but the weight across her shoulder urged her on.

It needed to be somewhere safe, and secret, and then perhaps she could rest for a while and mourn. But she thought not. Something inside her had changed during those terrible, violent moments. She felt so much more grown up than before, so much *older*. Perhaps her blood had grown as thick and old as that crone's.

"It's just across the bay," Neville said.

———◆———

"Won't they be so busy today?"

"Not really." He was trying to be fatherly, but Franca could see that he didn't really know how to converse with a child. He'd sworn that he would look after her and be her guardian, but though she respected his good intentions, she knew that soon he would leave. Perhaps on another expedition, or maybe back to the museum, buried in the dusty depths where old things lay in shadowed mystery. But that was all right. Franca could look after herself.

"Why not?" she asked. "So many dead. They say hundreds, but it'll be lots more, won't it?"

"I suspect we'll never know how many," Neville answered. "But Chapel of the Chimes…a special place. And you have to be a special person to be interred there."

"And mother was a special person." Tears blurred her vision. She was pleased, because she was still finding it hard to cry.

"She was," Neville said hesitantly. "And also, I know the people who keep the cemetery grounds. I've known them for a very long time. They granted me the favor."

The urn banged against her hip as they walked. It was far heavier than it should have been.

"I'd like to do it myself," she said.

"Of course. We're almost there."

Families huddled around fires in metal barrels, people walking with precious water in containers, impromptu stalls selling food in streets, weary men staring into the hellish distance across the bay, harried and hopeless. They smelled fire and death.

She sensed wretchedness and hope in abundance.

At last they reached Chapel of the Chimes. Neville stood awkwardly, trying to say a few words but eventually making do with silence. Franca smiled and nodded her thanks, then entered the strange building.

Shadows of this library of the dead welcomed her. Keepers of the mausoleum met her, as Neville had told her they would, and told her what to do. Then they left her alone in a room with her urn, and the book-shaped reliquary where her mother's remains would sit out eternity.

Franca opened the urn and stared inside at the contents. The grainy, gritty ashes of her mother softly cradled the jar, its fractured shell tightly sealed by the ancient crone's blood. She had killed herself to protect its contents, and in doing so prevented a full release of whatever might lie inside. She had also passed on a terrible responsibility to the person closest to the tragedy—Franca. A young girl, now destined to be the guardian of something so amazing, and so dangerous.

When she was finished, Franca would leave this place and return once again to the shattered San Francisco daylight. And then her new, long life would begin.

THE LIBRARIAN

4

You remember studying the 1906 San Francisco earthquake in school, or hearing about it from stories passed down from generation to generation: a high magnitude quake resulting in more than three thousand deaths. You wonder how many of those casualties endure in The Library of the Dead. The earthquake and resulting fire was marked as one of the worst natural disasters in U.S. history, with over eighty percent of the city destroyed, the greatest loss of life from a natural disaster in California's history.

Could the opening of Pandora's box—?

"That is only one recount," the librarian says, returning the books to their shelves. "There are others, but not in this room."

Your guide leads you up a set of stairs to the second floor, and then to the third, where more golden books await, more statues, more vestiges. From this level, overlooking the balconies to below creates a dizzying effect that once again seems to force you toward the walls and to the bookshelves. You follow your guide along bookshelf after bookshelf. A corner of the building houses corner shelves, which house even more of the dead; the books here have Chinese symbols on their spines instead of alphanumeric English. A memorial hangs on one wall, but the two of you move along too swiftly to read the text.

Another covered hallway surrounds you in books, then another walkway, another balcony overlooking below, and then another hallway and another set of rooms. Already you are lost, turned around in so many directions and led down so many paths that everything begins to look the same in a labyrinthine blur of books and urns and memorials, although each room is completely different from the last and quite mesmerizing. There is no longer a north, east, south or west, no direction at all, no discernible path leading to the entrance you first encountered, nor to any new means of exit. Panic does not settle in, however, for you are enraptured, taking it all in, as if enchanted by the building and what it contains. The place seems endless.

And then once again you and your guide overlook the two floors below, the height again forcing you toward the flat granite walls with their square tombs—which again you must touch—and the glass-encased bookshelves.

It is then you notice that next to most of the panes of glass, which front—and keep dust at bay, you realize—anywhere from one to half a dozen books each, there are black metal rings attached to their framework: one the diameter of the ring made from touching your middle finger to thumb, and one half that diameter just below it. Out of the hundred or so sets of rings on this particular bookshelf, only three hold bouquets of cut flowers.

How many of the dead are revisited each year?

How many forgotten?

JADED WINDS, reads the spine of the next chosen book. Nestled within the black metal rings next to it are three banded red roses.

"This is one such tale."

While mesmerized by the vibrant red, the hooded figure had somehow removed the book from behind the glass.

"Both this story and the last are of ancient ethnic lore, and claim responsibility for an event that transpired over a century ago, influencing the entire Bay Area. And one contains my story—the basis for a penance I have been paying for the last century as the librarian. But I will drop my cowl at the end of your tour and reveal my identity. Now, there are two others on these shelves you must see before we move on to another part of this library."

The other two books are of course those with the flowers. Someone alive recently visited these—

Phasing through the glass, as if not there at all, the librarian's robed hand reaches through to retrieve the second of the three books, for you realize he or she always chooses this magic number.

TEARS OF THE DRAGON reads the second book, and you wonder if the story likewise takes place in San Francisco because of the title, perhaps in the part of the city now known as Chinatown.

Before the librarian picks the third, you are drawn to its title and try to reach through for yourself, but your fingers meet what protects it: cold glass.

PHANTOM ON THE ICE, the spine reads, a title perhaps with more than one meaning, a title perhaps mocking your attempt at phasing through to grab the book as the librarian had so easily managed.

You want to ask the question, but the answer comes first:

"By the end of our tour, you will be able to do the same."

An answer with more than one meaning?

The librarian's covered hand does what yours yet cannot and retrieves the third book, placing it beneath the others.

The tiled floor tremors beneath your feet—the smallest of shakes—as the second tale of the San Francisco earthquake opens.

JADED WINDS

RENA MASON

Ming Li woke to the sounds of a skeleton in motion, flat percussions reminding him of primitive bamboo wind chimes. The clacking came from the bed mat behind him. Last week, on their third wedding anniversary, he'd strangled his wife to death as she slept there.

They married in Chinatown the first week of April in 1903, and she still hadn't borne him any sons. He had to get rid of her before he could get a new wife, one who would fulfill her duty. *Ridiculous Western laws.* Ming dumped the body in the Oakland side of San Francisco Bay. Now her *gu nu* bone demon returned for his soul.

Never one to fear a woman, supernatural or not, Ming turned over and opened his eyes. Face to face with Xi, he marveled at the way her long, black hair undulated in the air above as if under water. Her porcelain skin glowed and rippled in the moonlight. Stark eyes squinted at him, but Ming felt no remorse for what he'd done.

"Come closer," she whispered in a soft voice, a timid expression on her face. Xi parted her robe, exposing flawless breasts.

A pinch of excitement tweaked his groin. Then he rolled away from her. "Go, now."

"Not until you have me one last time."

With his back to Xi, Ming reached for a wooden box on the floor.

"No. Please don't," she said.

He struck a match, lit a candle, then turned toward her and held up the light. Xi's mouth opened wide and she screamed, her jaws unhinging until half her face became a howling orifice. Her cries grew louder as her flesh melted, leaving nothing but animated skeletal remains. She reached for him, but he moved the flame closer, forcing her back. Xi's bones clacked once more before falling away and disappearing.

Ming smiled, blew out the candle, and slept deeply.

Packed within a throng of other Chinese immigrants in black robes and beanies, many with queue braids swinging behind them, Lew Hong spotted his business partner Ming. They acknowledged one another with a nod, wove around people, and met in the middle. Together they shuffled to their small ironworks on Sacramento Street. Morning mist from the San Francisco Bay clung to the sides of brick buildings, vaporous specters defying the sun.

The men jostled forward in rhythmic surges with the crowd. Lew listened as Ming spoke in Cantonese. "The Dragon Boat Festival is only two months away. Are you certain ours will be ready?"

"Yes, of course. The men work hard to keep us on schedule. They know it's important."

"Will you be going straight to Oakland this morning?"

Lew paused before answering. "I planned to but shouldn't. Yu is due any time."

"May the heavens bless you with another son. Yes, they will. This is your year, year of the horse," Ming said.

Lew smiled and nodded. He'd thought the same thing when he left his wife sleeping. She nearly bled to death on the floor of their cramped living quarters after the premature birth of their first child. He'd made a vow then to work harder and give her a more comfortable living.

Images of a bigger house and a better life for his family occupied every moment of his days for the last decade. After the success of their small ironworks, they'd started a fishing boat manufacturing business, and he couldn't be happier with how well production moved along.

Lew's good fortune made him feel somewhat guilty after Ming's wife had recently run away and left him.

"I'll go," Ming said.

"You're a good friend and business partner." Lew patted Ming's shoulder.

After Lew entered their factory, Ming turned down Stockton Street. He despised walking alone outside of Chinatown where Chinese often became targets for prejudiced cruelty. Mechanical sounds thundered behind him as he crossed Kearny. He quickened his pace, stepped into a small crowd of Westerners and tried to blend in. Someone shouted, "Chinaman, stop!"

Every muscle tensed, he scowled and clenched his fists. People scattered with shocked looks of disgust. A covered motorcar pulled up alongside him. The metal demon twitched and sputtered. The driver ignored Ming's presence, kept focused on the road ahead. Dark curtains over the windows concealed everything inside.

A door opened. A familiar voice came from within. "Need a ride?"

Ming scanned the area then got in.

"Shut the door," said Carl Worthington.

Ming did, and the car rumbled forward.

"You headed to the docks?"

"Yes."

"Take the long way, Sam," Carl said.

The man up front nodded.

"Well, Mr. Li, have you talked to your partner?"

"No. Not yet, but—"

"You're not trying to get out of our little agreement, are you?"

"I need more time. My partner's wife is about to have a baby."

"No one on the city council cares. We made a deal, didn't we?"

"Yes."

"So?"

"Very soon. I promise."

"Soon isn't good enough, Mr. Li. If you want payment and more acreage around your boat business in Oakland then you need to be faster. You people aren't in short supply, if you know what I mean."

"No." Ming shook his head. He didn't understand, but even with the language barrier, the Westerner made his air of superiority clear.

"My goodness, your kind are slow in the head." Carl pointed to his temple. "I mean someone else will take my offer of money and land to move Chinatown across the bay if you don't want it—other Chinese. I bet you understand now."

The driver laughed.

White devil!

"Yes," Ming said.

"Next week, then. Sam and I will find you. Make sure you have the signed papers."

Ming nodded.

"Good. Now get out."

The motor car stopped and Ming had barely stepped down when the car sped off again.

Anger roiled his insides on the ferry ride to Oakland harbor. He walked up to the bow's railing, looked over, and vomited morning tea. It stirred the dark water below. A pale white, familiar face floated up to the surface. Xi! It couldn't be. He'd weighted the body.

The prow moved through her and into a thick fog bank. Damp, frigid air embraced him and squeezed the breath from his lungs.

Ming looked up and imagined a fleet of his boats fishing the waters. Dealing with the Westerner had its downside but not for long. Ming planned to outsmart them all. Once Lew signed over the ironworks, everything would be his. Why should he care if the white devils reclaimed Chinatown in San Francisco? Better success awaited them across the bay in Oakland. Lew would eventually see it and be forever grateful. Or join Xi at the bottom of the bay.

New business, a wife, wealth, and many sons would soon be his. He'd build his own Nob Hill to entice the other rising entrepreneurial Chinese.

Soft coughing came from nearby.

He looked over his shoulder. White, silky air stirred to his right. A petite shadow emerged from the fog in a slow twirl. The most beautiful woman Ming had ever seen. She stopped with one foot forward and bowed.

"Jiu wei," she said.

"Jiu...wei?" He gasped. *The Fox Demon?*

Bright red lips exposed an impish smirk across her perfect face. She nodded and he backed away.

"I know what you want, demon. Go away."

"I can be your new wife. Give you many sons." Jiu danced toward him. Pink lotus petals flowed from her imperial robes to cushion every step she made.

"You will take all my money."

"And your soul." Two fans appeared in her hands. She flicked them open and continued to dance. After a slow pirouette she held them side by side. "Look."

Watercolor scenes moved across the folds. A blurred image rode atop ocean waves toward Chinatown, to the ironworks building, and at the end, Ming's body lie in a widening pool of crimson.

"I know your tricks, demon!"

Jiu giggled. "Marry me, and I'll save you."

"Never."

Childish whimpers came from behind the fan to echo through the fog, but Ming couldn't look away. The blood from his body in the pictures spread, spilled off the sides, and trickled down Jiu's hands and arms.

"As you wish," she said.

The fans closed, spurting blood in all directions, forcing Ming to close his eyes. When he opened them again, a blast of seawater sprayed him. Jiu and all her vibrant colors vanished. Overcast skies hung low as far as he could see.

The ferry bumped the slip several times before docking. He used a sleeve to wipe his face and smiled. A good life must be in store if the Fox Demon chose to visit him. The old legends said she sought the riches and protection of men by seducing kings and emperors. Indeed, he would soon be the royalty of a new China-town—in Oakland.

Lew kept busy inspecting the work and safety of the employees. The factory specialized in working iron anchors and link chains. Generations of his family had a formula and techniques Lew brought with him from mainland China. With population increases forcing San Francisco to become a large port city, their small business quickly grew.

He always believed *too busy* paralleled good fortune and less time to squander. The workers seemed to appreciate their jobs and never complained about toiling too hard and past their time to keep up with demands. He felt they wanted the factory to be as successful as he did, and this gave him a great sense of pride—of family.

Chen stood atop a high ladder against a water-cooling vat, shouting orders to men working pulleys below. A large anchor moved overhead, inching toward the foreman as he yelled directions and climbed down. The workers slowly lowered the warm iron. Steam billowed up to the ceiling as a soft burble and hiss came from the vat.

"Nice work," Lew shouted. He walked over to his dear friend. "You make it look easy."

"It is." Both men laughed.

"Where's Ming?" Chen said.

"I told him I didn't want to be far from home. He offered to check the Oakland factory."

Chen looked away, stared at the evaporating steam. "He spends a lot of time there."

His foreman had never been the kind of a man to speak lightly of anything bothering him, which made the muscles between Lew's shoulders tense. "Someone has to monitor the progress…what do you mean exactly?"

"Every chance he gets, like when you go home for lunch to spend time with Yu, Ming leaves and doesn't always return."

"Maybe it upsets him that I go home to my wife when his left him only a short time ago."

"Even before that."

"I've known him a long time. We're like brothers, and I trust him. So unless you have some evidence he's been up to something, I think you should keep quiet about this."

Chen lowered his eyes and looked at Lew. "I'm sorry. It's just that—"

"Enough. I'll be in the office." He walked away, conflicting thoughts chasing each other in circles around his head like too many fish in a pond.

Lew rounded a corner and saw Ming shouting and running toward him. His partner came up then hunched over to catch his breath.

"What is it?" Lew said.

"On my way back…" Ming gasped for air. "It's Yu."

Lew put his hand on Ming's shoulder. "Is she all right?"

Ming nodded. "Yes, yes, I'm sure she's fine. A neighbor of yours asked if you would come see her before your usual lunch time."

"Ah, I should probably go, then."

"First, please sign some important papers for the Oakland factory."

"Okay, but let's do it now, so I can go to Yu."

Both men stepped into the office. While Ming went to his desk and rifled through papers, Lew went over to his and picked up a pen.

"What are these?" Lew said.

"Dock rental agreement."

"But—"

"Just sign. I'll take care of the rest. Your neighbor seemed a little upset when she told me Yu sent for you."

"You should have said that before." Lew signed the papers, and rushed out of the office.

As he sprinted the two blocks to his home, he prayed for everything to be all right. The concerned looks on the neighbors' faces who'd gathered outside his house only made his anxiety worse. Lew barreled through the door and saw Yu lying on their bed mat, her sweaty face twisted in a grimace of pain. A Chinese apothecary from across the street sat beside her. The man stood up and shook his head when he saw Lew.

"You must take her to the Western hospital. Something isn't right."

He looked at his wife. "How will we get there?" Lew said.

"My son will pull her in the rickshaw we use for deliveries. Don't worry, he's young and fast, but you'll have to meet them there."

"No. Please, don't leave," Yu said. She reached out to him.

Lew took her hand and knelt on the edge of the mat. Blood seeped from underneath her onto his knee. He fought back a wave of panic and spoke in a calm voice. "I must go now, but I'll be there soon, or maybe even before you." He forced a smile.

She nodded.

"You know I can run fast," Lew said.

"Yes. Run with dragon's breath behind you."

He kissed her hand then released it and looked up at the apothecary.

"Go now," the man said. "My son will be back any minute."

229

"Please, take care of—"

"Just leave," the apothecary yelled.

Lew bolted out the door.

Crowds blurred as he flew past Portsmouth Plaza, his long braid tapped his back in rhythmic thumps. Yu's words carried him. He prayed a dragon followed close behind and blew strong winds.

———▲———

Lew had waited near the hospital's reception desk for over an hour when he saw a Chinese man pushing Yu in a wheelchair toward him. A Western doctor wearing a white coat walked alongside them.

"She's your wife?" he said.

The Chinese man translated the Westerner's words.

Lew nodded. He understood English better than he could speak it, but having the translator made things easier.

"She needs to see a specialist south of here. We've done what we can for now, but if you don't leave soon it could be too late."

"South of here?" Lew scratched his head. "How far?"

"Several hours away."

His heart sank when the doctor told him. "But how will we get there?"

The Westerner shrugged his shoulders and left.

The Chinese man spoke up. "I know a way."

"Please, tell me. I'll do anything."

"You know the Tongs," he whispered.

"No. I, I can't. They're criminals. It's too dangerous to ask."

"Then your wife and baby will die."

Lew thought for a moment. "What do I have to do?"

"I know a Westerner who's a soldier from the Bo Sin Seer Tong group that owns a motorcar. You will have to pay him a lot. You have any sycee? He likes to collect our things."

Yu gripped the sides of the wheelchair and groaned.

"Yes, I have one. A gold one saved for—"

The man's eyes lit up. "He'll want it before."

"Just get him here."

"Meet us out front in an hour. I'll keep your wife safe until you get back."

Lew nodded and ran for home. *What had he done to deserve this?* He and Yu had survived the plague that had killed so many in Chinatown. He thought for sure this meant they should live. Not once did he ever think he'd have anything to do with the Tong gangs, and now he'd made a deal with the devils. With no other choices, perhaps he should feel lucky the translator had a connection to someone with a motorcar. Yes. It had been fortunate.

"Thank you," he said aloud.

Yu's pale face haunted his vision as he hurried down streets. On his return, the small sycee boat of gold with a dragon carved on the side, all his earned savings, weighed heavily on his mind as well as in his hand. Lew's other treasure, his first son, Bao, lightened his heart as he pulled the three-year-old along with his other hand.

———▲———

Ming got up and closed the door after Lew left. He separated the signed papers from the dock receipts he'd had on his desk and slid them inside his robe pocket. Maybe he should go find Worthington. No. *It's better to make him wait.* Feeling satisfied, he walked over to Lew's desk, sat back in the chair and put up his feet.

Chen peered in through a window. His eyes opened wide, and then he came around and entered the office. "Hey, what are you doing? So disrespectful to put those there." He tsked and pointed to Ming's dirty shoes.

"Get back to work and mind your own business."

The foreman scowled.

"You know, you're right," Ming said. "I've had a long day and should have my feet up at home. I'm certain you'll keep that watchful eye of yours on the factory while I'm gone." He got up and bumped Chen on his way out.

Dreaming of riches, Ming napped for an hour until clapping sounds woke him. He sat up and patted his robe for the signed papers. Although he wanted to make the Westerner wait, unease and restlessness nibbled the edges of his confidence. His decision to bring the contract to Worthington after opening the factory tomorrow morning gave him relief.

More claps came from outside. After putting on his slippers, Ming went to the door, opened it and looked out. Low clouds on the horizon glowed soft pinks above the setting sun. They reminded him of the beautiful Fox Demon. He stepped down and walked to the front of his apartment building.

Twilight faded to darkness as Ming stood and gazed out. Peripheral movement made him turn to the right. He gasped. A woman who could have been his wife's twin sat in a chair.

"Who are you?"

The woman smiled, raised her hands and clapped three times. Her head fell off and landed into her open palms.

Ming's eyes widened. She held up her hands and the head flew at him.

"Headless demon!" he said.

It circled him several times in the air, chomping its teeth while lunging for his face.

"Why are you afraid?" she said. "You are the one who called me here."

"I did not."

"You killed your wife and the bugs come. I'm here to eat them." She cackled then darted at him again.

He waved his arms to keep the gnashing maw away. The head landed on the pavement in front of him with a wet smack, eyes focused on the ground. An elongated, pointy tongue stretched out of its mouth and lapped at a trail of ants, inching the disembodied head forward with every swallow.

Ming ran back to his apartment and bolted the door. That hungry thing out there and the rest of the headless demon would leave when the ant supply ran out. Plenty of bigger bugs could be found elsewhere. He'd cleaned up good after strangling Xi. Ming had always taken pride in keeping a tidy abode. Still, little sleep would be had until it left. He lay back on his mat and listened to the moist, sticky sounds outside.

After several hours tossing and turning, Ming got up and washed his face. He didn't remember when the noises had stopped, not that long ago he guessed, but his body needed the hour of sleep it got when the Fei Tou Bie finally left. These supernatural visits had to end. He'd find a shaman to cleanse the way and lessen the demons' dark natures after he handed the papers over to the Westerner.

The sun wouldn't rise for a couple hours, but Ming couldn't wait. Outside, a fog had rolled in. The demon's body no longer sat patiently waiting for its head. Even the chair had disappeared. Wary, Ming watched his steps until he felt the familiar sidewalk underfoot.

Chen showed up fifteen minutes after Ming opened the factory doors. Ming wondered if the foreman had followed him in. He walked over to secure a pulley then went into the office. Moments later Chen yelled to Ming.

"What is this?" he shouted.

Ming looked through the office windows and saw Chen holding up papers. He patted his jacket and felt nothing. They must have fallen out! He opened the door and ran to Chen.

"Give them to me!"

Chen held the papers out of Ming's reach. Ming lunged at him, and the men fell to the floor, wrestling for the contract. Ming landed two hard punches to Chen's chest. The foreman let go. While Chen gasped for air, Ming grabbed the papers and climbed to his feet.

"Traitor," Chen said.

Before he could fully regain his balance, Ming rushed Chen, pushing him hard. The foreman stumbled and then let out a choked cry as the point of an unfinished anchor tore through his chest from the back. Blood dripped off shredded flesh that hung from the curved barb.

"Traitor," he muttered once more, blood running from his mouth. Then his eyes closed.

A loud crack sounded, and the floor between them split open. The deceased Chen, the anchor, worktable and its vice fell into the widening fissure. Everything rumbled, shook and swayed. Ming lost his footing and fell. With his free hand, he clawed at the floor and rolled over.

An ancient warrior dressed in full Chinese armor stood at Ming's feet. Maggots filled the sockets of the decayed warrior's head, giving him writhing, white eyes. The foul worms wriggled across his face in a pulsing trail.

"General Lang!" Ming said. Every muscle in his body trembled.

The warrior raised a massive sword engraved with a long list of names on both sides. A forged dragon decorated the hilt and part of the blade, one of its ruby eyes twinkled. Ming watched as his name appeared on the blade. He knew the names carved there had been traitors of the Chinese people.

Ming lay paralyzed on the factory floor. Lightning bolted from the tip of the general's blade and blasted through the ceiling. Burning pieces of the roof crashed down. Ming's body buckled, and he screamed as falling debris landed on top of his body. He gasped for air but his breath became blood. It seeped out around the brick pile that now covered him into a widening pool of crimson.

Pinned to the ground, he could do nothing but watch as General Chi Lang drifted upward, his vengeance done. Ming looked away and saw his hand catch fire. The skin bubbled and melted off the bones—bones that clutched an unharmed contract. A deal he never should have made with the white devils.

That morning, sunrise brought no light to Chinatown. Thick layers of smoke darkened the skies and black clouds massed overhead, circling into vortices of soot and ash that dropped toward Ming. Behind them, two dragons breathed fire.

The Western Tong soldier slid the sycee into his coat pocket and glanced at Yu.

"Let's get," the Westerner said, hurrying them into his motor-car.

The man raced south in silence, looking back occasionally with concerned expressions. Bao leaned against Lew's right arm and slept. Yu held his left hand and wrenched it when she felt pain. Several hours had passed since his upper extremities went numb. The Tong soldier dropped them off at the hospital entrance, nodded once to Lew, and sped away as the sun set. His wife gave birth to their second son Feng soon after. She didn't return from surgery for several hours. The Western doctors had stopped the bleeding but had to remove her womb.

Lew struggled with mixed feelings of loss and gratefulness until he saw Feng. One look at his son, and he'd never been so thankful. He watched over his family as they rested then fell asleep in a chair.

Thunder rolled through and woke him. He stood and quietly left the room. Outside, dawn never came. Black clouds hung low in the sky. Lew thought he saw dragons behind them. He yawned and rubbed his eyes.

Lew left his family in safety and headed back to Chinatown. It took two weeks for him to get through the carnage. He crawled over bricks and twisted metal that filled the streets ten feet deep in some areas. Thick, dirty air choked his every breath. Decaying bodies lay strewn among layers of rubble across miles of wasteland.

The entrance and one side wall of the ironworks remained erect. Lew had passed the collapsed building several times without recognition. He spent countless days moving debris, his hands raw and bleeding.

He climbed toward folded white papers jutting from a mound. Bricks slid underneath him as he scrabbled up. They fell away and left him looking down at charred remains. Skeletal fingers clutched the papers. Lew tugged on them and the tiny bones fell apart. He sat back, read the papers, and wept with joy and sorrow.

—————▲—————

Lew Hong sat on a bench in a small garden, burning the contract he'd found in Ming's hand. A funerary honor for his business partner, despite the story they told. Ming's deception saved his family from the great earthquake that had demolished San Francisco.

At their Oakland fishing boat warehouse, which hadn't been damaged, Lew provided housing and care to survivors. He'd been a part of the Chinese Six Companies that helped plan and propose rebuilding a new Chinatown to which the Westerners would agree.

After three years of keeping the scorched bones of his business partner in an urn, Lew had arranged for them to be exhumed and ground to ash. With a large, private donation, he handed the remains over to the caretaker at Chapel of the Chimes, ensuring Ming received the eternity of golden splendor he deserved after all.

TEARS

OF THE

DRAGON

MICHAEL MCBRIDE

I

Chapel of the Chimes
Oakland, California
(Today)

"My name is Dr. Sam Himura and everything about my life has been a lie."

An uncomfortable silence falls over those gathered to pay their final respects to one of the most generous and gracious men most of them have ever known. A nervous shuffling of feet and clearing of throats. Uneasy glances are exchanged. Men and women in black stare at the screen positioned in front of the ornate wall where the golden book containing the ashes of the great man will forever be displayed alongside other great men. The man himself stares back at them through the screen and from the other side of the grave. His expression is one of sadness and regret and appears strangely foreign on a face furrowed with the lines of laughter and joy.

The funeral director unconsciously retreats deeper into the shadows of the darkened room, a ghostly apparition limned with the golden light from the projector attached to the laptop on the memorial stand beside the urn and the framed photograph of the man in his younger days. It was the decedent's wish that this final recorded message be played for the intimate assembly of his most cherished friends and family. Judging by their curious whispers and confused stares, none of them have any idea what's happening. They all look blankly at the larger-than-life representation of the ninety-seven-year-old man, whose gaunt frame betrays the fact that he is not long for this world as he struggles to form words that appear to cause him physical pain.

"I am not who you think I am. I have lied to each and every one of you since the moment we first met. I am not the man with whom you have shared your laughter and love. I ask not for your forgiveness or your sympathy, for I deserve neither." His bony shoulders rise as he takes a deep breath. Closes his eyes. He seems to deflate when he blows it out and again looks at the future gathering of mourners. "I am a murderer. And even now, with death imminent, I feel no remorse."

II

Epidemic Prevention and Water Purification Department
of the Kwantung Army
Pingfang District, Manchukuo
(1945)

The days were filled with the horrible screams and sobbing of the damned, but the nights were so much worse. Lying in their dark cells, listening to the whimpers and the prayers and the bleating of the dying, like so many tortured lambs. Each new day promised the sweet release of death for those whose pain grew progressively

TEARS OF THE DRAGON

more exquisite, and the arrival of even more voices to replace theirs in the chorus of suffering.

And with the dawn came the men in boots.

The boy had never actually seen them, but he had heard them. Clomping down the corridor outside his locked door, speaking in muffled voices devoid of all emotion. They spoke in a tongue he could not understand. He knew on a primal level that he should consider himself fortunate for that small favor. Those who understood were taken first and it was their awful cries he would attempt to tune out when the crimson sunset bled once more into the all-encompassing darkness that denied him the mercy of sleep.

The smell was one of sickness, of vomit, and urine, and blood, and diarrhea. No matter how often the men in masks and rubber boots came to hose them down and swab the room with dirty mops, the stench grew exponentially worse. The boy believed it had seeped into the concrete floors and the cinderblock walls and bloomed like sweat from them during the sweltering heat of the day. Not even the ammonia that made his eyes sting and his skin burn could conceal the reek of what he now equated with the scent of unadulterated fear, the pheromone the body secreted in anticipation of the soul's violent release.

The men in boots. They were saving him. Like the others crammed into that barren cell with him. They were saving him because he was a child, but for what purpose he didn't know, nor did he care to speculate. His only certainty was that each day spent locked in here with his own filth was a gift of life to be cherished, for its passage brought him one day closer to the morning the men in boots came for him. Unfortunately for him, today was that day.

The sound of jangling keys preceded the clank of the disengaging bolt, which echoed from the far end of the hallway.

The others pushed and shoved and fought their way back against the rear wall, beneath the window that had been sloppily painted over from the outside, as far away from the cell door as they could get. Some of the other children cried, while still others

239

attempted to silence them with sharp whispers and even hands clasped tightly over their mouths.

The squeal of a heavy door on rusted hinges.

The boy's heart pounded so loudly in his ears that at first he didn't hear the boots.

Thump. Thump. Thump. Thump.

The stride was measured, relaxed, as though the man were strolling through a market, perusing the fresh fruits and smoked fowl to either side of the narrow aisle.

The boy summoned every last ounce of courage he possessed. He needed to be brave. Not just for himself, but for the others, too. At seventeen he was the oldest and largest of them and he understood that if he didn't protect them, no one else would. He balled his sweaty hands to fists at his sides. His legs trembled as a shadow passed across the seam of light under the door.

The shadow stopped. He watched the thick soles of the boots turn to face the door that separated them. A sharp, unintelligible command and a riot of footsteps filled the corridor.

The boy closed his eyes as tightly as he could to stall the tears. He would not give them the satisfaction. He took a hesitant step forward and prepared for the inevitable.

The clamor of keys again, mere feet away.

He glanced back at the whimpering silhouettes of the others, still scrambling to force their way behind each other in a final desperate game of hide-and-seek.

The lock disengaged with a thud he felt against his chest as a physical blow. The iron door shrieked as it opened outward.

In a moment of mental clarity, the boy realized that death lurked just outside of this chamber of horrors. More importantly, he decided that he wasn't ready to die yet. Not in this miserable place and not with his cries reverberating through the darkness.

A line of light knifed into the room as the door opened. A shadow momentarily eclipsed it and the boy seized the opportunity. He charged at the shadow and caught it by surprise, staggering it.

He swung his fists with everything he had left. Kicked and bit like an animal.

A crack on the base of his skull and he tasted blood in the back of his mouth. His legs went numb and his vision exploded with sparks. Another blow, this time to his face. When his vision cleared it was the floor he saw, slick with a widening puddle of the blood he could feel rushing through his nose.

He rolled over and looked up at a blurred trio of men whose outlines converged to form a single man in olive fatigues. A tuft of black hair adhered to the butt of his rifle in a smear of glistening blood. The man's face was concealed by a tan mask with circular plastic lenses and a tube like an elongated elephant's trunk. He helped a man dressed in black from head to toe back to his feet.

The man in black brushed off the front of a smock that hung to mid-shin like a dress. He wore rubber gloves and boots sealed to the smock by lengths of thick tape. He shoved aside the man in olive, who fell back into rank with the other soldiers. He crouched in front of the boy, tipped up his chin so that he gagged on the blood pouring down his throat faster than he could swallow it, and stared into his eyes through the plastic lenses of his black gas mask.

"My name is Dr. Isamu Himura." He spoke in Mandarin so the boy could understand him, and even then the words sounded somehow wrong when he spoke. "You have a strong will to live. Not like these other animals. I admire that. What do you say? Shall we put that will of yours to the test?"

III

International Symposium on the Crimes of Bacteriological Warfare
Changde, China
(2002)

Translated from the Original Chinese Transcript:

MODERATOR: Mr. Zhou, it is your assertion that you were confined at the Pingfang facility in Manchuria from October, 1944 until its abandonment and subsequent Russian occupation in August, 1945.

HUANG ZHOU: That is correct, sir.

MODERATOR: Please describe for the assembly what you witnessed inside this detention camp.

HUANG ZHOU: The majority of my days were spent confined to a dark room with many other children. The windows were painted over from the outside. We were subjected to routine starvation for days at a time until the weakest among us died. Some of us received what we were told were routine inoculations. To this day I do now know what those syringes contained, but I was one of the few to survive their administration.

MODERATOR: What can you tell us about the camp itself, Mr. Zhou?

HUANG ZHOU: It was an enormous complex with a surprising number of buildings. You must understand, I did not see it with my own eyes until much of it was either destroyed or on fire, and even then I was rushed through the devastation by armed soldiers who spoke only Russian.

MODERATOR: Your caveat is noted, Mr. Zhou. Considering this symposium was convened with the intention of understanding war crimes of a bacteriological nature, perhaps I should have been more specific. Did you see any part of the plague-flea breeding program responsible for the spraying attack on this very city that caused the deaths of nearly six hundred thousand civilians?

HUANG ZHOU: If I did, I did not recognize it. I did see several industrial-size cauldrons and an assortment of barrels I believe contained chemical agents. And I saw mounds of bodies ... or at least what was left of them. I heard ... we all heard ... the surgeries they performed ... [unintelligible]—

MODERATOR: The vivisections?

HUANG ZHOU: Yes, sir. The screams still wake me at night.

The things they did to us...

MODERATOR: Did you hear any of your captors verbally acknowledge their affiliation with Unit 731, which the government of Japan—even so many years later—refuses to acknowledge?

HUANG ZHOU: Not in so many words, sir.

MODERATOR: But you heard names, didn't you Mr. Zhou?

HUANG ZHOU: [Clears throat]

MODERATOR: Mr. Zhou?

HUANG ZHOU: No, sir. I thought I did, but I was wrong. I am an old man. My memory is not what it once was.

IV

Epidemic Prevention and Water Purification Department
of the Kwantung Army
Pingfang District, Manchukuo
(1945)

The boy stood naked and shivering in the morning mist. Every inch of his soaked body was prickled with goosebumps. The men with the hoses had finally taken a break to warm their hands, granting the children a momentary respite from the worst of the cold. The boy could barely see the outline of a gray brick building across the field through the chain link fence. Its broad smokestacks churned greasy ashes into the sky and produced a mouthwatering scent that made him salivate, despite knowing exactly what they incinerated inside. His stomach clenched and the pangs of hunger he had until now been able to effectively ignore forced him to double over. He gritted his teeth, stood upright, and stared at the men with the gas masks. They were going to kill him, but he would not allow them to break him first.

"You children look so cold," Dr. Himura said through his black mask. "Wouldn't you like to warm up?"

The other children stood in a clump behind the boy, shivering and sobbing and crying for the parents whose ashes fell upon their bare shoulders like snow. A cloud of their breath obscured their small faces until a gust of wind swept it away. It was unseasonably cold for August, especially with the monsoon winds racing inland from the distant sea. The air would warm as the day progressed, but the afternoon rains would once again drench them before the temperatures plummeted into the night.

The boy wrapped his arms around his chest and tried to squeeze his privates between his thighs to preserve his heat.

One of the soldiers wheeled a covered cart past him, tipped it, and dumped its contents onto the gravel in a heap. The boy looked away before he lost his resolve. The blankets were still warm enough to issue faint tufts of steam. He closed his eyes and heard the patter of bare feet racing for the pile.

"Do not take them," he said, but his voice lacked conviction.

"Would you prefer to watch them freeze to death?" Dr. Himura said. "Without anything to contain your diminishing body heat, your skin will first grow cold and then red. Your breathing will slow and you will become confused, sleepy. Your speech will become slurred and your body will stop responding to your conscious commands. Eventually, you will stop shivering. Your pulse will slow. And—I assure you—you will die, but not until long after the pain in your fingers and toes becomes unbearable. Then again, maybe you will survive until the sun rises again and dispels the cold rain. Everyone can endure a single night of suffering, right?"

"Do not take the blankets," the boy said again. His eyes locked on those of the doctor through the glass eyeholes of his mask. "We will huddle together for warmth and die together if we must—"

The man in black cut him off with a laugh.

"I suggest you turn around and watch the sheep don their wool."

The boy glanced back to see the others snatching blankets from the pile and scurrying to the rear of the pen, where they crowded together and buried themselves inside the coarse brown blankets. They hid their faces from the wind, but he could still hear their whimpers.

Only a single younger boy of maybe eleven or twelve stood paralyzed by indecision, looking up at the boy with wide brown eyes filled with terror.

"I will keep you alive with my own heat. I promise you...you will survive."

"I guess we'll find out soon enough." Dr. Himura turned to his entourage. "Collect the bodies in the morning and have them pre-pared for vivisection by the time I arrive."

The boy understood the comment had been for his benefit, for the man in black always spoke to his men in Japanese. He wanted the boy to know that it didn't matter what he said or did; they were all going to die one way or another. Some worse than others.

The boy watched his captors lock the gate behind them and cross the field until they vanished into the mist, then took the younger boy by the hand.

"What you did was very brave."

"I am so cold."

"Tell me your name."

"Huang. Huang Zhou."

"You will not die today, Huang. You have my word."

V

An excerpt from the article: "Biotechnology Value Investing for the Nineties: The ABOs of playing the synthetic blood market." by Liam Reubens, *Biological Engineering & Technology News* (June/July, 1989; *Vol. 2, Num. 3*)

As of the end of the fiscal year, the sale of perfluorocarbon-based (PFC) oxygen carrying blood substitutes comprised nearly seventy percent of Tradewinds Pharmaceuticals' gross domestic receipts and accounted for more than four billion dollars in revenue. In conjunction with the increasing usage of steady performers like its coagulation and fibrolytic agents and the recently announced developments in immunological agents and diagnostic reagents, Tradewinds promises to be a leader in the hemodynamic revolution through the end of the millennium and beyond.

Dr. Isamu Himura, founder and Chief of Development, claims this is only the beginning of the new golden era of medicine. He believes his blood products will be used as a springboard for the advent of new surgical procedures and techniques, as well as a host of potential cures for any number of diseases.

"This is an exciting time in the field of biotechnology," the reclusive Dr. Himura said in an interview conducted in his unassuming Napa Valley home.

"Our knowledge base is expanding at an astronomical rate and brilliant discoveries are being made every day. It's only a matter of time before preventative measures take the place of radical treatments and the entire human race is ushered into a new and enlightened age of health and prosperity."

When asked about his rumored involvement with the government-reputed Unit 731 and its alleged human experimentation during the Second Sino-Japanese War and World War II, Himura smiled indulgently.

"Since the inception of Tradewinds, I have devoted my life and not-inconsiderable resources to the betterment of mankind. From my first PFC synthetic blood to any number of blood-based products designed to increase the lifespans and overall health of our species, to the billions we donate to various scholarship funds and grants on an annual basis, Tradewinds has demonstrated that its mission is more than just a statement; it is a way of life. Whatever people may think, I believe the true measure of any man is defined by his contribution to society."

VI

Epidemic Prevention and Water Purification Department
of the Kwantung Army
Pingfang District, Manchukuo
(1945)

"You must save your tears." The boy's teeth chattered so hard he
could barely understand his own words. "Your body requires the
fluid to keep your blood flowing."

They boy wrapped his arms even tighter around his young
charge and buried his face in Huang's hair. He gritted his teeth to
keep from biting his bleeding lips, which only served to make him
shiver harder. Already he could tell his body was succumbing to the
cold. All optimism had faded with the setting of the sun. The darkness summoned a wicked wind that lashed his bare back and thighs
with whips of frigid rain that burned like fire. He struggled to keep
his eyes open. Patches on his skin turned first blue, then white, and
with that transition came a level of pain beyond anything he had
ever experienced, like molten fishhooks baited with razor wire
latching into his flesh. Each shuddering inhalation hurt his chest
and seemed to turn to ice in his lungs. Time jumped back and forth
in bursts of blackness that lasted longer and longer with each epi-
sode.

He briskly rubbed Huang's bare skin, shielded the younger
boy's body with his own, and monitored his slowing pulse as best
he could. He wished he'd been wrong about the men and the blankets so he and Huang could join the others and hopefully survive
the night, but their cries had commenced before the sun even
burned off the morning fog and the first rain started to fall. One
girl had cast aside her blanket and run screaming through the pen,
her body literally black with fleas. After repeatedly attempting to
shake out the insects, which found their way back every time, the
others had resigned themselves to the fact that the pain from the

bites was the price they had to pay for what little warmth the drenched blankets provided. The bites turned to florid welts and the infection swelled to the size of eggs in the lymph nodes of their armpits and groins. Many sloughed off their blankets when their fevers spiked and whimpered pitifully with each wave of vomiting or crippling spasm of diarrhea.

Huang and the boy distanced themselves from them, dug the deepest trench they could with their frozen and bloody fingers, and attempted to fool themselves into believing that they had a prayer of surviving.

"Can you ... hear me ... Huang?" The child made no reply. His shivering had waned to random twitches. "You have to ... have to stay awake."

"Let me ... sleep ... tired ... so ..."

The boy shook Huang hard enough to make his teeth rattle.

"No. You will wake up ... wake up this very instant. Do you hear me, Huang? Do you—?"

A great burst of light from the building with the smokestacks and a wall of heated air and smoke rolled over them. The ground trembled with a reverberating *thoom*. Scorched bricks and flaming debris rained down upon them.

Another explosion. Another still.

Shouting voices.

Apparitions moved through the smoke. Hauling as much gear as they could carry. Running. Abandoning this hell of fire. Destroying every trace that they had ever been here before the Russians, who had just liberated Mengjiang, advanced into Manchukuo.

"Get up, Huang. You must help me."

The boy exhausted his strength pushing himself to his knees, which felt like they broke when he straightened them, and dragged himself up the fence until his feet were beneath him.

"Free us," he tried to scream, but his voice made a sound like breaking glass. "Please. Don't leave us in here ..."

VII

Chapel of the Chimes
Oakland, California
(Today)

"You need to understand that we are all a product of our times. Morality is nothing more than the prevailing wind in a tempestuous storm. What I did was no better or worse than anything that had been done to me and my people, and I have spent my entire life trying to make amends. To those I've wronged. To all of you whose lives have touched mine. To the world as a whole."

None of the mourners speak, for there are no words to express the maelstrom of thoughts and doubts colliding in their heads. Here was a man each of them placed on a pedestal, and now he was telling them that the heights to which he had convinced them to aspire were built upon a rickety framework of deception.

"I will not blame you for hating me or the world for demonizing me. As much as I was a product of my times, you are the product of yours, and I know which way the prevailing winds of morality now blow. Before you pass judgment upon me, though, I implore you to look at the world as it was through the eyes of a young man full of fear and hatred and pronounce his verdict not for his actions at the time, but for the actions he has taken since."

VIII

Epidemic Prevention and Water Purification Department
of the Kwantung Army
Pingfang District, Manchukuo
(1945)

The others were long dead by the time help arrived in the form of a

Russian detachment unprepared for what they found in the remote installation, but by then the boy was on the verge of death. The soldiers had been unable to look at the small corpses partially covered by the wet blankets that flagged on the breeze as they incinerated the soiled remains. The scent of all of that sickness and disease was the last thing the boy remembered before being carried off in the arms of a man in full isolation gear. The man's words were sluggish and ugly, but the boy had never heard anything so beautiful in his life.

He cried out for Huang in his physically compromised state. One minute the smaller boy's cold body had been cradled to his, and the next it was gone. He could no more remember what happened than he could communicate his desire to learn the fate of the child from these men.

Everything was a blur. Hours passed. Days. He fell asleep in an olive tent and awakened in the cargo hold of a covered transport vehicle with a dozen people like him crammed inside. Some were missing entire appendages, others eyes and teeth. Some had wicked wounds haphazardly sewn shut where organs had been removed. All of them were emaciated and pale. Most didn't survive the journey. None of them had seen a boy matching Huang's description, nor did any of them hold out much hope for the child's survival.

Only the boy believed, and no amount of stories of mountains of body parts or pits filled with corpses or mass incinerations could sway his conviction.

His parents on the other hand ... he'd known from the start there had been no hope for them. He'd recognized their voices in the chorus of the damned and was thankful their suffering had lasted only a single night. In his heart, he believed they had sacrificed their lives in exchange for his—for the mere chance that he might survive—because that was the kind of parents they were. And he would revere them and their sacrifice for the remainder of his days.

He explained as much to the Ukrainian nurse who helped with his rehabilitation in Taiyuan. She spoke just enough Mandarin to patronize him with her sad smile and solicitous words, but she had also been the one to convey the rumors circulating through the ranks of the Red Army. The evil men in charge of the facility where so many had been tortured to death had been rounded up by the Americans. The problem was the rumors also spoke of shady deals brokered by the Supreme Commander of the Allied Forces, Douglas MacArthur, himself. In exchange for the scientific data gleaned from their experimentation, the Japanese doctors would be granted immunity.

The boy hadn't believed her, of course. No human beings capable of perpetrating such heinous atrocities could ever escape execution, let alone receive any form of immunity from prosecution.

It was the face of the nurse he saw, whose words echoed inside his head, when he witnessed the proof with his own eyes.

IX

Tradewinds Pharmaceuticals Global Headquarters
San Francisco, California
(1984)

"Dr. Himura." The tone of his receptionist betrayed the fact that something was wrong. "There are gentlemen here to see you."

The doctor had known this day would come for several years. Nearly everyone involved with his initial deal had either moved on to greener pastures or was buried beneath them. He'd been content to remain in America for the remainder of his days in exchange for freedom. And then INTERPOL had gone and thrown a wrench in the works. For nearly forty years, the International Criminal Police Organization had refrained from assisting with the capture and prosecution of war criminals thanks to a liberal interpretation of Article 3 of its constitution, which forbade intervention in matters of a quote-unquote political nature. Once they officially joined the

Nazi hunt, though, it became open season on all of them.

Dr. Himura reached for the intercom to tell his receptionist to send them in, but his door burst open before his finger found the button. He closed his eyes, straightened his tie, and greeted his fate with an extended hand. The first two men through the door wore matching suits and introduced themselves with little more than a flash of their badges. FBI. The next two men wore suits of a different style, the kind that screamed foreigners. The older of the two wore brown wool and had a cloud of white hair encircling his bald crown; the other wore gray and wasn't old enough to have been a party to the rebuilding of Europe. His curly dark hair and telltale complexion suggested a personal stake in the prosecution of those responsible for the decimation of his people.

The older man stared at Dr. Himura's proffered hand with distaste. When he spoke, it was with a British accent.

"Are you Dr. Isamu Himura?"

"Yes, sir."

"The same Dr. Isamu Himura who served as one of the staff physicians for Unit 731 of the Japanese Imperial Army at the Ping-fang complex—also known as the Epidemic Prevention and Water Purification Department of the Kwantung Army—from 1942 to 1945?"

Dr. Himura didn't answer. Either response was a lie that would damn him.

"You've done quite well for yourself, doctor. Just look at this place. The real estate alone has to be worth millions. And this building?" He whistled appreciatively. "Sure looks like your dear old Uncle Sam set you up nicely."

"My achievements are my own."

"And the research for the products you manufacture here? Is that your own, too?"

"I have several teams of devoted—"

"You manufacture blood products, don't you?"

"That's a bit of an oversimplification, but yes, we—"

"And you started up right after the end of the war, correct? By 1950 you'd already made your first million without ever having to stand trial for the atrocities you committed—"

"This man is an American citizen and has his rights," one of the FBI men said.

"And we have a witness," the dark-haired man in the gray suit said. His eyes locked onto Dr. Himura's. "Speaking of whom ... would you please come in and join us?"

Dr. Himura turned away and faced the window behind his desk. He didn't want them to see the expression on his face. Instead, he stared out across the choppy blue waters of the bay toward the distant Golden Gate Bridge as he listened to the tentative approach of footsteps from the anteroom. He needed to commit this view to memory. This was the one thing he wanted to take with him.

With great reluctance, Dr. Himura turned to face his accuser.

X

Hong Kong, China
(1946)

While in the hospital, the boy met a man from the Hong Kong Kowloon Brigade, a group of patriots who'd utilized guerilla tactics during the Japanese occupation to rescue prisoners-of-war. He said his men had been helping to smuggle people out of the war-torn zones of China and into countries where they would be able to start their lives over again. He believed that if Huang had survived, the odds were good he would have been helped to reach San Francisco, where there were people willing to take in orphans of the war, especially those who were young enough to be absorbed into existing family units. He'd even gone so far as to arrange for someone to meet with the boy down in Hong Kong. Even then, the boy

TEARS OF THE DRAGON

knew finding Huang was a long shot, but he liked the prospect of securing passage for himself on one of the American freighters.

It was while he was working on a container ship called the *Looby Louise* that he saw the face of the man who haunted his dreams. His eyes, anyway. He would have recognized the man's eyes anywhere, even in the briefest of glimpses across a deck crammed with containers.

And then he was gone.

It took the boy two days to find him again on a ship the size of a small town and the majority of the third day to locate the cabin in which the Americans had stashed him.

On the fourth day, when the mainland was a distant memory behind them, he waited until the man—dressed in the uniform of the merchant marine and speaking exclusively English—went above decks to take his midday meal, then broke into the cabin, where he waited in the darkness amid boxes and crates filled with notes and photographs, and detailed anatomic drawings and folders brimming with the tragic ends that befell men and women whose lives had been reduced to numbers.

He stood behind the door with a length of rope stretched tightly between his fists and waited until he heard the clap of footsteps outside the door and the key hit the lock.

Before the doctor could turn, the boy wrapped the rope around his neck, jerked him into the room, and closed the door with his hip.

The doctor died far too quickly and mercifully, but there was no avoiding that outcome. Screams would have drawn too much attention, and besides, the boy was nothing like this monster who had tortured so many. The act of taking this one life—the life of one who so clearly and desperately deserved it—was more than he could bear.

He vomited onto the floor while the dead man stared at him through eyes he would never forget, eyes that would continue to stare into the horrors waiting from him in the abyss until the crabs plucked them from his head and his remains rotted into the silt, not too terribly far from Pearl Harbor.

The boy had been prepared to take responsibility for his actions, but he had understood, even at such a young age, that the boxes and crates were what was important to the Americans, not the scientist responsible for collecting the data. They undoubtedly detested the doctor so much that they could barely stomach being in his presence, let alone look at him for any length of time.

So it was during the remaining eleven days at sea that the boy committed to memory as many of the files as he could and absorbed every word of English he heard. The worst of the files he purged in the boiler. The rest he turned over to the Americans when they docked in San Francisco. He dressed like the doctor. He acted like the doctor. He even talked like the doctor.

The fiends willing to trade their souls for his knowledge knew he was the epitome of evil and never once stared at the face of a physician who might have looked a lot younger than they expected if they had.

So little did they care about his past or what anyone might think of his presence, they set him up with a bank account under the name of Dr. Sam Himura and left him with the credentials of a dead man and new documents with his picture to go along with the life of a man whose intimate knowledge of blood and clotting factors he now possessed.

And he could think of no better way to disrespect the memory of the monster than by using that knowledge for the betterment of society.

XI

Tradewinds Pharmaceuticals Global Headquarters
San Francisco, California
(1984)

TEARS OF THE DRAGON

Dr. Himura stared into the face of a man maybe five or six years his junior. Even after so many years he would have recognized this man anywhere.

"Mr. Zhou?" the INTERPOL agent with the dark hair said. "Is this the man you remember from the Pingfang complex in 1945?"

Dr. Himura felt a lump rise in his throat. It was all he could do not to cry.

"Mr. Zhou? Is this the same Dr. Isamu Himura who subjected you to routine starvation and left you to freeze to death in the rain rather than accept one of the flea-infested blankets he used to infect the others with the bubonic plague?"

Huang looked him directly in the eyes and they shared a moment of recognition. Dr. Himura wanted nothing more than to embrace the man for whom he had always held out hope.

"No," Huang said. "I have never seen this man before in my life."

"This is Dr. Isamu Himura. The only man by that name who ever worked at Pingfang. The same one who copped a deal with the American military to save his worthless—"

"I think we're done here," the FBI agent said.

Huang looked Dr. Himura in the eyes for a moment longer, then, with a nod and the faintest hint of a smile, turned and left the office.

XII

Chapel of the Chimes
Oakland, California
(Today)

"My name is Jun Fang and I murdered Dr. Isamu Himura nearly seventy years ago. I am not ninety-seven years old; I am only eighty-six. I have lied to you all. Worse, I have betrayed your trust.

So it is with great dishonor that I pass from this life to the next. I pray you all know how very special each of you are to me and how very sorry I am for deceiving you."

The recording stops. The screen freezes on the image of the old man, his eyes downcast in shame.

An elderly man separates from the gathering and approaches the table upon which the decedent's golden book sits. He stands silhouetted against the image as he stares up at it. He wraps his arms around his chest as though to stifle a shiver. When he finally looks away, his eyes seek the old man's ashes. He kisses his fingertips and presses them to the golden urn. He turns to face the mourners with tears in his eyes and speaks in little more than a whisper.

"I would like to tell you a story about a boy..."

PHANTOM

ON THE

ICE

ERINN L. KEMPER

October 2, 1992, Eutsuk Lake Lodge, British Columbia, Canada

Jeremy Chambers checked the hockey bag for leaks.

They'd frozen the body parts, wrapped in garbage bags and duct tape, but he still smelled blood. Probably would for weeks to come. He strapped in to the co-pilot's seat and put on his earphones while his dad did a final pre-flight check on Roger's plane. Doctor Hannan took a seat in back, as far from the hockey bag as he could, and stared out the window.

Vancouver was three hours away. There they would turn over the body, what was left of it, to authorities who would ship to the family in Oakland for burial. A place called Chapel of Chimes.

Roger stayed behind despite evacuation orders. The fire was still on the other side of the hills. He said if it got too close he'd load what he needed in the jet boat and wait in the middle of the lake for pickup. The old caretaker watched from the dock as they taxied out for take-off.

Oakland Tribune, September 15, 1992

Is Sharp Benched for Good?
Local Player #22 Fails to Impress in
Pre-Season Matchup

San Jose Sharks power forward Brent Sharp was pulled from play last night in his first game against the Boston Bruins since the incident early last season that left him in a coma, and left the Sharks floundering for their first season on the ice.

"He'll be back and better than ever." Sharks Coach George Kingston sounded confident in an interview yesterday. The Sharks built the entire team around Sharp, the highest paid rookie in NHL history, claiming #22 as the next Gordie Howe. Without Sharp, the Sharks' second season looks likely to go belly up.

September 28, 1992, Eutsuk Lake, British Columbia, Canada

"It's a miracle he's still walking around." Ted Chambers rubbed his knee and shook his head. "One tough SOB. You see that game?"

"Nah. Missed it. But I did see the hit. They showed it on TV every day for a while there." Jeremy felt queasy remembering the incident. He poured coffee from the silver Thermos his dad kept full throughout the day, but passed on the whiskey bottle that sat between the sugar and the powdered creamer. Roger had already filled his cup on his way out to dump the garbage. He took the John Deere and a small thermos that held mostly whiskey. Took his gun, too, to scare off the bears that prowled the dump site.

"Head first into the boards. Like a dang torpedo. Kid kept getting up, trying to get to the bench. That's what got me. All jelly-

260

legged and swerving. Three tries before he stayed down." His dad pulled the checked curtain aside. "Look at him now. Fit as a fiddle."

In the news from two years ago journalists reported Sharp's brain had swelled up after the accident, and he lay in a coma while everyone—teammates, coaches, commentators—speculated on his fate. On the fate of the team. Then there was the recovery, months of testing and rehabilitation, and his miraculous return the next season. But it looked like the season was over for him now, possibly his career before it even really started.

Jeremy and his dad watched the hockey player in the amber wash of dawn. Brent Sharp sipped coffee and stared out at the lake and the mountains beyond. Even the grand expanse of wilderness couldn't make him look small. From the moment he stepped onto the Twin Otter, ducking through the pill-shaped door, hockey bag slung over his shoulder, Jeremy had marveled at the man's size.

Two people had come with him. His petite, dark-haired fiancée, Tamara. Her sunglasses and makeup almost hid the bruising around her eye. And Doc Hannan, built like a tennis player, with a quiet voice and a salesman's smile. Jeremy helped them board the float plane, handing up suitcases and fishing gear, the roar of the propeller behind him. When Brent Sharp stepped on the pontoon, the metal flexed. Next to them all, the man was a Goliath.

"You going to take him trolling, or casting?"

"Casting, I think. It occupies the brain a little more. Apparently he liked it as a kid. Mr. G said to keep his mind off hockey and whatever's going on with his fiancée."

"That'll be tough." Ted nodded out the window. Tamara, hair wrapped in a towel, the rest of her bound in spandex, approached Brent. She stopped a few meters behind and he turned, likely in response to her voice. He frowned and took another sip of his coffee. Her mouth moved rapidly and she raised her arms in a shrug of frustration, then strode back to their cabin.

Jeremy's dad cleared his throat. "Well, you boys catch us some dinner. Got the barge coming later with fuel and supplies. Good thing, too. With that fire over by Vanderhoof, people are going to be pretty busy up there."

———————▲———————

Mist rose from the lake in cumulous drifts that spun away from the bow. Jeremy headed for the far end, cutting through the mercury grey water to where the Eutsuk River spilled in with its load of kokanee and trout. The hockey player sat hunched in the front of the boat, turning his head to track a flock of ducks that sped low over the water.

From the plane the lakes spread like a circlet of glinting blue jewels, connected by rivers, on an undulating velvet of forested hills. But from the boat the lakes were huge, feeding one into the next, completely isolated.

Brent Sharp remained quiet, his gaze drifting like the haze on the water. They ran the boat up on the grassy point just east of the river mouth and unloaded their gear. Brent squatted with his rod laid out in front and tied on a weighted lure.

Once his own rig was ready, Jeremy walked over to check the hockey player's rig. Brent was testing the knot on his lure as Jeremy came up beside him.

"How are you—"

A fist hit him in the stomach like a sledge hammer and he fell, landing hard on his back. The rest of the wind knocked out of him when he hit the ground. He lay there, staring up at the sky, blinking back tears, body screaming for air.

"Shit man. I'm so sorry. I didn't know it was you." Brent stood over him, grabbed his hand and pulled him up. "Breathe, man. You'll be fine."

Jeremy tried to answer, but all that came out was a strangled groan.

"See, better already." Brent slapped his back.

When Jeremy could breathe again, he asked, "Who'd you think it was, if it wasn't me?"

Brent shrugged and grabbed the gutting knife. He trimmed the loose ends of line close to the knot, then laid the knife aside. "That's what the doc keeps asking. And Tamara. I don't know."

"Wow. This has happened before?"

"I take it you don't watch hockey?" Brent smiled and stood, giving the rod a few test sweeps before casting his line.

"Sorry. Not really my thing."

"That's why they pulled me this season."

Brent told his story while they fished, in short spurts between casts. He'd clearly been over it so many times his voice took on a flat, matter-of-fact tone.

"When I came out of the coma I bounced back pretty quick. I just wanted to get out on the ice. They did a few tests and then the doctors gave the green light. Practice went good. Just like before. I was in the zone, making plays." Brent swung the rod in nice easy strokes, then let the line fly.

"Our first game was with the Bruins. Same team as before. But I wasn't worried."

It started like any other, Brent said. At first the lights, the noise, the music overwhelmed him. But that quickly faded until all that was left was the scrape of metal on ice, the smack of the hockey sticks and the grunts and shouts of the players. Sharp focused on the game, the puck, the geometry of the play. It was easy…all the visualizing techniques their coach subjected them to, the Doc with his talk of embodied images and seeing the win…didn't factor. Go, puck, play. He sped across the ice, turned, and the puck came to him. Every time he was where he needed to be.

Halfway through the third period something fell out of place. Sharp skated behind the goal, bringing the puck around for a pass up the ice and someone came toward him from the side, fast. Faster than any Bruin could skate. Coming hard so his gut clenched in anticipation of the crunch against the boards. Sharp stopped, blades shearing a wave of ice off the rink, and changed direction, leaving the puck behind. The Bruins #8 came in, took the puck and the game-winning goal.

Brent watched the play later with his coach, watched himself flinch, stop short, and reverse. Alone in the corner. No one there bringing a challenge. And that was just the first of many. In the next few games he ducked, feinted, changed direction when there was no player checking him. He sometimes threw his arm or shoulder at someone skating by, his own teammate, the ref, on-ice and then off.

"So you thought I was a Bruin? That's what you saw?"

Brent landed the trout he'd been playing. It flopped on the mossy ground. He picked up a rock, held the fish down with one hand and crushed its skull in three sharp blows.

"Kinda. I don't know. I saw something. Anyways, Doc says he's gonna figure it out. They did lots of tests in case there was some damage, to my brain, I guess. Nada. They sent me home for a bit, me and Tamara, to my folks in Oakland. But the media kept at us. So I'm here under orders to relax. Talk to the Doc. Catch some fish. Make things good with Tamara...if that's possible." He reeled in, and set his rod down. When he turned to face Jeremy his eyes held a glint of desperation. "I just want to get back to the game. That's all."

———————▲———————

Jeremy spent the afternoon sketching while the hockey player had his therapy session. He sat on an outcropping under the main lodge. The expanse of lake stretched west, no end in sight. The wide dock in front, two planes resting like water bugs on either side. With charcoal sticks he tried to capture the contrasts, the mirrored gloss of the lake, the stone cast shadows of the shoreline, the way tree branches cut dark swaths from the sky.

He listened to his Walkman, flipping the Dire Straits tape back and forth, but clicked the music off when Brent Sharp walked into view.

In swim trunks that stretched over the bunched muscles of his legs, he strode along the dock, stopped at the end, wind-milled his arms and shrugged his shoulders, his back rippling and flexing with the movement.

Jeremy flipped to a new page and sketched—the convex curve of flesh on either side of the spine that rose from the solid arches of his buttocks, the smaller ligaments and tendons, like little animals wrestling under his skin. A different kind of landscape with power surging beneath. Jeremy held his breath as Brent launched himself into the Eutsuk Lake. He slammed into the water and surfaced with a whoop of exhilaration.

A creak from the deck above and Tamara's voice. "How did it go?"

Chairs scraped across the floor as two people sat to watch Brett swim the lake. Jeremy tried to tune them out and concentrate instead on his sketch. He tore the quick figure drawing out and started on a new page, wanting to create a more detailed image.

Doctor Hannan's voice caught his attention. "... might still be the trauma of the accident. That he's afraid of it happening again, afraid of another injury. Medically the doctors said he was fine." They were talking about Brent, his fiancée and his therapist. "We did some work on visualization, looked at some tapes to see if he could tell me more about what happened. He said there haven't been any incidents since we got here. At least that's progress."

"If he can't play next season... my dad says they'll have to take the team in a different direction. Without Brent."

"Let's hope it doesn't come to that. We need you to stick by him for this to work." Doc Hannon's tone was neutral and soothing. "You two are the Kennedys of the sport. Well, maybe that's a bad example. But you're hockey royalty. You can have it all. You just have to give him time."

"Well, if he doesn't play next season, I'm out. Without hockey, I mean, look at him. He's lost."

The hockey player surged through the water with force and focus, ripping across the reflected sky.

Jeremy lay awake in the dark, listening to the restless scuff of branches against the roof. He wondered if Brent remembered hitting him in the stomach while they were fishing, or if he was just keeping it from his Doctor. An intermittent snore permeated the wall from his father's room. The distant call of a loon haunted the dark, and then the sharp voices of Brent and his fiancée arguing cut across the water.

———————▲———————

Bristling undergrowth scraped at Jeremy's ankles as he ran. The morning light slanted through the trees, striping the ground with long shadows. He stayed in front, setting the pace, but he'd started out too fast and now he struggled to control his breathing and the cramp that sliced through his side. The hockey player ran behind, the rhythmic thud of his feet on the ground was the only sound he made.

They ran along the track that led to a weedy old airstrip, and on around the lake.

"Thanks for letting me tag along. Can't let the training slide too much."

Jeremy gave a thumbs up; it was all he could manage.

"Couldn't do this back in Oakland. In case reporters tracked us down. Especially after what happened with Tamara. Had to keep that out of the paper."

Jeremy was going to ask what he meant, but it really felt like Brent talked to himself, that if he had to deal with a question he might stop. Besides, earlier Jeremy had seen Tamara approach her fiancé, and when he turned in her direction, fist coming up fast, not knowing she was there, or what was there, she flinched and stepped back, her arms coming up to shield herself. They faced each other, saying nothing. Brent looked at his fist, uncurled his fingers and lowered his arm. Tamara left him standing there, hands limp at his sides.

"This is a great summer job you got. Mr. G said you're at Stanford. Good school. What are you taking? Art? I've seen you drawing. You look really into it."

"Law." Jeremy managed to speak without panting.

"Huh. You like that?"

All he could do was shrug. A loaded question, and in the face of Brent's honesty a real answer seemed like the right thing. "My grandfather was a lawyer."

"That's wild. Mine played hockey. My dad too. Both team captains and all that. It's the family business, I guess. Gramps is probably half of the money behind the team."

"But you like hockey, right?" Jeremy slowed down and turned to look back at Brent. He hadn't even broken a sweat.

"Like? I live hockey."

They hit the top of a rise and the path opened up onto rocky slope with a view down to the lake. They stopped running. Jeremy bent forward and put his hands on his knees, breath coming in short rasps, sweat raining down on the ground.

"Must be a lot of pressure." He gasped out the words.

"Pressure's part of it, man. Sure you can drop out. Come to a place like this and disappear. That's easy. But if it's something you love, you gotta stick with it. Otherwise you lose." The hockey player turned and set off for the lodge at his own pace. Jeremy didn't try to catch him.

———————▲———————

The mountains seemed to inhale the remaining light from the sky; they expanded, drew closer, as the remnants of day slipped behind.

Tired and sore, Jeremy approached the cabin he shared with his dad. The door stood open and from inside he could hear the rustle of papers turning. He peered in and watched as his dad flipped through the sketchpad. The first pages contained landscapes, detailed drawings of trees, flowers, a bear Jeremy spotted fishing up river—his dad flipped past those quickly.

Then he turned to a new sketch and recoiled visibly. But he didn't turn the page. It was the drawing of Brent Sharp, arms out to the side, poised and ready for his first dive into the lake. Ted

Chambers studied the drawing, then flipped slowly to the next. The hockey player, in a sweat-soaked t-shirt and jeans, chopping firewood. And the next. Brent sitting on the porch steps, staring intently at a photo of himself, #22, strapped in all his gear, stick up, poised to shoot.

"Hey, dad." Jeremy pushed the door open the rest of the way and walked in the cabin.

"Oh, hey there. Sorry. It was just sitting here." His dad held up the notebook, then looked at the last drawing again. "These are really good."

"Thanks." Jeremy waited a moment, but his dad didn't say anything more. "Well, good night."

⁕

Jeremy stumbled back to the lakeside, stomach clenched, hands shaking. The morning sun glared off the water, and he blinked the wash of red and dark that nibbled at his consciousness, thundered in his ears.

Brent was cleaning a fish. He rammed the blade into the stomach, splitting the flesh in a perfect incision through which entrails spilled on the rocks in a grey mound.

"You find Tamara?" Brent looked up.

Jeremy opened and closed his mouth, no idea what to say, so he just pointed. Brent stood, still holding the knife, hands coated in a sludge of gore. He stared at Jeremy a moment, then dropped the knife and ran.

Of course he had to go back. As Jeremy approached the clearing he could hear the hockey player's bellow of horror when he reached the pool, then his frantic cries for his fiancée that moved around as he hunted for her—or her body.

When Jeremy arrived at the spot where the hot spring bubbled up through the stone—where Tamara had shed her clothes and folded them in a neat pile, where the water was stained a dark rust, rocks slick with arterial spray, air heavy with the hot stench of fresh meat—he found Brent, on his knees, blood-streaked hands curled up on his lap like dead insects, eyes stunned flat with shock.

"She's gone."

———————▲———————

They spent the rest of the day looking. They took guns and flash-lights. Roger was the only hunter, but they all knew to follow the drag marks that tore through the underbrush until they lost the trail when the terrain got too rocky. Then they searched for caves that might be used as dens, for niches and ravines. Roger radioed the police in Vanderhoof. He got a dispatcher, but with the fire evacua-tion underway there it would be a while before anyone could come, he said.

Cougars, bears, wolves—Jeremy knew all the possible threats. Probably more coming this way as the flames drove them south. He pictured what must have happened. Tamara alone in the hot spring, relaxed, vulnerable. Then something—Jeremy imagined it as a black shadow—descended on her, ripping flesh, sending blood out in gusts, the dark tangle of forest swallowing her screams.

They searched until it was dark. From the boat as they mo-tored back to the lodge, a glow on the horizon, the faint red stain of fire in the distance...

———————▲———————

"I can't see it anymore." Brent spoke to his therapist, his voice slow, slurring, like he was hypnotized.

They waited in the lodge for instructions from the Vancouver RCMP. Jeremy sat on the deck, his Walkman earphones in, but the tape had ended and he didn't turn it over. Brent's voice seeped through the dining room window.

"I go through the steps you taught me. I'm in the theater, watching myself play. And I'm great. I'm on fire. Then I climb up to the screen and open the door and I'm in the game. But it's dif-ferent. The stick feels slippery, the ice is wet, you know, and it sucks at my skates, slowing me down. But it's not really me any-more. It's him. #22. And then it's there. It's so fast. Coming at #22 and he can't get away."

"What is it? Can you see it clearly now?"

"It's in a Sharks uniform. I can't see the number. I don't think it has one."

"And the face? Does it have a face?"

"Yes. I can see it. It lowers its head, charges towards me, but at the last second, before the check, it looks up. It's faceless ... then for a moment it looks like me ... just a moment ... then nothing. A phantom. It doesn't have a face. Nothing."

The Twin Otter idled, tethered to the dock. They had delayed their departure until the fog burnt off the lake. The RCMP would be waiting for them when they landed in Vancouver. There'd be questions before Brent and Doctor Hannan could go back to California. And someone would be dispatched to make a proper search of the area once the fire threat had passed.

Brent sat on the lodge stairs, his bag packed, and Tamara's set beside. He held the hockey photo, but looked instead at the mountains, at the black plumes of smoke that erupted in the distance. He curled and uncurled the photo, his huge hands awkward handling something so delicate. Those hands Jeremy had seen squeezed in a fist, gripping a knife and streaked with blood, hanging limp and helpless when they called off their search for his fiancée.

"I think something happened. By the river. Tamara was with me. Said fishing was boring. Suggested we go to the hot spring. Then—" Brent dropped his head to his hands.

"You can't remember?"

"You know what I said the other day. It's true, isn't it?" Brent's voice sounded muffled, rusty. "You gotta stick with what you love."

Jeremy nodded, a sick feeling churned in his guts. There was nothing he could say, so he said nothing.

His dad waved to them from the plane. They stood and walked down the path to the dock. Brent Sharp looked different, softer, his t-shirt hung like loose skin from his shoulders. The lake beyond them so still it vanished, like you could walk down into the reversed horizon, down into a mirror of the world, maybe one where there was only silence, only peace.

They walked along the dock, boards creaking, shifting with each step. The hockey player's feet fell heavy on the wood, hollow, slow.

Jeremy started loading their bags. His dad waved from the cockpit, mouth wide in a shout he couldn't hear over the engines. He turned to look. Brent had walked past the passenger door, around the wing and the propeller, to the end of the dock.

The hockey player stood a moment, took a deep breath of mountain air that seemed to fill him, bring him back to size. He started back to the plane, eyes glassed over with a wash of too many tears shed. He walked straight, then wavered and looked left as though something was there, coming at him over the water. He went sideways—fell, jumped, it was hard to tell. But he hit the plane's propeller hard. The blades sliced through him like an ax, sending chunks in all directions, splashing into the water, thudding onto the dock, against the plane.

Something hit Jeremy and he fell back under its stony weight. He grabbed on reflexively as a hot curtain of blood slid down his face, filling his eyes and his mouth, choking his scream. Blood covering everything.

He blinked his eyes clear and looked down at what he held. Brent Sharp's arm, muscles still bulging, still in motion, lay across his chest. Fingers clutched at his shirt in desperate convulsions, shuddered, then were still.

THE LIBRARIAN

5

Down, down, down you go, returning to the ground floor, or what you imagine is the ground floor, through a maze of never-ending hallways and rooms, past smaller yet more delicate rooms that serve as chapels with names labeled next to each arched entrance: names such as Chapel of Forgiveness, or Chapel of Hope, or Chapel of Redemption; through gardens that could be either indoors or out for the light shining through the ever-changing ceilings—flat, high-vaulted, peaked, domed, stained-glass—is bright and misleading; through off-level rooms that cascade one into the other that are full of greenery and trickling fountains, some with spires twice the size of man, some with angel figures adorning the walls, some covered in broken-tile mosaics.

Some of the rooms you pass appear entirely golden because of the light— every book, ornament, hand-carved molding, even the floor, looks as if dipped in pure gold—and it is in one of these golden rooms the librarian takes you to find the next three golden books on their glowing shelves.

The entire room warms you, yet you feel an impending finality as you somehow understand these will be the last three books of the dead your guide— this current librarian—will show you.

"You will be able to do the same," the voice haunts.

NIGHT
SOLILOQUY

SYDNEY LEIGH

Freddy "Flowers" Forsythe could not have loved Fern more. That's why the tragedy that laid his wife to rest in Oakland's Chapel of the Chimes was so strange.

For a time, all of San Francisco talked about her death. Many still do, and rightfully so. Had *you* been there, standing under the neon glow of a sign on those dark city streets, or perhaps watching from a window, or passing by in a car, you might still be talking about it, too. *If* you made it out alive, that is.

I wasn't so lucky myself.

———————◆———————

Freddy was a fixture on the floors of the San Francisco Flower Mart, and on the industry itself. He'd seen the grand opening of the Terminal in 1956, and thirty years prior, helped his old man wrap bouquets on Fifth and Howard. Freddy knew his flowers like no one else... but there was no blossom, no petal, no fragrance that he loved more than Fern.

Fern was a leggy brunette with a heart-shaped ass and a side smile that made men weak in the knees and firm in the rise. But she belonged to Freddy, and we respected that. Not because he was the jealous type; Flowers didn't have a mean bone in his body. At fifty-one, he had kind eyes that matched both his voice and his nature. As a straight man, even *I* can admit Flowers was as handsome as he

275

was gentlemanly. He worked hard, played hard, and deserved a woman like Fern. He was, quite simply, just a hell of a guy ... and, to be honest, I'd like to think I was, too.

———————————▲————————————

Fern sang at Griff's, a place named after my brother which we co-owned and I ran while he raised his family and tried to get a vineyard off the ground up in Calistoga. I never married, and suppose it's because someone who spends all his time behind a bar pouring drinks, sweeping cigarette butts, and wiping down countertops might not be a dream come true for a girl. But my name was Kingston Cole, and they called me "King" for short. And for a while, I felt as though that's exactly what I was.

Several nights a week, Fern enchanted Griff's crowds with a voice as rich and romantic as a dozen red roses. She really was something—a rare and elegant arrangement hand-picked by the gods themselves.

Not that there weren't other women, mind you. The clubs in those days were hopping with girls who loved the West Coast at night and were game to fly wherever the bay breeze took them. Some were single, some weren't, and none held a candle to Fern; but that still didn't deter me and the other boys on Nob Hill from trying to sweep them off their feet.

And boy, does *that* phrase carry a whole new meaning now.

———————————▲————————————

The year things went wrong had started off right for a lot of us, but then again, San Francisco was dynamic in the seventies. What remained of the city's denizens had survived the Zodiac and Zebra killings, saw the rise of gay pride, and the backlash against it.

Flowers and Fern were so happy it was almost contagious, and come September, Flowers made a big to-do about her fortieth birthday. Fern was eleven years his junior, an only child, and her parents never left their East Coast hometown. We were all she had, and didn't mind one bit. Fern was our mascot, if you will. But one you wanted to give more than a high-five.

She was a siren and a songbird; a prodigy, of sorts. That girl could play any instrument you put in her hands: guitar, saxophone, piano... she was even known to get behind a set of drums like she was Buddy Rich or Max Roach in high heels and a sequin dress. She moved here from New York to attend the conservatory right out of high school, and whatever she didn't learn there she already knew inherently, like a gift.

So when Flowers bought her an old Artley flute from the antique shop on Fillmore, we were all eager to see her put that long, magic silver whistle to her pretty little lips. Problem was, we were expecting the wrong kind of magic.

San Francisco was just coming off the heels of another tragedy that shook our city to the core and gave us all one more reason to look over our shoulders and expect the unexpected. The Golden Dragon Massacre had riled a lot of people up earlier that month and left a handful of innocents dead and, granted, none of the boys from either side ever spent any time at Griff's. But it made eating or working in restaurants a dangerous thing to do, much like the Zodiac made us feel unsafe sitting in parked cars, going to a library, driving a taxi.

It was a dynamic world.

And change can't always be for the better.

The first night Fern picked up that flute, we were hypnotized. She played a dreamy piece called *"Danse de la Chèvre,"* and not a soul in the joint was talking after the sixth note.

It was a different sound and mood to which we were accustomed. No one got up to dance, or sang along, or tapped their feet. We all just...listened.

After that, things *really* changed. And so did Fern.

Fridays and Saturdays were big for regulars, but also for honeymooners and tourists dropping by for a night to wet their whistles or break in a new pair of dancing shoes. I like to think Griff's was a place you could go for a good time: decent food, strong drinks, live music, hip crowd. We had something no other bar, lounge, or club in all of Nob Hill had—or beyond, for that matter. We had Fern.

So you can understand that a lonely, haunting melody on an unusual instrument like a flute might be captivating for a spell, but for a room full of young, sweaty people drunk on life, love, and lust, something a little jauntier than "*Nature Boy*" was in order.

"Get up there, Fern," I remember my waitress Gina yelling.

Fern tossed back the last of her martini before heading for the small stage. Rollo, our piano player, lent her a hand before sitting down at the Steinway.

"What'll it be, young lady?"

Fern reached for her flute case.

"Oh, girl!" Rollo pled. "Let's do something with a little more pizzazz." He tore into an intro of "*Whole Lotta Shakin' Going On*" and the crowd whistled and howled.

Fern leaned in close to Rollo while he played. Her long, silky hair fell in front of her face, and she tucked the auburn slip behind an ear. "I thought I would play something a little quieter."

But when Fern took the flute out of its bone and saddle-colored case, one of the boys near the stage quoted Ferlinghetti and yelled, "Fuck art, let's dance!"

Fern set down the flute, nodded to Rollo, and smiled.

Saul Beckman was the first to die. According to the others, he was no drunker than usual, but raising hell on the roof deck patio when he went backwards over a railing. It was late night, or early morning—however you want to look at it—and witnessed by the same crew that gathered topside most nights to howl at the moon and revel in the buzzy glow of a growing industrial skyline. The novelty of the Pyramid had yet to wear off, and some nights you could see it through the smog draped over the city.

The only thing different about this night was Fern, sitting in Freddy's lap playing Bach's "*Little Fugue*" while the gang knocked back their last drinks. I was behind the bar, and as a result caught a glimpse of Saul through the front window on his way down … though at the time I had no idea what I was seeing. It's hard to wrap your head around a dark shadow rushing past the glass being one of your customers kissing the sidewalk at thirty miles per hour.

Through tears and a spell of retching, Gina told me everything once the police cleaned up and cleared everyone to leave.

According to Gina, Fern was sitting in Freddy's lap playing her flute while everyone smoked, drank, and did all the same things they did late night on the roof of the bar. At one point, Freddy came downstairs to hit the head, and when he did, Saul slid into Freddy's chair and pulled Fern onto his lap. Normally, any one of the guys could have done such a thing and earned a playful slap. But Fern wasn't amused, and stood up. Saul patted her ass, and Fern whirled around with a glare.

"Fern, baby…what's with you?"

"Don't call me that."

"What?" Saul laughed. "But that's your name, baby!"

"That's *not* what I meant."

Gina said Fern's eyes were glazed over, angry.

Saul grabbed the flute out of her hands and held it to his mouth like a microphone. "*Baby come back*," he sang, words and judgment equally slurred. Fern ripped the flute out of his grip, and in the process gave his mouth a good jab with the lip plate.

"What the fuck, Fern?" Saul jumped up and brought a hand to his mouth. A bit of blood pooled in one corner. "Jesus! What the hell is wrong with you?"

Gina put an arm around Fern and led her to another corner of the roof.

"What are you doing with that thing, anyway?" Saul yelled after her. "This isn't the fucking *Philharmonic*, you know. It's a fucking *bar*, Fern. Put that thing away, for Christ's sake. We're sick of it."

Freddy returned and tried to calm things down rather than explode and belt the guy mouthing off to his wife.

Gina asked Fern to play another song to keep her occupied. Fern said she'd like to show Gina a special piece with a name Gina couldn't pronounce, some kind of Romanian funeral song.

What happened next is unclear.

Still pissed, Saul lit a cigarette by the edge of the roof deck as Freddy walked back toward the others. He waved his hand, said, "Just give him a minute."

Within that minute, Saul cried out and was gone. How he fell or managed to go over that railing is anyone's guess. I had theories, of course, but those came later. At the time, it was a shock and just bewildered the hell out of us all.

Either way, Saul ended up in a puddle of his own blood, piss, and shit, and looked just like the bodies you see in movies after falls—arms and legs sprawled out and facing all the wrong directions. That's not something you forget.

We closed down for a few days to honor Saul. After that, it felt better to be together, and in all honesty, a few drinks seemed to help put it out of our minds. There were moments and tears, don't get me wrong, but we tried to get back to normal and find some laughter. You know what they say—that's usually the best medicine. Usually.

The night we reopened, Rollo was working his side job playing progressive jazz at the *hungry i* in North Beach, and Fern was playing Debussy on her flute. Standing alone in the middle of the stage with a soft yellow light around her, she went into a trance that was both strange and beautiful at the same time. With her eyes closed, hips and shoulders swaying in an alternating rhythm, she appeared almost serpentine. I'll be damned, that hourglass figure was something to behold—her breasts heaved as she drew in air and pursed her lips—but I swear, the music sounded as if it played itself.

It was a quiet night, and while Fern played, Freddy sat at a small table chatting with Kitty McLean, a young nursing student at UCSF who went steady with Johnny Blackwell.

I had hit on her myself before she and Johnny hooked up, but I didn't begrudge the guy. There were plenty of skirts I chased before Kitty's, and plenty I'd chase after hers.

Flowers was as funny as he was kind, and could have you in stitches once he got on a roll. I slung a rag over my shoulder as he delivered his punchline; watched him use the same hands he wrapped roses and delicate greens with every day to measure an imaginary dick in the air. Nearly in tears, Kitty leaned in and put a hand on Freddy's knee, whipped her head back, and laughed so hard that I did too, despite not hearing the joke.

Kitty grabbed her throat, and at first, we thought she was putting us on. When she turned purple and her eyes got real wide, Freddy launched out of his seat like a rocket—but Kitty fell backward in her chair before he could reach her, and the sound of her head hitting the floor was so loud I could hear it over Fern's music. I jumped over the bar, but none of us dared to touch her in the event she had broken her neck. Before we could get through to the emergency line, she had turned an even uglier shade of blue and stopped breathing. When the paramedics arrived, they cleared the way and kneeled over her body before confirming she had choked to death on her gum.

<hr />

The cops were back at my bar with more questions less than a week after Saul fell to his death from my roof.

"What can you tell us about what happened, Mr. Cole? That's the second death here recently. Are you concerned about your business?"

"Concerned? Of course I'm concerned. My brother and I are both concerned. Two of our customers are dead. And just so you know, I considered them friends."

The cop shifted from one foot to the other and tapped his pen against a small spiral notepad. "Well, it's gone beyond coincidence at this stage, so we're gonna have eyes and ears on the joint. Consider yourself warned."

"Is there anything else, officer? I really need to get back to work. It's been a hell of a week, and a lot of people here could use a drink."

The cop tipped his hat back with his pen. "Well under the circumstances, I hope you're pouring doubles ... on the house. With two dead bodies, you may need more than a happy hour to keep your patrons coming back."

I closed the bar for the second time in September, and Griff drove down from Napa to deal with insurance paperwork and cover the bar while I went to Kitty's wake.

We reopened the day of her funeral, after which Johnny drowned his sorrows in a tidal wave of Jameson's. He'd bought Kitty a ring and was planning to propose. The mood was somber, an unseen but palpable melancholic weight bearing down on our shoulders.

Rollo accompanied Fern on piano for a slow song, which seemed fitting for the occasion, although in those days it seemed we heard more of Fern's flute than anything else. She hardly sang anymore. The once lively atmosphere of Griff's had faded, like a sun-bleached painting left to hang in the light for too long.

Griff walked in as I was stocking the bar the following day. He sat down and sighed.

"What the fuck, man? This is nuts. What the hell's going on? Is this place cursed?"

"I'm starting to wonder if there's a black cloud over this bar."

"There's a black cloud over this whole damn city, King. That's why I left. I don't know how you stand it."

"I love it here," I said. And at the time, I'd meant it.

"Well, something has to change. The mood of this place is so different. What happened? It used to be *swinging*. People dancing, laughing, coming in off the streets ... I'm hearing this place just isn't the same anymore." He shook his head. "I can't believe Kitty and Saul are dead. *Fuck.* And what the fuck's with Fern and that fuckin' flute? Word is it's giving Griff's a weird vibe, that people are having second thoughts about coming here. We'll be lucky to keep the damn doors open."

"I don't know, Griff. It's strange. It started off as something neat and different and now... I don't know. It's taken on a life of its own."

"I want you to get rid of it. Tell Fern she can't play it anymore. It's not the kind of music we play here. Enough is enough."

"Griff, I'm gonna be honest with you ... I don't think Fern'll give up that flute. She's really attached to it. It's all she ever wants to play."

Griff hopped off his stool. "Well it's too bad. She's been the heart and soul of this place for some time now. But if it comes down to our business or that goddamned flute, you're gonna have to get rid of Fern."

We both looked up to find her standing in the doorway.

"Aw, Fern," Griff said. "I'm sorry. I don't want to see you go. You know how we feel about you here. You're a legend. I just—"

"It's okay," Fern said. "I understand. I'll just sing tonight."

But after Griff left, I heard her up on the roof deck, alone, playing that thing like she was serenading the entire city and every life in San Francisco depended on it.

And I wondered then why it was so damn important to her.

———▲———

I didn't catch wind of my brother's boating accident in the South Bay until Freddy saw it on the news. He sat me down, poured me a drink, and told me to brace myself.

"Let me guess. Someone's dead."

"Yeah."

"Well it isn't you, it isn't Rollo, and it isn't Fern ..." I looked around the room and motioned to the few customers we had. "And it isn't any of these guys."

"No," Freddy said. "It's Griff."

I slammed my fist on the bar. "Is this your idea of a sick fucking joke?"

Freddy shook his head. "I would never kid about something like this."

"Well, I don't believe it. I just don't. This can't be happening, Freddy. Tell me how the fuck this is happening. Please."

"All I can tell you is *what* happened, King. But do you really want to know?"

I poured myself another shot, then another on top of it.

"They don't think he drowned." Flowers cleared his throat and poured himself a shot. "The news report said ..." he pushed out a hard breath, "... said his head was taken clean off by a propeller. So I don't think he suffered, either." He put his hand over mine. "They said a young boy in a nearby fishing charter snagged it with his rod. Kid was hysterical. He and his family are at the hospital—my guess is he's pretty traumatized." He paused. "Man, I can hardly believe the words coming out of my own mouth right now. I hate to be the one to tell you this, King."

I downed another shot and closed my eyes.

Heartache licked at my chest with a sharp, fiery tongue. Our parents had been dead for years. They were both only children. Griff was all I had left for family in this world.

"How the hell could this happen? Griff's been on boats his whole damn life. Did he fall? Get knocked off? Who else was there?"

"I don't know the details, bud." He patted my hand. "I'm sure we'll find out more soon enough. Why don't you close up shop, and I'll take you home."

"No, I need the distraction. I'll call the station and see what I can find out, but I don't want to close. I don't want to be alone."

"I'm so sorry, King."

"I know, Freddy." I squeezed his hand and fought back tears that came anyway. "I know."

That night, a Saturday, oblivious to the tragedies we had faced that fateful month, Lana Greenwood walked through the door like she owned the place in a low-cut, fire engine red dress, lipstick to match, and a pair of nylon stockings with a black line running up the back of her legs. She was a cross between Veronica Lake and Mamie Van Doren and came out of nowhere, already stocked with a little liquid courage and a point to prove. She ordered a Sloe Gin Fizz after allowing the room ample time to size her up. As I poured her drink, I could tell she had an agenda. I just didn't know yet what it was.

She tongued her straw for a few seconds and looked around the room, trying to find the only pair of eyes that wasn't on her. She made her way over to a high top where Flowers sat listening to Fern sing *"How Can You Mend a Broken Heart,"* a tribute he'd re-quested to Griff and the others.

"Who's the dame?" Lana asked.

"My wife," Flowers answered with as much of a smile as he could muster. "Her name's Fern. I'm Freddy." He offered a hand. "But they call me Flowers."

"Really." She leaned forward and made the most of her low-cut dress. "Well it's nice to meet you, Sweet Pea."

Now you can call it luck, fate, karma…call it what you will, but the fact that I turned around to grab a bottle of Tanqueray at that very moment is the only reason I caught a glimpse of Fern in the mirror.

Her eyes were fixed on Lana, and what I saw inside of them was one of the most frightening things I'd ever seen in my life. When she shifted her gaze and caught mine, I knew whatever had passed between us would be the end of me.

Next thing I knew, I was asking Flowers to make sure Rollo and Gina covered the bar while I went to the morgue to identify my brother's body. And as my car went off the bridge, it was not me driving. My hands were on the wheel, my foot on the gas, but I was not *thinking* or *willing* my body to do what my movements implied. I wasn't thinking at all.

The only thing I heard was the sound of a flute, the windshield breaking, and the rushing of water as the music faded and I plummeted to the bottom of the bay.

And then, just...darkness.

I was already back in the bar when Fern turned her sights on Lana, but no one could see me. They didn't even know I was dead yet. Hell, I don't even know how I got there. I just knew there was nothing I could do stop what happened next...not any of it.

"This might be your lucky night, Sweet Pea," Lana said. "If you can believe it, some creep stood me up, so I just happen to be available. And you know what they say ... one man's loss is another's gain." She sidled up to Freddy, who had no intentions of obliging her.

Fern ended her song to a round of applause. Then she picked up that accursed flute and began to play.

Lana asked Freddy to light her cigarette, and when he did, the Zippo exploded into a ball of flames. Lana's long blond hair caught fire and she just sat there, stricken, fire dancing all around her. Freddy ripped the tablecloth out from under their drinks like a magician and covered her head with it before she let out so much as a sound.

When Freddy pulled back the cloth, some of Lana's skin came with it, her movie star face raw and charred and blistered. Smoke drifted off her hair in little wisps.

I could smell the singe from wherever I was, and for a moment I was lost in thought about that whole side of things.

Lana's screams snapped me out of my daze, and all hell broke loose. Gina nearly went through me to get to the phone—perhaps she *had* gone through me—and I turned my attention to Freddy. He was staring at Fern, who was holding her flute in her hands and smiling.

Smiling.

Flowers reached up and grabbed her hand. He forced her down the steps and off the stage. "Come outside with me. I want to talk to you."

I followed them out while everyone else stayed behind, tending to Lana.

"What the hell is going on? Why are you smiling? Did you see what just happened back there?"

"Of course I did. That slut deserved it. And if you hadn't been such a hero, she'd be a lot worse off than she is now."

Freddy's face went white. "You... *you* did this?"

"So what? She deserved it. They *all* did."

"What do you mean? Who?" Sick recognition crossed his face. "But... I don't understand. You did this? How? Why?"

"Because I can," Fern said, and put the flute to her lips.

Freddy grabbed it out of her hands and stared at it. "What the fuck? Is this some kind of black magic?" He turned back to Fern. "What are you doing? What's happened to you?"

"You gave it to me, Freddy. We all have you to thank. Now give it back."

Freddy turned red with anger, as if he'd been burned by Fern's fire act. He put the flute to his lips. "You know, when I was a kid, I played the recorder. It can't be much different than this."

He blew into the silver lip plate, and Fern backed away.

"Stop it, Freddy!"

"Why?" he asked between breaths. "You don't like it? Let me play *you* a song for a change." He played a few more notes, pushing breaths into the blowhole and pressing the small silver keys. Fern stumbled wide-eyed into the street, her smile replaced with a fearful grimace.

For a moment, I almost recognized her. Fern, the love of Freddy Flowers' life; the elegant songbird who made my bar a success and even broke my heart a little by belonging to someone else. I tried to cry out, but my voice made no sound.

Fern was in the street now, hands in the air and tears in her eyes while Freddy played that thing like the Pied fucking Piper. And I don't know if he was possessed by it, angry, or just plain in shock, but he played on as the cable car passed. Fern's heel came out from under her and she fell back, got her hair caught in a wheel, and was dragged screaming up the dark street.

Freddy blew one last note on that old Artley Flute just as someone pulled the emergency brake.

By then, Fern's screams had stopped.

BROKEN LADY

GENE O'NEILL

1.

Saturday night in San Francisco's Tenderloin is always a time of spirited buying, selling, and trading. But, in addition to being Saturday, this is the first day of the month, with both SSI and General Assistance checks cashed hours ago. So the 'Loin is already rocking and rolling long before dark.

2.

At around seven thirty, Ellie meets her friend and next door neighbor, Taj Jones, just as they both step out of their rooms on the 2nd floor of the Hotel Reo, located right in the heart of the 'Loin.

"Hey, Elinore Nightwind!" Taj says, dark eyes flashing brightly, using Ellie's full name as she always does whenever they first meet, as if she were the M.C. at some nightclub announcing tonight's star performer. Then, after a slight pause, Taj punctuates the statement with a joyous chuckle.

3.

When they'd first introduced themselves a year and a half ago in the shabby lobby of the Hotel Reo, Taj had thought a moment, and then declared with her patented wide, full-toothed smile and lifted eyebrows: "Whoa, Nightwind? Y'all doan look Native American... But then again you doan look white either. What's going on in your background, girl?"

Ellie smiled back and explained: "Well, my pops was actually a full blooded Wappo. My moms was a mix of Irish and black."

Taj nodded and laughed, pointing at Ellie's booty. "Well, I know which side of the family *that* comes from."

Ellie couldn't help laughing. Even though Taj had a B.A. from SF State with a major in Black Studies and a minor in Drama, she insisted on sprinkling her speech with street vernacular, as if purposely masking her education. In any event, Taj's speech was always friendly, colorful, and personal. This woman was so truly good-natured and totally uninhibited that Ellie couldn't possibly be offended by anything she said. And most of what she had to say was right on anyhow. Ellie did indeed resemble her mother—at least the two old yellowing photos she still carried in her wallet. And of course she'd inherited Angie Nightwind's raspy singing voice and interest in the blues. But, her dad? Well, maybe she got a little of his rugged constitution and temper, but not too much of anything else... except, of course, his taste for booze.

Ellie and Taj got along great from the moment of that first meeting. On a couple of special occasions, when Taj wasn't dancing at The Mitchell Brothers, they'd gone out together and partied down hard, including once at The Greeks.

Ellie had watched her friend perform a number of times in the renowned strip joint up on O'Farrell Street. The tall black girl was elegant and tastefully erotic. Had all the customers—mostly male—staring with bright lust in their eyes, clapping enthusiastically when she finished her routine, and reaching for their wallets. But Taj never got involved personally afterhours with any of those paying customers, even the high rollers. Didn't even have a real boyfriend. "Doan have the time," she'd replied when asked why. "'Cuz, I plan to be dancing in Vegas soon." Ellie thought her friend had the sufficient amount of talent and drive for the big time. Knew she lived in the lower rent 'Loin only to save money, which she mostly spent on formal dancing lessons from two very expensive teachers, one who'd danced on Broadway and the other in Vegas shows.

4.

Standing near her door, Ellie says: "Time for work already?"

Taj glances at her watch and nods. "Where y'all heading tonight, girl?"

"Cashing my *two* checks, then, I guess, down to The Greeks."

With Taj's encouragement, Ellie has been fooling around working on some new songs during the last four or five months, finding herself initially rusty, but eventually getting a little better after she cut down on her drinking, at least during the daytime when she's writing. But today Ellie has finished a rough draft with some really promising lyrics—she *knows* this song is going to be really good. She can barely resist showing it to Taj. But she forces herself to wait until it's polished and perfect.

Nevertheless, tonight she is going out to celebrate. And, actually, she's pretty comfortable drinking at The Greeks, even though it has a biker and mostly working-class, rough crowd ... But then, she reminds herself, I ain't such a high-rent package anymore myself.

"Girl, you need to quit drinking at that dump," Taj says with an uncharacteristic frown. "You keep on dragging them scruffy dudes home, and one's gonna do more than just rough you up. Remember *Looking for Mr. Goodbar?*"

Ellie smiles wryly. Taj is always reminding her of this old Diane Keaton movie about a school teacher, who cruises low rent bars at night, picking up young dudes for one-night stands. Until this psycho guy finally frosts her ass big-time. But Ellie definitely prefers the younger, bigger guys. She has never shared with Taj a kind of weird dream she has after she's been really juiced up. She imagines one of the young, strong dudes squeezing her so tightly it magically welds together all her invisible scars and cracks.

"Where else am I going to go, Taj?" she says, shrugging. "The bartenders take pretty good care of me down there, you know. Point out the real crazies. Even physically intervene when some obnoxious drunk can't keep his hands to himself or is overly aggressive."

"How 'bout the new club near The Mitchell Brothers, jus' around the corner on Van Ness? The O.K. Corral is a little classier. Got your kinda rockabilly sound, girl. They even have live music on weekends. Maybe you can get a gig there, you know what I'm saying?" It's Taj who has been constantly pestering her to cut back on the booze, write her own songs, and try singing again. And Taj had convinced her to sing two songs when they were out at a club with an open mic a month ago. After hearing her sing, Taj had declared: "Wow, that's some sexy growl, girl. Needs a little bit of polish, but indeed reminds me of Janis Joplin."

Of course, despite her friend's generous encouragement, Ellie knows her rusty singing voice is pretty much shot. Too many cigarettes, too many years of heavy boozing. No real range left, just a hoarse, deep-throated, grating rasp. Ha, she thinks, not much of a commercial market for a female imitation of Tom Waits.

"Hey, I may just check out the Corral, Taj," Ellie finally says, smiling at her friend. "Catch you later."

She takes off for A-I Check Cashing, which is open late, a couple blocks over on Geary Street. Her social worker, Caitlin O'Shea, has helped her finally get her first small General Assistance check from the City today. And with another one coming on the fifteenth, along with her SSI, she just might get by each month without having to panhandle, *if* she cools it.

One of the reasons she likes The Greeks is because she doesn't have to buy *all* of her own drinks, when the young guys are flush, like they will be tonight. Of course, they all have their sly intentions for getting into her Harley Davidson shorts, even though she is at least twenty-five-years-older than most of them. Thankfully, the majority of these working class guys don't put on a total full-court press; so she usually has some breathing room, and can return home alone, despite what Taj thinks. But the O.K. Corral is unknown turf. And if it is indeed rockabilly it will attract an urban cowboy crowd. She remembers that the Canadian cowboys she knew at one time were usually pretty tight, expecting some immediate gratitude for any money spent. They buy a girl two drinks, and automatically figure the first one entitles them to a blowjob and the second to some pussy. She smiles again wryly, actually feeling really upbeat with her two checks in hand. She can buy her own fucking drinks tonight at the O.K. Corral.

5.

Ellie steps out onto the crowded street in front of the Hotel Reo, immediately assailed by a mix of sounds: horns honking, people laughing, music blaring from open windows and bar-fronts, people shouting loudly in English, Spanish, Vietnamese, and some other indecipherable language. She grins, because even Ole Reverend Louie-Louie is out late tonight, ranting his usual daytime religious screed, and trying to proselytize another parking meter.

6.

Earlier, just after the first checks were cashed, it was *steak burritos around*; and, *yes please, both French fries and onion rings with that double burger*; and, *oh yeah, make that first one a Jameson's with ginger*; and, *hey, hey, pal, no, this one is on me*; and, *yo, darlin, get youself somepin nice*; and, *yep, give 'em bof a double scoop*; and, *yeah, thas right, da dawg do luv a lil taste of a cold brewski.*

By late afternoon, the sidewalks were swarming, a tingling sense of excitement palpable in the foggy air, like smoky ringside at a big fight in Vegas. The Vietnamese kids coming home from the playgrounds and parks were picking up on the vibe, skipping along, dodging joyfully in and out of the crowd. Some johns were juiced up early, the electric vibe an invisible finger stirring their collective libidos. A pair sporting a painted lady on each arm, both guys anticipating a basic sweaty afternoon all-skate. Even the drug dealers with tombstones in their eyes were up and outside by four o'clock, wearing wolfish grins. Ole Daisy Mae, on the corner of Post and Geary, was completely sold out of her flower bundles by six, many of her younger customers hoping to score some spiced huggings with their dates. Sweet Jane-the-Fiddler's hat was full of bills, no skimpy coin tosses this afternoon. The homeless, the winos, the junkies were all doing pretty well, shaking their stuffed paper cups, smiling nice and thanking their donors kindly.

Oh, it was a joyful and exciting evening, and the high spirits carried over later into the night, when the serious buying, selling, and trading started, the night people eventually taking over the street.

7.

After cashing her checks, Ellie decides to definitely forego a visit to The Greeks and hike up O'Farrell and around the corner on Van Ness to check out the O.K. Corral...

The place is jammed. But she manages to find a recently vacated empty stool at the far end of the bar, near the jukebox. She has to wait to be served though because all three bartenders are busier than a hot craps shooter on a twenty-roll winning streak.

Gives Ellie time to look into the bar mirror and do a self-assessment.

Not too bad, she decides. The invisible scars were still holding the etched wrinkles tightly together, her face fairly attractive in this dim, partially revealing light. Yep, not too bad for a forty-nine year-old babe, who has definitely been around the park. But looking at her experienced face in the mirror reminds Ellie of the recurring nightmare she's been experiencing. In the dream she is staring into a big mirror when suddenly there is an almost melodious plinking-cracking sound, like a large sheet of plate glass developing cracks and shattering apart in slow motion. But as she stares closer, she realizes it isn't the mirror breaking into pieces … No, the sound comes from her face, which is cracking apart, as if she were under-going some kind of a sudden face-quake—

She always awakens at that point in a clammy sweat, panting for breath and thinking: I'm breaking up!

After several minutes, Ellie, still shaken by the memory of the surreal dream, finally gets her first double Black Jack, and with a trembling hand, she drains the glass, immediately signaling for an-other. While waiting for the whiskey to take effect and begin relax-ing her, she thinks back to when her run of bad times first began.

8.

One night when Ellie was ten and living in Oakland, her dad came home early from work, but really drunk. This time he stumbled into the kitchen and glared at them hatefully, scaring both badly. He shouted: "I've been fucking fired! It's all your fault. You two bitches are smothering me to death. Leaching every ounce of my energy and spirit." Then, he spun on his heel and went out, slam-ming the front door.

They hid in Ellie's tiny bedroom under the stairs, thinking they'd ride out the storm there if he came back later that night. But the next morning he wasn't back. And, in fact, they never heard from John David Nightwind again.

Ellie and her mom did okay by themselves for the next year, Angie working as a waitress at a local bar, Julio's, even singing the blues live on Friday and Saturday nights. The mostly male custom-ers appreciated the music and always tipped her well. Then, early one morning, just after her eleventh birthday, Ellie found her mother unconscious in the bathtub, a trickle of blood running from her nose, her breathing ragged. Ellie called 911. But Angie Nightwind died that same night at Highlands Hospital. Brain aneurism. A congenital problem, apparently, undiagnosed until too late.

With no relatives in Oakland to take her in, Ellie bounced around ten different foster home placements in Alameda County over the next seven years. At eighteen she was released from Foster Care and out on her own—no education, no skills. On the street she did whatever she could to keep a studio apartment together with two other teenage girls. Including hustling tricks on The Track on International Boulevard—the major hazard there was avoiding the aggressive pimps. By that point, she had chosen her drug of choice, using booze to dull her sensibilities.

But then, like out of some kind of fairy tale, Gabriel, her shining knight, showed up at the Silver Spur, a popular East Oakland C&W club Ellie could get into even underage. She fell under the spell of the charismatic drummer on the spot. And she took him home that first night. She returned to the club every night during the next week that the *Radar Angels*—a Canadian rockabilly band that sounded a little like *Creedence Clearwater Revival*—played at the Spur.

The night before the second week of the band's gig, Israfel, their female lead Angel was in an auto wreck, breaking a leg and two ribs. So, Gabe convinced Ellie to fill in the rest of that week. She'd sang to him, including a Janis Joplin number during the week days they were living together, and he truly thought she had a terrific voice—a natural. She filled in that week nicely for Israfel. But the Spur was packed that last Saturday night and the crowd went nuts when Gabe convinced Ellie to eventually do *"A Piece of My Heart."* She followed it up with her personal favorite: *"A Woman Left Lonely."* But the crowd demanded even more Janis from Ellie, shouting out a dozen numbers. She only sang one more Joplin song she knew well enough and that the *Angels* could back up: *"Me and Bobby McGee."*

Later that night Gabe kissed her on the lips, hugged her tightly, and announced: "Everyone in the band agrees, you're going north with us, girl, as our new lead singer!"

And she was saved from the misery of East Oakland… for a while.

9.

A huge cowboy decked out in a black Stetson, black and white checkered shirt, jeans, and polished black boots has sent a drink over to Ellie. He's young, but kinda cute, so she smiles and toasts him, just before he gets up and comes over to the nearby jukebox. The music here isn't strictly C&W or even Rockabilly, but mostly bluesy rock and roll numbers. The big guy takes his time, looking over everything, carefully selecting five more songs. The second one begins playing—

Ellie is stunned!

She hears herself… *herself*, at least thirty years ago, singing her own song, *"Broken Lady."* She hasn't heard it played publicly for… at least twenty-five years.

10.

After a couple of years, the *Radar Angels* were landing gigs at top C&W and Rockabilly clubs and venues on their tours, playing all the big cities across Canada from Vancouver to Toronto. And then finally setting up new digs and headquarters, south of Toronto.

The group recorded their first real album, *Heavenly Blues*, featuring several songs Ellie had written, including *"Broken Lady."* And on that one she indeed sounded a lot like Janis Joplin, belting out in her raspy, bluesy voice.

The album and *"Broken Lady"* rose rapidly and eventually crossed over onto the pop charts in Canada, reaching as high as number five.

Two months after release of the album and its climb in sales, Ellie walked into their bedroom one afternoon and stopped short. There in plain sight, on the end table by the bed, sat a book of matches, several tiny balloons, and a wrinkled-up piece of aluminum foil with one side stained a dirty nicotine brown.

When Gabe finally came home late that night, she confronted him with the aluminum foil and balloons. "What's all this, Gabe? What's going on here?"

He frowned, not able to avoid looking guilty and more than a little sheepish. "Well you know, Sweetie... Ah, like it's been getting a little harder to come down at night after some of these gigs. Everything so crazy now. Too jacked up to sleep, eh."

"I know, but why this? Dope? And the fucking dangerous stuff?"

He shrugged dismissively. "Ah, I'm just chasing the dragon... nothing too serious, you know. I'm not shooting up any dope." He shook his head. "Wouldn't do that, babe."

Ellie knew exactly what he was doing. Mixing a drop of water with a dab of black tar from one of the penny balloons on the aluminum foil, heating it with three matches from underneath, and then inhaling the smoky heroin fumes. This produced an almost instant nerve-deadening high; not quite as intense as mainlining the stuff with a spike, but, nevertheless, dangerous and highly addictive. And she'd noticed lately that their sex life had tapered off to almost nothing. She had attributed everything to the grueling bouts of overwork. They'd just done another two weeks of back-to-back nights at local gigs followed by long daytime hours of studio time, honing themselves for another album and road tour at the best venues across Canada. Intense, demanding, and exhausting. Of course, she also felt the constant pressure.

"Gabe, you're going to get your ass hooked and take the whole fucking band down with you—"

He scowled, his defensive expression turning slowly to anger, and after a moment he countered in an accusatorial voice: "Okay.

But what about *you*, babe? Uh-huh. You've been doing a nearly perfect imitation of Janis Joplin, except you've been downing a quart of Jack Daniels every day instead of Southern Comfort."

He was right about the drinking, and the guilty impact of his stated observation immediately choked her up. Wiping her eyes on her wrist, she cleared her throat, and replied: "Okay, okay. We both need to clean up our acts, Gabe. Get ourselves straight ... for the sake of us, the band, and the music."

He looked into her eyes for a long moment and then said the words that sent an icicle stabbing into her heart: "I think I can do it, babe, but I don't think you can. You've been hitting the sauce heavy even before we first met in Oakland. And now you *need* at least a quart a day to just maintain. Forget my bullshit excuses about the added pressure of the increasing fame. You needed the booze long before any of that. You can't quit, Ellie, or escape your shitty background. You're living in your own song."

She wasn't about to admit what he was suggesting. "No, you're dead wrong, I can easily quit drinking ... any time I want."

And she did quit, for exactly *one* day. Then, she snuck out for a drink after finishing at the recording studio two days later.

Ellie came home slammed late that next morning, her lipstick smeared, her hair and clothes disheveled. Of course, she knew Gabe instantly realized what was going on. She could hide the booze, but she couldn't hide its effect on her.

It went on like that for weeks, their agent delaying their next tour, until she discovered his full rig—the balloons, the spike, the surgical hose, the spoon—wrapped neatly in a towel. She couldn't help noticing the bruises on the inside of both his arms. Unable to help herself, much less Gabe, Ellie drank even more to compensate for everything.

"I can quit anytime, babe," Gabe had insisted, when finally confronted again. But his voice and his eyes lacked confidence.

She shook her head, tearing up, and saying: "I don't think so, man."

He frowned and shrugged. "And you, Ellie? What about you? The apartment is filthy, empty bottles stashed all over the place. We are both going down. It's all unraveling, coming apart: us, reality, the music."

"What do you mean, coming apart?"

"You're slurring your vocals, babe, and it's showing in practice. Michael and the other *Angels* have noticed. They've been asking me for months to help tone down your drinking. I told them I've tried—"

"But it isn't only my drinking, Gabe," she said defensively. "It's also you, the dope is fucking you up, too. Yesterday at the studio in the middle of a piece, you dropped one of your sticks."

"Uh-huh…" After a moment, Gabe held up his hands in a surrendering gesture. "We both need to try and quit." He dug a wrinkled scrap of paper with some writing from his pocket. "Our agent gave me this. The name and address of a good 28-day program right here in Toronto."

"Okay! We can do it, starting tomorrow morning," Ellie cried out, nodding her head with enthusiasm

Of course, they never made it to the program, tomorrow never really coming for either of them. A month or so later, Michael told her the band had made a reluctant decision: they would *both* have to go. They'd already auditioned a new drummer, who they called, Raziel. And, Israfel, their old lead singer, was ready to come back.

Two nights after being booted from the band, Gabe told Ellie he couldn't let her drag him down lower. He was leaving, returning to Montreal where he grew up, and getting his act cleaned up…

Ellie found Gabe the next morning, when she woke up with a ferocious hangover around noon. He was slumped on the couch in their Toronto apartment. He hadn't left, he'd OD'd, sometime during the night, the spike still dangling in his tied-off arm.

Grief-stricken, Ellie fled to her hometown, Oakland … only to discover she had an additional problem.

She was pregnant.

She tried going to AA meetings every night, and pull herself together, hold the booze at arm's length, but she fell off the wagon repeatedly, going on blackout binges. She always climbed back onboard the next day—shaky, but committed to *never drinking again until after the baby is born.*

Gabriel, Jr. finally came, after a very tough delivery ... but he was delivered a stillbirth. Devastated, Ellie scraped together enough money to bury him right there in the upscale Oakland crematorium, Chapel of the Chimes. Then, she hit the booze with a big-time vengeance, creating an alcoholic buffer between her and reality.

After years of steady boozing, she decided to wander across the Bay Bridge to the Tenderloin, joining the others there—*the forgotten and the never-known.* She managed to eventually get onto SSI, rent a room at the Reo, and somehow survive, which often required panhandling during the last days of each month ... Fortunately, she met Taj, who encouraged and inspired her to cut back on the drinking and recapture part of her musical past. Miraculously, she'd been making some good progress on both the boozing and the song writing.

11.

The ignored cowboy, now sitting next to her, finally bumps Ellie's shoulder, and offers to light her cigarette, which has apparently been dangling while she's been tripping out in her dark past.

"You liked some of the rockabilly blues I played, right?"

She nods, taking a deep drag on her Marlboro, not bothering to tell him who sang *"Broken Lady."* He probably wouldn't believe her anyhow.

"Name's Jake. Visiting a sick friend tonight here at San Francisco General Hospital. Work on a cattle ranch up north in Pope Valley. Staying at the Holiday Inn on Van Ness. Stopped in here for a drink, and you sure caught my eye, pretty lady."

Man, she thinks, he's a *real* cowboy. Kinda cute. And he has a nice smile, a child-like facial expression, even in his eyes ... although he's big enough to play tight end for the 49ers.

"Hi Jake, I'm Ellie," she says, smiling.

The cowboy keeps the drinks coming, so they get along just fine, Ellie not saying much, just enough to be polite. He finally gets up again to play some more music on the jukebox. "What do you want to hear, little girl?"

She almost laughs at that last, *little girl*, but says, "Oh, how about some more Janis Joplin if they got it on there. Maybe some Joe Cocker, too, if you can find him."

There is a lot of both on the jukebox.

They drink and listen, Joe Cocker finally finishing Jake's six plays with "*Ain't No Sunshine When She's Gone.*"

Then it's closing time, 2:00 AM...

Ellie is pretty much in the bag, as she leads Jake back to *her* room at the Hotel Reo.

He doesn't pay much attention to her tiny, shabby room, even the bright new pictures she's just hung around. Instead, he turns away from Ellie, and begins to peel off his clothes—a cowboy version of foreplay. Completely naked, he turns to face Ellie, and the child-like expression is gone, replaced with a mean, surly look. She finds it chilling.

"Best peel out of them clothes, girl, unless you want them ripped off."

Even unsteady on her feet, Ellie put her hands on her hips, and with some attitude says, "Well, I guess it's 'bout time for you to go, Cowboy."

"Hah." Moving quickly across the room, the big man grabs the front of her shirt in a mitt, and with one clean jerk, tears it completely off. He pushes her back on the bed, and holds her down with one hand around her neck, fumbling with her jeans.

Frightened, she squirms, lashing out at him, and finally gets his attention when she rakes a long gash across his right cheek with her fingernails.

Jake bleeds heavily, but he doesn't flinch away.

"Ha, you like to play rough, little girl?" He laughs, then punches her solidly right square in the face, making a scrunching sound… but Ellie knows something inside her head, in addition to her nose, is broken.

Entire face and head exploding with pain, everything begins to fade out, as Ellie sinks into a black abyss…

She holds on though, struggling to maintain consciousness, while gasping for breath on her side. She blinks, wiping a stream of blood from her nose. Then she turns her head slightly, and sees the nude cowboy standing on the other side of the bed, an enormous erection in one hand, and his big cowboy belt in the other. He leans across the bed and strikes her with the buckle, the blow raising an instant red welt on her hip. But the cowboy makes a big mistake, pausing a moment, giving Ellie enough time to wiggle off the bed and grab the industrial flashlight near her nightstand.

The drunken giant is roaring with laughter now, as he shuffles around the bed in pursuit. He reaches out to grab Ellie when she whirls about, and strikes out with the heavy flashlight, hitting him squarely above his right ear. He drops face down on the floor… and begins to convulse.

Ellie leans over the stricken cowboy and says: "What part of *no* didn't you understand, asshole?"

Jake doesn't answer. His eyes glaze over, and he finally gasps out a rattle-groan from deep within his throat.

Ellie knows then that Jake is dead, and the perception sobers her up. She glances around the room, blood specks splattered across her bed. She groans, realizing that again she is responsible for a death—

A series of pings sound from inside her damaged head—the sounds tight rubber bands make when snapping apart.

And Ellie knows this is the last straw, that those mental rubber bands were the only things holding her together. She staggers to the mirror above the dresser—

"No," she moans in protest, because as she suspects, the wrinkles, *all* the deeply etched wrinkles on her face, slowly widen and pull apart.

She's a broken lady...

A few seconds later, next door, Taj blinks awake. It's quiet, but she gets up. A palpable, ominous tingling sensation lingers in the air—

Then, she freezes in place, because she hears a faintly melodious plinking-cracking sound coming from next door in Ellie's place, like the sound of a plate of glass or perhaps a large mirror shattering apart.

12.

Broken Lady

"...forever now apart,
everything so dark and shady,
time can heal a broken heart,
but nothing can heal a broken lady."

– song and lyrics by Elinore Nightwind

TALES
THE
ASHES TELL

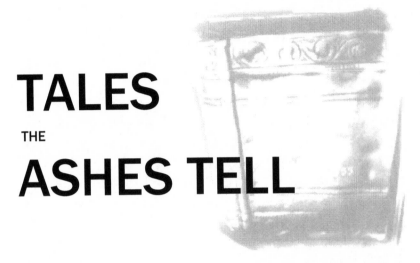

GARY A. BRAUNBECK

I was in the darkness;
I could not see my words
Nor the wishes of my heart.
Then suddenly there was a great light—
"Let me into the darkness again."

– Stephen Crane

Some nights, when the visitors have left and everything within me
falls into dismal silence, when even the Librarian grows weary of
drifting through these halls, maintaining these chambers, and looking at these glass doors behind which rest the golden books, when
the rain spatters against the roof and the flashes of lightning create
glinting reflections swimming against my marble floors, when I am
at last certain there will be no one and nothing to disturb me, I allow myself, for a little while, to flip through these books as one still
among the living would flip through the pages of an old family

photo album; only where the living warm themselves in the nostalgic glow of reminiscences, I sustain myself on the memories of those housed within the books arranged on my shelves, behind my glass doors with their golden hinges, here in my corridors with marble floors. I have no memories, being born of wood, iron, and stone as I was. But those who slumber here, within these golden books, their memories remain with them, and many are so lonely that they gladly share them with me on nights such as this. I house them from the elements; they sustain me with their stories. I prefer it this way, on nights such as this, when it is just the ashes, the rain, and I...and the tales the ashes tell.

Tonight it's old Mrs. Winters who's the first to start in with her story of her grandson's death in Vietnam and how it broke her own son's heart and led to the ruination of his marriage and career, ending when her son took his own life in a squalid motel room somewhere in Indiana. Every time she tells this story, her neighbors listen quietly, politely, patiently, for they—like I—have heard this a thousand times before, but she always changes some small detail so it's never *quite* the same; tonight, the scene of his death is not some sleazy roadside hovel but an expensive, five-star hotel in the middle of downtown Manhattan, and this time her son does not decorate the blinds with his brains but instead stands on the roof of the palace, arms spread wide, a joyous smile on his face as he falls forward off the edge and for a moment almost flies until he ... doesn't.

Like her neighbors I am pleased by this new trick of the tale. Each time she changes a bit of the minutiae the story resembles itself less and less, and one night it will be a completely new story that she will begin revising almost immediately. We like this about her. She was never married, our Mrs. Winters. She had no children. She died alone, on a bus-stop bench, a forgotten bag lady whose mortal remains were cremated and placed here by a sympathetic police officer who still comes by once a month to bring flowers and pay his respects; it seems Mrs. Winters reminded him of his own grandmother; beyond that, no one here has any further idea of his reasons, and if Mrs. Winters knows of them, her memory is too fragmented to know for certain if those reasons are true or not. We do not press the matter. Even here, certain privacies are respected.

I find it curious how many of her neighbors were interred here by strangers, or family members they were never particularly close to. Many of them come here from cities and towns that are hundreds—sometimes *thousands*—of miles away. I know that I am a glorious edifice, and am honored that so many of the living wish to bring their loved ones here to rest. I am a tranquil place, a quiet place, a place of serenity and sanctuary. I know all of the stories of nearly everyone who slumbers here, but not all.

Tonight, we have new neighbors on my shelves, behind my glass doors. I heard only a part of the explanation given by the slightly hunched, spirit-broken man who brought them here. Something about his brother and his niece and a boy his niece once knew. I wonder whom it is he has left with us. I exchange pleasantries with all my friends between the golden covers of their books, and as I do each of them asks, *What do you know about the new arrival?* I have no answer for them, not yet, but being the curious sorts they are—and always so lonely, even when all of them are chattering away—they want me to find out but are too polite to ask. They know they don't need to; I will discover it in time.

I see that the glass doors have been freshly washed and dried so that our new arrival is welcomed into a clean space. She is whispering to herself, our new neighbor, and I become very still, empyrean, allowing the rain and lighting and the slow turning of the Earth to cast shapes of angels in the primum mobile of night.

She speaks not of herself, but of *we*, of the uncle who brought *us* here.

Could it be? There are so few books here that contain more than a single person's remains; the last was five years ago, when an elderly husband and wife who died within hours of each other left specific instructions that they were to be burned and interred together, their ashes, like their souls (or so they believed), intermingled for eternity. I find that sort of sentimentality pitiful, but I never speak my judgment to those who need to believe in such antiquated notions. Do not misunderstand—the souls of that elderly couple are intermingled here, but not in the way they were raised to believe; there are no fields of green they run through, hand in hand, laughing as the afternoon sun sets their faces aglow and the scent of autumn leaves fills the air. They are simply *here*, and so shall remain. But it is enough for them, this fate, and that pleases me.

The girl still speaks of *we* and *us*, very seldom does the word *I* make an appearance. At least not at first.

I'm here, I tell her or them. *As are we all, and we are all listening.*

She continues to whisper, but whether she is telling the story to me or to those who live inside my walls, I do not yet know. But she tells her story as if she has told it a thousand times before and expects to tell it a thousand times again; and, perhaps, like old Mrs. Winters, she will begin altering details as the years and decades and centuries go by, until it is a new story, one she finds can spend eternity with and not be crippled with regret.

Mute, voiceless, abandoned and all but forgotten, she begins, *my father's house does not so much sit on this street as it does crouch*; an abused, frightened animal fearing the strike of its keeper's belt, the sting of a slapping hand, the rough kick of a steel-toed boot. No lights shine in any of the windows, which are broken or covered with boards or black paint or large sections of cardboard that now stink of dampness and rot. The paint on the front door long ago gave up fighting the good fight and now falls away, peeled by unseen hands, becoming scabs dropping from the body of a leper in the moments before death, but with no Blessed Damien of Molokai to offer up a final prayer for a serene passage from this cheerless existence into the welcoming forgiveness and saving grace of Heaven. This was once a house like any other house, on this street like any other street, in this town that most people would immediately recognize and then just as quickly forget as they drive through it on their way to some place more vibrant, more exciting, or even a little more *interesting*.

But we can't blame them, you and I; we can't impugn these people who pass through without giving this place so much as a second glance. If things had worked out differently, we would have burned rubber on our way out, making damn sure the tires threw up enough smoke to hide any sight of the place should one of us cave and glance in the rear-view for a final look, a last nostalgic image of this insufficient and unremarkable white-bread Midwestern town, but that's not the way it works around here; never was, never will be. You're born here, you'll die here; you're a lifer, dig it or not.

We sometimes wonder if people still use that phrase, *dig it*, or if it's also passed into the ether of the emptiness people still insist on calling history, memory, eternity, whatever, passed into that void along with *groovy, outta sight*, *"That's not my bag," "Stifle it, Edith,"* Watergate, Space-Food Sticks, platform shoes, Harry Chapin flying in his taxi, and the guy who played Re-Run on *What's Happening?*

Wouldn't it be nice if that drunken Welshman's poems had been true, that death has no dominion, or that we could rage against the dying of the light? Odd. It occurs to me that if we were still alive, we'd be looking right into face of our fifties about now, feeling its breath on our cheeks, its features in detail so sharp it would be depressing.

But this never does us any good, does it, thinking about such things? Especially tonight of all nights. Don't tell me you've forgotten? Yes, that's right. This night marks the anniversary of the night my father buried us under the floorboards in my bedroom after he came home early from work and caught us in my bed. It was my first time, and when he saw you there, with his little girl, it was too much for him to take; not this, not this dirty, filthy thing going on under his roof, it was too much; his wife was gone, three years in her grave after twice as long fighting the cancer that should have taken her after nine months; his job was gone, the factory doors closed forever, and he was reduced to working as a janitor at the high school just to keep our heads above water because the severance pay from the plant was running out.

"At least the house is paid for," he'd say on those nights when there was enough money to buy a twelve-pack of Blatz, sit at the kitchen table, and hope with every tip of every can that some of his shame and grief and unhappiness would be pulled out in the backwash.

You never saw it, you never had the chance, you didn't know him as I did. I couldn't look at his eyes and all the broken things behind them any longer; I couldn't listen to his once booming voice that was now a disgraced whisper, the death-rattle of a life that was a life no longer, merely an existence with no purpose at its center ... except for his little girl, except for me and all the unrealized dreams he hoped I'd bring to fruition because he no longer had the faith or the strength to fight for anything. A hollow, used-up, brittle-spirited echo of the man he'd hoped to be. Even then, even before that night, he'd ceased to be my father; he became instead what was left of him. I tried to fill in the gaps with my memories of what was, what had been, but I was a teen-aged girl, one who hadn't paid any attention to him during the six years my mother was dying, and so I made up things to fill in those holes. I pretended that he was a Great War Hero who was too modest to boast about his accomplishments on the battlefield; I dreamt that he was a spy, like Napoleon Solo on *The Man from U.N.C.L.E.*, hiding undercover, using his factory job to establish his secret identity, his mission one so secret that he couldn't even reveal the truth to his family; I imagined that he was writing the Great American Novel in hidden notebooks late at night, while I slept in my room with the Bobby Sherman and David Cassidy posters on the walls, their too-bright smiles hinting that someday soon my father's novel would make him so rich and famous that the two of them would be arguing over who would take me to Homecoming, and who would take me to the prom.

But he was no war hero, no spy, no secret great notebook novelist; only a factory worker with no factory who'd exchanged a lathe machine for a mop and a bucket and pitying looks from faculty members. To the students, he was either invisible or an object to mock.

No, I don't remember your name. I don't remember *my* name, but what does it matter now? Our names, like our flesh, were only a façade, an illusion to be embraced, a falsehood to be cherished and mistaken for purpose, for meaning. We have—*had*—what remained of our bodies to remind us of that, beneath the floor, flesh long decayed and eaten away, two sets of bones with skulls frozen forever into a rictus grin as if laughing at the absurdity of the world we're no longer part of.

Let's not stay here for now, let's move outside, round and round this house, watching as the living ghosts of everyone who once passed through the door come and go in reverse; watch as the seasons go backwards, sunshine and autumn leaves and snow-clogged streets and sidewalks coming and going in a blink and ... and let's stop here. I want to stop here, in the backyard, just for a few moments, just to see his face as it was on that night.

Watch; see how pretty it all is. Murky light from a glowing street lamp snakes across the darkness to press against the glass. The light bleeds in, across a kitchen table, and glints off the beer can held by a man whose once-powerful body has lost its commanding posture under the weight of compiling years; he's overweight from too many beers, over-tense from too many worries, and overworked far too long without a reprieve. Whenever this man speaks, especially when he's at work, especially when he's holding the mop and bucket, his eyes never have you, and even if they do you cannot return his gaze; his eyes are every lonely journey you have ever taken, every unloved place you've ever visited, every sting of guilt you've ever felt. This man's eyes never have you, they only brush by once, softly, like a cattail or a ghost, then fall shyly toward the ground in some inner contemplation too sad to be touched by a tender thought or the delicate brush of another's care. To look at him closely, it's easy to think that God has forgotten his name.

He lifts the can of beer to his mouth. It feels good going down, washing away the bad taste in his mouth that always follows him home from work. He drains the can, sighs, goes to the sink and pours himself a glass of water. He is thinking about his days as a child, about the afternoons now forgotten by everyone but him, afternoons when he'd go to the movies for a nickel and popcorn was only a penny. He thinks about how he used to take his daughter to the movies all the time when she was still a little girl and her mother, his wife, was still alive. He remembers how much fun they used to have, and he longs for the chance to do something like that again, something that will put a bright smile on his daughter's face and make himself feel less of a failure.

He stands at the sink listening to the sounds of the house, its soft creaks and groans, still settling after all these years. He thinks about his dead wife and doesn't know how he'll be able to face the rest of his life without her by his side. She was a marvel to him. After all the mistakes he's made—and, God, he's made a lot, no arguing that—her respect and love for him never lessened.

He tries to not think about the things his daughter has done for him the past few months, things he didn't ask her to do, but things she's done nonetheless. To help him relax, to help him sleep.

And then he hears a sound from his daughter's room. A squeak of bedsprings. A soft sigh. The muffled laughter of a boy.

His face becomes a slab of granite and the broken things behind his eyes shatter into even more fragments. Unaware that he's doing it, he reaches over and picks up the hammer he left lying on the kitchen counter last night while he tried repairing the loose cupboard door above the sink. He turns and marches toward his daughter's bedroom, knowing what he's going to find when he opens the door and—

—what? All right, just this once, we won't watch the rest. He wasn't really *there*. Anyway. I'm glad we know that now. He just wanted to scare us but his frustration, his anger, his heartbrokenness took control.

Let's pretend that we still have hands, and let's pretend to hold them as we play "Ring Around the Rosie" once more, going back just a little more, a year, maybe less, because I've been saving this for you, for this anniversary, this most special anniversary. Why is it special? That's a secret I need to keep just a little while longer. Take my hand and let's go, round and round and round and—

—stop right here. Yes, this is the place, the time, exactly right.

There's a young girl of seventeen sleeping in her bed who, for a moment, wakes in the night to hear the sound of weeping from the room across the hall. She rises and walks as softly as she can to her door, opens it, and steps into the hall.

"...no, no, *no*..." chokes the voice in the other room.

"Daddy?" she says.

"...no, no, *no, oh, God, honey, please*..."

She knows he can't hear her, that he's dreaming again of the night his wife, her mother, closed her eyes for the last time, of the way he took her emaciated body in his arms and kissed her lips and stroked her hair and begged her to wake up, wakeup, please, honey, what am I supposed to do without you, wake up, *please*...

She takes a deep breath, this seventeen-year-old motherless girl, and slowly opens the door to this room stinking of loneliness and grief. She takes a few hesitant steps, the moonlight from the window in the hallway casting bars of suffused light across the figure of her father as if imprisoning him in the dream. She stares at him, not knowing what to do.

Then his eyes open for a moment and he sees her standing in the doorway.

"Arlene," he says, his voice still thick with tears. "Arlene, is that you?"

"Shhh," says the young girl, suddenly so very cold at hearing him speak her mother's name in the night. "It's just a bad dream, go back to sleep."

"...I can't sleep so hot, not without you..."

She can hear that he's starting to drift away again, but she does not move back into the hallway; instead, she takes a few steps toward the bed where her father sleeps, tried to sleep, fails to sleep, sleeps in sadness, sleeps in nightmare, wakes in dark loneliness, drifts off in shame and regret.

For the first time, she realizes the pain he's in, the pain he's always been in, one way or another, this man who was no war hero, no spy, no secret notebook novelist, just a sad and decent and so very lonely man, and she feels useless, insufficient, foolish, and inept; but most of all, she feels selfish and sorry.

Her eyes focus on one bar of suffused moonlight that points like a ghostly finger from her father's sleeping form to the closet door a few feet away, and she follows the beam, opening the door that makes no sound, and she sees it hanging from the hook on the inside of the door: her mother's nightgown, the one she'd been wearing on the night she died.

"Oh, *Daddy*..." she says, her voice weak and thin.

Still, her hand reaches out to lift the gown from the hook and bring it close to her face. Her mother loved this nightgown, its softness, its warmth, the way it smelled when it came out of the dryer after a fresh washing, and this girl holds the garment up to her face and pulls in a deep breath, smelling the scent of her mother's body and the stink of the cancer still lingering at the edges.

From the bed her father whimpers, "...no, no, *no, oh, God, honey, please...*"

And she knows now what she can do for him, what she has to do for him, and so she removes her nightshirt and slips on her mother's death-gown, crosses to the bed, and slips beneath the sweat-drenched covers.

"...Arlene...?' says her father, not opening his eyes.

"Shhh, honey, it's me. Go back to sleep. Just a bad dream."

His hand, so calloused and cracked, reaches out to touch her face. She lies down on her mother's pillow and is shocked to find that it still carries the ghost-scent of her perfume. She remembers that her parents liked to spoon, so she rolls over and soon feels her father's body pressing against her, his legs shifting, his arm draping over her waist as he unconsciously fits himself against her. After a moment, she feels his face press against the back of her—her mother's—gown, and he pulls in a deep breath that he seems to hold forever before releasing it.

She does not sleep much that night, but her father sleeps better than he has in years.

We can watch now, you and I, and see his face, see my father's face when he wakes the next morning and sees her next to him. Shadows of gratitude, of shame, of self-disgust, of admiration and love flicker across his face as he stares down at her now-sleeping form. He feels her stir beneath his arm and realizes with a start that his hand is cupping one of her breasts, the way he used to cup his wife's breast before the cancer came and sheeted everything in sweat and rot and pain.

Still, his hand lingers for a few moments as he realizes how very much like her mother's body does his daughter's feel. Then he feels her stir, waking, and closes his eyes, pulling his hand away at the last moment.

His daughter rolls over and sees how deeply asleep he is, and realizes that she's now given herself a duty that can never spoken aloud, only repeatedly fulfilled. Only in this way can she comfort him, help him, thank him.

She slowly rises from the bed, crossing to the closet where he replaces her mother's gown on its hook, then slips back into her own nightshirt and leaves, closing the door behind her.

As soon as the door closes, her father opens his eyes and stares at the empty space in the bed next to him that now hums with her absence. So much like her mother. So much like her mother. So much like her mother.

This goes on for nearly a year, her assuming the role of her dead mother in the night so her father can sleep. In a way, both know what's going on, what they have become, the roles they are playing, but neither ever speaks of it aloud. And even though nothing physical ever occurs between them in the night as they keep the grief at bay, a little part of each of them falls in love with the other. In this way they become closer than they had ever been, and though the house is never again a happy place, the shadows begin to retreat a little ... until the night when her father hears the muffled laughter of a boy coming from his daughter's bedroom and storms in with a hammer that he does not intend to use but does, nonetheless, then collapsing to the floor afterward, vomiting and shaking with the realization of what he's done, what he's become, and it takes only a few frenzied hours for him to mop up the blood and tissue and tear up the floorboards and move the piles of human meat underneath, burying his daughter in her mother's nightgown. He takes great care replacing the boards, hammering them into place, then covering them with an area rug taken from the living room before gathering a few things—some clothes, what little cash is in the house, some food—and stumbling out into the night.

Shhh, listen—do you hear it? That sound like old nails being wrenched from wood? The front door is opening, someone is coming in, someone who walks in a heavy heel-to-toe fashion as if afraid the earth might open up between each step and swallow him whole.

We watch as the old, hunched, broken thing that was once my father makes his way toward my bedroom. He carries a battery-operated lantern with him, a small backpack, and so much regret that its stench reaches us even in this non-place we wander.

He sets down the lantern, then his backpack, removing a hammer from inside. The same hammer.

In the light we see how he's changed. Well over seventy-five, and the years have not been kind. He looks so much like Mother did toward the end, a living skeleton covered in gray skin, slick with sickness. He moves aside what little remains of the rug and sets to work on the floorboards, which offer little resistance, and within a few minutes, he is staring down at us.

"I'm home," he whispers.

Hello, Daddy. I've missed you.

He sits down, his legs dropping down beneath the hole in the floor, his feet resting between us.

"I thought about the two of you every day," he says. "I've dreamed about the two of you every night...those nights that I can sleep. Ain't too many of those, especially lately."

It's all right, Daddy. I understand. We understand.

He reaches into his backpack and removes something we can't quite make out, because he's deliberately keeping it hidden from our gazes. We're back in what remains of our bodies now, staring up at this lost, broken, sick old man whose face is drenched in sweat, in pain, in the end of things.

"I had no right," he says. "I had no right to love you like that, in that way. I had no right to be jealous, Melissa."

Melissa. So that was my name. How pretty.

"I didn't mean it, I didn't mean to do it." And he brings the object into the light so we can see it. But we already knew, didn't we, you and I? His old gun from the war where he never was a hero, just a simple foot soldier who helped fight the enemy and serve his country before coming home to marry a good woman and build a life for his family.

He begins to speak again: "Oh, *honey*, I ..." But the rest of it dies in his throat, clogged by phlegm and failure and guilt.

It's all right, Daddy. We understand. We're not mad anymore.

But he doesn't hear us. He clicks off the safety, jacks a round intro the chamber, and pushes the business end so deep into his mouth that for a moment we expect him to swallow the entire weapon.

He hesitates for only a moment, but that gives us enough time to move, to rise up as we are now and open our arms as he squeezes the trigger, and we are with him, and he is with us, and as the human meat explodes from the back of his head we lean forward and take him into our embrace, cold flesh and tissue meeting bone and rot, and he embraces us both, does my father, and we hold him close as his blood soaks into the tattered, rotted remains of my mother's nightgown, and we can smell her, she is within us, around us, part of us, and in the last few moments before we pull my father down into hole with us, I find some remnant of my voice in the release of his death, and have just long enough to say, "I forgive you, Daddy, And I love you."

Then he is in the hole with us and in this way are our sins of omission at last atoned.

We remember the way we mingled as we decayed, how we were then found and identified; we remember the way Uncle Sonny claimed our bodies—even yours, my teenaged lover whose name I still can't remember—and had us taken to the place of cardboard coffins with plywood bottoms where we were fed one at a time into the furnace, our tissues charred and bones reduced to powder. We remember the way the workmen swept us into the containers and then into the machine that shook back and forth, filtering out gold fillings and pins once inserted to hold hips together.

And now we are here, all three of us. Our new home; our hushed home; our forever home.

And you are welcomed here, I tell them.

Mrs. Winters thinks Melissa sounds like an nice girl, the type of girl her grandson might have married if he hadn't died in Vietnam, and oh, by the way, don't let me forget, young lady, to tell you all about my son who was a pilot, who flew so high above the clouds you would have thought he was some kind of angel.

I'd like that, Melissa replies. I smile, insomuch as I am capable of performing such a thing, and I continue through my corridors with their marble floors, looking through my glass doors at those who reside behind, and I know that I will never know the loneliness and hurt of those who reside here, for I will always have these hushed and hallowed nights, I will always have those who rest here within me, and—most of all—I will until eternity is no more have the tales the ashes tell.

THE LIBRARIAN

6

So ends your tour of Chapel of the Chimes, or The Library of the Dead.

The librarian—your robe- and cowl-covered guide—places the last three golden books on their respective shelves: NIGHT SOLILOQUY, followed by BROKEN LADY and TALES THE ASHES TELL, a most fitting title considering the works contained in this strangest of libraries.

"I told you earlier that I would reveal myself to you," he or she says, and removes the cowl. And there is nothing there.

The headless figure holds out his or her hands, or more aptly where his or her hands should be, for there is nothing there but empty sleeves.

"I'm not there," the figure says, repeating the title of a book read earlier. "Yet I am everywhere. I am the librarian. I exist with those who shall never be named, with the raven in the dove's nest, with the chimera, with Cthylla, and with the broken lady. I exist and relive through chemistry, within the tales these ashes tell, through jaded winds, with those who dwell on the shaking grounds of these fault lines on which The Library of the Dead was constructed. I exist in the reflection of dragon tears, on the ice amongst phantoms, on the notes of soliloquys played in the night. I exist and I am getting closer and closer to becoming free of this penance."

The golden glass behind the figure reflects the librarian's true appearance: no longer nonexistent, but full and alive; and it is then you realize which of the two tales of the earthquake contain the ashes of your guide.

"It is time to serve your penance."

The librarian—or what used to be the librarian of this place—removes the cowl and disrobes, dropping both garments to the golden tile floor.

Only one reflection remains, but not yours.

In this library of the dead, you realize that is exactly what you are: dead, and understand the penance you must serve before it is your turn to become free. Each of the books in this place—the seemingly countless cinerary urns—has a unique story to tell, and you must read them all in order to find your own, to discover the story amidst your ashes.

You assume the robe and cowl, wondering where to start.

"With the latest addition," the reflection tells you before disappearing.

On the topmost shelf, a book glows brighter than any other, and you float gracefully toward the vaulted ceiling to read the spine.

Your hand phases easily through the glass this time.

AFTERWORD

The idea of there being a library of the dead is, to me, an intrinsically beautiful one. In this world, so much of death and loss finds its way into our lives. When we can, I think we try to detach from it; this is simply a survival tactic, meant to override a sense of empathy that would make us fear and hate the unstable world around us. Sometimes, though, a death strikes the deepest chords of our emotion and we can't turn away from it. To do so would be a dishonor to the one who has passed, a cruelty to the loved ones left behind, and plainly, a wound to ourselves, leaving a cold rift in our souls unable to be healed. For these deaths, these painful losses, the notion of a library of the dead comforts. To me, it speaks to the concept that even if we die, our story isn't over; we live on, immortal, every time our book is taken down from the shelf to be read and reread and told to others. Like souls, our stories are immortal, both the ones we create as writers and the ones we live as people. And that means the best of us is never truly gone. Death has no real power over us; it is simply a transition from one beautiful form to another—a form that cannot be touched by the ugliness of this world.

The passing of Jesus "J.F." Gonzalez is just such a loss as I described above. I can't think of a more fitting final resting place for one of Jesus's last stories than this library of the dead. Jesus left a legacy, not just as a beloved father, husband, son, and friend, but also as a writer and a librarian of sorts in his own right. He is a story worth telling and retelling; his tale in this anthology alone is testament to that, and I can only hope this afterword is a worthy addition to the final pages of his life.

I met Jesus back in 2001, I think at a World Horror Convention. He looked like a California bad-ass with a leather jacket and long hair, swigging a beer and having fun with his boys, so of course, that was the group of guys I spent that evening with. But I quickly saw there was more to Jesus than that—he was a true example of a gentleman and a scholar. Five minutes of talking to him was enough to show he was smart and witty in a quiet, sharp sort of way, the kind of man who thinks before he talks and says what he means. He was honest and loyal, and when he cared about you, it meant something, because Jesus didn't waste time on people he had no patience for.

I remember asking Jesus once what he would choose if he could have any superpower, and whether he'd be a hero or a villain with it. He said, "I'd be invisible. As to whether I'd be a hero or a villain, I'd be like Dexter and kill predators. So I guess I'd be a hero." This response—it makes me smile now to think about it—just seems to sum up the Jesus I called a friend. He didn't look for spotlight, he didn't need to shout to be heard, and he spent more time listening—and learning—than talking. But Jesus had a sense of honor and justice, and of loyalty to friends and family. He kept his friends grounded. He was a shoulder to lean on. And although I think he'd shirk off the title if he knew I was using it, he really was a hero to many—to fans and readers, to aspiring professionals in the horror field, and to those who were privileged enough to call him friend.

Jesus was the author of almost twenty novels and a number of collections and chapbooks. He got his start learning from several prominent Splatterpunk authors during the genre movement's initial rise, authors like David J. Schow, John Skipp, and Craig Spector. He also copy-edited a novel of Richard Laymon's before moving on to becoming a writer and editor himself. Probably his most well-known works are his novel, *Survivor*, which has been optioned by Chesapeake Films, and the *Clickers* series, optioned by Cooked Goose Productions, that he co-wrote with Mark Williams and Brian Keene, respectively. He's worked with many of the genre's top horror and suspense publishers, such as Leisure Books, Kensington Books, HarperCollins, Cemetery Dance Publications, Delirium Books, Bloodletting Press, Thunderstorm Books, and others. In addition to novels, Jesus has written over eighty short stories. He has also written dozens of articles, starting back in the late '90s with his long-running nonfiction column, "Diary of a Madman," which ran in *Afraid* and then in various other venues after the newsletter folded. His most recent series of nonfiction articles on the history of the genre has been published by *LampLight* magazine. His articles on horror writing and publishing contained a wealth of knowledge that spanned three decades, and ought to be, in my opinion, required reading for any practicing horror writer.

Jesus was also an editor for a time. He co-founded Iniquities Publications in 1990, serving as co-editor and publisher of *Iniquities Magazine* and *Phantasm Magazine* until 1997. He also edited an anthology, *Tooth and Claw*, which was published in 2002. As both writer and editor, Jesus was in the business a long time, and he had seen the genre through ups, downs, quirks, and changes of all kinds. He was well-read and well-informed and discussed the genre academically, citing works and events in horror publishing to forward an idea or prove a point. Jesus understood the importance of diversifying as a working writer and also of giving back to the writing community: in addition to full-length and short fiction, he also did work for hire, screenplays, technical writing, interviews, memorials, forewords, afterwords, and everything in between.

He used to joke about quitting the horror business and becoming a forest ranger or a tugboat captain, but Jesus's heart was in the genre. He was a fan before he was a professional, and that enthusiastic love of horror literature never failed him. It was what made his work, both fiction and nonfiction, so compelling.

Jesus was no stranger to loss of friends and family, but he knew a fundamental truth about stories—that the ones we love live on in the stories we tell, and a part of us lives on with them. And when we write them down, those stories keep on even after we do.

I meant what I said at the beginning of this afterword, that a library of the dead can be a comfort. And what is horror fiction if not, in a way, a library of the dead? What are these stories if not justice by way of illuminating real horrors left unavenged in the dark? Aren't they tributes to the little deaths and losses? This anthology examines the sinister and often terrifying aspects of death and loss and the innate horror of tragedy. With these stories, the reader gives the writer permission to prevent detachment and to mark the soul indelibly with a memory, a piece of soul. This is, at the heart of it, what horror fiction does. It provides a means of vicarious experience, sometimes thrilling, sometimes cathartic. It provides a way of processing the little and the monumental horrors of our own lives, the tragedies, the losses. This anthology is a mausoleum of shelves upon which the human condition has been examined and recorded in little volumes. It is a place of solitude to visit, remember, relive, and remind ourselves that someone like J.F. Gonzalez hasn't left us; he is still with us in the pages onto which so much of his soul was poured.

So read on—read his books, his articles, his stories. His piece of soul.

His work influenced and inspired generations of writers. His story—the life he lived—touched the lives of many of us. He was loved, and his story cherished. Take his book and read on…

Library Archives, New Jersey
2014

J.F.GONZALEZ
1964-2014

VISIT THE LIBRARY OF THE DEAD

Chapel of the Chimes
4499 Piedmont Avenue
Oakland, California 94611